CRITICS RAVE FOR
KATIE MacALISTER AND
NOBLE INTENTIONS!

THE BEST LAID PLANS . . .

"The trouble with you, Gillian, is that you indulge yourself in every ludicrous scheme and thought that passes through your head."

"Noble."

"If you would learn to deal with things in a calm, organized manner, you would be well rewarded, wife, with serenity and tranquility."

"Noble—"

"You are young yet, despite your years, so I will not make a point of your headstrong nature and heedless manner of flinging yourself through life. You do not know better. Your upbringing is to blame, of course. It will be my pleasure to instruct you in all the joys of a well-ordered, temperate life."

"Noble!"

"What?" He was annoyed at her interruption. Didn't she understand that he was trying to help her organize her life into something satisfactory?

"I am not the one chained naked to my mistress's bed with a broken man part."

KATIE MACALISTER

NOBLE INTENTIONS

LEISURE BOOKS NEW YORK CITY

A LEISURE BOOK®

October 2009

Dorchester Publishing Co., Inc.
200 Madison Avenue
New York, NY 10016

ISBN 10: 0-505-52847-9
ISBN 13: 978-0-505-52847-6

My heartfelt appreciation goes to Noble's mistresses—Beverly Brandt, Libby Muelhaupt, and Lori Grube—who cheered me on and offered sage advice.

And to Vance Briceland,
who made me laugh with his tinglemeter.

NOBLE INTENTIONS

Chapter One

Gillian Leigh's first social event of the Season began with what many in the *ton* later labeled as an uncanny warning of Things To Come.

"Well, bloody hell. This isn't going to endear me to the duchess."

Gillian watched with dismay as flames licked up the gold velvet curtains despite her attempts at beating them out with a tasseled silk cushion. Shrieks of horror and shrill voices behind her indicated that others had spotted her activities, which she had hoped would escape their notice until she had the fire under control.

Two footmen raced past her with buckets of water and soon had the fire extinguished, but it was too late, the damage was done. The duchess's acclaimed Gold Drawing Room would never be the same again. Gillian stood clutching the sooty cushion to her chest and mournfully watched as the blackened curtains were hastily bundled past the small clutches of people who stood talking intently, looking everywhere but at her.

"Sealing my fate as a social pariah, no doubt," she muttered to herself.

"Who is? And what on earth happened in here? Lady Dell said something about you burning down the house, but you know how she exag . . . oh, my!"

Gillian heaved a deep sigh and turned to smile ruefully as her cousin, and dearest friend, caught sight of the damp smoke-stained wall.

"I'm afraid it's true, Charlotte, although I wasn't trying to burn down the house. It was just another of my Unfortunate Accidents."

Charlotte gave the formerly gilt-paneled wall a considering look, pursed her lips, then turned her gaze on her cousin. "Mmm. Well, you have certainly made sure everyone will be talking about your debut. Just look at you! You've got soot all over—your gloves are a complete loss, but I think you can brush the worst off your bodice."

Gillian gave in to the urge and snorted while Charlotte affected repairs to the sooty green muslin gown. "My debut—as if I wanted one. The only reason I'm here is because your mother insisted it would look odd if I remained at home while you had your Season. I'm five and twenty, Charlotte, not a young girl like you. And as for setting the *ton* talking—I'm sure they are, but it will no doubt be to label me a clumsy colonial who can't even be a wallflower without wreaking havoc."

Charlotte rolled her eyes as she clasped her hand around her cousin's wrist and dragged her past the excited groups of people and out the door. "You're only half American and not clumsy. You're . . . well, you're just enthusiastic. And slightly prone to Unfortunate Accidents. But all's well that ends happily, as Mama always says. The curtains can be replaced, and I'm sure the duchess will realize the fire was simply one of those unavoidable events. Come, you must return to the ballroom. The most exciting thing has happened—the Black Earl is here."

"The black who?"

"The Black Earl. Lord Wessex. It's rumored he's going to take a bride again."

"No, truly? And this is an event we must not fail to witness? Is he going to take her right there in the ballroom?"

"Gillian!" Charlotte stopped dead in the hallway, blocking people from either direction. Her china-blue eyes were round and sparkling with faux horror. "You really cannot say such things in polite company! It's shocking, simply shocking, and I cannot allow you to sully my delicate, maidenly ears in such a manner!"

Gillian grinned at her cousin and gave her a little push to get her moving again. "Honestly, Charlotte, I don't see how you can tell such awful whoppers and not pay the price."

"Practice, Gilly, it's because I pay the proper attention to perfecting a shy, demure look for an hour each morning. If you would do the same, it would do wonders for your personality. You might even catch a husband, which you certainly won't do if you continue to be so . . . so . . ."

"Honest?"

"No."

"Forthright?"

"No."

Gillian chewed on her lip for a moment. "Unassuming? Unpretentious? Veracious?"

"No, no, no. Green, that's what you are. Utterly green and without any sense of *ton* whatsoever. You simply cannot continue to say what you think. It's just not done in polite circles."

"Some people like honesty."

"Not in Society, they don't. Now stop dawdling and fix a pleasant expression on your face."

Gillian heaved a little sigh and tried to adopt the demure look that spinsters of her age were expected to wear.

"Now you're looking mulish," Charlotte pointed out with a frown, then gave in to a sudden impish grin. She linked her arm through her cousin's and tugged her along the hall. "Never mind, your face doesn't matter in the least. Come, we don't want to miss Lord Wessex. Mama says he is a terrible rake and isn't welcomed into polite circles anymore. I can't wait to see how depraved he looks."

"What has he done to make him unacceptable to the jades, rakes, and rouges that populate the *ton?*"

Charlotte's eyes sparkled with excitement. "Lady Dell says he murdered his first wife after he found her in the arms of her true love. He is said to have shot her in the head, but missed when he tried to murder her lover."

"Truly? How fascinating! He must be a terribly emotional and uncontrolled man if he didn't tolerate his wife having an inamorato. I thought that sort of behavior was de rigueur in the *ton.*" Gillian and Charlotte slipped past small groups of elegantly clad people and paused before the double doors leading to the ballroom. The heat generated by so many people inhabiting the confined space left the room stifling and airless. Charlotte fanned herself vigorously as she continued to tell Gillian what she knew of the infamous earl.

"He doesn't wear anything but black—'tis said to be a sign of his guilt that he's never been out of mourning even though he killed his wife more than five years ago. She cursed him, you know, and that's another reason he wears black. And then there are rumors of a child . . ."

Charlotte's voice dropped to an intimate whisper that Gillian had a hard time hearing above the noise of several chattering matrons standing nearby. ". . . and was born on the wrong side of the blanket."

"Someone is a bastard?" Gillian asked, confused.

"Gillian!" Charlotte shrieked and, with an appalled look toward the matrons, pulled her cousin closer to the ballroom doors. "God's teeth, you're as uncivilized as a Red Indian. It must be living among them as you did that makes you so unconventional. Do try to curb your tongue!"

Gillian muttered an insincere apology and prodded her cousin. "Who is illegitimate? The earl?"

"Gilly, really! Don't be such an idiot. How can he be illegitimate and an earl? Make an effort to pay attention, do—I was just telling you how Lord Wessex murdered his first wife because she refused to bear him a son and turned to her lover for comfort. Isn't that thrilling? It's said she pleaded with him to give her a divorce so she could marry her lover, but he told her that if he could not have her, no man would. Then he shot her while her lover looked on." She sighed. "It's so romantic."

"Your idea of romantic and mine are most definitely not the same," Gillian said, looking around at the dandies, macaronis, fops, elderly gentlemen in silk breeches, and other assorted members of that small, elite group who possessed the combination of fortune, rank, and reputation to admit them as members of the *ton*. "And this man is here tonight? Which one is he? Does he look evil? Does he have a hump on his back and a squint and walk with a limp? Will he ogle the ladies?"

Charlotte frowned. "Don't be ridiculous, Gilly. The earl is not a monster; at least, not to look at. He is quite handsome if you like large, brooding men, which I most definitely do. When they're earls, of course. And perhaps viscounts. But nothing lower than a viscount, you understand." She forestalled Gillian's questions by turning toward the doors. "Come stand with me and we will watch to see if the rumor is true."

"Which rumor—that the earl killed his wife or that he is looking for a new one?"

"The latter. I will know soon enough if he is—men cannot keep a thing like that secret for very long."

"Mmm, no, I imagine not. If their intentions are not clear in the speculative gazes they impart on every marriageable female who can still draw breath, it's in the way they check the bride-to-be's teeth and make sure her movement is sound."

Charlotte tried to stifle a giggle. "Mama says I am not to listen to a thing you say, that you are incorrigible and a bad influence."

Gillian laughed with her cousin as they entered the ballroom arm-in-arm. "It's a good thing she doesn't know I've learned it all from you, my dear cousin. Now, after we view this rogue of

15

the first water, do tell me who has caught your fancy. As I told Aunt Honoria, I'm determined you will end your Season with a stunning match, but I cannot help you become deliriously happy if you do not tell me who your intended victim is."

"Oh, that's simple," Charlotte replied with a beatific expression of innocence that was spoiled only by a perfectly wicked smile. "Everyone knows rakes make the best husbands. I shall simply pick out the worst of the bunch—one riddled with vices, bad habits, and a reputation that will make Mama swoon and Papa rail—then I shall reform him."

"That seems like a terrible amount of work to go to just to find a suitable husband."

"Not really." Charlotte whipped open her fan and adopted a coy look. "After all, you know what they say."

"No, what do they say?"

"Necessity is the mother of intention."

Gillian stopped. "Invention, Charlotte."

"What?"

"Necessity is the mother of *invention.*"

Charlotte stared at her for a moment, then rapped her cousin on the wrist with her fan. "Don't be ridiculous, where would I come up with an invention? Intentions I have a-plenty, and that's quite enough for me, thank you. Now let's go find this delicious rake of an earl. If he's as bad as Mama says, he might just suit."

Gillian laughed at her cousin as the pair resumed their course across the brightly lit ballroom. Three men standing nearby turned at the sound of their merriment and considered the pretty picture in contrast the pair made.

"What have we here?" The shortest man, stylishly dressed in salmon satin breeches and an embroidered ivory waistcoat, lifted his quizzing glass and gazed at the two women. "Ah, it's the Collins chit. Who's the Long Meg with her?"

The tallest member of the group lifted a dark eyebrow at the question. "I haven't the slightest idea, Tolly. You're the expert on members of Society. You tell us who she is."

Sir Hugh Tolliver toyed with his quizzing glass. "You'd know, too, if you came to town more often, Wessex. 'Struth, you haven't even come for Parliament for the past five years! It ain't healthy to bury yourself in the country like that, my friend. A man of your consequence should be in town, taking your rightful place in society. You owe it to your title and your family to do so."

The Black Earl gave the young man a tolerant look. Tolly had always been a bit of a romantic, nattering on about chivalry and the rights of the nobility for as long as the earl had known him.

"You sound like my mother, Tolly," he said with as much gentleness as he could muster, then turned his gaze back to consider the two women. "I'm here now, that will have to suffice."

Sir Hugh flushed at the set-down. "But how long do you plan to stay in town? Don't look at me like I'm a candle short, man, it matters a good deal if I am to smooth your path into society."

"I'll stay as long as it takes. And as for smoothing my path— I've told you, Tolly, I don't give a damn what the *ton* thinks of me. I'm here for one purpose only, and once I've achieved my goal, I shall return to Nethercote."

"Ask St. Clair who the Amazon is, Tolly. He's tight with Collins and is sure to know." The third member of the group, who had also been watching the two women make their way to the opposite side of the room, nodded toward a door leading to the card room. Sir Hugh obligingly turned to find his quarry but was stopped by a soft voice.

"Get me an introduction."

Sir Hugh stared at his saturnine friend in surprise, the flush slowly fading from his face. "You're serious then, Wessex? You're looking to get leg-shackled again? I would have thought after Elizabeth . . ."

The words dried in his mouth as Lord Wessex gazed at him

with a look he did not care to investigate further. "Er . . . yes. Which one?"

"Which what?" Wessex drawled in a bored voice that made Sir Hugh even more nervous. His palms began to sweat. Wessex was at his most dangerous when he appeared bored.

"Which chit did you want the introduction to?"

Wessex sent an uninterested glance to where the pair had joined a flock of young women. "The redhead."

"She's a bit long in the tooth, don't you think? On the shelf, and all that." Sir Hugh regretted his comments the second they left his lips. One didn't inquire into the reasons behind Wessex's actions. Although his gray eyes might be hooded by apparent disinterest, Sir Hugh knew how quickly they could turn frigid. His hands immediately stopped sweating and turned to blocks of ice.

"Tolly," the third man warned, taking on his accustomed role of peacemaker, "just get the introductions. Wessex has my curiosity up now as well—the Amazon is damned pretty, even if she is a head taller than you."

Flushing again at the comment, Sir Hugh nodded curtly at the marquis and scurried off to garner the necessary information.

"Don't tell me you're shopping for a wife as well, Harry?"

Grimacing at the thought, Lord Rosse adjusted his spectacles and took another look down the line of this year's crop of debutantes. "Lord, no. But you never know what lovely bit might be agreeable to carte blanche."

"You're looking in the wrong spot, old friend. Allow me to direct you away from the virgins. The widows and bored wives are kept on the other side of the room."

Rosse ignored the gentle ribbing and continued his perusal. "If you hadn't told me yourself you intended to wed again, I wouldn't have believed it. I suppose you're doing it for Nick's sake?"

Wessex took two glasses of whiskey off the tray of a passing footman and handed one to his friend. "My son is part of the reason, my nursery another. It's time I fill it."

"Damned shame you didn't marry Nick's mother."

The gray in Wessex's eyes turned to icy silver, but Rosse wasn't daunted by the waves of almost palpable hostility that emanated from the man next to him; they'd been through too much together not to speak their minds in private.

"If you recall," Wessex said softly as he directed his gaze back toward the Amazon, "I was already married at the time."

"Ah, yes. The lovely Elizabeth."

Wessex's gut tightened, as it did every time her name was mentioned, his lips thinning into a cruel parody of a smile as he fought down waves of bitterness and deep pain. It never failed to surprise him that he could feel such pain; for the last five years it was the only emotion that breached the icy numbness that was his constant companion. The lovely Elizabeth. By God, he would make sure his second wife was nothing like that cold, heartless bitch.

He surprised himself by putting his thoughts into words. "My next wife will be a quiet, unassuming, biddable woman who will not draw attention to herself or cause scandal. She will be pleased to stay in the country, take care of my son, and provide me with heirs."

Harry smiled. "In other words, this paragon of virtue will be everything your first wife wasn't."

Wessex's answering smile, icy as a fjord in February, matched the coldness he felt within. "Exactly." Unbidden, his eyes wandered back to where the tall redheaded woman towered above the handful of dandies dancing attendance on her blond companion.

"Rosse, good to see you." A deep voice rumbled behind the two men. Rosse and Wessex turned to greet the Duke of Sunderland, but the greetings froze on their lips when the duke continued with a frosty, "I can't say as much for your companion. Bad company you're keeping, Rosse, bad company."

Rosse stared after the retreating figure with an unhappy frown. "That was a direct cut, Noble."

Wessex tossed back his whiskey and nodded, rubbing his hands to warm then.

"It was indeed," he answered, turning back to gaze across the ballroom.

"But damn it, man, it's unfair! He's your cousin! If you'd just let me speak about what happened that night—"

Wessex made an abrupt movement. "It's not important, Harry. Sunderland is a fool. I don't particularly care what he thinks."

"But—Noble, this is getting worse. You've been in town only a fortnight and already you're being given the cut on the street, in your clubs, and now here! If you don't take steps soon, you won't be recognized in polite society."

Wessex snorted, pleased to feel the whiskey burning a path down to his stomach. At least he could still feel that. "Polite society. The day I care about what *polite society* thinks, Harry, is the day hell will freeze."

His brows drew together as he watched across the room where Sir Hugh and another man approached the woman who had caught his eye. Tolly was paying far too much attention to the redhead, gazing up into her eyes as if she was the most fascinating woman on earth.

"Looks as if Tolly has cleared the path. Shall we?" Lord Rosse gave his friend an inquiring glance.

"Yes." Surprised by the sharp bubble of emotion remarkably akin to jealousy, Wessex gathered the mantle of boredom he habitually wore and sauntered after his friend across the inlaid wood floor toward the gaggle of tittering misses.

Charlotte's keen and eager eye, ever on the alert for a titled rake, saw the two men heading toward them from across the room. She was certain after the interested looks the Black Earl had been shooting at Gillian he would claim an introduction and couldn't decide what attitude to adopt about this unexpected turn of events. A hasty evaluation of the number of suitors gathered around her went far to assuage her plans for reforming the Black Earl, so it was with no sense of pettishness or ill feeling that she turned to mind to plotting the future happiness of her dearest cousin. A quick glance at said cousin showed that Gillian was in her usual state of disarray: her gloves were wadded up into sooty balls, tendrils of unruly red hair were fighting their way out of the once tidy coronet on her head, and her gown showed signs of losing the battle with the fire. Unfortunately, there was no time to rush her off to the ladies' withdrawing room to affect repairs, but Charlotte was not one to go down without a fight—not when her cousin's future was at stake.

"Would it be an inconvenience to ask for a cup of punch, Sir Hugh? I fear the warmth of the evening has made Miss Leigh rather thirsty, but she's much too shy to ask you herself."

She dimpled charmingly at him as he shot a curious look at an equally surprised Gillian, then let her smile fade as he left to fulfill her request. As soon as he was out of hearing, Charlotte swung around to her cousin and began dabbing at the faint soot marks on Gillian's bodice. "Cousin, pinch your cheeks."

"I beg your pardon?"

Charlotte cast a glance over Gillian's shoulder to where the two men were approaching. "Oh, never mind, they're too close, they'll see you. Bite your lips."

Gillian wondered if the stifling heat of the ballroom was affecting her dear cousin's mind. "Is it the heat, Charlotte? You look flushed. Are you ill? Shall I call your mother?"

"Oh, heavens no! You know how Mama is, she'll rattle on about nothing and monopolize all the conversation." Charlotte waved her fan in a vigorous manner and slapped an artificially bright smile on her face.

"Monopolize the conversation with whom?" Gillian was becoming concerned; although Charlotte was in truth a vivacious, exceptionally headstrong woman, she made it her habit to adopt the pose of a shy, timid maiden when in public, the better, she said, to snare a husband. Yet here she was smiling with a ferocious intensity that would scare the spots off a leopard.

"Smile," Charlotte hissed at her cousin as she deepened her dimples. "Look pleasant. He's been watching you. I think he's interested."

In a flash, Gillian understood. She'd heard of this. Obviously her cousin had fallen victim to a temporary derangement. She put an arm around Charlotte's shoulders and gave her a little squeeze. "It's all right, dearest. Don't worry, I'll see that you get home without your mother becoming aware of your . . . your unfortunate condition."

"My what?"

Gillian took charge, gently turning Charlotte, intent on making their escape before anyone else noticed her cousin's sad mental condition, when the sight of Sir Hugh approaching with two tall men halted her. Her eyes widened as they met the gaze of the dark man who stopped in front of her. God's elbows, he took her breath away!

"Lady Charlotte, Miss Gillian Leigh, may I be permitted to introduce the Earl of Wessex and the Marquis Rosse?"

Gillian's mouth formed an O, but she couldn't get any words out. The earl's gray eyes were flecked with bits of silver and ringed with the darkest, lushest lashes she'd ever seen. She felt her toes curl in her green satin slippers when the Lord of Lusciousness raised her hand to his lips. As his touch sent frissons of fire down her hand, she thanked heaven she had ruined her gloves.

The earl raised one beautiful glossy black eyebrow. "Indeed. It makes an introduction so much more *personal* when the lady has a bare hand."

Gillian felt the flush sweep up from her chest as she realized her Unfortunate Habit had once again made itself known. "Oh, blast!"

A second dark eyebrow climbed upward. The flush reached

Gillian's face. "I'm sorry, my lord, it's my Unfortunate Habit, you see. It makes me speak without thinking." She tried for an insouciant smile, but it came out watery instead.

The corners of the earl's mouth twitched. Gillian's knees threatened to buckle at the sight of it. She tried to drag her gaze from his mouth but was fascinated by the sensual curve of his lower lip. Lips like that ought to be made illegal. Sending blasphemous thoughts heavenward about the unleashing of such a stunning creation willy-nilly upon unsuspecting and highly susceptible women, she made a desperate attempt to calm her wildly beating heart. It wasn't as if she was a silly, naive miss who knew nothing of the way of things—heaven knows, she had been to Boston! She was a woman experienced in the ways of the world, after all. She would not shame herself by expiring on the spot, overcome by one man's masculine beauty.

The bespectacled man next to Lord Adonis bowed over her hand, but she missed what he said, so enthralled was she by the earl. She let her eyes wander over the sharp, masculine planes of his features and wondered how he felt about the softening effect the cleft in his chin gave his otherwise harsh face. She knew how she felt about it. Looking at it made her lips burn with the desire to scatter kisses along his jaw and dip her tongue into the indentation . . . oh heavens, what was she doing, thinking such sinful thoughts? Another wave of heat washed over her as she clutched her hands together in an attempt to get hold of her wild imagination. She shouldn't be thinking about kissing an earl. Especially an earl who, if the gossip flying around the ballroom was true, quite possibly murdered his wife.

The earl's fascinating mouth was moving. Oh, Lord, he was speaking to her and she hadn't been paying the slightest bit of attention.

"I beg your pardon?"

A corner of his mouth twitched again. She didn't know if it was in irritation or amusement, but she hoped for the latter. "Woolgathering, were you?"

23

She smiled, happy he understood. "Oh yes, I'm afraid I was. Another bad habit, you see. You were saying?"

If she didn't know better, she'd swear the gray eyes softened for a moment. But they wouldn't soften—he was a rake earl, and she was a penniless, half-American nobody. Gillian suddenly felt it important that he know she wasn't one of the *ton*.

"I asked if you would honor me with the next waltz."

Gillian was sure she wouldn't be able to drag her gaze from the earl's eyes if her life depended on it. She mused upon the black flecks interspersed with the silver. The effect was mesmerizing. "I'm afraid I do not waltz, my lord."

A flicker of annoyance passed over the earl's face. "Do not, or will not, Miss Leigh?"

"Cannot, Lord Wessex." Gillian put her hand on his sleeve and leaned forward. "It's shameful, I know, but you see, I was raised by my aunt and uncle in Boston."

Wessex leaned closer. She was drowning in his eyes. Happily, eagerly, willingly drowning. A heady, spicy scent wafted up from him and tickled her nose. She greedily inhaled it, feeling it permeate down to her bones, sure that if she *were* to expire on the spot, she'd die a happy woman.

"Do they not waltz in Boston?" His voice rumbled intimately around her. Gillian's mouth went instantly dry.

"Yes, they do," she croaked.

"Then why?" Wessex took her hand and held it between his palms. Gillian felt the touch burn up her arm and directly into her brain. "Why will you not waltz with me?"

"Um." She was lost in the sliver and black and gray of his fascinating eyes. Why was he trying to distract her with talk? And what was he talking about? Waltzing? What was that? "My uncle would not allow me to learn how. He was a very devout man. A Shaker, as a matter of fact."

Gillian's eyes rounded and she stepped back under the influence of Wessex's sudden, feral smile.

"Then you must grant me the privilege of teaching you how. The next waltz?" He squeezed her hand gently.

"No, my lord, you mustn't," she gasped, horrified at the thought of learning to dance in such a public venue. Given the accidents that inexplicably seemed to shadow her, he'd probably end up with a broken leg—or worse.

"Ah, I see. You have not yet been given permission to waltz? I will speak with Lady Jersey on your behalf."

Gillian frowned up at the quirked brows. "Good heavens, my lord, I don't care about having permission to dance. It's not as if I'm . . . that is, I should warn you . . ." She glanced over at her cousin for help, but Charlotte had turned away in an obvious attempt to give them privacy. Gillian leaned forward again. "I'm not supposed to be here, you see. On virgin's row, that is."

"Virgin's row?" One side of the earl's mouth curved up. Gillian watched it, fascinated. She'd do anything short of murder to run her fingers along those lips.

"Yes, that's what I call it. I'm not really here to have a Season, I'm merely accompanying my cousin, Lady Charlotte. I'm not an heiress, you know. I don't have any illustrious family connections other than my uncle, and I'm not an Original or an Incomparable, so you needn't feel obliged to dance with me."

The other side of that lovely mouth curved up, and Gillian blinked with pleasure at the surprising warmth of the Lord of Sunshine's smile. She felt her own lips curving in response. Perhaps she had been a little hasty in ruling out murder.

"I assure you, Miss Leigh, I do not have a standing requirement that my waltz partners be heiresses, titled, or Incomparables."

"Or Originals?" Gillian asked with a decidedly mischievous look. Wessex noted with interest that her dark green eyes had brilliant little gold flecks that seemed to light up when she smiled.

He pressed her hand, then released it. "I suspect, my dear,

25

that you fit that title rather well. Ah, it sounds as if that's a waltz beginning. Shall we?"

He held out his arm for her.

"Oh—but—are you sure? I wouldn't want to hurt you." She tilted her face up to peer into his eyes.

Wessex noted the fine bone structure of her heart-shaped face. She was heavily freckled on all her exposed surfaces—obviously she was one of those redheads who freckled at the slightest hint of exposure to the sun, and if the golden hue of her skin was any clue, he suspected she spent a good deal of time outdoors. Rather than finding fault with the flaw in her complexion, he found himself wanting to stroke the silky, freckled skin. The warmth of her presence drew him like a moth to a flame.

He took her hand and, placing it on his arm, led her out onto the floor. "I have survived many worse situations, I assure you."

"Not with me," she mumbled, looking momentarily disgruntled, but immediately that look fled and one of sheer terror replaced it.

"Just follow my lead," Wessex said, speaking softly into her ear, "and listen to the music. A waltz moves to the count of three."

He tried to maintain his amusement at her terror, but truth to tell, he found himself drawn to the warming glow that seemed to surround her. Her unsophisticated display of emotions beguiled him; if she wasn't voicing her every thought, they were quickly discerned by one look at her easily read face. Wessex found such candor refreshing in a society that did its best to hide honesty and truthfulness.

"Oh, my!" Gillian gasped as he moved her expertly into the dance. She caught her lower lip between her teeth as she concentrated on matching his steps. Despite her stiffness and awkward movements, the earl felt a sudden flash of lust knife through him. His attention was drawn to her lips. They were mirrors of her emotions, twisting into a rueful grimace as she made a misstep or curving into a stunningly brilliant smile when she caught the rhythm of the dance.

"Look at me, not your feet," he quietly commanded, wanting to bask in the glory of that smile again. She tipped her head back and flashed him an impish grin that he felt deep in his chest.

"You'll be sorry, my lord. Or rather, your toes will."

"How old are you?" Wessex asked before he could stop himself.

"Five and twenty. How old are you?"

"A decade older than you," Wessex answered, amused by her brashness. She was forward, that was certainly true, but he didn't see any signs that she was putting on an act of innocence for his benefit. One look in her guileless eyes convinced him that she was indeed an Original—open, honest, and completely untouched by the debauched society that made up the *ton*. The glow from her innocence and gentle femininity washed over him in a wave of sudden welcome warmth. He entertained a pleasant picture of her sitting by the fire in his library, her head bent over a bit of feminine frippery, their evenings spent in quiet, tranquil companionship.

Charlotte watched as the pair danced, a smile playing about her lips. Gillian and the Black Earl were well suited, in her opinion, Gillian's height matching the earl's well. She grimaced when Gillian stepped on the earl's toes yet again, stifled a giggle when Gillian laughed at the earl's response, and watched with surprise when the earl suddenly stumbled and came to a halt for a moment before picking up the tempo of the waltz again. What had Gillian said that disconcerted him so?

Gillian couldn't believe her mouth had blurted out the words she had been thinking. The earl's eyes glittered silver as she held her breath for his response, and hoped he'd realize that she hadn't meant to be impertinent, it was just natural curiosity. If he hadn't distracted her by staring at her lips, she'd have been paying attention to their conversation. God's toes, he drove her wits straight from her mind when he looked at her lips like that. It was surely his own fault if she babbled at him as a result.

"I must decline the opportunity to answer your question, my dear."

Put in my place, and rightly so, Gillian thought with relief, and gave herself up to the heady pleasure of being in the arms of the handsomest man at the ball. She wasn't concerned with what people were saying about him—she prided herself on being an excellent judge of people and was quite confident that he was innocent of the crime society had pinned on him. No man could hide a soul capable of such a heinous act behind those forthcoming, open, beautiful eyes.

"Is there a particular reason you wish to know?" Wessex was curious as to why a well-bred young woman would approach him of all people with such a question. She must have been listening to the gossip, and yet she had enough courage to ask him about it. Her bravery annoyed and pleased him at the same time.

"There usually is a reason for everything I ask," Gillian replied dreamily, dismissing his frown as she gave herself up to the music and the magic of the dance. The earl was right—there wasn't much to the waltz once you remembered to count. She felt pleased she had picked it up so quickly, stepping on his toes only eight or nine times in total, and wondered if Charlotte was watching her triumph.

"Oh, I beg your pardon! I forgot to count. Did I hurt you badly?"

The wry twist to the earl's lips belied the attempt he made to brush off her apology. Gillian cursed her clumsiness as the music ended and the earl escorted her back to her aunt's side. Wessex expressed his appreciation for the dance with Gillian, bowed over a speechless Lady Collin's hand, and made a graceful exit.

Lady Collins stared at her hand as if there were hairy, eight-legged insects crawling on it, but quickly recovered both her poise and her voice.

"My dear, do you think—was that at all wise accepting—he is an earl, but—Lavonia is so certain—oh, why wasn't Theodore here when he asked you to dance?"

Gillian frowned as she tried to follow her aunt's convoluted thoughts. "Lord Wessex? Why would Uncle Theo have an objection to my dancing with him?"

Lady Collins looked at her niece as if the insects were now on her. "My dear Gillian, surely you must know—I was quite certain Charlotte would warn you—but then, you've been around no society but that of Red Indians—and such a nice-looking man, too. Tragic. Always in black, you see—but still, murder! No, indeed! And the Duke of Sunderland has cut him, they say. Just this evening! His own cousin! Not good *ton* at all, not even with eighty thousand pounds a year."

It took a strong person in their prime to follow her aunt's thought process, but Gillian was learning the knack. If you didn't listen too closely, and allowed your attention to wander slightly, it was possible to glean enough kernels of information to respond.

"You mean I should not have waltzed with him because it's said he killed his wife? Aunt, I'm surprised at you for believing such a ridiculous and patently untrue falsehood. Why, one only has to spend a short amount of time in the earl's presence to ascertain his innocence. Of all the maligned men of my acquaintance, he certainly has suffered the most at the hands of the very people who should stand at his side, offering him support and succor rather than tearing his reputation and character to shreds. Society should be ashamed of itself for slandering him in such a manner! I for one won't tolerate the sort of base lies and cruel implications that seem to delight the *ton,* and I must say, Aunt, I'm appalled that you would be cozened into believing such blatant untruths and can only hope you do nothing to encourage similar vile and reprehensible fabrications! Indeed, I would hope you do your part to help that poor, lonely, troubled man regain the sterling reputation that was tarnished by the unexpected death of his no doubt very beloved wife. I know I shall do all that I can to help him!"

Lady Collins wilted under her niece's blistering attack. Gillian felt an immediate rush of guilt at having raised her voice at her aunt—truly, it seemed as if half the occupants of the ballroom had heard her, and held their collective breaths while they waited for her tirade to continue. Thankful that the Black Earl was not present to witness her unladylike display, Gillian made a moue of chagrin and turned back to her aunt with a fixed smile.

"Such a lovely evening, isn't it?" she said loudly, for the benefit of the people who were attempting to eavesdrop. "And the weather—my, how lovely the weather has been for June. Delightfully warm, wouldn't you say, Aunt?"

"Warm, yes, it is warm. Lilacs and lilies—strolls in the garden and picnics at the riverside—Oxford, you know—oh, there is Her Grace. I will just pay my—yes."

As Lady Collins made her escape, Charlotte tore herself away from her group of admirers and hurried over to speak with her cousin. She laid a dainty glove-clad hand on her cousin's arm, flashed a dimpled smile over her lace fan at a passing admirer, and, with a grip that would do a stevedore proud, hauled Gillian into a sheltered spot guarded on either side by two large palms.

"What on earth were you thinking, Gilly?"

Gillian's stomach felt as if it were filled with lead shot. She had been unaccountably rude to her aunt and had no excuse for her behavior. She hadn't the slightest doubt that her cousin was about to dress her down, and she would deserve every harsh word. "I'm sorry, Charlotte. I had no right to speak to your mother that way—"

Charlotte stared briefly at her, then made a face and waved the apology away. "Oh, fustian! Mama drives me to distraction too. But why did you let the earl get away? The supper dance is next, and if you were to intimate that you were free, he might ask you for it. You should have kept him by your side with amusing anecdotes and witty repartee until that time."

"What amusing anecdotes and witty repartee would that be?"

Charlotte waved her hand around vaguely and bobbed a curtsy to a pair of elderly ladies as they passed. "Oh, you know—stories of your life among the Red Indians. Tales of your harrowing journey to Civilization. Surely you must have a large collection of lurid tales to enable you to do something as simple as keeping a man enthralled at your side for an hour or so."

Gillian choked back a laugh. "The only lurid tales I know are the ones the sailors told me on the ship when I sailed here, and I doubt if they would interest a man of the world like Lord Wessex. I'm surprised you would want me to try and keep his attention, Char. Your mama just told me he's bad *ton.*"

Charlotte shot her cousin a disbelieving look. "Oh, pooh, who cares about that? He is an earl and *that* is all that matters. Well? What did he say to you? What did you say? Did he ask to call on you?"

Gillian felt her face flame as she remembered her appalling gaffe. "He taught me how to waltz, then asked how old I was."

Charlotte's blue eyes widened as she snapped her fan closed and smacked her cousin on the arm with it. "Good! That means he's interested in you!"

"Don't be ridiculous," Gillian said, suddenly exhausted and wishing she were at home, where no silver-eyed rakes lurked to torment her with lascivious thoughts and strange yearnings. "He's an earl and I'm—well, I'm me. No one in particular. Even if he had been temporarily interested, he is no longer."

"Now who's being ridiculous?" Charlotte dimpled. "Of course he must still be interested. What could you possibly do on the dance floor to disinterest a man of his reputation? Even stepping on his toes wouldn't stop the likes of him."

"I did that quite enough, I'm afraid," Gillian admitted, feeling an ache starting at the front of her head. She rubbed her fore-head wearily. "But I went beyond stepping on his toes."

Charlotte looked a mute question at her. Gillian summoned up a feeble smile. "I asked him if he murdered his wife."

Chapter Two

"Miss, if you please, you're wanted in the house."

Gillian looked up from where she squatted in the straw. "I'm sorry, Owen, I can't come now. I believe Ophelia is down with colic again."

The footman sniffed, frowned, looked around the stall, and spotted the two large brown forms lounging against a bundle of hay. "You'll pardon me, miss, but I thought MacTavish said your hounds were not allowed in the stable. I thought he said they made it uninhabitable for man or beast."

Gillian stroked the mare's head where it lay in her lap. "He did, but Lord Collins banished them from the house due to their . . . uh . . . unfortunate tendencies. They have to stay somewhere. I raised them from pups and they are very devoted to me."

Owen sniffed again, blanched, and backed up a step or two. Even with the normal smells associated with a stable, the hounds' problem was noticeable. "As you say, miss. What shall I tell Lady Collins?"

"You may tell her I'm tending my mare. She's ill."

"Yes, miss. Although what Lord Wessex will think—"

"Lord Wessex?" Gillian's shriek unnerved the mare, who rolled back her eyes and curled her upper lip in protest. Uncouth noises from the corner of the stall indicated that the dogs were exhibiting their typical reaction to being startled. Gillian calmed her mare with one hand while fanning her face with another. What on earth was the Lord of Coldness doing here?

Owen grimaced and backed up even farther. "Yes, miss, Lord Wessex. He's called for you."

Hmph. More likely he called to purposely ignore her and pay attention to those people who didn't ask him about his late wife and the suspicious circumstances surrounding her death. Well, he was welcome to them. She would stay out with her animals. They didn't mind what questions she asked. "You may tell my aunt that I will be in as soon as I'm sure Ophelia is out of danger."

Gillian smiled as Owen muttered something about the horse acting like a spoiled child and continued crooning softly to the mare.

"I wonder why he has really called, Ophelia." Gillian scratched behind the mare's ear and tried to puzzle out the unexpected visit. As it had all day, a vision of the darkly handsome face with its vivid silver-gray eyes rose before her. Her heart beat faster as she relived waltzing in his arms. "He must be visiting Charlotte. 'Tis the truth that after I made that blunder about his wife, he couldn't get away from me fast enough. No doubt someone has told him about the little discussion Aunt Honoria and I had last night, and now he's called to tell me not to defend him at the top of my lungs in public."

Ophelia declined to commit herself to any opinion. The dogs snored and emitted periodic statements that Gillian refused to consider as a comment on her situation.

"It would serve me right for trying to aid such a maddening, obstinate man. No"—her anger turned quickly to sadness as she mused upon her sorry situation—"it must be Charlotte whom

Lord Wessex has come to call upon. After all, he's an earl and I'm . . . I'm . . ."

"Completely fascinating."

Gillian's heart leaped up to her throat as the Lord of Magnificence leaned negligently against the stall door. Her breath caught as she stared at him—it simply wasn't fair. No man should be as attractive as he was.

The earl's left eyebrow rose. "Thank you. I'm flattered you think so."

Gillian groaned and dropped her head to her hands. Her Unfortunate Habit had appeared again. "Is it possible to die of embarrassment, my lord?"

"If it were, there would scarce be a handful of people left. Good Lord, what is that smell?"

Gillian blushed even harder and peeked out from between her fingers at him. "It's my dogs. They have a little problem with their inner workings."

As if to emphasize the point, both dogs released proof of their affliction.

"I've been varying their diet weekly," she said, fanning the air in front of her, "but I don't seem to have struck upon the right combinations of food yet."

Wessex flinched but stood his ground. "Keep trying. What are you doing with that mare's head in your lap?"

Ophelia rolled an eye back to look at Wessex and blew loudly out of her mouth.

"She's ill. She tends to colic when I am unable to ride her."

"Hmmm." Wessex entered the stall and squatted down next to the horse, prodding her gently on the belly. Gillian couldn't tear her eyes from the two large and extremely well-muscled thighs directly in her line of vision. He was wearing gleaming black Hessians and buckskin breeches that fit like a second skin. A midnight blue waistcoat and jacket and a modest cravat completed his informal outfit. She wondered what would happen if she were to reach out and run a hand along that thigh.

"Are you all right?"

"Yes, fine, thank you," Gillian choked out, tearing her eyes and her mind from her unseemly imaginings. "I seem to have swallowed wrong. I thought you always wore black?"

"I beg your pardon?"

"Black. I was told you always wear black as a form of penance, and yet you are here wearing buckskins."

"You shouldn't believe everything you hear."

A noise from the corner proved the verity of his statement. Gillian pretended the dogs weren't present and covertly wiped at her stinging eyes.

"Has she been biting at herself?"

"What? Oh, no, she's quite content to lie here and have her head stroked. It keeps her calm."

Wessex's eyes ran quickly over the thin blue muslin of Gillian's dress, paying particular attention to the rounded curves of her breasts and the long length of leg outlined. "Yes, I can see she's content. She's not off her feed?"

"No, but she isn't always when she has colic. MacTavish— he's the head groom—he claims she's just shamming, but I don't believe he likes Ophelia very well. She tries to bite him whenever he's near."

The earl clapped his hands loudly, jumping back quickly as Ophelia leaped to her feet, then held out a hand for Gillian.

"The groom is correct, Miss Leigh. Your horse is fine. Come with me."

It took some doing, but Wessex finally convinced Gillian that her mare was not really ill and just indulging in a bout of self-pity. He escorted her back into the house, through the long hallway and, without pausing, out the front door.

Gillian looked at the scarlet and black phaeton in front of her.

"Your aunt gave you permission to go for a drive with me in the park. I assume you are not adverse to taking the air, especially after having been confined with those dogs?"

"No, of course not. I'd be pleased to go for a drive, but I'm not dressed for it, my lord. You must allow me to change my gown."

Wessex made a show of examining the faded blue muslin. "You look delightful. Come along now, my bays have stood long enough."

Startled at the authority behind the softly spoken words, Gillian found herself accepting his hand and was boosted up into the phaeton. She made one last attempt at propriety. "My bonnet?"

The earl accepted the reins from his tiger and slanted a glance across at her. "Do you burn easily?"

Gillian grimaced. "No, I just freckle."

"You don't need a bonnet." With a click, the lovely bays were sent on their way, and Gillian's spirits soared. The Black Earl had paid a call to see her, to take her for a drive in the park. An afternoon drive, when all of Society would be out seeing each other.

She chattered excitedly as Wessex skillfully maneuvered his team through the crowded streets toward Hyde Park. He listened with only half an ear, more concerned with the growing fascination he felt for Gillian than with paying attention to her babble about whatever it was women talked about.

"I don't know why everyone in England believes that we live with the Indians, but I can assure you we do not. Although I did have the opportunity to discuss the old days with a very interesting Indian who was staying with a merchant on our street. The Indian gentleman shared the technique of scalping with me and even promised to give me one, but he never did." Gillian sounded disappointed for a moment. "On the whole, however, Boston is a very civilized city."

She seemed to expect some sort of response to whatever it was she was saying, so Wessex murmured his agreement and continued to examine the problem his unwelcome attraction to her presented. It was surely madness that allowed her to be

37

Katie MacAlister

constantly in his thoughts. She was a woman, merely a woman. Pretty, yes, lively and entertaining, true, but underneath her innocence and high spirits she was the same as every other woman—manipulating, conniving, and wholly untrustworthy.

"I wasn't really responsible for the man being caught and tried, you understand, my lord. 'Tis the truth it was a coincidence I should bump into him just as he was escaping the jeweler's and, of course, only an accident that our collision resulted in his breaking his arm. So you see, there is no reason the jeweler should have called me a heroine."

"Of course," Wessex replied without thinking, and continued the dissection of his feelings. Given her many faults, why was it he felt like a hollow shell of ice when he wasn't in her presence? He shook his head at his confusion and set out to methodically sort through the jumble of emotions that was clouding his good sense and organized mind.

"Truly, my lord, it is beyond my understanding why the sailors would think it was my fault the mast snapped, and although the captain *might* have been correct when he blamed me for letting it loose, I feel confident that my knots were just as well tied as anyone else's." Her voice stopped briefly as Wessex bowed to an acquaintance who sniffed and quickly looked away in response. When he turned back to her, she was smiling.

"Sailors are a very superstitious group, I've found, hence their belief that women onboard ship are bad luck. Don't you agree, my lord, that such a belief is ridiculous?"

She placed her hand briefly on his arm as she spoke. Wessex smiled in return, mumbled something inane, and felt as if he had been struck.

He wanted her.

This was madness. The answer was simple—he had been too long out of the company of women. Despite having recently taken a mistress, base physical need must be the answer. There could be no other reason why he would be overwhelmed with the desire to brand Gillian as his own, to bask in the warming

38

glow of her innocent sensuality, to bend her until she admitted she was his and his alone. He shook his head again. Surely this was insanity. He knew his duties as well as the next man; he was to pick a suitable wife from those women deemed eligible by Society. Daughters of fellow peers, or perhaps even a titled young widow, but not a penniless, unconnected, thoroughly unconventional woman. He would have to choose a wife from among the insipid, mindless chits that were dangled in front of him, and no matter how much he appreciated Gillian's spontaneous laughter, no matter how bright her eyes glowed when she laughed, no matter how golden she appeared in the sunlight with her hair a beacon of flames dancing in a halo around her head, he could not marry her.

"Why the hell not?" He spoke the words without thinking.

Gillian looked startled at the rawness in his voice, but her delectable pink lips curved into a smile as she begged his pardon. "Why the hell not what, Lord Wessex?"

Lord, he enjoyed her brashness. "Nothing; it's of little consequence. Make your bow to Lady Fielding, she's trying to get your attention."

He pulled up the team briefly so Gillian could speak with her aunt's sister, and watched her closely as she conversed. She was the granddaughter of an earl, and her manners were suitable, if a little rough. Training would help her overcome most of her gaucheness, although Wessex recognized instinctively that he only wanted to tame her spirit, not break it.

Why shouldn't he offer for her? She was a pleasant companion, appeared to be well read and conversant with the topics of the day, a fact that came to light when she shyly admitted that she read her uncle's daily *Times* whenever she could. Wessex approved of her inquiring mind and curious nature—up to a point. It would be his task to see to it that she learned her proper duty and place as his countess. She would be a good mother to his son, he mused as he gave the signal to the leader, and would provide him with the heir he needed. Her pleasant, unassuming nature boded well for her happiness; she would be content with life in the country, a dutiful wife who would tend to his needs and not interfere in his life.

Indeed, the more he thought about it, the harder pressed he was to find any fault with her at all. She was witty, amusing, and at the same time possessed a gentle nature and dignity that . . .

"Stop!" she screamed in his ear, startling him into compliance. Gripping his arm, she leaped over his legs and flung herself off the phaeton.

Dear God, she was going to get herself killed weaving in and out of the heavy traffic like that! Wessex snarled an oath to himself, tossed the ribbons to his tiger, and leaped out after his soon-to-be-bride before she was flattened.

He was shaking by the time he reached her side, but whether from anger or fright he didn't know. He suspected it was both, and clenched and unclenched his hands in an attempt to keep from strangling her on the spot. He took a deep, calming breath, mopped his handkerchief across his perspiring brow, and reminded himself that he was by nature a calm man, a placid man, a man fully in control of his emotions, and he would be damned before he allowed the daft Amazon to get the better of him.

"What the devil do you mean, leaping off the phaeton like that, madam?" he bellowed at her. "Have you no brains, woman? You might have been killed!"

Gillian looked up from where she was kneeling on the sidewalk next to a ragged street urchin and scowled at him. "Hush, my lord. You're frightening the child."

Wessex boggled at her. Did she just order him to be quiet? He shook his head. No one, not even a clearly deranged woman like Gillian, would be so foolish.

"Miss Leigh," he ground out between his teeth, trying desperately to leash the raging volcano of temper seething inside him. She'd taken at least ten years off his life, scaring him with her heedless actions. "Would you be so kind as to inform me why you saw fit to leave the safe confines of my phaeton to dash recklessly across the road?"

Gillian was crooning softly to a small, extremely dirty street Arab. Wessex guessed the child was female only because there was a wilting clump of pathetic violets clutched in the urchin's filthy fist.

"My lord, surely you must recognize that this poor child is in distress and in need of our care."

Two soft brown eyes peered up at him through a curtain of matted hair. The imp had the cheek to grin at him as she cuddled closer to Gillian.

Wessex counted to ten before he addressed the woman kneeling before him. "I appreciate the fact that you have a kind and sensitive nature, Miss Leigh, but now is hardly the time to impress me with your good works. You could have been kil—"

"Impress you with my good works, my lord?"

If Wessex didn't know better, he'd believe the glitter in the eyes of the woman who slowly rose to her feet before him indicated annoyance. He nodded and waved toward the child, who had her eyes greedily fixed on the earl's watch chain. "It is obvious to me that you seek my approval and wish to demonstrate your concern for the less fortunate, but it is not necessary."

Gillian stared at him openmouthed. God's nightgown, the arrogance of the man was overwhelming! Impress him, indeed! If he hadn't addled her brains so thoroughly by standing there looking every inch the handsome rake she knew he was, she'd give him a piece of her mind. What remained of it, that is. A tug at her sleeve reminded her of her duty, however.

"My lord, a coin, please."

"A coin?" Wessex frowned at her outstretched hand.

"Yes, a coin for the child."

So surprised was he by her request that he handed her a coin without thinking. She knelt before the child. "Now, my dear, don't fret. I shall take charge and you will not have to live on the streets any longer, subject to cold and hunger and the abuses of strangers. I'm sure my aunt and uncle will be happy to take you in and see to your welfare. You'll be educated, of course—perhaps trained as a lady's maid? Would you like that? Yes, of course you would. You don't happen to speak French, do you? 'Tis of no matter; take my hand, sweet. Lord Wessex will drive us somewhere we can feed you, and then he'll escort us home and you'll have a bath and—"

Wessex started to interrupt but was cut short when the child spat out a curse, snatched the coin Gillian held, and dashed off into the crowd.

She watched the child disappear, then closed her mouth with an audible snap and turned to face the earl. "Don't say it."

He looked for a moment as if he would take exception to her instruction, then without a word held out his hand and escorted her back to his phaeton.

An hour later, as he was handing her down in front of her uncle's house, she couldn't help but shiver at the sight of his cold, unmoving face. Surely a man who had gone through as many trials as he had during their drive should be showing some emotion by now—annoyance over the scene with the street urchin, exasperation when she argued vehemently that they were traveling in the wrong direction based on the position of the sun and the direction of the wind, and finally, there was that painful episode with his horses . . . but no, it was best to put that behind them. The Lord of Granite held her hand for a moment longer than was proper, and when she looked up into his eyes, he held her gaze.

Her mind went completely blank of all thoughts but those of the man standing before her. Slowly he raised her hand to his lips. Gillian gulped at the shock of the touch and tried to think of some way to apologize for the disastrous outing but couldn't form words under the penetrating scrutiny of those silver-gray eyes.

"Tomorrow, madam." He bowed and turned to leave. Gillian floated up the steps and through the opened door with only a brief greeting to the footman.

Tomorrow? What could he mean?

"What does he mean?" Gillian asked three hours later, as she lay prone on her stomach on Charlotte's bed, kicking her feet in the air and watching her cousin's maid create long blond ringlets out of the girl's mass of hair.

"For heaven's sake, Gillian, you are a goose! I can't believe you're seven years older than me. He's paying court to you, of course. Just as the dangerous Raoul did to Beatrice in *The Castle of Almeria.*"

Gillian looked thoughtful as she picked at the soft shawl in front of her. "Was that the novel that opens with the heroine covered with blood after she believes she murdered her father who tried to rape her and is later befriended by the kindly vegetarian?"

"No, that was *Louisa*, or *The Cottage on the Moor.*"

Gillian tapped a long finger on her lower lip. "Is it the one that had the heroine beset with wolves and marauding strangers after she's kidnapped by her sinister father's men, only to be nearly ravished in a French chateau?"

Charlotte frowned briefly, then shook her head. "No, that was *Romance of the Forest.*"

"Then it must be the one where the heroine strangles the nefarious lord who attempts to sully her virtue, and the evil villainess gets an unspeakable disease due to her lust for anything in trousers."

"Yes, that's Almeria, although I don't understand why Madam de la Rogue was made out to be such an evil woman. I quite understood her fascination with the count. And the blond footman. And, of course, that rogue of an under-gardener. However, as I was saying, Lord Wessex is clearly made of the same romantic material as Raoul. Just as Raoul fought the kidnappers, pirates, and the evil brandy-swilling monks of Clermont in order to be with his true love, so, I feel sure, would Lord Wessex fight for you."

Gillian rolled her eyes and made an unladylike snort. "Oh, yes, why didn't I see that? Of course, it makes perfect sense. Here is a man—wealthy, enormously attractive even if he is thought to be a murderer, and in possession of a title—and he falls madly in love with untitled, poor, freckled, opinionated, *clumsy* me. How could I have missed such an obvious fact?"

"Don't be sarcastic, cousin, it will give you spots. You have many charms, even if you don't have a dowry or a title. Perhaps Lord Wessex is enamored with you. After what you've told me about your drive this afternoon, such a romantic gesture would certainly fit with his actions today."

Gillian sucked in her lower lip and considered Charlotte's comments. She possessed enough self-awareness to realize that the attraction she felt for the Black Earl went beyond what was acceptable for casual acquaintances, and in an honest moment she even put a name to the emotion. That same honesty forced her to admit that such instantaneous and overwhelming attachments were rare and not, as a rule, duplicated on the gentleman's side. Pride drove Gillian into wanting the earl to spend time in her company not because he was bored and had nothing better to do, but because he found her witty, amusing, and completely captivating.

She frowned at the figure seated before the dressing table. "What charms?"

"I beg your pardon?"

"You said I have many charms. What, in particular, do you consider my many charms?"

Charlotte waved away her maid and turned to look at her cousin sprawled out across her bed.

"Stand up."

Gillian sighed and rose from the bed, trying without success to smooth the wrinkles out of her new gold evening gown.

"You're tall," Charlotte pronounced, circling her cousin and eyeing her from ears to toes.

"I know that," Gillian replied tartly. "I'm taller than most men."

"But not taller than the earl. In fact, you come only to his nose. That's good."

Gillian rolled her eyes again but kept her comments to herself.

"You carry yourself well."

"Oh, come now, cousin! I fall over my own very substantial feet!"

"Only when you aren't watching where you are going. Henceforth, and especially when you are in his lordship's presence, you will watch where you are walking."

"This is ridiculous." Gillian waved a hand in a gesture of defeat. "He's not really interested in me; he's only passing time until he finds someone suitable to wed."

"Why would he pass time with you when there are suitable women available now who would throw themselves at his feet?"

Gillian thought about that for a moment. Her hopes and reality were separated by a deep, dark abyss. "I believe I amuse him. His mouth is always twitching, as if he wants to smile but won't let himself."

"Aha! Compatibility! It's very important in married life. I wouldn't want you to dislike your husband. Now, let's see . . ." Charlotte continued her tour around Gillian. "You're intelligent. You can speak three languages and you're very well read."

"Only in the classics, although I have been enjoying the novels you've lent me. Uncle Jonas wouldn't let me read them—he said they are sinful and depraved and would lead to the downfall of society as we know it."

It was Charlotte's turn to snort. "Wessex is surely a man who appreciates a mind in a woman, no matter what she reads. I can't see him with a simpering idiot like Diana Templeton, can you?"

"She does have a large dowry. And a large . . . er . . . bosom. Men like that too."

"She's also the daughter of a marquis, but she has the wits of a common garden toad. No, your brain is sure to appeal to Lord Wessex, and your bosom is just as large as hers, so you've met both of those requirements." Charlotte tipped her head as she considered her cousin. "I hope you're not afraid to speak your mind in front of him."

Gillian smiled. "Have you ever known me to be able to hold my tongue?"

Charlotte continued to look thoughtful. "No, but I don't anticipate that that should be too much of a problem. I fancy Wessex enjoys honesty."

"So I have all the necessary ingredients to make me the perfect wife to the Black Earl?"

"Yes, I believe so," Charlotte replied cheerfully and checked her own figure in a long oval mirror.

"Except one."

"What's that?"

"He's not in love with me."

Charlotte turned and looked at her cousin with a gentle, pitying smile. "What has love got to do with the earl asking you to wed him?"

"Charlotte! I couldn't possibly marry a man who didn't love me." Charlotte gave her a weary look that spoke of wisdom beyond her eighteen years. Gillian looked at her hands twisting the gold gauze of her overskirt. "I suppose a love match is out of the question—no one marries for love any more."

"Only romantics and women of a low station," Charlotte agreed.

Gillian released the handful of gauze and smoothed her palm over it. Meeting her cousin's eyes in the mirror, she smiled. "As if it matters—we're talking foolishness, my dearest Charlotte. The earl has much plumper pigeons to pluck than me."

Charlotte gave her gown a final tweak and spun around.

"We'll see what happens tomorrow. If he calls for you again, we'll know he's serious. Mama wouldn't allow him to dally with you if his intentions weren't honorable. Heavens, there goes the second gong. Papa will be furious if we hold up dinner!"

The two women hurried down the hallway.

"What will you wear tomorrow?" Charlotte asked, pausing to pirouette before a mirror at the top of the stairs.

"What does it matter?"

Charlotte made an annoyed sound and started down the stairs. "What you wear matters greatly! You don't want to appear before the earl in another of your work gowns," she tossed over her shoulder. "You should strive for a look of sophistication and elegance, as I do."

"A gown isn't going to make me sophisticated and elegant." Gillian laughed. She glanced at her reflection in the mirror, made a face, then turned and sprinted down the stairs. "I have red hair, green eyes, and freckles, Charlotte, and I'm not in the least sophisticated or elegant. You can put your faith in the fact that no matter how well suited you might believe us to be, the earl will not pay his addresses to me."

Charlotte gave her cousin a mysterious smile as she swept into the dining room.

Unaware that he was the object of discussion, Noble Britton, known to the *ton* by the exciting sobriquet of the Black Earl, sat in the smoke-filled card room of White's and proceeded to win most of the family fortune of Manfred, Lord Briceland. Despite his reputation as a merciless, cold predator, Noble did not enjoy destroying men, even foolish young men like Lord Briceland.

"My vowels, Lord Wessex." The young man's hand trembled as he scrawled his signature.

"You will, of course, be by in the morning to redeem them?" Wessex drawled as his long fingers stroked the tablecloth. The earl had every intention of refusing to accept the viscount's money, but he wanted him to spend a sleepless night considering the implications of his foolish behavior first.

Pale and looking distinctly ill, Lord Briceland nodded and staggered out of the room, calling hoarsely for a whiskey.

"Well done, Noble; you haven't lost your touch. I do hope the young man is duly appreciative of the fact you saved his fortune from the likes of Mansfield and the other vultures who have been circling him all evening."

"Thank you, Harry." Wessex acknowledged his friend's compliment and waved him and Sir Hugh into nearby chairs. "Brandy, gentlemen? Peel! Three brandies."

The Marquis Rosse adjusted his spectacles and took the offered balloon of brandy. Like Wessex, he was in his evening blacks, creating a somber counterpoint to Sir Hugh's emerald waistcoat and indigo coat and breeches. Wessex thought the younger man looked like a peacock as he sat casting nervous glances around the room to see who was present, fiddling with several watch fobs, his quizzing glass, and two large emeralds on his pudgy fingers. He had reason to know those emeralds were paste and not the real thing.

"Where have you been?" Rosse leaned back and questioned the earl. "I thought you were taking Mariah to that play at the Lyceum. It's all she and Alice talked about today."

Wessex rubbed a finger across his lips as the brandy snaked its way down his throat and formed a warm pool in his stomach. His eyes narrowed as an acquaintance began to move toward the threesome, then, catching sight of the earl, turned on his heel and left the room. Another cut. They were getting bolder about it, too. "Does it occur to you that our mistresses are entirely too forthcoming with one another about our private plans?"

Sir Hugh snorted as Rosse grinned. "They are twins, Noble. And they do like to talk. I suppose it's only natural that they share us, so to speak."

"I suppose so, although it matters not. I will be giving Mariah her congé tomorrow." Wessex pulled a silver case from his coat and offered a cheroot to his friends. A servant dashed forward to light the men's cigars.

"Tired of her already?" Sir Hugh asked, surprised. Although Wessex did not often employ a mistress for any length of time, he had set up Mariah only two weeks past.

"Tired of her incessant chatter, yes, but that's not the reason I am dispensing with her services. I will be marrying in three days, and much as it would shock the *ton* if they knew, I intend on honoring my marriage vows."

Rosse and Sir Hugh both choked on their brandy. Five minutes later, when Rosse was once again able to breathe without gasping, he replaced his spectacles and stared at his friend.

"Who's the lucky chit?"

"Gillian Leigh."

"Leigh? The Amazon?" Sir Hugh squeaked, almost dropping his brandy. "Good Lord, Wessex, have you lost your mind? She's nobody! You can't marry her, even with her connection to Collins."

In his distress, Sir Hugh did not notice the menace in the earl's sudden stillness, but the marquis did.

"Tolly . . ." he began warningly.

Wessex raised his hand. "No, let him continue, Harry. I would hear what words of wisdom our young friend has to impart to me."

Sir Hugh sputtered under the gaze of the mocking gray eyes. " 'Pon my word, Wessex, you're jesting with me! You can't be serious—a man of your consequence can't marry some penniless chit from the colonies, no matter how badly he wants to bed her. Offer her your house in Kensington if you're finished with your bit of muslin, but for God's sake, man, don't waste your name on an undesirable!"

Wessex's eyes never left those of the gently perspiring baronet before him. No expression flickered across his impassive face, but Rosse noticed that the long fingers clasped about the stem of the glass he held were white with tension. "Have a care, Tolly, you speak of my future bride," Wessex replied in a soft, dangerous voice.

Rosse moved uneasily in his chair. Although he had known both men for several years, he did not believe a long acquaintance would stop the situation from escalating into a challenge if Tolly continued along his present path. Rosse decided to remedy the situation as best he could.

"I'm sure Tolly didn't mean to interfere, Noble. He's as surprised as I am by your announcement—you haven't wasted any time picking out a suitable countess. I know you're the master of efficiency and organization, but don't you think that you need more than two visits to acquaint yourself properly with the young woman?"

"I do not."

The look Wessex shot his old friend was fraught with warning, but Harry grinned in response. "And then there is your choice of bride—forgive me, old man, but did you not just two evenings ago specifically detail the list of attributes your wife would possess?"

"I did." Rosse was relieved to see one side of Wessex's mouth quirk up as he answered. Only Harry was granted permission to tease and challenge the earl, owing largely to the fact that the two had grown up together on estates that touched. That, and the unspeakable event five years past that had drawn them closer than most brothers.

"I'll admit Miss Leigh possesses a particularly luscious body"—Sir Hugh ignored Wessex's warning frown—"but she can hardly be considered countess material. Surely there must be some other chit—a *nobly born* chit—who would suit you better."

Ever the peacemaker, Rosse hurried to distract his friend. "I like her, Tolly. She's a bit of an Original, but I'm sure Noble knows what he's about."

Wessex gave his friend a slight bow of acknowledgment.

Sir Hugh fiddled with the ribbon of his quizzing glass and

appeared to be lost in thought. His eyes were bright, almost feverish, as he watched the earl closely. "Why her?" he asked suddenly. "You've only seen her twice—why the Amazon?"

Wessex gazed down at the brandy he was absentmindedly swirling. "Any man with an intelligent and well-ordered mind would be able to choose a bride upon the first meeting, and as I pride myself on the latter, if not the former, I did not find it a difficult situation to look over the available crop and make a rational choice."

"You're aware that she is the one who set fire to the Lincolns' house the other night? From what Lady Dell says, your intended is not the most adept of creatures," Sir Hugh pointed out.

The other side of Wessex's mouth curled as he recalled the waltz they had shared. She had tried her best but had succeeded in stepping on his feet more than the ballroom floor. Still, he had felt in her a hidden innate grace, and noted that when she was not self-aware, she was as lithe and graceful as a swan. And then, of course, there was the warmth she generated, warmth that fingered its way through all the layers of ice that coated his soul, leaving him with a gentle glow deep within.

"We'll rub along well together."

"What about . . ." Rosse hesitated to speak on the subject but was worried that his friend was making an uncharacteristically hasty decision. "What about Nick?"

Noble raised one sable brow. "What about him?"

Rosse glanced at Tolliver, then back to his friend. "Will you trust her with him?"

"I believe she will be very good for Nick. Is there a reason I shouldn't trust her with my son?"

Rosse considered his brandy. "No, of course not. I had just wondered whether you would be . . . comfortable allowing her to have access to him after what the poor lad has gone through, losing his mother when he was just a year old, and then with . . ."

An icy wind howled inside of Wessex. "Elizabeth?"

Rosse nodded, a frown creasing his brow. "You swore you'd never trust him with any woman again. I find it hard to believe that after only two meetings, you have such a high estimation of Miss Leigh that you are willing to entrust your son's care to her."

"She will be an excellent stepmother," Wessex replied, the set of his jaw belying the stubbornness behind the statement.

Rosse leaned forward. "Noble, what is it about her that is making you act so . . . so spontaneously?"

"I never act spontaneously, Harry, you know that. As I told Tolly, I am a man of order and control. I viewed the available stock, I took into consideration a number of desirable characteristics such as temperament, intelligence, and pliability, and I winnowed down the choices to one obvious woman. There was no spontaneity involved."

Rosse stared at him for a minute, then stood as Wessex rose and offered his hand. "I do hope you'll allow me to be your groomsman?"

"Of course. I will procure the special license in the morning, then acquaint the bride and her family of her good fortune."

The marquis gave a sharp bark of laughter that he quickly converted into a cough. "You haven't yet offered for her?"

Wessex brushed an infinitesimal bit of dirt from his immaculate sleeve. Sir Hugh hesitated for a moment, then joined the duo and strolled with them out the door and down the stairs leading to the hall.

"No, I haven't. Is there a reason why you believe I should worry?" Wessex drawled the question in a voice laden with indifference.

"None, other than the fact that she might reject you," Rosse responded. "The gossip about Elizabeth's death has taken the *ton* by storm, Noble—already you've been cut by a number of prominent men. Even you have to admit that your reputation is a daunting obstacle. The Amazon's uncle might refuse to allow you to pay your addresses."

The Black Earl shot his friend a disbelieving look as he accepted his cloak, hat, and walking stick, then stepped out the front door. "I care little for what the *ton* thinks of me, as you well know. They cannot harm me, so let them say what they will. As for the other, I doubt if Collins will refuse the marriage settlement I am prepared to make."

"For the Amazon," Sir Hugh said, his voice thick with emotion.

The three men paused outside. Noble rubbed his hands to warm them as he looked up at a waxing moon. "For, as you say, the Amazon."

Rosse looked curiously at the baronet's face, wondering briefly at the expression behind the pale blue hooded eyes, then turned and walked with Wessex to the earl's carriage. With one hand braced on the side, he leaned in through the open door. "Does Tolly know it is you saving him from bankruptcy?"

"No, and I'd rather it stayed that way. If he found out it was I offering more than the land was worth, it would cause him no little embarrassment."

Rosse considered the Black Earl for a moment. "Saving his neck by keeping the bank from foreclosing goes beyond friendship, Noble."

Wessex looked away and shrugged. "I had a debt of honor to his father."

"Which you paid in full when you bailed Tolly out of that gambling mess two years ago."

Noble shrugged again.

"About this other situation . . ." Rosse gave in to the grin he had been battling for the last half hour. "You might be right in your choice of brides, Noble. A word of warning, however—in addition to being very good for Nick, you might just find your Amazon will turn out to be very good for you as well." With a tip of his hat, he strolled off toward his own carriage whistling a jaunty tune.

Katie MacAlister

Sir Hugh watched the two depart before gaining his own carriage and giving his coachman an address in Kensington.

Gillian sat on the scullery maid's chair the following afternoon and thought.

"Table scraps are not helping matters."

A tiny, shriveled woman no bigger than a seven-year-old child perched on a chair across the table. "No, miss, it just seems to make them worse."

"Have we tried Mr. Mystico's advice? He is lauded in the *Times* as being a genius with digestive complaints. What works for people must certainly work for dogs, don't you think?" Gillian waved toward the booklet she had recently purchased from a street seller.

The tiny woman snorted. "You don't pay no heed to those things you read in newspapers, miss. Those writers are a bunch of scoundrels and scallywags they are. No, the answer is in here. We'll find it, miss, don't you worry none." She tapped the side of her wizened head and screwed up her face in thought.

"But we've tried everything, Cook. I'm at my wit's end—Piddle is bad enough, but Erp is becoming a positive leper among dogs!"

The Collins's cook pursed her lips and counted off her fingers. "We've tried meal, game, and stewed vegetables. Potatoes, turnips, and beans."

Gillian shuddered. "The beans were a disaster. What haven't we tried?"

"Corn?"

"Two months ago. It didn't work."

Cook's eyes roamed the kitchen as she mentally reviewed the pantry. "Rice?"

Gillian sat up straight in her chair. "Rice? No, I don't believe we've tried rice. Do you think it would help? Perhaps if we—"

Owen the footman interrupted the discussion of the bloodhounds' diet with a request for Gillian's presence in Lord Collins's study.

Knowing that nothing raised her uncle's ire more than tardiness, Gillian promised to return to the discussion and raced up the backstairs to the first floor. There was no time to pin up the strands of hair that had come down from her haphazard chignon, or to change into a less wrinkled gown. Gillian took a deep breath and stepped forward as Owen announced, "Miss Leigh, m'lord."

Miracle of miracles, Uncle Theo was smiling. Gillian blinked in surprise. Her uncle was not given to noticing her much, let alone finding something about her that would please him, but she dutifully beamed back an answering smile. She held on to her smile until a dark shadow removed itself from the wall and strode forward. Her smile wavered and crumpled into a soft gasp that only Wessex heard. For some reason her reaction pleased him immensely.

"My dear, I believe you know why Lord Wessex is here?" Lord Collins asked archly.

Gillian's stomach dropped into her boots. Oh, yes, she knew why he was here. The Lord of Traitors must have decided her behavior yesterday was so horrifying that he was compelled to report it to her uncle. She frowned at him, annoyed. Did he not promise to never mention the embarrassing incident with the street urchin? Did he not accept her apology when she startled one of his matched bays into stepping on his foot? Did he not admit that it was a minor wound only, that the boot could be easily replaced, and that William, his tiger, had wished for a rest in the country, and thus the slight injury to his back was really a blessing in disguise as it would allow him to rest for three to four weeks, depending on the doctor's recommendation? He had indeed! She remembered quite clearly him insisting the episode was nothing but an accident, and not her fault at all. And now here he was tattling on her! Gillian narrowed her eyes at him and decided quickly on a course of complete indifference. It wouldn't matter one whit what tales he carried to her uncle; she would deny knowledge of everything.

"Yes, I believe I do know why his lordship is present," she replied with a dignity that would do a queen proud. She would cut him cold, that's what she would do. Imitating his annoying habit, she raised one eyebrow and gazed at him coolly.

"Ah, excellent, excellent. And what do you have to say about the situation?" Lord Collins asked.

"What do I have to say?" Gillian turned to her uncle with a gay little laugh. "Why, nothing! The matter is so trivial it is beneath my notice."

Theodore Hartshorne, Lord Collins, stared at his niece and wondered if she had gone completely mad. "A matter so trivial it is beneath your notice, madam?"

Gillian stepped back when his voice hit a note an octave higher than normal, but she was determined to stick to her plan. Without glancing at the dark figure looming immediately to her right, she straightened her shoulders and lifted her chin.

"That is what I said. A trivial matter. One I cannot even recall, it is so very trivial. Infinitely trivial, if you comprehend my meaning."

She wondered idly how it was possible for a person to turn crimson in the face as her uncle had, then quickly became concerned when he seemed about to succumb to a fit of apoplexy. His mouth opened and shut but no sound came out. His eyes bulged. The hair on his ears stood on end. "Uncle? Are you quite all right?"

"Trivial?" was the only word to escape the earl's lips.

"I will fetch Aunt Honoria," Gillian said as she turned to leave. A hand gripping her arm painfully stopped her.

"I believe, madam, that you owe me an explanation."

"I owe *you* an explanation?" Gillian fumed at the scowling earl. "How dare you! You promised you would not mention this and yet here you are, tattling to my uncle. If there are explanations to be handed about, my lord, you are the one who should be offering them, not me."

Wessex loosened his grip on her arm and narrowed his fascinating eyes. "What are you talking about?"

Gillian shot a glance at her uncle, who looked as if he would swoon at any moment, then leaned forward and hissed into the earl's ear, "Yesterday. Your horses. When I startled them—you said it did not matter in the least!"

The sound of laughter rolling around the small study snapped Lord Collins out of his brush with apoplexy. Both he and Gillian gaped at Wessex in surprise. The Black Earl was laughing. No, not just laughing; he was holding on to his side and wiping tears.

"I hardly think it is that funny," Gillian muttered with a disgruntled look as she watched the earl wipe his eyes. " 'Tis not you who has to live with these things."

"On the contrary, my dear, I fear it is me who will have to live with these things. Lord Collins, if I might have a moment alone with your niece?"

Gillian waited until after her uncle left, then looked cautiously at the earl. "Am I?"

He stepped forward and took her hand. "Are you what?"

"Your dear?"

Wessex stilled and held her green-eyed gaze with his own. "Your uncle has given me permission to pay you my addresses. I would not offer for a woman unless she was very dear to me indeed."

"Oh." Gillian tipped her head to one side and wondered that she didn't float away with this feeling of happiness. "Very well. I accept."

She smiled to herself over the fleeting look of surprise on his face. She had a feeling it wasn't easy to disconcert the earl, and she relished this experience. A little giddy, she watched as he made a bow, kissed her hand, and matter-of-factly informed her that unless she had objections, they would be married immediately. He had secured a special license and suggested two days hence as their wedding day.

"I have no objections at all, my lord; your plan is quite agreeable."

Wessex stared at her, surprised by her quick acquiescence. It was his experience that even the most eager of brides demanded declarations of love or assurances of undying devotion before they accepted a man. "Do you have any questions? Concerns? Comments?"

This last was said with an emphasis Gillian couldn't help but notice. She gave in to a smile and shook her head. "No, none at all. Do you?"

The corner of his mouth twitched. "No, I believe my questions have all been answered. Gillian—" He stepped forward and brushed a strand of hair from her cheek. Gillian held her breath as the feather-light touch raised goosebumps on her arms. "You are easy in your mind about this match? I would not have you fear me. Despite what you may have heard, I am not a cruel man, nor am I given to mistreating anyone who depends upon me."

While he spoke, he pulled her into an easy embrace. Gillian had to remind herself to breathe as the spicy essence that was the Lord of Miracles curled up and around her. She met his unblinking gaze with a steady look that she fervently hoped belied her racing heart and shaking knees. "I am quite easy in my mind, my lord. I believe we will suit very well indeed. You seem slightly concerned about my reaction, however. Are you having second thoughts?"

"No, Gillian, I am not. As we are now betrothed, do you think you could use my Christian name?"

"Certainly, my lord. What is it?"

"It's Noble."

Gillian smiled. "I am sure it is. Your parents would hardly bestow an unsuitable name on their firstborn son. What is your name?"

Wessex closed his eyes briefly. "My name is Noble."

"Yes, I know." Gillian nodded encouragingly. "And it is . . . ?"

"Noble," he ground out, cursing his mother's whimsy and his father's lack of foresight. "My name is Noble."

Another smile lit Gillian's face. "Oh, your name is *Noble*. How interesting. Is there a story behind it?"

"No."

"Ah."

The pair stood looking at one another. Wessex felt obliged to break the silence. He leaned in closer to her. "Gillian—"

At the sound of her name on those wonderful lips, the goosebumps trailed up her arms and down her back. She was willing to wager her entire year's pin money that he was going to kiss her.

"I wouldn't take that wager," he said with a smile just before he leaned down and brushed his lips briefly against hers. The embarrassment she felt that she had once again spoken her thoughts was quickly drowned in the overwhelming surge of emotion generated by his touch. He stepped back, watching her carefully.

"Oh," she said, words failing her. She wondered what he would do if she threw herself back into his arms and claimed the kisses she had been dreaming of the last few nights.

"Do you think it is possible, my lord, that one or both of us might die in the very near future?"

Lines appeared between the two lovely black wings that were his eyebrows. "Do you know something I do not?"

"No. I just think it is best to live one's life to the fullest. I would hate to die leaving something undone."

Wessex stared at her for the count of seven. Then, as if he couldn't help himself, he asked, "What is it you wish to do?"

"This," she replied, and threw herself on him. Unfortunately, having his newly betrothed fiancée spring upon him was the last thing the Black Earl was expecting at that moment and, caught off balance, he fell backwards against an incidental table, knocking over both the table and a large vase of flowers. The vase struck him squarely on the head, rendering him unconscious.

Gillian Anne Honoria Leigh married Noble Edward Benjamin Nicholas Britton, twelfth Earl of Wessex, two days later by special license. The groom, presenting a dramatic picture with his forehead swathed in bandages, was dignified and appeared his usual expressionless self. The bride, owing to a somewhat stupefying state of shock, managed to get through the ceremony without maiming or disabling anyone.

Chapter Three

Gillian looked out the open window of the carriage at the figure of a large man riding a dappled gray horse, then back at the two large hounds residing on the seat across from her. She didn't blame Noble, not really. Although she had arranged for Piddle and Erp to start a diet based mostly on rice, boiled chicken, and a variety of wholesome vegetables, there was no time to tell if the change was successful. They were still a bit much in confined quarters. One look at her traveling companions had prompted her husband of two hours to declare that he would ride his horse the distance to Nethercote. Although Gillian would have preferred getting to know him during the four-hour journey to his estate, she found it hard to fault his reticence.

Leaning across to open the other window, she returned to her corner of the carriage and continued watching her husband's broad back.

"Husband," she said to the dogs, rolling the word around on her tongue. It felt good. It felt right. It felt large and masculine and absolutely thrilling.

"I have a husband. An earl husband. Lord of Kisses." It got

better the more she said it, especially when she recalled the kiss of peace that had sealed her marriage vows.

"I think I took him by surprise," she told the dogs. Erp thumped his tail, but Piddle just gave her his usual melancholy stare. "I do hope his lip heals quickly." She thought for a moment. "And his head. And the toe that one of his bays crushed."

She looked back out the window. He really was the most amazing man. She couldn't wait until tonight, when he would finally answer all the questions that had arisen when Aunt Honoria sat her down to have a talk about wedded life. She knew her aunt had meant well, but surely Honoria must have had some of her facts confused. It wasn't as if she, Gillian, were naïve, after all—she was five and twenty, not a girl fresh from the schoolroom. Ah, well, tonight it would be straight in her mind. She smiled at the thought of having Noble all to herself, alone, with no distractions, and mindful of her propensity for unfortunate events, she made a mental note to clear the room of all potentially lethal objects. It wouldn't do to accidentally strike down her bridegroom while her curiosity was still piqued.

Three hours later the carriage turned between two massive wrought-iron gates and rolled up a smooth drive edged with tall oaks.

"Nethercote," she breathed, her heart racing, and peered out the window for the first glimpse of her new home. Rounding one last curve, the house finally came into view. A large four-story structure with wings extending on either end, it was built of a warm gold-colored stone. Seemingly hundreds of windows glittered in the early evening sun, dazzling the eye.

"Turrets!" Gillian exclaimed as she grasped her husband's hand and alighted from the carriage.

Noble looked at her bemused face and felt her pleasure warming him deep inside his chest. Her cheeks pink with excitement, her green eyes the color of emeralds in sunlight, Gillian was the picture of delight personified. She turned to Noble and gifted him with a blinding smile. The warmth in his chest spread as

he placed her hand on his arm and took her forward to introduce her to the staff gathered on the front steps.

"This is Tremayne, my butler."

Gillian shot the earl an amused look. "Your butler, indeed,
my lord. Pull the other one, it has bells on it! Good afternoon,
Tremayne. How did you get here from London so quickly?"

"My dear, this isn't Tremayne my head coachman; this is his
brother."

"No! Truly? They look identical! How unusual." Noble nodded and introduced her to Mrs. Hogue, the housekeeper, then
followed behind as she was introduced to the rest of the female
staff. When Tremayne took her to meet the male staff, she came
to a halt and giggled.

"You're playing tricks on me, aren't you Tremayne? You must
have ridden very hard indeed to arrive here before us." She
waggled a finger in front of his face.

Noble took a deep breath. There were times when he felt his
life resembled a French farce. "This is my valet, my dear. He
isn't Tremayne the coachman."

Gillian looked from the valet to the butler. "Triplets? Identical
triplets?"

The two men nodded. Gillian bit her lip to keep from laughing. Wessex sighed again and, taking his wife's arm, escorted
her over to where two people stood aside from the staff.

"This is Rogerson, the tutor. And Nicholas, my son," he said
as she was in mid-curtsy. Her knee seemed to buckle for a
moment, but she caught herself and whirled around to face him.

"Your son? You have a son? You have a son and you didn't
bother telling me? A *son*, Noble?"

Noble narrowed his eyes as he watched surprise, astonishment, then anger flit over her face. Her eyes glittered back dangerously at him. He was about to suggest that they step inside
to continue the conversation when she threw herself into his
arms, kissed him directly on the spot she had accidentally

nipped during their wedding ceremony, then was out of his arms and hugging his son.

"Imagine that; I have a son and I didn't even know it," she chirped at the nine-year-old boy, who looked just as flabbergasted at the turn of events as his father. "You look just like your father, you know. The same lovely gray eyes and black eyelashes. And the same chin. Oh, I'm so happy! I have acquired a husband and a son on the same day!"

She took Nick by the arm and started toward the house, chattering as she went. A bit dazed, Noble followed, wondering when she would notice that the boy didn't speak.

"A cold supper, Mrs. Hogue," he told the housekeeper. "My dear, Mrs. Hogue will show you to your rooms. I will meet you in the library in an hour. Nick, Rogerson, my study if you please."

Noble waited until Gillian went upstairs, the two hounds trailing morosely after her, before following his son and the tutor into his study. He had fully expected his troubled son to reject his stepmother, but so far the earl noted only stunned astonishment on the boy's face. He hoped his instincts were right and that Gillian would be just the antidote Nick needed to bring him back to the world of the living.

Noble knew only too well what had driven the boy into the hell that had robbed him of speech, and although he had been patient and followed the advice of the doctors, the lad still refused to speak. Since Noble himself had built formidable walls against the pain and heartbreak of loving unwisely, he knew just how hard it would be for Gillian to breach the boy's defenses, but he had hope that if anyone could do it, she could. Ignoring his son and the tutor, he stared out the window and thought about his wife. She had a way of getting under *his* defenses that made him extremely uncomfortable. His plan to leave her in the country for a month while he finished up business in town became more appealing with every minute he spent in her presence. She would settle in at Nethercote and begin to work her magic on his son, while he would be away from the danger her innocence and lively mind posed.

He turned and asked for a report from the tutor. Once completed, he spoke at length to his son about his expected behavior with his new stepmother and inquired after the boy's pursuits. Nick shrugged at the questions and looked impassively back at his father. Noble had no way of knowing, but the look was identical to the one he himself affected in public. Rogerson noticed, however, and, genuinely fond of both his charge and his employer, sent up a prayer of hope that the new countess would be able to reach the father and son where others had failed.

"How did you find your rooms?" Noble asked his wife a short while later, when the two were seated in front of the library fire, a cold repast spread before them.

"I turned right at the top of the stairs," Gillian replied.

The Black Earl looked up from where he was slicing ham. "That is an old chestnut, madam."

Gillian smiled. "I know, but I couldn't help myself. Truly, my lord, the rooms . . . well, to be honest, I clash with them."

One delectable eyebrow went up. Gillian's fingers tingled with the desire to smooth back the hair that fell over his brow and brush the satiny eyebrow.

"How so?"

"They're pink, my lord."

"Noble."

"They're pink, Noble. Very pink. I look terrible against pink."

Noble carved a slice of duck and added it to her plate. "Gillian, you are now the Countess of Wessex, mistress of this house and three others. If something displeases you, you may change it."

"Truly? Anything?"

Noble nodded. "Within reason, of course."

"Of course," Gillian agreed. Fortunately for his peace of mind, her husband was busy with his own plate and didn't see the speculative look in his wife's eyes.

Supper, a quick tour through the house, and a visit to the stable to settle the dogs passed the remaining evening hours quickly. With some surprise, Gillian found herself alone in her repulsively pink bedchamber, dressed in her best nightrail and a rather worn dressing gown, awaiting the appearance of her husband. She was mildly disconcerted by the pitying look her newly assigned maid had given her as she left, but her anticipation of the day's culmination kept her from worrying about it too much. She just hoped she wouldn't do anything to hurt Noble before he had a chance to explain everything to her.

"Woolgathering again, my dear?"

Gillian jumped a foot and spun around to see her husband close the connecting door. He was dressed in a rich blue velvet dressing gown that didn't quite go to his ankles. Gillian stared at his feet. They were as bare as hers.

"Um. Woolgathering. Yes. Your feet are naked."

"So are yours." Noble took her hands in his and gently pulled her forward until she was leaning against his chest. "You are allowed to be frightened, my dear, given the circumstances. I give you my word that I will do my best not to hurt you, but I'm afraid there will be a certain discomfort the first time."

Gillian looked up into his gray eyes and wondered how she could ever have thought them icy. They blazed now with a fiery heat that warmed her down to her bare toes. She didn't care how much discomfort the evening held; he could pinch her black and blue, he could torture her, he could stretch her out on the rack in his dungeon—just so long as she could stand in the blaze of those glorious eyes.

He slid his hands around her waist and pulled her tighter. "Nethercote doesn't have a dungeon. Did your aunt explain to-night's proceedings to you?"

"Well, she tried. I am afraid I lost track of what she was saying at some point. I had hoped you would explain it all to me." Gillian looked so wistful Noble couldn't keep the smile from his face. He knew from her reactions to the few chaste kisses they had shared that she had an untapped font of passion simmering just below the surface, but he had assumed that like most virgins she would view her wedding night with trepidation or horror.

"I'd rather show you than explain it," he murmured against her hair, slipping her dressing gown off her shoulders. Gillian shivered as the air reached her through the delicate linen of her nightwear.

"Cold, sweetheart?" Noble asked, nibbling his way down the ivory column of her neck and along her collarbone. Gillian clutched both hands in his hair and held on for dear life. She had no idea what he was doing—Aunt Honoria certainly hadn't mentioned anything about him *tasting* her—but she didn't want the wonderful sensations to stop. He dipped his tongue into the hollow behind one ear and suckled on an earlobe.

"Dear God in heaven," she moaned. Surely this wasn't right. Surely Noble shouldn't be sending flames of desire licking down her body. Licking, oh lord, he *was* licking her! Gillian's skin prickled as her nightrail was pushed down over her shoulders, over her hips, and left to pool around her ankles. Before she had time to comment on the embarrassing situation of her nakedness, he picked her up, headed for her bed, paused, then turned and carried her through to his chamber. Gillian didn't have a chance to take an inventory of the bedchamber before she was settled with exquisite gentleness on his bed. She propped herself up on one elbow and watched closely as he disrobed.

"Well! *That* answers a good many questions," she muttered, staring at his arousal. Then, to Noble's complete surprise, utter amazement, and undying gratitude, she reached out and touched him.

"Yes indeed, it explains much. Am I hurting you?" she asked, concerned about the grunt of pain that had accompanied her touch.

Gently, ever so gently, Noble pried his wife's hands off his nether regions and, gritting his teeth with the determination not to shame himself ten minutes into his wedding night, he pushed her back onto the bed and lay down beside her, panting slightly.

"You are perspiring. Are you too hot? Should I open a window? Fetch you a cold beverage? Would you like me to fan you?" Gillian snuggled closer and placed a hand on his chest. Her fingers drew lazy circles around one flat brown nipple. He slapped a hand over hers and held it tight. He'd never make it through the night. If he didn't shame himself first, she was going to kill him with her innocent erotic seduction. He ground his teeth together in an attempt to distract himself from the thought of plunging deep inside her.

"Nothing. Just lay there. Don't move. And if you have any mercy in your soul, stop touching me there!"

Gillian jerked her hand back. "I'm sorry. I thought it was allowed."

Noble tried hard to swallow past the lump that had suddenly appeared in his throat. "It is allowed; nay, encouraged under normal circumstances, but this, my lady wife, is not a normal circumstance."

"Oh." She lay next to him and wondered if his breathing was always so ragged. Surely it couldn't be good for him to be breathing so shallowly for any length of time. Perhaps if she stroked him as she did the hounds when they became distressed, he would calm down and his breathing return to normal. Disengaging one hand, she lightly caressed his chest from shoulder to navel.

"Oh, God." Gillian didn't think he meant that as a prayer; it sounded more like a groan of agony. His head must be paining him. She tilted her face up until her lips were a hairbreath away from his.

"Do you hurt, Noble?"

He moaned softly against her lips and with one hand cupped the back of her head so he could plunder her mouth.

"Is it your head?" she asked, the words catching in her throat.

Now her own breathing was erratic, but there didn't seem to be much she could do about it, what with Noble's tongue probing her mouth like an enthusiastic explorer in a particularly moist cave. Unable to withstand the surge of emotions and desires flooding her body, she pressed against him, eliciting another moan from deep within his chest. Then suddenly she was on her back and he was poised over her.

"I meant to do this right, I swear I did," he said hoarsely as he positioned himself. "But you're so damn hot. Bloody hell, I'm only human! You can't blame me for being human! Tell me you don't blame me!"

He seemed to require some sort of reassurance, so she stroked his arms and back gently. "I don't blame you. You're beautiful, Noble. Even your muscles have muscles. You're made very differently from me."

Wessex stared at her for a moment that seemed to him to last at least a lifetime, then slowly, with a patience he thought beyond human control, he sank into her.

"Well, I think this just about answers all of my questions," Gillian gasped, her voice simultaneously huskier and higher than she had ever heard it. There was a sharp jab of pain, but it quickly faded into unimportance in the rush of other, much more pleasing feelings.

Her husband didn't answer her—hell, he was incapable of words at that point. All that mattered was making Gillian his own, bonding with her, joining with her until they ceased to be two entities and were one.

Gillian uttered his name in a brief shriek and arched up beneath him. Sunlight exploded behind his eyes as he drove into her one last time, crushing her beneath him, pulling her into his soul just as surely as she pulled him into hers. Noble and Gillian ceased to exist; there was only a united pair. Together, joined, one body, one breath, one heartbeat.

An eon later Gillian gave a contented sigh, and wrapped her arms around the man lying limp on top of her. Her husband.

Her life. Her Lord of Lovers. Forever he would be hers and hers alone. She stroked one hand down the damp muscled planes of his back and sent profusions of thankful prayers heavenward. Suddenly her hand paused.

"Noble?" She nudged him. He didn't move.

Oh lord, she had killed him!

"Noble?" Her voice rose to a near scream. He bucked upward and sucked in one huge breath like a drowning man surfacing for air. Gillian was surprised there was any oxygen left in the room.

"I thought I had killed you!" she cried with relief, and placed a cautious hand over his heart. It was beating madly.

"You almost did," he replied grittily; then, grinning, he wrapped his arms around her and rolled them both onto their sides.

"It's amazing how well we fit together, don't you think? Considering how very large you are and all."

"Mmm."

She snuggled into his chest and let a languorous sigh of fulfillment escape. "When can we do it again?"

Noble drew a deep breath. "I might have recovered enough to give it another try in eight or nine years. We'll have to see how it goes."

Gillian tipped back her head to see whether or not he was jesting. His eyes were closed, but the corners of his mouth were quirked.

She snuggled back onto his shoulder. He was jesting.

". . . and that is how I met your father. Isn't it a romantic story?" Gillian strolled with Nick and the two dogs around the rose garden early the following morning. Nick peeked at her out of the corner of his eyes and shrugged his shoulders. Gillian had realized that something was seriously troubling her new son but was content to let him come to her with the problem rather than force him to tell her his woes. Mothers, after all, had an instinct about such things. He would come to her in his own time and explain everything.

"Oh, dear, Piddle, I don't think the gardener is going to appreciate that." Gillian ignored the soft snicker beside her and avoided looking at the dogs altogether. She loved them dearly, but they did have a penchant for embarrassing her at the worst time. All she needed now was for Noble to pop up and notice the gift the dog . . . oh, no, both dogs, had left in the middle of the formal, pristine, not-a-leaf-out-of-place garden.

"My lady—"

Gillian shrieked at the deep voice behind her and spun around, clutching her heart to keep it from flinging itself out of her chest.

"Lord, Tremayne . . . er . . . which Tremayne are you?"

"I am Tremayne the butler, my lady."

"Oh, Tremayne Two. Well, Tremayne, you startled me. Has Lord Wessex sent for me?"

The butler looked outraged over something. Perhaps he had noticed the dogs' activities. "No, my lady. His lordship has returned to town. He asked me to—"

Gillian turned a blind eye to what Erp was doing to a particularly fragrant pink rosebush and frowned at the butler. "He what? You must be mistaken; we have just arrived from town. Perhaps he went into the local village or out to visit the tenants."

Tremayne Two shook his head. "I'm afraid not, my lady. His lordship ordered his things packed and he left early this morning with his valet. He left this letter for you—"

"He left me? The day after we were wed, he has *left* me?"

Gillian stared at the man in front of her with an expression that mingled horror with a magnificent display of anger. Tremayne watched her, fascinated by the ability of her eyes to darken from brilliant green to almost black.

"After the most satisfying wedding night in the entire history of the world, he left me, Tremayne?"

"I'm afraid I know nothing about your wedding night, my

71

lady, indeed I do not, but his lordship did leave you a—"

"That poor man!" Gillian shouted at the top of her lungs.

Tremayne blinked at her in surprise. "I beg your pardon, my lady?"

"That poor, misguided, *foolish* man!" she bellowed in return.

"Misguided, my lady? That man left you after your wedding night! You, an innocent young bride!" Tremayne was yelling just as loudly as Gillian, a point that did not escape her attention. She motioned her stepson back into the house, took a deep breath, and addressed the agitated butler in soothing tones.

"Tremayne, calm down, it's quite all right. I understand his lordship's reasoning—"

"He left you, my lady! Just up and packed his things and left you like you were yesterday's breakfast! Such a callous, uncaring man doesn't deserve your kindness!"

"Tremayne, I understand—"

"He's got to be mad to leave a bride alone the day after he wed! Especially you, my lady! Especially after the most satisfying wedding night in the entire history of the world! He's lost his reasoning, that's what it is!"

Lord, she'd soon be deaf if he continued to defend her. "Tremayne!"

He stopped his tirade and stared as Gillian stomped her foot on the soft grass. "You will stop this slanderous talk about Lord Wessex immediately. He is your employer. He is an earl. And he is my husband—I won't have you chastising him when he's not here to defend himself."

The butler stared at her in disbelief.

"But, my lady," he said weakly, waving his hands about in a helpless manner.

Gillian noticed the cream envelope clutched against a silver tray. "Is that for me?"

"Er—yes, my lady. It is from"—he took a steadying breath and spat out the words—"his lordship."

Gillian read the brief contents of the note. It consisted of three lines, stating that Wessex felt it important that he be in London while Parliament was sitting, and since he knew Gillian would be infinitely happier in the country with her dogs, he trusted she would amuse herself until his return.

She carefully folded the note and, ignoring the expectant look on Tremayne's face, turned her back and scanned the lush, perfect grounds of Nethercote. Life was funny—one moment you could be deliriously happy with everyone and everything, the next moment that happiness seemed to crumble and fall to pieces. Gillian felt as if she was standing on a threshold: one step forward and her life would follow one path, a step backward and it would go in another direction. The question of which path to choose was not at issue—she would follow Noble. He needed her, whether or not he knew it. Last night's intimacies made that quite clear in her mind. No two people who could share the experience they shared could doubt that they were soul mates, intended from the very beginning of time for each other. She sighed heavily. Bringing the Lord of Obstinacy around to see that truth was another matter. The walls he had erected around his heart were formidable ones, and she wasn't quite sure how she was going to scale them.

She sighed again. "I am, however, quite good at climbing trees, and I shouldn't think there is too much of a difference."

"Beg pardon, my lady?"

Gillian turned back and met his confused countenance. "It is of no consequence. Tremayne, would you have my maid pack my things in preparation for a trip to London?"

"I will indeed, my lady, with all due haste. And may I say, good for you, my lady?"

She matched his jubilant smile. "Would you also have my son's things packed? Nick will be accompanying me. I believe we will ride rather than take the carriage."

"Very good my lady, I'll order . . . did you say you would ride rather than take the carriage?"

She nodded and started toward the house. "We shall leave in

an hour. You can follow later with the trunks and any servants who are needed at the town house. Oh, dear, Piddle and Erp; I forgot about them. It wouldn't be fair to leave them here with strangers. . . . Tremayne, I don't suppose—"

"No, my lady, I couldn't. Please don't ask me to."

"But they are very well-behaved dogs, and I could not stand the thought of leaving them behind."

"It's not their behavior I object to, my lady."

Gillian sucked on her lower lip for a moment. "Has Lord Wessex an old carriage? One that is not used frequently?"

The butler met her gaze with a slow smile. "He does, my lady. I shall see to the hounds' removal to London myself."

"Pettigrew likes them," she said as they strolled toward the house. "Tell him we'll need a boots in town, and send him to guard over their safety."

"As you wish, my lady."

Gillian paused at the bottom of the steps leading up to the veranda and looked up at the warm stone of the house. "Don't worry, Tremayne Two. I'm not giving up on him."

"I'm eternally grateful for that, my lady."

The two shared a brief smile, then Gillian skipped up the stairs and into the house to change into her old green velvet riding habit. A brisk ride was just what she needed to clear her head.

Chapter Four

Gillian swung her leg over the perch of the sidesaddle and slipped down to the ground in a manner reminiscent of a sack of bulldogs plunging the same distance. She stifled the groan that threatened to escape as she hobbled over to help Nick from his horse. The lad leaped down without assistance and looked about him with interest, as fresh as a daisy despite the grueling four-hour ride.

"Children," she grumbled under her breath, and handed the reins to the groom who had accompanied them on the journey.

"Nick, please use the knocker," she instructed and, hobbling to the front steps, attempted to straighten her appearance into something resembling that of a countess. A perspiring, dusty, unkempt countess whose riding habit had an unfortunate tendency to rick up on one side, but still, Gillian reminded herself as she raised her chin and tried to summon a haughty look, a genuine countess.

" 'Ere, what's that noise yer makin'? Can't you see the knocker's off the 'ouse? Don't that mean nothin' to ye? We don't want ye hereabouts!"

Nick, faced with a door without a knocker, had affected entrance by simply pounding on the door with his fists. He was as startled as Gillian when the door suddenly swung open and a monstrous figure appeared, one huge hand on his hip as he glowered at the three people standing before him.

God's ten toes, the man was huge—even bigger than Noble. He was as dark as sin, with a frown that could scorch the sun, but what really worried Gillian was the strange apparatus that lay glinting against his hip.

In place of his left hand was a highly polished bright brass hook.

"Good lord, pirates have taken over your father's house!" Gillian yelled, snatching her son back and pushing him behind her in a protective gesture. "What have you done with my husband, you reprehensible, dastardly brute? By all that's holy, if you've harmed him, I'll do you bodily injury!"

The giant's scowl deepened. A gold hoop hanging from his ear swung gently as he shook his head at her. "I 'aven't done nuthin' to 'is lordship, lady, I works for 'im. Ain't much ye could do to me, either, 'cept maybe to rabbit an' pork me to death."

He took a step toward her and waved the menacing hook in her face. Rabbit and pork? Why was the huge, behooked pirate meandering on about supper at a time like this?

The giant gave Gillian a look that could only be described as disgruntled. "Ain't no one mentioned supper, missis, nor meanderin' fer that matter, whatever that might be. If'n ye don't want to feel the flat of me 'and on yer bottle and glass, ye'd best be quick with tellin' me who ye is, and what ye want with 'is lordship. I don't 'ave all day to natter with ye, no matter how fetchin' ye are."

Gillian's stomach contracted into a ball roughly the size of a runtish walnut. The barbarian was threatening to do some physical harm to her, of that much she was sure, even if she was confused by his sudden reference to bottles and such. Well, he certainly was due for a stern lecture about his manners with guests. She was convinced Noble had no idea his pirate was answering the door in such a surly manner.

"I am Lady Wessex. Please stand aside and allow my son and me to enter our house."

The pirate looked taken aback for a moment or two. His massive black brows actually retreated to either side of his forehead as he carefully studied Gillian, absently rubbing his jaw with the wickedly sharp end of his hook. She watched the tip of it, mesmerized. "Well, I'll be blowed! The Duchess of Fife!"

Gillian frowned at him. Although she didn't, as a rule, approve of employing pirates to answer one's door, he was now a member of her staff and, as such, she was responsible for his well-being, both physical and moral. It was obvious to her that worry over his unfortunate infirmity had caused some damage to his mental state. Keeping this fact in mind, she corrected him in a gentle voice. "No, the Countess of Wessex. I'm Lord Wessex's wife. Gillian, Lady Wessex, to be precise."

"That's what I said. Yer 'is lordship's trouble and strife."

Gillian forgot to be mindful of his defective mental humors and bristled at the uncalled for accusation. "We've only been married one day, sir; I hardly feel that gives me time to be of any trouble to Lord Wessex, let alone cause him strife. And whether or not I am, that is certainly none of your affair. You will cease making such ridiculous and completely unjustified judgments and allow me to pass by your large and, I regret to say, uncouth person."

The giant looked confused. "Don't get yerself riled up now, m'lady. I wasn't makin' no judgments against ye."

"You said I was nothing but trouble and strife!"

"Aye, and ye are. Trouble and strife. Gooseberry puddin'."

"Pudding! Did you just call me a pudding?"

"Aye, gooseberry puddin'!" The scowl was back on the pirate's face as he shook his hook at Gillian. "Are ye daft, woman?"

Gillian took exception to his manner of debate on the front steps. This was not how she had envisioned making her entrance in her new home, in front of her new staff. "I am not the daft one here, Mr. Pirate. Will you please stop waving that thing in my face? Didn't your mother ever teach you it was impolite to point your hook at others?"

The giant gawked at her, a dull red washing over his cheeks.

"That's better. You should be more careful with that—that—apparatus. You could put someone's eye out with it. Now please move aside, and then you may explain your propensity to speak in riddles."

"Er . . . if I might intercede, my lady. He means you're his lordship's wife. Trouble and strife, gooseberry pudding, and Duchess of Fife are all popular cant used to mean wife." A short, round man pushed the behemoth aside and bowed at what would be his waist if he weren't shaped like an orange. "I'm Devereaux, Lady Wessex, your husband's man of affairs. Welcome to Britton House. I wasn't aware that Lord Wessex was expecting you, however I'm sure the news merely slipped his mind."

As he spoke, the dapper little man waved her and Nick around the now mute gargantuan, politely escorting them into an oak-paneled hallway. Gillian gave the pirate a good glare to let him know she was not happy with him, then peeled off her gloves and looked around her. The hall was tastefully paneled in a warm, honey oak, and had the loveliest parquet floor she'd ever seen.

"You must forgive Crouch, my lady. He meant no harm; he was as taken aback as I was by your unexpected, albeit welcome, arrival."

Nick was standing next to the looming colossus, admiration clearly evident in his eyes as he watched the man nonchalantly pull out a cloth and, spitting on the hook, polish it with a grand gesture. Gillian was aware of her stepson's approving eyes and made a mental note to discuss the impropriety of expectorating in public, let alone doing so upon one's personal apparatus.

"Indeed. Well, Mr. Devereaux, would you please take me to

Lord Wessex? I shall discuss Crouch's behavior with the butler at a later time."

The giant smiled. It made the jagged scar running across the bridge of his nose pucker, pulling the corner of one eye down slightly. The result was not one to inspire hilarity.

"Crouch is the butler, my lady," the round man said softly, wringing his hands in apparent distress over this news.

"Aye, m'lady. I've been with 'is lordship nigh on five years now."

He nodded so forcibly that his earring swung madly back and forth. Gillian smiled broadly, gave a little mental shrug over the eccentricity of her husband's staff, and turned back to the soft-spoken round man. "My husband?"

"Is not here, my lady."

"Will he be back soon?"

"I'm afraid I do not know, my lady."

"Where has he gone?"

"I cannot say, my lady."

"Cannot or will not?"

"Alas, cannot, my lady. His lordship is on the reticent side when it comes to sharing information."

"I see. When exactly did he leave?"

Devereaux shot her a pitying glance. "I am unsure of the exact time of his departure, my lady, as he left instructions for me and did not meet with me in person."

Gillian felt oddly disappointed at the news, although she had prepared herself for Noble's absence, knowing he had returned to town for the sole purpose of conducting business. Still, she would have liked to see her bridegroom again, especially when she had spent most of the agonizing ride into town reliving just how she came to be so uncomfortable in the saddle. It was worth every twang and ache, she reflected idly as she allowed the pirate butler to introduce her to the house staff and show her around the ground-floor rooms. She was very much looking forward to seeing whether another intimate encounter would prod her husband into bellowing at her about being only human. She hoped it would. She felt certain it was good for him to lose his vaunted control now and again, especially if she was on the receiving end of his magnificent display.

"My lady?"

She blinked and looked around as the butler twitched dust-cloths off delicate rose-colored furniture.

"What display would that be?"

Oh lord, would she never learn to think without involving her mouth in the process?

" 'Tis nothing. You were saying?"

"This is yer sittin' room, m'lady."

She looked around and flinched visibly. "It is pink, Crouch?"

The pirate surveyed the room, hand and hook resting on his hips. "Aye, that it is. A right nasty shade of pink too, I'm thinkin'."

"I am agreeing with you, Crouch."

" 'Twas 'er ladyship's favorite color. 'Er late ladyship, that is, yer being 'er new ladyship an' all."

Gillian took a deep breath and smiled at her stepson, who was staring with openmouthed fascination at a rather indecent painting involving an enthusiastic group of satyrs, nymphs, and cherubs. She took him firmly by the shoulders, then pushed him out the door after the butler, ordering him to wash up from the dusty ride before going downstairs.

Twenty minutes later the silent boy stepped into a small room lit by several stands of candles and a cheerful fire.

"Hungry, Nick?" Gillian waved a hunk of yellow cheese at him and pointed toward the end of the mahogany desk, where a light repast had been placed. She sat behind the desk, sorting through the post that had arrived that day, looking for a clue as to Noble's whereabouts. "I'm hoping your father returns for dinner, but until then, I thought we might refresh ourselves. What have we here?" From beneath a stack of account papers peeped an edge of expensive-looking lilac paper. Gillian pulled it out and examined it, wrinkling her nose as she did so.

"Hmmm. Perfumed."

Nick looked up from his bread and cheese at the disgusted tone in her voice. Gillian examined the direction on the front of the letter closely, sighed, then waved the letter back and forth gently as she nibbled on her lower lip.

"It is unethical to read a letter that is not addressed to you, Nick."

Nick shrugged noncommittally and stuffed a large piece of cheese in his mouth.

"Close your mouth when you chew, dear, you're spewing bits of cheese on your father's desk. No, it is unethical and quite probably illegal as well."

Gillian considered the two purple seals on the back of the letter. They had clearly been slit, indicating that Noble had read this letter. She glanced over at her stepson.

"You would not want your private correspondence being available to just anyone, now would you?"

Nick thought for a moment, then shook his head and washed down a big hunk of bread with a swallow of milky tea. Gillian watched the fascinating process, momentarily reminded of a large South American snake she had seen the year before.

Shaking away the image, she tapped her finger on the letter. "However, there are times when one has to breach protocol, such as in the case of an emergency. For instance, what if someone near to you—oh, let us just pull a person out of thin air and use your father for this example—if you knew that your father was in peril, and that you could save him if only you knew his whereabouts, and that those whereabouts might be ascertained if you were to read a letter addressed to him in a very definitely feminine hand on paper so scented with lilac that it could drop a horse at thirty paces; why then, you would be fully justified in reading that letter, wouldn't you? Even though you would not consider such an action under normal circumstances?"

Nick tipped his head to one side as he watched his step-mother, then nodded again. He wondered why she didn't just read the letter, instead of making a fuss about it. He shrugged again and popped a whole apple tart into his mouth.

"I am *so* glad you agree with me, Nick. We shall get along just famously, I can tell. Now, since we are in agreement about when it is appropriate to throw the niceties out the window, I believe I can say without hesitation that the situation of your missing father clearly falls under the heading of an emergency."

Nick looked up from the apple tart crumbs and raised an eyebrow in perfect imitation of Noble at his most quizzical.

"You do not agree that the letter should be read?"

Nick blinked at her.

"Or you do not agree that your father is missing?"

He nodded.

Gillian waved the letter gently back and forth as she thought about this. She considered explaining to him just what a fragile state of emotion his father was in. She considered telling him her plan to breach the walls Noble had built around his heart. She considered explaining that there were things that she, as an adult, saw that he did not. She considered whether or not she wanted to make up any more excuses, decided against it, and read the letter.

Two minutes later, Nick, his hunger abated, watched Gillian as she paced the room and muttered expletives under her breath. He had been prepared to dislike the woman his father brought home as his new mother, but something about Gillian had put him immediately at ease. She was unlike anyone he had ever met. He didn't understand why she had immediately accepted him as her son—despite his father's attempt at shielding him from the worst, he understood the harsh words the villagers used toward him. He knew that for some reason he was defective and wasn't the heir his father needed, but he didn't dwell on that shortcoming. It brought back too many painful memories of another mother and a terrifying night that had seemed to last for years.

He watched Gillian now as she paced and mumbled to herself. Was she talking about his father? He assumed she was, but her attitude didn't make sense. One minute she was saying things about a poor, deluded man who had suffered so much he didn't know how to love, the next minute she was threatening to emasculate him if he thought to play her false, especially after the most satisfying wedding night in the history of the world. Nick wondered just what exactly emasculating consisted of, decided by the expression on Gillian's face it wasn't pleasant, and settled back in the chair, content to watch her.

She seemed to struggle with a thought for a moment as she stood before the window gazing out at the darkening sky, tapping a finger on her lips; then she nodded twice and turned to face him.

"I have decided to save your father."

He looked at her in surprise. Was his father in need of saving? Nick couldn't imagine anyone as big and powerful as his father in need of help. He frowned. Despite her height, Gillian was thin and didn't have much bulk. He doubted she would be of much assistance.

"He needs saving, Nicholas, and I am just the woman to save him. He's too pigheaded to admit that, and 'tis the truth part of that fault could lie with the fact that we are not very well acquainted yet. Still, he is my husband now, and I owe him my help as well as my loyalty. You can stop shaking your head at me, Nick. I have made up my mind. Do you wish to come with me?"

His father's obsession with order and control had seen to it that life at Nethercote, while pleasant, was dull and unexciting. Gillian's arrival had brought a swirl of adventure that struck a deep chord in the boy. Nick yearned to ask his stepmother where they were going, but the visions of that black night long ago were too strong. He nodded instead.

She nodded back, and then started out the door, calling over her shoulder, "I will be back shortly. We don't want any gossip, so I must change my clothing. The boots, I think, will suit. He is about my size."

Gillian scratched at the rough neckcloth as she sat back against the uncomfortable squabs of the hired hack and peered out the grimy, flyspecked window at the darkened house beyond. It was a modest-sized house of red brick, situated in a conservative, pleasant neighborhood. She frowned at the staid front of the house and nibbled on her lip. This wasn't the sort of domicile she had expected Noble to keep his mistress in. She took another look down the gently curved street. God's knuckles, it was all wrong—this was not the sort of neighborhood she expected would tolerate a member of the demimonde. Did all mistresses live so well?

"Well, there's nothing for it but to knock," she muttered and, pulling at the boots' waistcoat, she straightened her shoulders and allowed Nick to help her out of the hack before turning back to the driver.

"Please remain here, sir. I will have need of you again in a few minutes."

The driver nodded. Holding tight to what remained of her quickly evaporating confidence, Gillian strode up the stairs with her son in tow and wielded the knocker briskly.

"Perhaps they are all abed," she commented to Nick two minutes later. As he was wont to do, he raised one eyebrow in a youthful imitation of his father. Gillian bit back a smile and used the knocker again, rapping loudly against the white door.

The sound echoed through the house.

"No one appears to be home," she said thoughtfully and, with a quick glance at her stepson, put her hand on the latch.

The door swung open. Gillian and Nick peered into the darkened hallway and listened. There was no sound but a muffled thumping from somewhere upstairs.

"Good evening?" Gillian was ashamed of the brief quiver in her voice. It was ridiculous to be afraid. This was her husband's house, after all, and no matter whom he chose to install in it, she had a right to be here. A movement by her side made her realize she had taken Nick's hand and was clutching it tightly. She made herself relax the grip, and with a smile she felt far from meaning, stepped over the threshold.

"Is anyone at home?"

Her voice echoed eerily around the small hallway illuminated faintly by the streetlights. To her right was a white staircase that presumably led upstairs, although all she could make out was a ghostly parade of steps dissolving into complete and utter blackness. She fought back a shiver, then froze as Nick suddenly dropped her hand and disappeared into the inky darkness.

"Nick, return to me this instant! You have no idea what sort of . . . oh, thank you!" The scrape of flint brought relief to Gillian as her brilliant and resourceful son lit a rack of candles found on a small ornate table at the foot of the stairs. The hall didn't look nearly so menacing once it was lit by the soft glow of candles. Nick lit the tapers in another rack; then, taking it in hand, he tipped his head toward the stairs and looked an obvious question to Gillian.

"I suppose," she said softly, stepping into the hall, "that you would like us to investigate those mysterious noises coming from somewhere upstairs?"

Nick nodded and held out his hand. Gillian was touched by the gesture. She took a step forward and captured his warm hand in hers.

"You are very brave, do you know that? Much braver than I, for 'tis the truth that although I am just as curious as you, my knees feel as if they are made of water. Well, come my valiant knight, shall we see what is making those thumping noises?"

Nick graced her with another of his rare smiles and the two mounted the stairs with much stealth.

"Bloody . . . ow . . . hell!" A cat's outraged yowl curled up and around Gillian as she trod an intricate dance trying to avoid stepping on the small black animal as it wound around her ankle. Nick clutched her by the lapels of her coat and tugged her away from the stairs as she detached the cat's claws from her ankle.

"I'm sorry, puss, I did not see your tail there, although I must say the landing is not the best place to keep it." The cat shot Gillian a belligerent look, and with a haughty flick of its abused tail, marched down the stairs, voicing its opinion of people who didn't watch where they were stepping.

Gillian and Nick smiled at one another, but their smiles faded as the thumping seemed to gain a new energy.

"The second floor, I believe," Gillian said thoughtfully after listening to the rhythmic noise for a moment. It was not, as she had hoped, a loose shutter banging in the wind. There was clearly someone or something upstairs making the noise.

"Perhaps it is only another cat, trapped in a closet," she said hopefully, trying to calm her jangled nerves as they climbed the next flight of stairs. Nick didn't look as if he believed her suggestion. 'Twas the truth, she didn't either. "Stay behind me, Nick."

The pair looked down a dark hallway. The noise was definitely coming from a room to their right, a bedchamber, she assumed. Gillian patted the pocket of the boots' jacket nervously, then pushing Nick behind her, took a deep breath and started down the hallway.

"If there's any trouble, I want you to fetch the hack driver," she whispered over her shoulder to him. "Tell him to bring the watch."

Nick nodded abruptly, then pointed to the closed door before them. The muffled thumping sounds were louder, clearly originating in the room beyond the door.

Gillian's mouth went dry as she reached out to open the door. What was making the horrible thudding noise? A corpse, hanging from the rafters and swaying against the wall? A huge, unchained beast throwing itself around the room as it bit with slavering jaws at anything it sighted? A deformed and mutilated person too hideous to be let out of the room, forced to drag his legless torso around his chamber prison by walking on his twisted and grotesque arms?

Almost swooning at the thought of the horror to be found within the room, Gillian patted her pocket again, sent a quick glance at Nick standing several paces back, and, holding the candle rack high, threw open the door.

"Oh my God!" Gillian screamed and stared at the atrocity before her. It was terrible! It was heinous! It made her skin crawl with the sheer, unadulterated abomination of it all!

It was her husband. Naked. Spread-eagled. Shackled to the bedposts. And if the expression on his face was anything to go by, ready to kill the first person who came within reach.

"Noble! What on earth are you doing? Is this some sort of strange game you are playing? My aunt told me that some men enjoy such rough bed sport, but really husband, I had not thought it of you."

He was also gagged, a fact for which she was briefly grateful since the look he gave her was enough to peel paint.

Nick peered in the doorway, astonishment clearly writ on his young face. Gillian sidled up to the bed and tried to avoid her husband's infuriated, icy gaze.

"I take it by your silence that your participation in this . . . uh . . . pose is not voluntary?"

Noble banged his head back against the headboard.

"I assume one thump means no, husband?"

His eyes narrowed at her. She let her gaze wander over his bared form, looking for signs of injury. There were none, except . . .

"Dear God! Noble, you're . . . you're broken! What happened? Oh, those villains! How could they do this to you? You poor, poor man, how you must have suffered!"

She reached out a hand to touch that portion of his anatomy

that lay limp along his thigh, intending to cradle the beloved injured part, but Noble's sudden agitated movements and head bangings stopped her. Of course, how cruel, how unthinking she was. He was obviously embarrassed and didn't want her sympathy in this, his time of need—not when his son was standing by watching with bright, intelligent eyes. She fought back a tear and gave her husband a reassuring nod, then turned her attention to the shackles around his ankles.

God's truth, although it looked to be an uncomfortable position, and her husband was clearly spitting mad, it did display his masculine attributes to advantage. If only the dastards hadn't broken one of his more interesting bits. Gillian gave herself a moment or two to grieve the damage to that item, then turned her attention to admire his heavily muscled thighs and calves before another muffled protestation had her prodding the manacles.

"They are locked," she said, looking up. Truly, she hadn't realized the Lord of Masculinity's chest was quite so broad, although perhaps having his arms stretched out had a broadening affect on it. She considered the manner, eyes narrowing with concentration as she let her gaze wander over his torso, imagining his arms to his side. No, 'twas the truth his chest was really that broad and not just an optical illusion. She wondered briefly how many hand spans wide his chest was, and was just reaching out with the intention of satisfying that curiosity when another gargled and furious noise stopped her in midstretch. Noble banged his head against the headboard twice and rolled his eyes at her.

"Oh, of course, the gag. Why didn't you say you wanted it off first? Here, lift your head and I will reach behind . . ."

The knot was tied tightly, and it took Gillian, draped across Noble's heaving chest as she wrestled with the obstinate cloth, several minutes before she could pull the obnoxious item from his mouth.

The spate of profanities that followed confirmed her earlier thoughts. He was *very* angry. Casting periodic nervous glances at Nick, who gazed at his father with a placid expression that didn't fool her for one moment, she finally interrupted what appeared to be a lengthy discussion of the tortures Noble was going to inflict upon whoever had placed him in this position.

"I think your plan with the iron maiden and saltpeter is a good one, my dearest, but first I would have you released from this bondage."

Several minutes later, when Noble could speak without incorporating further plans for revenge in his comments, he replied hoarsely to Gillian's earlier statement.

"The key is on the dressing table. I've been staring at it all bloody evening."

Nick headed for the table while Gillian sat down on the bed next to her confined husband and absently laid a hand on his bare chest. He was warm. Very warm. "Who did this horrible thing to you, Noble?"

The Black Earl closed his eyes. "I don't know, although I have a suspicion."

"You didn't see who stripped you naked and chained you to a bed in your mistress's house?"

"No. I was struck on the head when I entered the house." Noble groaned slightly as Gillian's hand gently stroked his chest in a reassuring manner. Rather, Noble corrected grimly, it might have been meant to reassure him, but unfortunately his wife's presence was having another effect that would be all too evident if she continued her present attentions.

His wife's presence?

"What the devil are you doing here?" Noble roared, startling Gillian out of her reverie. She jumped, her fingers still entwined in the soft hairs on his chest. Noble gave another roar, this time of outraged pain. "You're supposed to be at Nethercote! I do not recall giving you permission to leave!"

Gillian glanced over toward the dressing table. Nick held up a key and cocked a brow. Gillian shook her head slightly.

"I was not aware that I was a prisoner, to be held captive until you decided to set me free."

"You're not a prisoner, damn it, but I expect you to stay where you're put. When I give an order, it is to be carried out without question." Noble took a deep breath. Lord but she was pretty, even dressed in the ratty clothes of a boy. As a disguise, it was hopeless. Long tendrils of red hair fell out of a blue knit cap, and no man with eyes in his head could mistake the rounded feminine curves displayed by a tightly fitted black waistcoat and breeches. A movement beyond her recalled his son's presence to mind. The wave of heat flushing his cheeks was immediately cooled, as if he had been dowsed with a bucket of snow.

"I see," Gillian replied to his statement stiffly and, disentangling her hand, stood and moved to the foot of the bed. "I was unaware that you had give me an *order,* my lord."

"I did. And you have disobeyed that order."

Gillian said nothing, but her expression told Noble she wasn't pleased with that comment. Obviously, she needed instruction on how to order her own life so that she wasn't always finding herself in situations out of her control. There was no time like the present to begin her training.

"Without order, wife, there is chaos, and chaos in our lives is not to be tolerated—it wastes our time, drains us of energies better spent at other endeavors, and creates worry and concern when the mind should be calm and peaceful. Would you agree with that statement?"

Gillian's eyes widened and her lips trembled at his words. Clearly she was overcome by his masterful use of imagery. Still silent, she nodded her head abruptly, then crossed her arms over her chest, pulling the short jacket up and throwing the gentle curve of her hips into relief against the wall behind her. Noble cleared his throat and continued.

"I'm doing my best to make order out of the chaos that seems to follow you everywhere, but God knows it isn't easy." Had her legs been this long the night before? The breeches seemed to go on forever, stretching over lush, long thighs. Noble thought briefly of the way her legs had wrapped around his hips and decided they were the same length, then dragged his mind back to the task at hand. He wouldn't think of her legs while his son was present. He wouldn't think of how long they were, or how the shapely contour of her calf made his mouth go dry, or the silken feeling of her leg as it rubbed down his own. . . . God's teeth, he'd be shaming himself in a minute. Grimly, Noble envisioned scenes of war, pestilence, and mutilation.

"In order for your life to become the calm, enjoyable existence that I know you long for," he continued in a gritty voice, his jaw tense and tight, "you must abide by my rules and not question them. Through me, you will gain control over your life and will no longer be subject to such unpleasant experiences as you have encountered since I have known you. You are undisciplined, wife, but not beyond hope of redemption."

Nick went to stand beside Gillian. She turned and put an arm around his shoulders, pulling the jacket up even higher. The breeches did nothing to hide the sweet outline of her derriere. In fact, Noble thought with a rising sense of panic, they enhanced it. Not even the vision of his son clutched to her side could stop the memory of just how warm that backside had felt nestled against him intimately when he had woken that morning, nor how he had been possessed to waken his bride by means that would guarantee to keep a smile on her face all day. Two pairs of eyes leveled seriously upon him suddenly drove home the point that he was lecturing his wife while stretched out nude, manacled to a bed. "Gillian, the key."

Gillian took the key from her stepson. "I have one or two questions, if you please, Noble."

"Release me and I will be happy to answer all of them." Gillian nodded and reached toward his feet, but instead of unlocking the shackle, she idly stroked the top of his foot instead.

"It's about this concept of order you have." Her brow wrinkled as she puzzled it out. "I do not think I understand it fully. When you say chaos, do you refer to those little surprises that make life so very interesting?"

Her fingers ran from the top of his ankle down the slope to his toes. He doubted that she even knew she was touching him. Noble had never before thought of the foot as anything but a useful appendage, but a thousand nerves he did not know he possessed jumped to life and pulsated under Gillian's magic fingers. He laid his head back and groaned. He heard his wife gasp as she suddenly clutched his foot.

"Noble—that part of you. The broken part. It's moving!"

It took every bit of willpower, but he didn't look, nor did he meet his son's eyes. Instead he kept his voice calm and level and thought of the affects of the bubonic plague on the human body.

"Gillian, unlock the blasted shackles." His voice sounded thick with strain.

"But—are you sure all is well? I believe the damage to your . . . part . . . is causing a delayed reaction. One moment you're swelling, and the next you're deflating. You cannot tell me that is right."

He kept his eyes closed. He didn't have the energy to explain the whys and wherefores of male anatomy to her. Not now, when his head was throbbing, his arms were aching, and his foot was on fire.

"The key, Gillian?"

She gave his nether regions one last wary look, as if she wouldn't be surprised to see that part of him stand up and dance. "I am trying to understand you, Noble, truly I am. If you could just answer my question about what you mean by chaos . . ."

His head snapped up as he shot her a blistering look. "Will you release me if I do?"

Her eyes widened in innocence. "Of course, my dearest."

"Then the answer is yes, wife, those *little surprises*, as you erroneously call them, are what make your life so hectic and chaotic. No other lady of my acquaintance would leap off a moving phaeton in order to comfort a thieving street urchin."

"But—"

"Nor do I know anyone who has set fire to a house while they attended a ball."

"That was the merest of accidents—"

"You startled my horses, injuring my tiger."

"One of them was limping! I was just trying to show you that the horse must have had a rock in its shoe."

Noble grunted in disbelief. "And the day we become betrothed?"

Gillian's expression took on a pouting appearance. "That was yet another accident."

"You wanted me to kiss you. If you had acted with control and indicated such in a discreet manner, I would have been happy to oblige you. The trouble with you, Gillian, is that you indulge yourself in every ludicrous scheme and thought that passes through your head."

"Noble."

"If you would learn to deal with things in a calm, organized manner, you would be well rewarded, wife, with serenity and tranquillity."

"Noble—"

"You are young yet, despite your years, so I will not make a point of your headstrong nature and heedless manner of flinging yourself through life. You do not know better. Your upbringing is to blame, of course. It will be my pleasure to instruct you in the joys of a well-ordered, temperate life."

"Noble!"

"What?" He was annoyed at her interruption. Didn't she understand that he was trying to help her organize her life into something satisfactory?

"I am not the one chained naked to my mistress's bed with a broken man part."

93

"It's not broken!" he bellowed, glaring at her. She returned his look with one of utter disbelief as she stared pointedly at the part of his body in question. Noble felt her heated gaze as if she was touching him.

"There, you see, that part of you is swelling again. I'm going to find some cold water. A compress is what you need now." She started for the door, but his bellow of outrage drew her back. As she unlocked the manacles she tried to reassure her that nothing was broken, and with a frown at his son, promised to explain the situation at a more appropriate time.

Five minutes later Noble was rubbing the feeling back into his wrists as Gillian and Nick examined the tall wardrobe. It was empty, as were the bureau drawers.

Ten minutes later he was storming naked up and down the long, darkened hallway with one branch of candles in his hand, scattering orders and expletives behind him as Gillian and Nick scurried from room to room in search of clothing.

Fifteen minutes later the hack driver got the surprise of his life when a furious man emerged from the house clad in nothing but a bedsheet draped around his massive frame, followed by the woman dressed in boy's clothing and the dark lad who looked as if he was trying hard not to laugh.

"You! Take us home! Now!" the sheet-clad man ordered in a plummy voice that brooked no opposition. The driver considered voicing his admiration of the bedsheet knotted into a bow on the man's left shoulder, but one glare from the man's piercing gray eyes killed that idea. Despite his unusual apparel, the tight, grim line of the man's mouth, not to mention the muscles that bulged and rippled across the bared portion of his broad chest, bespoke unwillingness on the gentleman's part to engage in a little friendly ragging.

"Bloody queer toffs," the driver huffed to himself and, touching the horse with his whip, set off through the warm night.

Noble continued to mutter rude things under his breath during the ride to his town house. Every lurch of the poorly sprung hack made his head throb worse. It felt as if someone were sitting on his shoulders, using his head for an anvil. He wanted nothing more than to lie down with his head in Gillian's lap and let her trail her long, cool fingers over his aching head. How had he come to this? he wondered idly as he watched his wife through narrowed eyes. Wanting—no, *needing*—a woman's touch. He shied away from the blossoming suspicion, but honesty compelled that he recognize the existence of the uncomfortably restricting feeling that banded about his chest for what it was.

His desire for his wife went beyond the purely physical.

Nobel was disgusted with himself. He had never sought anything but physical relief from a woman. Had he not learned from Elizabeth that to allow anything more led only to deep, bone-searing pain? God knew, the lessons learned at her feet were enough to turn a man away from women altogether. Women were not to be trusted, no matter how demure they looked, no matter how innocent and naïve and wholesome they appeared even when wearing the clothes of a servant. No, he might be weak enough to secretly yearn for more than he ought, but he would not let that weakness control his life. There was comfort in an ordered and structured life. He had learned years ago how to beat down those feelings of need, the desire for succor, the best-forgotten longing to be cherished and loved. He would not let those unwelcome emotions flare to life again, no matter how tempting he found his wife.

"Does your head hurt, Noble?"

The words were softly spoken, but they seemed to hang in the evening air for a moment, before melting and blanketing Noble in a warm glow. His jaw worked, but he could not get the words of denial past his lips.

Gillian slid across from the opposite seat and gently drew him toward her puny woman's shoulder. Noble thought briefly of pushing her away. He knew it was the sheerest folly to allow himself into a situation where a woman offered more than mere physical release, but her touch was as gentle as her words. With one small hand she pulled him down until he was lying back drunkenly across the seat, his head cradled against her breasts. God's knees, but she smelled good, even wearing his boots' clothes.

Gillian murmured tenderly to him as she stroked his head. Odd, but her touch seemed to make the pounding in his temples lessen. Noble knew he should be lecturing his unruly wife on the dangerous nature of London at night. He knew he should forbid her to ever leave his house again without several footmen in attendance. He knew he should interrogate her as to her reasons for following him to town when he had purposely left her at Nethercote. He knew all of this, but for the first time since he had been so brutally betrayed by Elizabeth, he told the righteous side of his conscience to get nobbled.

Gillian knew the moment Noble stopped fighting his inner demons. His head lay heavy on her bosom, but she reveled in its weight, in their closeness, and in his trust. Lightly she stroked her husband's dark hair and marveled that such a man—such a domineering, overpowering, *large* man—should have hair that felt like silk slipping through her fingers. The finest rich brown silk, shot through with threads of walnut and occasional silver. Noble sighed as she delicately traced the contours of his brow and let her fingers trail down to the angular plane of his cheek. His skin was rough with stubble, a strangely pleasing texture that seemed to set her fingers afire. She stroked past the indentation in his chin that never failed to thrill her and followed his jaw line up to the sensitive spot behind the back of his ear. The black crescents of eyelashes—surely there must be a law against a man possessing such long, thick eyelashes—fluttered briefly but remained resting on the tanned skin of his cheek. Her fingers followed the path of his cheekbone to a swelling near his temple. Prodding the area with a gentle touch, Gillian breathed a sigh of relief when it became apparent the wound was not a serious one.

Taking advantage of the Lord of Bliss's unexpected acquiescence, Gillian explored her husband's face to her satisfaction. She looked up once, when the hack bumped across a hole in the road, to find her stepson's bright eyes watching her.

What had Nick thought when he saw his father powerless, his vulnerability—among other things—exposed? It had to be a felling blow to a boy who worshipped his father, but he didn't express any emotion or misbehave in an attempt to garner attention, as Gillian's brothers always had. He simply watched them with an uncanny silence and an expressionless face. Gillian suddenly felt a chilling sense of sadness for her two men— Noble was trying so hard to deny his need for affection, and his son was following his path to self-control and denial. If she didn't step in and put an end to the intolerable situation, soon it would be too late and both would be lost to her. Gillian's fingers tightened around a fistful of Noble's hair. She had no intention of letting that happen.

A soft snore drew her attention down to the smooth lines of her husband's face. An unaccountable pricking behind her eyes surprised her; Noble looked so young, so untroubled as he slept resting against her. A fierce wave of possessiveness washed over her as she watched him sleep. *Mine*, she thought. He's mine and I won't let anyone hurt him again—either of them, she amended, glancing across the carriage to where Nick leaned in the corner, his eyes closed. A fire burned in her breast as she made a vow on the happiness of those most dear to her. If Noble wanted an uncomplicated, structured life, he would have one. From that moment on, Gillian was going to ensure that her lord was going to be happier than he thought possible. Their life was going to be one of peace and serenity, or by God, she'd know the reason why.

Chapter Five

Their life was pandemonium and turmoil. Gillian's determination for a quiescent life flew out the window with a rare Chinese vase. Unfortunately, the window was closed at the time the vase was sent on its way; even more unfortunately, the hired hack had just pulled up before Noble's town house when the delicate china hit the cobblestones before them and exploded with a noise that startled the horse into rearing and almost tipping the carriage.

Gillian and Nick clutched the squabs as the driver calmed the horse and the hack settled back onto its wheels. Gillian said a little prayer that Noble did not wake up when, just as the driver was climbing down from his perch, the door to the house opened and several men spilled out onto the sidewalk, screaming and pummeling one another. Gillian shifted Noble's head slightly to get a better look at the sight of the two butlers trying to throttle each other. As Crouch was a good foot and a half taller and several stone heavier than him, Tremayne Two wasn't having much luck getting a firm grip on his associate's neck.

Dancing around the pair was the small round form of Devereaux, who was evidently championing Crouch as he urged the pirate on to further violence. Gillian made a mental note to have a word with Devereaux about his proclivity to brutality, and pulled Nick back from where he was in danger of falling out of the hack's window.

Behind Tremayne Two was another Tremayne, attempting to pull his brother from the giant by means of what appeared to be a fire iron. But Two stuck to the man like a burr to a particularly hairy Shetland pony. A roar ripped through the night, and the third Tremayne—One or Three, Gillian wasn't sure which—suddenly leaped from the top of the steps and flung himself onto the grappling men. The mate to the shattered window opened and two housemaids leaned out to yell advice as the clutch of four men swayed, then fell to the ground and rolled around like a pack of demented hedgehogs, arms and legs bristling everywhere as the foursome tried to tear each other apart.

Things quickly deteriorated after that.

The three Tremaynes stopped trying to kill one another only after Noble leaped from the hack, roaring his displeasure at the foursome. Gillian wasn't sure if it was the volume and impressive string of invectives that sprang from Noble's lips or whether it was the sight of their huge, scowling employer clad in a white bedsheet that affected the men. She suspected from the stunned looks and open mouths that it was the latter but had no chance to verify her suspicion before Noble, with a flick of his powerful wrists, tossed a few of his employees aside, then stalked stiffly into the house.

"I do believe it was the bedsheet after all," she mused some two hours later as she sat propped up in her husband's bed, watching him pace the floor before the fireplace. "Crouch commented on how lovely the bow at your shoulder was, while Tremaynes Two and Three just stared at you as if you had suddenly sprouted toadstools on your head."

Her words had an immediate effect. He stopped in mid-pace, spun around to face her, and gave her a look that would do Medusa proud. Gillian cautiously moved her legs to make sure they hadn't been turned to stone. "On the other hand, both Tremayne One—at least I think it was One, it is so difficult to tell them apart, perhaps we can affix upon them some sort of identifying mark—both Tremayne One and Mr. Devereaux seemed to take your unconventional apparel in the best of spirits."

Noble's admirable body stiffened. The pulse beating wildly in the side of his neck was clearly visible from across his bedchamber. It was shameful, Gillian chastised herself. The poor man had been through a terrible evening, and she was clearly not doing her duty by offering solace and comfort. It was, after all, her job to help him relax so he could forget his troubles and enjoy his tranquil and serene home. Gillian blinked back a tender tear at the thought of his travails, and proceeded to buoy his foul mood.

"When I say good spirits, my dear, I do not mean they were laughing at you," she reassured him. If possible, his silence and accompanying scowl grew even stonier. "Although I must admit they were laughing, but I'm sure it was not *at* you, but rather *with* you, if you see what I mean."

It was obvious he didn't share her perceptions. It was also evident that at that moment he was hard put to keep from strangling her. Since she wanted to have more than just one night of wedded bliss, Gillian decided not to press the point further. She would ask him in the morning, once he possessed a less belligerent attitude, who wished him ill. He would no doubt be happy she was so interested in his well-being and would, despite his earlier statement, be forthcoming with the whos and whys that so consumed her with curiosity. She smiled sweetly at the choked, guttural noises Noble was making in response to her buoying attempt. He was obviously overcome with gratitude for her tender solicitation.

"Madam." Noble finally got his jaw unclenched long enough to speak. "You will have the decency to never mention the blasted bedsheet within my hearing! For that matter, you will not, under any provocation, refer to this evening again. You will forget about the entire day. Cast it from your thoughts. Wipe it from your memory. I do not wish to *ever again* be reminded of the humiliating events that have made up one of the most miserable days of my blighted existence."

Visions of the well-muscled, masculine, shackled form of her very naked husband danced before her eyes. She had serious doubts as to her ability to obliterate such a fascinating image. She had doubts as to whether she ever wanted to. Weighing his command to forget the image against a lifetime without that particular entry in her mental picture library offered little difficulty. The infuriated male before her in battle stance, however, his legs braced apart, his hands fisted on his hips, clearly indicated that outright refusal of obedience was not an option.

"Well, my lady? I'm waiting for your agreement." He looked mad enough to kill, but she wasn't going to start her marriage by courting distrust with falsehoods.

Unable to agree to his demand, Gillian shrugged. The edge of her faded blue dressing gown slipped off her shoulder. Noble's gaze pounced on the exposed flesh, the pulse in his throat suddenly accelerating as his silver-eyed gaze caressed her skin in a manner that raised goosebumps of excitement on her arms.

A warm kernel of womanly knowledge blossomed and spread inside her. Could it be this easy? Noble was an intelligent man; surely he wouldn't be susceptible to something so mundane as a bit of exposed flesh. Slowly, with deliberate movements, she shrugged her other shoulder and let the dressing gown slide down her arms. She was wearing nothing underneath.

Noble stopped breathing.

She felt her skin prickle even though he had yet to touch her. With great purpose, Gillian rose to her knees, allowing her dressing gown to fall to her hips.

Noble made an inarticulate, choking sort of sound.

It couldn't be so easy, but it evidently was. Her Lord of Eyes, who moments ago had looked as if he'd like nothing better than to wrap his hands around her throat, had stopped speaking and was staring at her, his gaze devouring her torso. A flush of a hitherto unknown emotion washed over her—this must be the power of seduction. God's nightgown, it was a heady thing indeed! Gillian was light-headed with this newly discovered knowledge, and filled with great design, she slid out of bed, leaving the dressing gown behind as she stood before her husband.

She curled one hand around the back of his neck and combed her fingers into his silky hair. "Breathe, Noble," she murmured as she traced the corner of his mouth with the very tip of her tongue.

His eyes crossed.

She trailed kisses over to his ear and sucked on his earlobe before whispering, "Are you breathing, my love?"

"I doubt it." His voice sounded like cracked rocks, but she smiled as she felt his ragged breath on her neck. He stood rigid, his hands clenched into fists at his side as she mumbled against his ear.

"It must be all these clothes you have on. Too constricting." She licked a path down his stubbled cheek to his jaw, nipped his chin, then continued down to lathe his Adam's apple. Although he hadn't donned his normal evening wear upon returning home, he had clad himself in trousers, shirt, and waistcoat. Gillian was thankful he didn't have a cravat to interfere with her exploration. With one hand still curled in his hair, she unbuttoned the buttons on his waistcoat, pushing it off his shoulders as she kissed the hollow of his throat.

He moaned.

A little disturbed to find that her own breathing was on the rough side, Gillian welcomed the warmth that seemed to flow out of Noble, warmth that sparked a slow burn that started somewhere in her stomach and spread out to her limbs. She was consumed by fire, but she craved his heat to make the fire burn even hotter. One by one she unbuttoned the mother-ofpearl buttons on his shirt, following each with scattered kisses on the exposed area of chest. His soft curls tickled her nose, but she was fascinated by the ripple of muscles that tightened beneath her trail of kisses. She moved lower, pulling his shirt off as she sank to her knees before him.

Noble's mind stopped working at the sight of his wife kneeling before him, her hand on his waistband.

Gillian sucked her bottom lip nervously. She wasn't sure if he was pleased with her boldness, but the fire his nearness had ignited was burning too strongly to let her back off. Eyes darkened with passion, she looked up at him for direction. A muscle in his jaw twitched. Twice. She took that as permission to proceed.

With both hands she unbuttoned the twin row of buttons on his trousers, then pushed them down over the sleek, muscled line of his hips, down his steely thighs, and after removing his slippers, over his long, narrow feet.

She lifted her head to find herself staring at his genitals. Joy filled her at the sight.

"You were right, Noble. You are not broken. You look just fine now. More than fine." She reached out a hand to hold his silky hardness and delighted at his gasp of pleasure. "Look, you bounce when I do this."

A shudder ran through him.

She held him with both hands, one tugging gently on the softness lower down, the other curled around the length of his arousal. "So hot. You're as hot as the fire you have started inside me."

With great delicacy she leaned forward and placed a gentle kiss on the tip of him.

Noble was convinced he had died and gone to heaven. He just hoped St. Peter wouldn't notice the long list of his transgressions until his wonderfully uninhibited wife had finished her exploration. Idly he wondered how long it would be before his control snapped. He took into account his history with women, his vaunted control, the fact that he was a sophisticated man and not a base animal driven by primitive urges, as well as the earlier anger he'd held toward his wife, and reckoned he had less than ten minutes.

"I hope you will not be offended . . . I hope you will not mind if I . . . that is, if I. . . ." She rasped her tongue on the sensitive underside of the head and felt his body shake in response.

Noble quickly recalculated. He would be lucky if he lasted four seconds.

The look of ecstasy on his face astonished her—she had hoped she would give him pleasure, but evidently her touch was more powerful than she had presumed. She didn't have a chance to dwell on this thought, however. Three seconds after she took him into her mouth, he yanked her up, and with a move too swift for her to follow, tossed her on the bed, covering her immediately with his own hard body.

"Now it's my turn," he said hoarsely just before his mouth took possession of hers.

Noble rolled off his wife and lay on his back, exhausted. He would have expressed the immense, overwhelming pleasure she had given him, but he didn't have the energy to move his lips, let alone prod his brain into stringing together more than two words that made sense. That thought scurried around his mind, nibbling at the edge of his awareness until it attracted his full attention. Why was making love to Gillian so soul-deep satisfying? Why did her warmth seem to penetrate even the iciest corner of his being? It wasn't right that a man should be so consumed with thoughts of his wife, his control so easily cast over. If she could do that to him now, just a scant two days after they had been wed, what sort of power would she wield after a week of marriage? A month? A year?

Gillian nudged his arm. He knew what she wanted but was too shaken by the turn his thoughts had taken. For it had come—although he had tried to tamp down on it, he had known that it would eventually emerge. That horrible knowledge, that black truth, that darkness slithering around inside him with insidious slowness, gathering before it a familiar feeling of coldness and dread. He closed his eyes and reluctantly acknowledged it.

If he gave her power over his heart, she would betray him.

Gillian nudged him again, then rose up on one elbow when she noticed his frown. "You did not enjoy yourself? That part of you is not bounceable any more. I assumed that meant you enjoyed yourself. Have I got it wrong?"

He couldn't give in to this attraction. He couldn't give her the chance to tear his heart out as Elizabeth had. He couldn't go through that pain again—as bad as it was with his first wife, he knew instinctively that it would be unbearable with Gillian. Elizabeth's betrayal had crushed his heart; Gillian's betrayal would destroy him completely.

"Noble?" She placed a hand on his chest where his heart still beat wildly. "Have I done something to displease you?"

She sounded hurt and confused at the same time. Noble gritted his teeth against the urge to pull her to him and murmur words of reassurance, to bury his head in her sweetly scented neck, to hold her until the cold, dark thing that roiled inside him was banished by her light, but he held back. He could not give her what she wanted. He could not allow himself to be vulnerable again.

A burning pain pierced his chest, searing through ice and tissue and bone with unerring accuracy straight to his heart. He reached up to rub the spot and felt the wetness of a single tear. Guilt washed over him, making his breath catch as he roughly pulled her into his arms, tucking her head beneath his chin, knowing he was damned but aware there wasn't anything he could do about it.

"Hush, sweetheart. Go to sleep. You haven't done anything to displease me."

She murmured something against his throat, but he couldn't

hear it over the blood pounding loudly in his ears.

Gillian felt his body tense, then slowly relax as she lay in his arms, her lips pressed against a pulse point on his neck. His inner demons had returned with a vengeance, driving him away from her again. It was the intimacy of their lovemaking that brought them out, she knew—such overwhelming oneness, such an expression of love no doubt forced to the surface all the pain he still felt over the death of his first wife. Gillian listened to his pounding heart slow and settle into a strong, steady beat as she considered a future that suddenly seemed bleak and endless. How was she to combat a ghost that Noble would not admit existed? How could she make him love her when it was obvious he still mourned his beloved first wife? She wondered for the thousandth time what had happened the night Elizabeth died, and why Noble was blamed for her death. How could any man who still grieved so be thought a cold, heartless murderer?

The only way to rid their marriage bed of the specter of Elizabeth was to lay her spirit to rest. Noble snored softly above her, then grunted and rolled to his side, taking her with him. He pulled her back against his chest, spooned his legs up behind hers, and draped a heavy arm over her waist. Gillian smiled drowsily to herself as she let his warmth wrap around her. She would see to it that Elizabeth's ghost no longer haunted their marriage. The faint outline of a plan formed in the hazy, sleep-muddled corners of her mind. She would take a leaf from Charlotte's beloved novels and investigate both Elizabeth's untimely death and the mystery of who wanted harm to befall Noble. Once she knew the truth, she could help Noble overcome his fears and teach him to open his heart again. She snuggled back against his warm chest and gave herself up to sleep. Tomorrow she would begin her investigations. Tomorrow she would see that their life was one of order and serenity.

* * *

"I won't have my orders defied, wife. You would have us live in the most disordered, disorganized, turbulent lifestyle, and I won't have it! We *will* have order and structure in our lives. You *will* obey my dictates."

"I'm not defying them, husband, I'm asking you to reconsider."

Noble pointed the knife he had been using to spread marmalade on a piece of toast at the two dogs sitting at his side, their dark eyes hopeful as cascades of saliva issued from their flews.

"You ask too much, Gillian. Charles! Make yourself useful and escort these dogs outside to the stable. Piddle is puddling on the carpet."

"That's Erp who is drooling so. Piddle is the one tending to his personal equipment. Truly Noble, if you would just see that my presence here—"

"At least they are no longer offensive by other means," he sniffed, giving the hounds a black look as they followed after the footman before turning back to his wife. Gillian felt her stomach wrap into knots around her breakfast. It was for his own good. Someday he would go down on his knees before her and thank her for her intervention. She just had to be strong until that time. She straightened her shoulders and looked him firmly in his lovely silver eyes.

"If you send me back, I shall simply return."

His eyes darkened as a muscle twitched in his jaw. It was odd she had never noticed twitching muscles on him before. "Do you threaten me, madam?"

Her words had to be considered carefully, lest he feel she was challenging him. Men, she had found, hated to be challenged. "No, I do not threaten you. I am *asking* you, Noble, to reconsider. We have been married but three days, and I simply do not wish to be separated from you."

His frown deepened. She ignored the presence of the remaining footman standing at attention behind her and placed her hand over his. "If you send me back, I will miss you."

Noble recoiled as if she had struck him. He waved the footman out before, eyes narrowed, he confronted her. "Again you threaten me! What steps would you take to end your loneliness? Would you seek comfort in the arms of another?"

Gillian felt as if she were the one who had been struck. "Threaten you? Noble, I'm not threatening you, 'tis the truth I'm not. I can't believe you would think I am so faithless that I would seek the attentions of another man."

Noble's jaw tightened at her words.

"Do you believe it is possible for me to engage in those . . . in the wonderful and thrilling things we did last night with someone else? How can you imagine that I would want to? Do you not value my lo—" She caught herself before she let the word slip out. He wasn't ready to hear about that yet, that was quite evident.

"Do I not value what, madam?" Really, if those brows arched any higher, they'd fly off his face.

"Do you not value my . . . my . . . longings for your touch?" Yes, that was good. Longings. It would make him feel that she was pining for him. That she was, was neither here nor there.

"Er . . . yes, of course, but that is not what I—"

"Indeed, I was not threatening you, my lord. As for the other—'tis the truth I would be lonely, but I would never seek the arms of another man. I wish only to be with my husband."

She hoped he hadn't heard the tremble in her voice as she spoke. The urge to throw herself on him and smother him with kisses until she eased the pain evident in his eyes was almost overwhelming. Although admittedly such an inclination was tempered with a healthy dose of self-pity. She hurt too. The fact that he loved Elizabeth so deeply that he could not welcome her into his life pierced her deeply, but she consoled herself with the knowledge that he needed a bit of time before he would realize just what a lucky man he was to have married her. She'd be patient. A week or two ought to be enough to bring him around.

"I doubt that a week or two will be sufficient for anything concerning you, my dear, but I am not an unreasonable man. You may stay for a fortnight," he said grudgingly, reclaiming his hand and turning his attention to his breakfast. "The Season will be over by then, and at that time you will return to Nethercote."

She blushed over her Unfortunate Habit but had other things to worry about than her tendency to speak every thought. It was on her lips to ask about his plans in a fortnight, but she bit the words back and muttered a soft statement of appreciation instead.

"About last night, Noble . . ."

A dull red flush washed over her husband's face at her words.

"I wish to discuss what happened last night, if I might. I am not sure I understand . . ."

"Dickon, you may leave that," Noble ordered, a frown playing across his manly brow. Gillian watched as the footman placed a fresh platter of sirloin before the earl, then left them alone again.

"I would rather you did not discuss our . . . er . . . evening activities in front of the servants, my dear. Now, as to your questions, I'm sure you have several about what we did last evening, it being . . . uh . . . new to you. I'm sure you were as surprised by your actions as I was, stimulating and enjoyable though they were."

"Well, I'm not as new to it as you might think," she interrupted, and heaped a spoon of marmalade on her toasted bread. "I have done it before, you know."

Noble felt as if someone had slapped him in the face with a wet fish. A salmon, perhaps. Or a very large flounder. He gaped at her. "I beg your pardon? Did you just say you had done it before?"

"Oh yes, once or twice. My uncle used to say I was a particularly wicked girl to do so, but I couldn't help myself. Sometimes I just had to, you know. It feels so different, so . . . so . . . oh, I don't know how to describe it. I suppose I didn't have to, as you well know the feeling."

Noble's face grew as black as a thundercloud and he seemed to be having difficulty swallowing. "I do indeed know, although I had not thought that my wife would come to our marriage bed in possession of such knowledge!"

What on earth had gotten into the Lord of Fury? "Well, really, Noble, I know it's not proper, but I wasn't aware that it would be something that so upset you. I shan't do it again, of course, since you are so unhappy about it."

"I should hope not!" Noble thundered, ignoring the memory of the utter bliss her mouth had given him. "I will have names, Gillian, names of the men with whom you have disported yourself in such a fashion."

Gillian looked at him in surprise. "Names of men? I never did it with men, Noble."

He dropped his fork and shook his head. He wasn't hearing her correctly, that was the problem. Perhaps he had water in his ears. Perhaps he was having a hallucination. Perhaps he was having the most realistic nightmare of his life. The thought that his wife, his lovely innocent Gillian, had engaged in oral acts with another man was enough to make his blood boil. To think that she had done so with a woman—it was inconceivable. He shook his head again and took a deep, deep breath.

"Gillian—"

"In truth, husband, I wasn't with anyone in particular when I did it. I just wanted to see how it felt, you see, and, well . . ." She shrugged. "Since they were available, I took the opportunity."

"They? *They* were available? As in more than one?"

"Well, yes, Noble. You don't think I'd go about with just one, now do you?"

Madness. This was sheer madness. That must be the explanation. He'd gone mad and he just hadn't noticed that fact.

"You don't think I would have wanted to appear indecent?"

He tried to formulate words, but his brain failed him. He just sat and stared as his wife calmly ate her breakfast and informed him that she'd had relations of a sexual nature with more than one woman in order *not* to appear indecent. Madness. Or hell. He could be dead and this could be hell. Either explanation would suffice.

"So when the opportunity came up to do it again last night, I couldn't resist. But I did do it properly, I hope you noticed."

Noble's mind ceased to function. He blinked a few times. Oh, he had noticed. She had done it more than properly; she had driven him past the point of his control within a few seconds of touching him. The fire she had started with her lips and tongue was still burning deep within him, melting layers of ice he hadn't known existed.

"And, of course, I had Nick with me, so that was all right."

His mind snapped back to attention. "What?"

"I had Nick with me."

A suspicion slowly began to materialize. "Gillian, of what, exactly, are you speaking?"

She frowned at him as she reached for another slice of sirloin. "Of going out to rescue you last night. In the boots' clothes."

The boots' clothes. She was talking about wearing the boy's clothes, and he had thought she had meant . . . a wave of relief washed over him, making him chuckle at his own foolish thoughts. Foolish, silly, couldn't happen, wouldn't happen sorts of thoughts.

"You're not angry with me still, are you?"

He was, but his relief was so great that he decided to be magnanimous. He spent a little time lecturing her on the magnitude of his generosity in forgiving her transgressions.

Gillian tolerated the lecture with as much good grace as she could muster, then decided to take advantage of the sudden

111

change in mood of the Lord of Chuckles and ask him what was uppermost on her mind.

"Who would want to do you harm, Noble?"

He pushed back his plate and frowned at her. "That is no concern of yours, my dear, except insomuch as you can be assured I will see to your protection."

"Me?" Gillian looked in surprise at her frowning husband. Why was he concerned about her when he was clearly the victim of a nefarious plot? "It wasn't me who was struck on the head and stripped—"

"Yes, yes, we both know what happened. Regardless, it should not concern you. I will see to it that it won't happen again. For your own safety, I will ask Crouch to accompany you when you go out. What are your plans for today?"

"But, Noble, if you'd just let me help you, I'm sure that together we can determine who—"

"Your help is appreciated but not needed," he said firmly, then cocked an insolent eyebrow at her. Really, he was so maddening. If he would just see that she could help him, that he needed her . . . she sighed and answered his earlier question. "I had planned to call on Charlotte, my lord, and perhaps visit Lackington's bookshop. I trust that meets with your approval?"

He nodded. "As long as you take Crouch with you." He stood, then tapped on the table for a moment as he pondered something. "Yes, Crouch and one of the footmen; they ought to be sufficient. Regarding this evening, I have accepted an invitation to the Countess Lieven's ball. Do you plan on attending as well?"

Gillian blinked at him. He couldn't mean that he had no plans to see her throughout the day, could he? And worse yet, that he would go to a ball, their first ball since they had been married, without her? And an important ball, one held by the infamous Countess Lieven! No, he couldn't mean that, surely he wasn't that cold and unfeeling. Not the man who had, just a few hours before, swept her up in his warmth and sent her spirit flying in one of the most sensual experiences of her life. No. Not her Noble.

She smiled. "I would be happy to attend the ball with you, Noble."

"Excellent. I shall see you there later, then." He started for the door, pausing when he reached it. "I will be out this evening, my dear. I'm sure your aunt and uncle will be attending the ball and would be happy to escort you there. I will, of course, accompany you home should you desire it."

Should she desire it? Should she desire the company home of her very own husband of three days? From her first public appearance as his countess? Gillian stared at him, stunned and hurt by his coldness. Tears pricked her eyes. How could he be this way? How could he be so unfeeling toward her when he had been so warm and wonderful that morning?

Noble nodded as if she had answered and left the sunny breakfast room. Gillian, her high spirits suddenly channeled into fury, threw her fork across the room and watched as it bounced off the cheerful yellow-and-white-striped wallpaper and onto the floor. "If I would desire him to accompany me home! Ooooh! I'll . . . I'll . . . oh!" She slapped her hand on the table, unable to think of anything horrible enough to satisfy her anger, then picked up her plate and threw it at Noble's chair. Eggs, sirloin, marmalade, and the remnants of kippers dripped down the front of the ornately embroidered yellow material. Her spirits rose at the sight of it. Noble thought he could cut her out of his life, did he? She eyed a dish of oatmeal speculatively.

"I have finished," she said a few minutes later to the startled footman who had been lurking outside the breakfast room, staring at the door with a worried expression on his face. "You may want to alert the housekeeper to a little problem with the upholstery on his lordship's chair. And there seems to be a spot or two on the wallpaper. Well, it looks to be a lovely day outside. I feel quite energized. I believe a little stroll around the square is in order. Piddle! Erp! Come along, no dawdling now."

She marched out with the two dogs, a hastily scrambling footman in attendance, while both Crouch and Tremayne Two stood gazing in horror through the doorway into the breakfast room.

Upon her return Gillian sent word to the nursery that she would like Nick to pay a call with her, and went upstairs to change her gown. As she was making a list of things she wanted to discuss with Charlotte, sounds of an altercation in the front hall drew her attention. Eerily counterpointing the noise of shouting and loud thumping were two mournful notes that twisted around and around as they raised in both volume and pitch.

"Blast! What are they up to now?" Gillian muttered as she raised her skirts and dashed down the stairs toward the hall. That was all she needed, for her two dogs to be causing trouble when she was on tenuous ground with Noble.

Leaping down the last few stairs like a gazelle, she skidded to an astonished stop at the sight before her. The three Tremaynes were locked in battle, pummeling and lashing at each other with an energy that surprised Gillian. Heretofore, the Tremaynes, with the notable exception of the disagreement the past evening in front of the town house, had always maintained a dignified bearing that reminded Gillian of an elderly penguin she had seen at a zoological gardens. And yet here the brothers were, arms flailing, the air rent with hurled accusations while grunts and muffled groans indicated when a blow was landed.

Crouch the pirate butler danced around the edges, yelling advice and generally getting in the way. The two dogs sat in a corner and howled. It was when one of the Tremaynes landed a particularly unsporting blow to one of his brothers' kidneys that Gillian noticed there was an extra person in the melee.

"Who is that gentleman?" she asked Deveraux, who stood with a phalanx of footmen, watching the battle with an unhealthy gleam in his eye.

"Beg pardon, my lady? Ah, that gentleman? The one just there?"

"Yes, Deveraux, the one who is currently lying flat on the floor. The one who is being sat upon by two of the Tremayne triplets, evidently having been knocked unconscious. The very same one who appears to be bleeding profusely from the nose."

Deveraux scratched his bald little head. "Ah, that gentleman. Well, madam, I'd be hard put to say just who he is. Perhaps Crouch knows. Crouch! Attend her ladyship for a moment."

"Aye, mistress? Ye be needin' me?"

Crouch jumped over the thrashing leg of a Tremayne and raised his voice to be heard over their din.

"Yes." Gillian likewise raised her voice. Really, the noise the three men were making was prodigious. How Noble put up with them was beyond her reasoning. "Piddle! Erp! Cease that howling immediately! Crouch, do you happen to know who that gentleman is?"

Crouch looked around himself in surprise, his earring bobbing wildly. "Gen'leman, m'lady? What gen'leman would that be?"

"That one. There. On the floor. Bleeding on the parquet."

" 'E's bleedin' on me bloody parquet?" The roar Crouch gave startled the three Tremaynes into quietude for a moment, but soon one shoved another and a third laughed, and all three were back on the floor, rolling around on each other and the poor unfortunate bleeding man.

" 'Ere now! That bloody swine is spillin' 'is claret all over me floor! Charles! Dickon! Remove the ruddy trasseno!"

"Trasseno?" Gillian spoke Italian, but had not run into that word before. "I don't believe I'm familiar with that occupation. What exactly is a trasseno?"

" 'E is, m'lady. 'E's a right speeler for all 'e's a swell." Crouch watched with satisfaction as two of the footmen picked the gentleman up.

"Oh, I see." Gillian didn't see but wasn't about to let her staff know that she wasn't current with the latest cant. "Has he speeled on the floor then?"

Crouch's eyebrows telegraphed wildly as he considered her. "Ye shouldn't be usin' such words, m'lady. It ain't right ye should know about such things. 'Is lordship wouldn't like it."

Gillian turned to Deveraux as two of the Tremaynes, having knocked out the third sibling, stood and glared at one another.

"Is speeling an unfortunate occupation, Mr. Deveraux?" she asked.

"Yes, it is, madam. A speeler is an undesirable."

Gillian was about to inquire after trasseno when Noble appeared from a back room where he had been attending to matters of a personal nature. "What the devil is going on here?"

"The Tremaynes have caught a speeler, my lord. Isn't that excellent of them?"

Noble shot Gillian a quick glance of disbelief, then strolled forward to have a look at the bleeding man held by his two footmen. With one hand he grabbed the gentleman's hair and yanked upwards, peering into the bloodied face. "Bloody . . . it's McGregor!" he roared and waved his hand at the footmen. They released their burden. The poor Scottish speeler hit the ground like a sack of marble. He groaned and muttered quietly as he tried to move his arms and legs.

"Charles! Dickon! You dropped the speeler! Pick him up this instant," Gillian demanded. A right speeler the gentleman might be, but he was a gentleman, anyone could see that by his elegant clothing. The two footmen bent and picked him up again.

"Not in my house you won't. Drop him," Noble ordered. They grinned and let go of McGregor again. He groaned even louder and lifted his head. One eye was swollen shut and a cut on his forehead was responsible for the blood covering the left side of his face.

"Oh, you poor man," Gillian started, kneeling next to him, dabbing at the cut with her handkerchief. "Pick him up, Charles, Dickon. He's injured."

Alasdair McGregor, Lord Carlisle, groaned again and pushed himself into a shaky sitting position. "If you don't mind, madam, I believe I'll take my chances with my own two legs."

"Wife, you will cease attending that blackguard and remove yourself from this hall," Noble demanded, marching over and prodding the Scot with the tip of his boot. "I shall see to it this refuse is removed promptly."

"That's right, my lady, you just step back and let Crouch and me take care of the gentleman," one of the Tremaynes said as he stepped forward, cracking his knuckles in a menacing manner. Tremayne One, Gillian thought.

"Aye, mistress, we'll take care of the bloke. We'll tuck him away in lavender, we will."

Gillian smiled at Crouch, who had assisted the gentleman to his feet by one powerful tug to the back of his waistcoat. "That's very sweet of you, Crouch, but I doubt lavender is the scent the gentleman prefers. Do you need further assistance, sir? Might I offer you a restorative strong beverage?"

Carlisle squirmed out of Crouch's hold, stepped over the body of the prone Tremayne, and made an effort to tug down his waistcoat. "Indeed, madam, I do not require either your assistance or a strong beverage. I thank you for your kind concern, however, as it is certainly a welcome oasis in what has otherwise been a vast desert of hospitality."

Gillian tsked over his cut and offered her handkerchief.

"Out!" Noble thundered, stepping protectively in front of Gillian.

"My lord, your manners!" Gillian prodded him to move. Noble stayed where he was. Gillian prodded again. "We have a guest who has suffered an unfortunate accident."

Crouch snickered. Charles and Dickon snickered. Tremayne One and Two snickered, looked at each other in surprise, and immediately frowned at the floor when Tremayne Three snored.

Noble growled. "Out, damn you. Now!"

"Noble!" Gillian pushed to her husband's side and tried to make her apologies. "Sir, I do apolo—"

"You do not. My wife does not apologize to the murdering bastard McGregor."

The Scot dabbed at his split upper lip and grimaced in what Gillian thought was a smile. " 'Tis no concern of yours, my lady. I've received enough apologies for your husband's behavior from the prior Lady Wessex to last me a lifetime."

With a snarled oath, Noble's right fist shot out and caught the Scot on the chin. His head snapped back, and he would have fallen over backward but Crouch, standing behind him, grabbed him and held him up in case the earl wished to thrash him soundly.

"If you ever come near my wife again"—Noble grabbed the poor man's cravat and hauled him over until he was just inches from his face—"I will cut out what passes for your black heart and dance the Highland fling on it."

"You can try," the man croaked in response, not seeming to be intimidated by Noble's threatening countenance. Gillian gave him full marks for bravery, although she was forced to subtract a few for lack of common sense. One didn't beard the Black Earl in this sort of a mood unless one had a death wish. "You can try, but we both know what will happen. You've tried to best me before, Wessex, and failed. What makes you think you can do it now?"

Noble's fingers tightened on the cravat. McGregor's face turned red beneath the blood, and he struggled to free his arms from Crouch's grasp.

"Now I have something worth fighting for. I warn you, McGregor, stay out of my life or prepare to forfeit your own."

Noble released him so suddenly that the Scotsman would have hit the floor if Crouch hadn't been holding him.

"Get rid of this rubbish, Crouch," Noble said, and turned on his heel for the library.

"Did you think I would forget so easily, Wessex? Do you

think I will allow you to murder another innocent woman the way you did Elizabeth? Do you think I'll let you torture this woman the way you did your first—"

Gillian flinched when one of the Tremaynes, who was assisting Crouch help the gentleman speeler out the door, accidentally shoved his elbow in the poor man's mouth. She made a mental note to have a talk with the staff about the manner in which they helped wounded guests down the front steps, then turned to face the library. If Noble thought he was going to let that scene pass without comment, he could just think again!

She poked her head around the door. Noble had his back to her. She was about to speak when he slammed his fist down on the desk.

Oh, dear. He didn't even flinch, and she was sure that had to hurt. She closed the door softly and eyed the members of the staff, engaged in cleaning up the mess on the hall floor. They suddenly refused to meet her gaze and attempted, with the exception of the Tremayne sleeping on the floor, to escape her presence.

"Tremayne Two." She pointed at the butler. "I should like to speak with you."

"Certainly, my lady," he replied, tugging down his sleeves and straightening his neck cloth. "I shall be with you as soon as I have assisted Mr. Crouch."

"Now, Tremayne." Gillian frowned and tried to imitate Noble at his most haughty. It wasn't a very successful imitation, but it did the job. Tremayne made one or two more attempts to escape but followed with lagging steps after Gillian as she went upstairs to her small sitting room.

"You've been with Lord Wessex the longest." She attempted to keep her voice stern, but the butler's long face was making her feel like the meanest sort of ogre. "You may tell me what that scene in the hallway was about."

"Actually, Hippy has been with his lordship the longest," Tremayne said, shuffling his feet.

Katie MacAlister

"Hippy?"

"Hippocratus. My eldest brother, his lordship's head coachman. Mother was of a classical bend of mind."

"I see. And . . . ah . . . I cannot help but asking, but Tremayne the valet . . . ?"

"Plutarch, my lady."

"No, truly? Well, that is different. And you?"

Tremayne lifted his chin and stared down his nose at her. "Odysseus, my lady."

Gillian considered this new bit of information and tried very hard not to allow the slightest peep of laughter to escape her. She swallowed hard several times and eventually was able to speak without her lips twitching.

"I cannot help but notice, Tremayne, that there appears to be an argument between you and your two brothers. Would you care to tell me why that is?"

Tremayne shuffled his feet and cleared his throat. "It's a bit of a long story, madam."

Gillian cast a glance at the carriage clock on the mantel. "I don't have time for a long story, Tremayne Two, so if you could abridge it, I would be most grateful."

The butler cleared his throat again and clasped his hands before him, much in the manner of a small boy about to recite his lesson. Gillian sat back with a sigh. Evidently she was not to have the abridged version.

"It began many years ago, madam, when we lived in Oxfordshire. There lived in the house next to ours a sweet girl by the name of Clara . . ."

"Ah, a woman is involved!" Gillian said with satisfaction. "I do love a story with plenty of romance. How old was this sweet Clara?"

"At the time of the Misunderstanding she was eight, my lady."

Gillan stared. "Eight? Not eighteen, but eight?"

"Yes, my lady. It was a very long time ago, as I said."

"What on earth could have happened to cause such a rift

120

between three brothers that you must battle with them to this very day?"

Tremayne looked pained. "She—that is, Clara—promised to attend the fair with me, my lady."

"And I take it she did not keep that engagement?"

"No, my lady."

"Did she attend with One?"

"No, my lady."

"Three?"

"No, my lady. She attended the fair in the company of one Jabez Willson."

Gillian felt a little dizzy. "Then why," she asked carefully, "are you still fighting if she slighted you all evenly?"

"That is a good question, my lady."

Gillian waited for him to say more, but nothing else was forthcoming. "And?" she prompted.

"I'm afraid we can no longer remember."

Gillian fought the urge to throttle him, decided not to pursue the origin of the feud, and turned back to her original question. "The gentleman speeler in the hall, Tremayne, who was he?"

"That would be Alasdair McGregor, my lady. He has recently become Lord Carlisle."

"Yes, well, that tells me who he *is*, but not who *he* is, if you understand."

Tremayne looked confused.

"What is his history with Lord Wessex?"

Tremayne looked stubborn.

"Why is Lord Wessex so angry with him?"

Tremayne looked unsure.

Gillian frowned at him and was about to speak quite harshly when he gave a little shrug and sighed. "Lord Carlisle is an old acquaintance of Lord Wessex, my lady."

"And?"

"They had a falling out five years ago."

"Oh. A friendship gone sour?"

Tremayne grimaced. "Something along those lines, my lady. If you'll permit me, madam, I have taken it upon myself to instruct Mr. Crouch as to the proper method of polishing a fish knife. His idea of polished would shock the feathers off a parrot."

"Yes, that's fine. Thank you." Gillian gnawed at her lip as Tremayne left. The Black Earl had certainly displayed a temper worthy of his name. She was quite prepared to believe he fully meant every threat he had uttered. If she had thought him cold in his manner to her earlier, she had now corrected that impression. Noble's anger was fueled by a fire hotter than that of hell itself. Still, McGregor's involvement with the earl was just one more thing to add to her list of items to investigate. Gillian heaved a sigh and went off to find the Lord of the Underworld.

"Noble?" She stuck her head around the library door and spoke softly. "Are you busy?"

Noble looked up from the blackmail letter that had come in the morning's post. "I am."

"Ah. Well, I can see you are, since you are holding a letter and what appears to be a paintbrush if I am not mistaken, but I had thought to ask you—do you paint, husband?"

Noble blinked at her. "You interrupted me to ask me if I paint?"

"Well, no, actually I interrupted you to tell you that I am off to see my cousin Charlotte, but I couldn't help but notice the paintbrush in your hand." Gillian stepped into the room and closed the door carefully behind her. Noble looked puzzled rather than furious, which greatly relieved her mind. "It's rather a curious thing to have in a library, I believe. A paintbrush. Unless, of course, you paint, but as I see no easel, nor any canvas or paints, I would have to assume that if you do paint, you paint elsewhere, which, as I believe I've mentioned, makes it curious that you are, in fact, holding a paintbrush. Here, that is. In the library."

She paused for breath and hoped Noble wouldn't notice that

she was babbling incoherently about a paintbrush.

A slight frown pushed down Noble's eyebrows as he carefully placed both letter and paintbrush on the desk, then rose and started toward her. "Why the devil are you babbling incoherently about a paintbrush, woman?"

"I—well, you have that paintbrush—"

Noble stopped scant inches away and frowned down at her. Gillian felt a flush sweep up from her chest. Really, it wasn't at all fair that he could so disconcert her with just a look. What on earth had she been thinking, marrying the Lord of Manliness and Virility? How could she expect to live a peaceful life with him constantly around, sending goose bumps up her arms, making her knees go weak with his nearness, causing her breath to catch when he looked at her as he was looking at her at that very moment, making her stomach ball up with the heady scent of his shaving soap, which lingered on his neck and cheeks.

"Oh, Noble," she gasped as she suddenly lunged at him. He rocked backward for a moment, surprised by her leap forward, but quickly regained his balance and returned the caresses she was unable to withhold any longer. The poor man, he needed her so much; she just couldn't help but show him how much he needed her. She nibbled on his earlobe, pulling it gently with her teeth as he grasped her behind and pulled her up closer to him. "I apologize for interrupting you, my lord," she said breathlessly, turning her head slightly so her lips met his.

"No apology is necessary," he groaned, then claimed her lips, stroking the roof of her mouth and the sides of her tongue with his own. She moaned and felt her knees buckle. Wonder of wonders, Noble buckled with her, and they both fell to the floor. Gillian was mindless of anything but the sudden desire that burst into flame between them.

" 'Tis the truth I should apologize," she murmured as he kissed a hot, wet trail down to her breastbone. How the devil had he tied his cravat? In knots? She bit back a sob as her hands, frantic to untie it, tugged and pulled until the cloth loosened and she could bare his neck.

Noble continued his path of kisses down to the top of her gown. He looked at the neckline with calculating eyes, wondering if he could just push it down, or if he'd have to tear it off her. Either way, he'd have her lovely breasts bared. "I've told you, sweetheart, no apology is necessary. I'm quite willing for you to interrupt me whenever you feel the need."

"That is indeed most gracious of you, my loooooooooooooorrr—" Gillian's voice rose as Noble's mouth closed around her breast, suckling her with a passion that started fires all over her body.

He pushed her gown off her shoulders and tugged it down to her waist, exposing all of her chest. "Not at all," he breathed, his mind happily frolicking in a land made up solely of Gillian's breasts. "Was there something in particular you nippled?"

"Something I what?"

"What?" Why was she bothering him with talk? Couldn't she see he was busy?

"Did you just ask me if there was something in particular I *nippled?*"

"Yes, lovely, aren't they?" he murmured, turning his attention to the quivering twin of the first. Lovely, adorable, tasty little pink nipples.

"Never mind, it doesn't matter," Gillian said, unable to hold a thought any longer than she could catch her breath, not with the Lord of Tongues lathing her breasts like that. "I, ah . . . uh . . . Nick. I wanted to . . . oh, lord, Noble, do that just once again."

He took her rosy little bud of a nipple gently between his teeth and tugged ever so slightly. She arched her back and thrashed her head. He gave in to a smug, masculine thought of how easy it was to arouse her but lost that thought when her hands slipped beneath his shirt. To be honest, he lost all thoughts, especially when she pushed him onto his back, straddling him, her breasts bobbing in a merry little taunting fashion as she worked to unbutton his shirt. Then she bent down and took his nipple in her mouth. Dear God, why had he never noticed his nipples before, and when had they caught on fire?

"Did you want to speak with me about Nick?" he gasped, sliding his hands up the outside of her silken thighs, pushing her gown upward. Dear God, her legs were longer than he remembered. And smooth, so very smooth. If only his nipples weren't on fire, distracting him just when he wanted all of his concentration for mapping out the contours of Gillian's endless legs.

Gillian squirmed under the onslaught of his fingers, relentless as she nibbled and sucked on first one nipple, then the other. Surely by now the fire must have consumed them, he thought wildly, his fingers sliding around to the fronts of her thighs. Surely he must have nothing left but little charred nipple nubs.

"I wanted to tell you how much he's enjoying . . . oh my God, yes, enjoying . . . enjoying . . . ah . . . London! Yes, London!" Gillian shrieked. She scooted down and plunged her tongue into Noble's navel while her hand reached for the buttons on his buckskins. He held his breath, waiting, feeling her light touch as she slowly released the tension of the material restraining his arousal.

"Oh," she squealed when the last button popped off and flew across the room. She was delighted to see that he was as excited as she was, and reached out with both hands to clasp that dear, dear unbroken man part of his. She smiled fondly at it, and would have bestowed a kiss upon its happy little head, but suddenly she was flat on her back, with Noble's tongue counting her teeth. At least that was what she thought he was doing. She let him check a few, then sucked on his tongue and pressed up against him as his fingers found that lovely secret spot that only he knew how to warm.

"Good," he groaned once he had retrieved his tongue, and

gave a moment of attention to the twin breasts clamoring for his notice.

"Oh, my, yes, very good, my lord," Gillian squirmed, wanting to close her legs around his probing fingers and pull him in closer. "Very, very good."

Noble chuckled as he shucked his breeches, then slid both hands along Gillian's legs, spreading her for him. "I meant it was good Nick is enjoying London."

"Oh, yes, that." Gillian watched as Noble began kissing her thighs, her thoughts as scattered as dandelion seed in a storm. Was he going to . . . would he do what he did last night? That thing with his tongue? Oh, lord, he was going to. She grabbed onto the carpet beneath her and felt her back arch as Noble's hot breath steamed over her most private area. "He told me he was happy here, and I wanted you to know . . . to know . . . oh dear heaven, Noble, don't stop!"

He didn't. Not until she bucked beneath him, clutching his hair as she called his name over and over again when he lifted her to a height she hadn't known possible. He rose up over her, settling between her thighs, gazing at her flushed face and passion-filled emerald eyes.

Noble's last coherent thought just before he plunged into his wife's sweet depths was that he hoped to God none of the servants would choose that moment to open the door. He didn't think he could stop, not even if the entire staff trooped in to watch.

"What did you mean he told you he was happy here?"

Gillian, squashed up against her husband's chest, sated, drowsy, happier than she'd ever been, lifted her head from where it lay on his biceps. Noble was on his side facing her, his arms wrapped around her, their breathing in perfect synchronicity, as, she was sure, were their heartbeats. She raised a languid finger to trace the length of his nose. How was it possible that each time Noble made love to her, she felt less and less an entity made up of herself, and more one made up of the both of them?

Did he feel that he was part of her, too? She hoped so. She wanted him to give his heart into her keeping just as she had given him hers. She sighed, wondering if he knew she had relinquished to him her most prized possession.

"I know," he said with a dark, unfathomable look, and pulled her closer so that his chin rested on her head. "I'll keep it safe, sweetheart."

She would have blushed at the reappearance of her Unfortunate Habit, but then, she reasoned, she was lying naked on the carpet in the library in the middle of the day, after having engaged in activities that were not usually conducted in such a place. Surely there were many other worthy things to blush about!

"How do you know that Nick is happy to be in London?"

"Hmm? Nick? He told me." Her Lord of Loins was certainly a man who explored a subject thoroughly before letting go of it. Her lips curved into a smile as she recalled just how thoroughly he had explored her. Thoroughness was not necessarily a bad quality in a man.

"He told you he is enjoying it here?"

"Yes." She tipped her head back and met his gaze. He looked puzzled.

"He *told* you?"

She made a little moue of annoyance. Didn't she just say that? "How else did you expect him to let me know he's enjoying his stay in London?"

Noble frowned. "You are aware, are you not, madam, that my son does not speak?"

"Well of course I'm aware he doesn't speak. It's rather obvious, Noble." Gillian pushed back from his chest and looked mildly insulted.

"And yet you tell me he has spoken to you. You will understand how I find this difficult to believe."

"There are more ways of speaking than by tongue, husband. I'm a mother. A mother understands her children."

"You have been a mother exactly"—he looked at the clock on the mantel—"forty hours. Hardly the experience I would imagine that was needed to read my son's mind."

"Regardless, I know Nick is having a wonderful time, and I would like him to accompany me on my visit to Charlotte."

Noble was about to refuse when it struck him that he might be defeating his own purpose if he interfered too much. He had promised to give her a fair chance with Nick, and since she obviously wanted to include him in her plans, he thought it best to let her proceed. With a few precautions set in place, of course. He wasn't about to expose his son to a nightmare like the one the lad had barely survived with Elizabeth.

Noble was about to suggest they reclaim their clothing when Gillian placed a hand on his chest and stroked him. "Noble, I will happily take as many footmen as you like with me, but I worry about you."

He was having a hard time thinking about anything but the fire she was starting deep inside his belly. "About me?"

"Yes. This attack on you, Noble, was clearly carried out by someone who wants to harm you. If you would just share your thoughts with me about it, I believe I may be of some help to you. You said last night that you had a suspicion of someone who might have abducted you?"

Noble had a suspicion, all right, but it wasn't about the person who had lured him to his small house in Kensington and left him naked on his mistress's bed. It was a suspicion that Gillian had just used him, turned his desire for her against him, and used him physically in a manner much like Elizabeth had used him so long ago. Elizabeth, who viewed lovemaking as a means to an end, as a way to force him into acquiescing to whatever it was she wanted. With Elizabeth it was jewels or baubles; with Gillian, it was his soul. His muscles stiffened beneath the gentle caress of her hand. Elizabeth and Gillian—this turn of events was surely proof that they were both the same after all, both only after whatever they could get from him, by whatever means necessary. He struggled to keep his voice emotionless. "I have told you that is no concern of yours, my dear. Now perhaps you should get dressed if you wish to visit your cousin."

Gillian continued to stroke his chest, heedless of the icy grip of torment that was creeping over her husband. It was true she could melt the ice encasing his soul with her passion, Noble thought as the pain from her betrayal seared a bloodless wound deep into his heart, but she could also be a thousand times colder than Elizabeth ever had been.

"If you would just tell me, Noble. Who is it you suspect? Who would do such a thing to you? Who knew where your mistress lived? Why would someone target you in such a way?"

"If you are quite through, madam . . ." The words fell from his lips with chilly formality. Briskly he pushed her away and fumbled with his breech buttons, his fingers numb with cold and fury. "I have work I wish to do. Your attentions, although welcome, are unnecessary to procure my permission for Nicholas to accompany you. The next time you seek such permission you might just ask me first."

Gillian paused in the act of righting her gown, feeling as if she had just been slapped. She stared at Noble, stunned and shocked by the frigid tone of her husband's voice. What had happened? Just a few minutes ago he had been whispering the most erotic, passionate words in her ear, praising her, thanking her, shouting out her name when their souls twined together in one blinding moment of ecstasy. What had happened to take that warm, lovely, *loving* man and change him into this cold automaton? She fought back the tears that threatened to choke her and finished arranging her gown, wondering all the while if she could explain to him the effect he had on her. Perhaps if she could, he would understand.

"Noble," she said a moment later, and reached out to touch him. Her hand froze in midair as he flinched away from her. She couldn't keep the tears back then. They welled up and spilled over as she choked out an apology, then ran from the room. What had she to do to banish the ghost of Elizabeth? Why couldn't Noble give her a chance? Wasn't there room in his heart for them both? Was she doomed to receive only the adoration of his body, but not his soul? She rushed blindly for the sanctuary of her bedchamber.

Nick watched his stepmother race past him on the stairs. She was crying and hadn't even noticed him. His shoulders slumped a little lower as he sat down on the step. Had it already begun, then? Had she started to hate him the way his other mother had? He went over a list of his actions in his head—no, there was nothing there that would upset her, nothing that would give her cause to hate him as the other one had. He had been very careful ever since she had come into his life a few days before—he liked her and wanted her to like him. He had made a mental promise to be good, but maybe that wasn't enough. Maybe she would turn away from him as his other mother had. He didn't think he could bear that.

"Nick." He looked up. His father was standing in the hall, Crouch helping him on with his coat. "Nick, come with me a moment; I wish to speak with you."

Nick watched as father took his hat, gloves, and stick, then waved him toward the library. He sighed. There would be no help from that quarter. He had failed his father just as he had failed his mother.

"Your stepmother wishes you to accompany her on her calls this morning. I am sure that you would much rather be attending your lessons, but I have given my permission for you to go with her. It goes without saying that I expect you to act in a manner befitting my son."

Nick closed his ears to the rest of the lecture. He'd heard it before. Sometimes the words changed, but the meaning was always the same. He was to behave in a manner befitting his father's station. That was of the utmost importance, just as Nanny Williams had said it was. "Your papa's an earl, and that's a very important man," she had told him. "Someday he'll have a son to follow in his footsteps and be an earl after him, but until then, he's got you, so you'd best do him as proud as you can. Not that it matters, in the end, since you can't be the son he needs, but still, you're here, so you'd best be showing your papa how grateful you are that he recognizes you."

"Nick." He looked up to find his father squatting before him, the big hands warm on his knees. "Nick, you do like Gillian, do you not?"

He nodded.

"Good. I like her too. I think—" His father stopped, looking toward the library doors, a wistful expression on his face. Nick had never seen it before, but the sight of it made something deep inside him want to hug his father, and be hugged in return. "I think she likes us too."

Two pairs of almost identical gray eyes surveyed one another for a moment, exchanging thoughts and emotions without words. Nick blinked back the wetness in his eyes when his father suddenly took him in his arms and squeezed him tight. He buried his face against the stiff neck cloth and wrapped his arms around his father's neck.

Maybe things would turn out all right after all. Clasped firmly in his papa's arms, Nick did something he hadn't done in almost five years. He began to hope.

Chapter Six

"Honestly, Gilly, I thought Mama would never leave us!" Charlotte said, slumping back against a watered-silk rose settee and kicking off her slippers.

"I think she just wanted to gossip a little, Char," Gillian said with a smile, watching as Nick sat on the floor, his knees to his chin as he contemplated Roget, Charlotte's bad-tempered cat. "You forget that I am now a countess, and therefore someone worth gossiping with."

Charlotte snorted and threw a fat pillow at her cousin. "Stop your gloating and tell me how you are."

Gillian tossed the pillow in the air and caught it with a little laugh. "You heard me tell your mama I was fine. What is it you really want to know?"

"Perceptive as ever." Charlotte giggled, then tipped her head meaningfully toward Nick.

"Nick darling, why don't you go down to the kitchen and see if Mrs. Tennyson has any of her delicious fruit tarts left? I'm sure Cousin Charlotte would let you take that four-legged curmudgeon with you."

Nick gave her a long glance that let her know he was aware

he was being sent out of the way, but scooped up Roget and left without delay.

"There, I have sent my son away for you, now what did you want to discuss that we couldn't in front of him?"

Charlotte leaned forward and clasped her hands together. "*That.*"

"That what?"

Charlotte prodded her with her foot. "You know. *That.*"

Gillian narrowed her eyes. "You don't mean . . . *that?*"

"Yes, I do. *That.*"

"No, truly, *that?*"

"*That!*"

"Oh." Gillian thought for a moment. "You know, it really is strange. I don't feel changed, but now that I am married, things are different. For instance, it wouldn't be at all proper for me to discuss *that* with you."

"Fudge about what's proper. Did you enjoy it? Was it as pleasurable as Penny says, or horrid like Mama told you?"

Gillian blushed. "Honestly, Charlotte, you shouldn't believe everything your maid tells you. And I don't believe I'm supposed to discuss *that* with you—I'm sure it's breaking some sort of married women's rule or possibly a law or some such thing."

Charlotte scooted over to the edge of the love seat and took a firm grip on her cousin's arm. "If you do not tell me about *that*, I shall tell Mama about the time I saw you kissing that scrumptious stableboy."

Gillian raised her chin. "Do your worst, cousin. I am beyond your mama's reprimands now."

"But not your husband's."

Gillian blanched at the thought of that. "What in particular did you wish to know about *that?*"

Charlotte told her.

A half hour later Nick returned to the sitting room to find both Charlotte and Gillian doubled over in laughter.". . . but it wasn't really broken at all, I just thought it was! It worked quite well later—oh, hello, Nick. Did you have a nice time in the kitchen? Did Cook give you a tart?"

Nick nodded and looked shyly at Charlotte. Gillian held out her hand for him and, scooting over, pulled him onto the seat alongside her. "I was just telling my cousin about last night. Now you're up to date, Charlotte."

Charlotte appeared thoughtful and watched absently as Gillian ruffled her stepson's hair and gave him a little hug. "Whose house was it that Lord Wessex was found in?"

"His own! It is the house he keeps for his mis . . . uh . . . his *lady friends.*"

"Gillian! How can you be so blasé about that?"

"I'm not in the least. But you see, I happen to know that Noble has dispensed with his latest *friend's* services."

"Oh. Do you think she had something to do with his abduction?"

"I'm not sure," Gillian said thoughtfully, her hand resting on Nick's shoulder. "But I mean to find out. Which is where I need your help—to uncover this dastardly plot against Noble and bring the miscreants to justice. Then I will have his full attention and can begin to lay the ghost of his beloved Elizabeth to rest. Once I've done that . . . well, things will be better."

Charlotte patted her free hand sympathetically. "I'm sure he loves you, Gilly; he wouldn't have married you if he didn't. And after such a short courtship—only a gentleman very much in love would marry someone after just a few meetings."

Gillian smiled at her cousin and flicked the fat cushion back at her. "You need not look so cautious, Char. I promise I won't fill your ear with lengthy does-he-love-me-doesn't-he-love-me dialogues. Now, you have far more experience than I in this— how do you think I ought to begin the investigation?"

Charlotte toyed with the cushion's gold tassels. "I have experience? What are you talking about?"

"The novels, cousin, the novels! You have read so many more than I have, and I know you pay closer attention to them than

I do, for you are forever anticipating a crime, or you know who the villain is before I do. Thus you are better equipped to deal with this situation. As I see it, we have two mysteries to solve— first and foremost, who is behind the attack on my dear Noble, and second, who killed the late Lady Wessex?"

Charlotte stopped spinning the cushion on her fingertip and stared at her cousin. "But I thought—surely I mentioned— didn't Mama tell you—Gillian, don't you remember that I *told* you Lord Wessex was responsible for his wife's demise?"

"Oh, of course I've heard that bit of cruel hearsay," Gillian responded, waving a hand airily. "But it's all false. Completely false. Noble would never harm anyone." She paused and remembered his actions that morning. "Well, no one of the female gender, that is. No, someone else is responsible for her death and is quite happy blaming Noble for it. I intend to get to the bottom of that, too. Perhaps then I can persuade Noble to give our marriage the same chance he gave his first."

Charlotte frowned at the wistful note in her cousin's voice, tossed the cushion to Nick, then turned her mind to the task at hand. "Well, it seems to me that if you wish to find out who abducted Lord Wessex, you must first find out who his enemies are. Then you may question them and eliminate the ones who do not seem to be the type to kidnap him and shackle him to his ex-mistr . . . uh . . . *friend's* bed."

"I see your point," Gillian said thoughtfully, eyeing Nick as he made the tassels dance a little tassel dance on his bony knees. "It is not an everyday sort of enemy who would do that; more a special enemy with a particular goal in mind?"

"Exactly. Someone who wanted to embarrass Lord Wessex as well as endanger him."

Gillian thought about that for a moment, watching Nick balance the cushion on his head. She said slowly, "Oddly enough, Char, I do not believe Noble was in any danger. He was confined, but there were no signs of occupation in the house, no signs that someone might have wished to harm him physically.

Katie MacAlister

It seems to me that whoever did this wanted . . . well, just wanted him found shackled naked to that bed."

"You mean it was a jest? Someone did that to him as a lark?"

"Nooo," Gillian said, chewing on her lower lip, being careful to hold her head still since Nick had transferred the cushion to her fiery crown of braids. "No, I don't believe it was a prank. I believe it was a warning of some sort."

"How are we to find out what that warning was? And whom it was from?"

"We shall have to do as you say—find out who Noble's enemies are and interview them." The tassels bobbed rakishly over one eye as she nodded her head emphatically.

Charlotte looked doubtful. "How are you going to find his enemies?"

"Well . . ." Gillian balanced the cushion on the toes of one foot as she thought. A slow smile spread over her face as she kicked the cushion high in the air. Nick leaped up and caught it. "I shall ask the people who knew him best."

She patted her cousin on the shoulder and stood. "Who knows a man better than anyone else, Char?"

"His friends? His family? His valet?"

Gillian shook her head at each. "Put the cushion back, Nick, and make your good-bye bow to your cousin. No, Charlotte, I want someone who will know all of the *on-dits,* someone who is familiar with all of the *ton* gossip, and who is willing to share it with me. I shall meet with"—she smiled a triumphant little smile—"his ladybugs."

"Ladybugs?" Charlotte snorted and clutched the cushion to her chest as she fell over backward laughing. "Ladybugs? I think you mean ladybirds!"

"Oh." Gillian made a little moue of chagrin. "Whatever they're called, I shall ask them. They will surely be able to tell me what I want to know."

"Do you know, cousin," Charlotte said, still laughing, "I believe that if anyone can do it, you can. No one else would have

136

the gumption, let alone the desire, to interview her husband's former mistresses. Leave it to you unschooled Colonials to simply ignore the precepts of good breeding and gentle manners when it suits you. Oh, I do wish I could be there when you question them. I would give an entire year's pin money to see the looks on their faces when you ask them about Lord Wessex."

Gillian pushed her son gently toward the door. "Shall I see you tomorrow to help me plan my strategy?"

Charlotte nodded and twirled the cushion. Gillian bid her good-bye and started out the door.

"Oh, Char?" Her cousin looked up, a slight frown of puzzlement wrinkling her brow. Gillian smiled. "Don't be spending any of your pin money. You will be helping me interview the ladybirds. I couldn't possibly interview them myself, being as unschooled and ignorant of the precepts of good breeding as I am. I'm sure your gently bred, noble touch is just the one needed to get them to unbend and tell us everything we want to know."

Gillian escaped out the door just a few seconds before the cushion hit it. She chuckled at the undignified and unladylike language coming from behind the door and hurried down the hall after her son.

"Crouch, I wish to go to Lord Carlisle's house. Do you have the direction?"

"Ye be wantin' to do what, m'lady?"

"I wish to go to Lord Carlisle's house. Tomorrow."

Crouch stared at Gillian as he handed her into the carriage. "Lord Carlisle, m'lady?"

"Yes, Lord Carlisle, Crouch. Is there a problem?"

Crouch's eyes glazed over at the thought of all the problems his mistress's unusual request would generate. The number alone staggered the mind. "Aye, m'lady, ye could be sayin' there's a problem. A right big problem it be, too."

"You don't know his direction?"

"Eh . . . well, as to that, m'lady, as ye've asked me out-right . . ."

"Excellent. Then I shall assume that you will be able to accompany Lady Charlotte and me tomorrow to pay a call upon Lord Carlisle."

A stunned Crouch climbed onto the seat next to John Coachman. "I'm all-a-mort, Johnny. What do ye think of that, then?"

"She fair bewattles me." John Coachman shook his head. "I wouldn't want to be in your shoes, Crouch, having to tell his lordship that."

Crouch, known to inspire terror in men with just one sneer of his scarred face, blanched with horror at the thought of what his employer would have to say.

"It's not so much what 'e'll say as what 'e'll do," he corrected himself.

"Aye, you're right there. He'll have your head if you let the mistress go calling on his hated enemy."

Crouch cupped a protective hand around his most prized possessions and stared ahead through the leader's ears. "I could live without me 'ead. It's what else 'e might take off that turns me blood pale!"

At the very time Gillian was on her way home, explaining to her son that she and Noble were going to be out that evening, Noble stepped down from his friend Rosse's carriage and glanced down Bond Street. Lord Rosse squinted against the afternoon sun and followed his friend's gaze. "I see Poodle Byng is back in town, stouter than ever. Who's that with him?"

"Sefton."

"Oh, yes, should know that nose anywhere. Shall we stay a moment and greet them?" Rosse looked speculatively at his friend. "Or is there a need to?"

"My dear friend, you may pass your time as you like, but I intend on expelling a bit of energy on whoever might be willing to oblige me." Wessex started up the steps to Gentleman Jackson's rooms.

"I gather this laissez-faire attitude means either, or both, men have given you the cut?"

"You may gather whatever you like, Harry. Remind me to mention a little problem I need your advice on once we've taken a bit of exercise."

Rosse smiled and followed his friend up the stairs. "I don't recall you having a need to expend energy at Gentleman Jackson's before, Noble. I used to have to beg you to come with me, despite the fact that you're a great hulking brute perfectly made for dashing a fellow's brains about the ring." He shook his head in mock concern. "How comes a newly wedded man to have so much excess energy? It can't be good, my friend. I sadly fear you are not doing right by your new countess and will have to take the issue up with you when you are finished expending all this energy you seem to possess."

The two gentlemen were greeted and conveyed to the dressing room. "If I were another man, Harry, I should take offense at your comments."

Rosse, secure in the knowledge that he had been practicing faithfully at Jackson's for the last two years while his friend rusticated in the country, grinned. "Is that a challenge?"

"If you like."

"My dear sir, I accept your challenge of a round of fisticuffs. Shall we set a boon upon the winner?"

"An excellent idea," Noble said as he slid his arms out of his waistcoat and allowed one of the attendants to remove his neck cloth.

"Have you something in particular in mind?"

"I do."

"And it is . . . ?"

"To be named at the winner's discretion."

Rosse grinned again, carefully removed his spectacles, and

handed them over to the man waiting, then swung his arms back and forth to limber them up.

"I should warn you, Noble, I've had several lessons while you've cloistered yourself away on your estate. I'm counted as quite handy with my fives. Even Jackson himself says I show considerable promise."

Noble allowed himself a smile. "I'll try not to hurt you too badly, old friend."

"I believe I'll stick to pistols from now on," Lord Rosse said meditatively, rubbing his swollen jaw and fingering his torn lip. "Less dangerous. I think you loosened a tooth."

"I did nothing of the sort," Wessex replied, wincing at the sunlight as they stepped from the building. "I told you I wouldn't hurt you too badly. However, I shall have a bit of explaining to do when Gillian sees my eye."

Rosse smiled a lopsided smile. "That's quite a mouse. As the satisfaction in landing a blow to you goes a long way in easing the sting of my defeat, I'll ask you now what it is you want my help with." He paused a moment to direct his hack driver. "St. James's, John." Then he turned toward his friend. "White's or Boodle's, Noble?"

"White's, don't you think?"

"White's it is. Ah." Lord Rosse sank back into the plushly upholstered seat and gingerly flexed his fingers. "Now tell me what sacrificing my good name and excellent reputation in favor of yours has cost me."

Wessex fingered the swollen tissue around his eye. A momentary distraction in the form of the sudden mental image of Gillian on the floor in his library, gown askew, hair tumbling down upon her golden shoulders and spilling onto those mouthwateringly lovely breasts had been all the opening Rosse had needed to land a powerful left.

"McGregor's back in town."

Rosse nodded. "I saw him a few days back at the theater. Didn't acknowledge him, of course."

"Of course. He paid me a visit."

Rosse blinked behind his spectacles. "Why would he do that?"

"To threaten me."

"Threaten you with what? Oh. Gillian?"

"Exactly. He muttered some deranged comments about wanting to warn her, but I know the truth. He's never forgiven me for marrying Elizabeth and will do his best to steal Gillian away as he did her."

Rosse relaxed. "I don't blame you for being angry that the bastard called on you, but I wouldn't worry that he can melt the heart of your Amazon. She's made of sterner stuff."

"She's a woman, and thus is capable of whatever deceit is necessary to achieve her goals."

Rosse watched the pain flit over his friend's face with a sorrow that had its origins deep in a night five years past. "Any other woman, perhaps. I don't claim to know everything about the species, but I know this—you've captured the heart of your Amazon."

Wessex grinned suddenly, then grimaced against the pain the action caused his swollen eye. "So she has informed me."

"There you go, then. Nothing to worry about."

"There's everything to worry about. Harry, someone has been out to cause me trouble ever since I returned to town."

Wessex told him about the plea for help from his former mistress that had sent him out to the house she was to be vacating and ended with a description of how Gillian and Nick rescued him.

"If you are quite finished," Noble said some time later, watching his friend wipe his eyes. "I wasn't aware that it was an episode that would bring so much amusement to you."

"Ah, Noble, if only I could have been there. In a bedsheet, you say? Yes, well—" Rosse saw he had pushed his friend to the limit of his tolerance and turned his attention to the matter at hand. "Has all the hallmarks of a jest of a grand nature."

"I considered it but disregarded it as an explanation. No one I know would dare commit such a jest upon me, and——" He looked out of the window as the carriage rolled up St. James's Street. "I do not believe the perpetrator knew Gillian was in town and prepared to go to outlandish lengths to rescue me from what she perceived as life-threatening danger."

"You don't think your life was in any danger?"

Wessex studied the silver head of his walking stick. "I'm not sure, but I doubt it. If whoever arranged for the scene had wished me harm, he had ample opportunity to do so after knocking me out."

Rosse thought this over for a minute. "I believe you are correct, Noble. That being the case, what is it you want me to do?"

Noble smiled as the door to the carriage was opened and the steps lowered. "I want you to use those talents you showed an aptitude for during the war," he said and nimbly leaping out of the carriage, turned back to face his friend. "I want you to become a spy again, Harry."

"Lady Wessex, how delightful it is to meet you."

"The pleasure is all mine, Countess Lieven. Please excuse my hand. I was admiring the colored lamps you have concealed in the flowers, and I wasn't aware the paint was still wet. Are you acquainted with my uncle, Lord Collins, and his wife, Lady Collins?"

Countess Lieven, a small, dark, vivacious woman with a gracious manner and a lively eye, looked with surprise at Gillian's blue palms, noted the blue hand print on the left side of her gold gown, and gave a mental shudder. She would never, ever understand the English. She turned with a smile to greet her guests, then placed a hand on Gillian's arm and guided her away from the receiving line. "My maid, Clothilde, will attend to your hands . . . and gown, my dear Lady Wessex. But before she does, allow me to express my utmost sympathy for your unpleasant situation. My heart, it bleeds for you in your time of trouble."

Gillian blinked and stared into the dancing black eyes before her. She very much doubted that Lady Lieven felt anything but a burning desire to gather and exchange gossip. "I appreciate your sympathy, Countess, but I am sure the paint will come off."

The countess's famed smile slipped a little as she glanced down quickly at Gillian's hands. "No, my dear, it was not that unpleasant situation of which I speak. It is the other situation that rends my heart in two on your behalf."

Gillian mentally reviewed her most recent unpleasant situations and flushed to the roots of her hair. "I beg your pardon, Countess. I will, of course, replace the trellis. I had no idea that the paint would be so very flammable, you see, but after I accidentally tipped the lamp over, it set a bit of the trellis on fire. Just a small bit, really, and I doubt if you can see it without being very close to it, which of course I was in order to put the fire out, and you can be sure I will replace those lovely rosebushes as well."

The countess stared at her as if she had suddenly grown a third eye in the middle of her forehead; then with a little shake of her head, she made a gesture of dismissal. "It matters not, dear Lady Wessex. What are a few roses and a bit of trellis between friends, eh?"

"That's very generous of you, Countess."

The countess seemed to be having trouble gathering her thoughts, but she gave Gillian a brilliant smile and spoke in a most conspiratorial tone of voice.

"It is not these trivial matters of which I speak, my dear. I speak of that which a little bird has told me, and I wish to reassure you that you may always consider me a friend should you need a sanctuary."

Gillian covertly glanced around her. There was quite a crowd surrounding them, and despite the low drone of chatter, they all seemed to be quite interested in what the countess was saying to her. The countess evidently realized that as well, for although she leaned in closer to Gillian, she raised her voice. "I refer primarily, of course, to your husband's unpleasant situation. You may be assured that whatever anyone else says about him, he will always be welcome at Ashburnham House."

Several people sniffed, and one man gave a bark of harsh laughter. "Thank you," Gillian said, confused by the innuendoes. Had she done something to make Noble an outcast? She snuck a glance down at her blue palms and was horrified to see a blue smear on the countess's lovely pale apricot and gold gauze gown. She tried to edge backwards, but a cluster of people waiting to greet their hostess kept her captive.

"Your support will mean a great deal to Lord Wessex, Countess. And to me, of course."

"And with regards to that other unpleasant situation of which the little bird spoke"—the countess tipped her head to the side, her ostrich plume swaying gently in the breeze from the open windows—"you must always think of me should you need respite from your . . . troubles."

Gillian smiled and tried to turn her face away from the sweep of the long ostrich feather. "That's most generous of you. I shall remember your kindness always."

The countess smiled again and, with one last pat to Gillian's arm, she moved off to greet the new arrivals.

Gillian gave in to the eye-watering itch the feather had started and rubbed her nose quickly before turning around to face Charlotte.

"What the devil was all that about?" Gillian asked her cousin.

Charlotte took one look at her and rolled her eyes. "For heaven's sake, Gilly," she said as she grabbed her cousin's arm in a grip that never failed to command respect, pushing her to a small room at the back of the long hall. "You've got a blue nose! I've never seen anyone who has the propensity you have for getting into trouble at a ball. If you'd only kept your gloves on, none of this would have happened."

"But I don't like wearing gloves," Gillian complained; she tried to explain about her desire to see the colored lamps but was summarily hushed and turned over to the waiting, if less than enthusiastic, hands of the ladies' maids.

Half an hour later she reappeared, minus a blue nose, but with a blue hand print on her left flank and wearing a pair of gloves that were too small for her. She picked nervously at them and peered around the ballroom, looking for a friendly face.

"Lady Wessex, you look . . . ah . . . charming as ever."

Gillian smiled at the man in front of her. "Thank you, Sir Hugh. That is quite gallant of you, considering I have a blue hand print on my gown and am wearing borrowed gloves."

"My dear Lady Wessex, no one will notice the slightest thing once they have beheld your radiant smile."

Gillian laughed at the dandy. " 'Tis the truth, Sir Hugh; you do raise my spirits so with your words. That's a particularly lovely shade of plum, by the way. It sets off the royal blue very nicely."

The baronet preened a bit as he smoothed out his waistcoat and checked quickly to make sure his watch fobs weren't tangled in the ribbon to his quizzing glass.

"You always wear the loveliest colors," she continued, hoping to return the kindness by paying a compliment to his vanity. "You quite remind me of a peacock with all the lovely shades of blues and greens and purp . . . why Sir Hugh, is something amiss?"

"A peacock?" he sputtered, his face flushed and perspiring.

Gillian was quite concerned that he might have an apoplectic fit on the spot. She hastened to soothe his ruffled feathers. "Why, yes, but I meant it in the nicest way, of course. I quite *like* peacocks, Sir Hugh. Oh, Sir Hugh, please do forgive me, I didn't mean to . . . oh, blast."

145

"It's a waste of your time talking to the popinjays like that, gel."

Gillian glanced over at the settee to see who was addressing her. An extremely elderly man was seated on the green cushions, so wizened and frail that he looked more like a shriveled-up child than a grown man.

"Well, I daresay I am more of a shriveled-up child than a grown man, now. I've seen a hundred-and-one summers, gel."

Gillian blushed at her rudeness and sat down carefully next to the man. "I do apologize, sir. I meant you no disrespect. I have this Unfortunate Habit, you see, and sometimes I speak without knowing it. You most certainly do not look like a shriveled-up child. You just look . . . mature."

The man wheezed a few times, worrying Gillian until she realized he was laughing. " 'Tis of no worry, gel," he cackled, and spent a few minutes catching his breath. "I've been called many a name in my day, and if shriveled and wizened is the worst, then I've naught to complain of."

"You're very sweet," Gillian said with a gentle smile. "Who are you?"

"Palmerston's the name."

"Lord or Mister?"

"Just Palmerston'll do. Faugh, did you ever see such a sight?" One of the old man's gnarled hands rose, and a crooked finger stabbed into the air. "Gels in naught more than their chemises. In my day, a gel would have been whipped for appearing in nothing but their folderol!"

Gillian looked at the parade of fashionables as they strolled past her. "I'm sure it must look that way to you, but I can assure you that fashion has at last taken a step forward. My mother used to complain something terrible about all her corsets and panniers and hoops and such. Don't you think these gowns are much simpler and more elegant?"

"Damn sight more pleasing to the eye, but I'll not be admitting that to a chit like you. You're Wessex's bride, ain't you?"

"Yes, I am. My name is Gillian."

Two sapphire blue eyes, still brilliant in color despite the age of their owner, turned their gaze on her and considered her from beneath two mammoth bushy white eyebrows. The shaking, gnarled hand made another appearance and poked at her arm. "You've taken up quite a challenge, gel. Are you up to it?"

Gillian stared back into the old man's eyes. "I believe so."

"It won't be easy; he's a long road to travel. There's bound to be highwaymen about, trying to drive you from your path."

Gillian found herself drawn into the deep, deep blue of his eyes. They were so clear, so pure, it was like looking into the eyes of a child. What was his connection to Noble? How did he know that Noble had a long journey ahead of him? "I know there will be; we've already met with one. I hope, however, that we will make the journey together."

The old man nodded, and gave her arm another poke.

"Tell me, sir, if you would—you must be acquainted with Noble if you know of his troubles."

"Aye, that I do."

"Then perhaps you would tell me—do you think I will be successful in my quest?"

The sapphire eyes slowly turned away from her and gazed out into the crush of people meandering by. "You'll need to uncover secrets, gel."

"Secrets?"

"Aye, secrets and lies, each begetting the other, one ending where the other begins. If you can figure out that puzzle, you will be successful."

She pondered his answer for a moment, decided it was, on the whole, optimistic, and smiled and gave his hand a little squeeze. She was about to ask him how he knew Noble when Charlotte found her.

"Dearest cousin, you'll never guess what Mama . . . for heaven's sake, Gilly, can't you keep those gloves on for five minutes? Oh, never mind them, come with me. I have the most shocking news to tell you!"

Gillian was appalled by her cousin's rudeness to the old man, but before she could protest, Charlotte dragged her off to a relatively quiet corner near an alcove containing a bust of Paris.

"What is it, Char? I was having a fascinating conversation . . ."

Charlotte's face screwed up suddenly as she whipped around to face the wall while she bit back the beginning of tears. Gillian put her arm around her shoulders and gave her a reassuring little squeeze. "Oh, blast, I'm sorry, Char, it's so warm in here, my hands must be perspiring . . . I'm sure that will come out."

Charlotte stared as her cousin tried to wipe the blue fingerprints off the silver tulle on her shoulder. "Gilly! This goes beyond your normal ineptitude and lack of social graces! What are we going to do? Papa just told Mama not to have you present me to anyone. Gillian—"

Charlotte turned and started to take her cousin's hands in hers, then remembered the paint. She made a quick check of Gillian's arms, then clutched her by the elbows instead. "Gillian, you don't seem to recognize how serious things are for Wessex. He's been cut by just about everyone, Papa says, and soon won't be recognized by anyone nice."

"Countess Lieven said he'd always be welcome."

"Countess Lieven says one thing one day and another the next. Gillian, you don't seem to understand the gravity of this situation—if Lord Wessex continues to be persona non grata, I won't be able to be seen with you."

Gillian blinked at her. "You what?"

"I'm sorry, Gilly, truly I am, but Mama says we won't be able to recognize you if things do not begin to improve for Lord Wessex."

"I see," Gillian said coldly, and shook off her cousin's hands. "Thank you for alerting me to the situation, Charlotte. I wouldn't wish to blight your chances with either my or Noble's unwelcome presence."

"Oh, Gilly, I just knew you were going to go all haughty on me and take it like that. Gilly—Gilly! Let me explain—"

Gillian suffered her cousin to pull her back to the alcove. She pretended to examine the bust, tracing a finger around a marble ear, not wishing to admit she was wounded to the bone by her cousin's words.

"I promise, cousin, no matter what the *ton* says about your husband, I'll always stand by you."

Gillian gave her cousin a grateful smile and a quick hands-free embrace. "Thank you, Char. I didn't think for a moment you'd abandon us."

"Well, it won't be easy, but we'll worry about that when it happens. Dear heavens, look what you've done to the countess's bust! Come, let us go over there where you can do no harm."

Gillian followed her cousin meekly, scanning the room for signs of a familiar form.

"Will you stop peering around like a long-necked giraffe and tell me what it is you're looking for?"

"Noble, although why I should want to see him after the atrocious way he treated me, I couldn't say."

Charlotte looked over the crowd with her cousin, then motioned toward the door leading to the veranda. "Why are you so angry with your husband? What atrocious thing has he done?"

Gillian explained about the cold way Noble had mentioned he would escort her home if she desired.

"This is my first ball as his wife, Charlotte. You can imagine what people must be saying about us when he can't be bothered to attend with me!"

"Well, about that." Charlotte paused for a moment, wondering how to break the news to her cousin. She opted for the easy way. "Look, there's Aunt Fielding. Do let us go and greet her. She always has the latest gossip."

Gillian agreed reluctantly. "Just for a moment, though. I want to look for Noble."

Charlotte tsked at her and herded her outside onto the veranda to where her aunt sat surrounded by a group of chattering women. Upon seeing Gillian, the women exchanged raised eyebrows and knowing nods and moved off.

"What was that about?" Gillian hissed to her cousin.

"Nothing. Behave yourself. Good evening, Aunt."

Gillian exchanged pleasantries with her cousin's aunt, a woman of indeterminate age and French background, and sat in a small chair when so ordered. "I wish to speak with you, Gillian. I know that our relationship is not one of blood, but I think of you as I would my own flesh-and-blood niece, and hope I've treated you with as much care and attention as I have dear little Charlotte."

"Oh, yes, indeed," Gillian said, watching the people parade past on the veranda, enjoying the lovely evening.

"You have become very dear to me, which is why I will say to you that I could not help but notice that Lord Wessex is not with you this evening. I do hope there are no difficulties?"

"Difficulties?"

"Difficulties—a little contretemps between you and the earl, perhaps? It is not uncommon, I believe, for a bride and groom to have little disagreements and unpleasantnesses as they settled in."

"I thank you for your concern, Lady Fielding, but I can assure you—"

"My dear Gillian—" The older woman interrupted her and leaned toward her. "My dear, allow me, one who is older and wiser, to counsel you in this matter. It is said that you and the earl have had a rather heated disagreement. You must not allow such differences to drive you apart. These things will pass, and if you treat them as they should be treated—that is to say, ignored—then your life will be a most happy one."

Gillian stared at the baroness. "Someone is spreading rumors that Noble and I have had an argument?"

The feathers in the baroness's elaborately arranged hair

bobbed as she nodded. "It is quite the talk, although I beg you to pay no notice to it. It is quite evidently false, as your appearance here tonight has proven."

Gillian's hands tightened into fists. How dare anyone spread more rumors about poor Noble! Wasn't it enough he had to contend with the false ones about his late wife? How on earth could someone know that they'd had an argument that day, and who was spreading the news? "Who is telling you these things, Lady Fielding?"

"Oh, I've heard it from here and there. Talk of the Black Earl and his treatment of you is all anyone speaks of now. No one truly expected that he would manage to marry and keep his wife, no matter how"—she eyed Gillian's bare arms, blue hands, and palm-printed gown—"unorthodox that wife might be."

"Well, this really takes the cake," Gillian fumed a few minutes later, when she and Charlotte had escaped Lady Fielding's presence. "Someone is spreading the most appalling rumors about Noble, trying to create trouble for him, and it's working! Everyone is blaming Noble for a little argument we had."

"What was it about?" Charlotte asked following her to the veranda railing.

"That's the problem, I don't know!" Gillian slapped her hand down on the stone railing. "One moment he was all warm and loving, and the next moment he was as cold as marble. And now this! Noble leaves me to attend our first ball on my own!"

"You've been in England long enough to know how these fashionable marriages work. Your husband goes his way and you are free to go yours. As long as you're discreet, of course."

"I'm always discreet," Gillian muttered, turning around and peering through the crowd, then back across the lawn. "Noble hates crowds; perhaps he's gone to see the garden. Blast the man, he said he'd be here tonight. Where is he?"

"Don't be in such a dither, Gilly." Charlotte took a deep breath, looked toward the doors to the ballroom and, with a muttered prayer that her mother wouldn't discover her antics, followed her cousin out into the garden. "Oh, look at the lovely cascade! Did you ever see such a sight?"

"Never," Gillian muttered, giving short shrift to the countess's fantastic display of colored lights set up to illuminated the water flowing along the mossy paths. She craned her head to catch sight of any tall, handsome earls who might be hiding out in the scented shrubs, trying to avoid their wives' eyes.

"Look, a waterfall! Isn't that lovely?"

"Lovely. Oh, blast! He doesn't seem to be out here."

"You know how men are—they have so many other important things to do. They visit their friends at their clubs, or they gamble, or they visit their mis—"

Gillian turned to face her cousin. "Visit their what?"

Charlotte peered around her in the softly lit darkness. There was a group of people at the foot of the stairs, near the waterfall, but no one close by. "Mistresses. Gillian, it's time you face facts. I don't want to see you hurt any more than you are, dear cousin, but you really must face the truth. Men like Wessex simply are not the type to give up their freedom just because they are married. I know you believe Wessex no longer has a mistress, but you are not being terribly realistic."

"I agree," Gillian said pleasantly after a moment's thought, and started to move toward the stairs. Perhaps he had gone into the cardroom.

"You do? You agree? Just like that? No argument?"

"No argument."

"But Gilly—wait, Gilly." Charlotte hurried to catch up to her cousin's long stride. "Did you not say you were certain Wessex had disported of his mistress's services?"

"Dispensed, and yes, I did, but I was wrong. He does have one."

"Oh, Gilly, I *am* sorry. I had hoped for your sake that Wessex was different—"

"I am his mistress."

Charlotte stopped dead. "You? You think you're his mistress?"

Gillian stopped and looked back at her. "I know I am."

"You can't be his mistress!"

"Whyever can't I?"

Charlotte waved her hand around. "Because . . . because you're his wife."

"So?"

"You can't be both."

"Why not?"

"Well . . . just because! Wives and mistresses—Gillian, they're just two separate people. Wives are . . . wives, and mistresses—well, you know what they are."

Gillian tipped her head to one side. "Perhaps I don't, Charlotte. What exactly is the difference between a wife and a mistress? Oh, don't stare at me like I'm an idiot. Other than the obvious, what is the difference?"

Charlotte looked around helplessly, hoping for inspiration. "Well, for one thing, mistresses show affection in public. Did you hear about La Bella Dona and the Duke of Ainstey two nights past?"

Gillian shook her head.

"They were in the King's Theater, you know, and it's said that she sat right on his lap. In front of everyone. *And kissed him!*"

"That certainly is in poor taste, but hardly—"

"While the duchess was in her box directly across from La Bella Dona's!"

"Oh. Well, yes, then I will agree that your example certainly does show a shocking lack of manners, but that hardly has anything to do with my situation."

"Yes, it does. The point is that you can hardly behave in such a manner, even with your own husband."

Gillian thought back to the morning's activities in the library. "I'm not so sure of that—"

"Oh, look!" Charlotte squealed, and grabbed her cousin's arm. "There he is."

"Noble? Where?"

"No, not Wessex. His friend. The handsome one. By the shrubs to your left."

"Lord Rosse? I don't see him either. All I see is that little man Sir Hugh—"

"Gillian! How can you be so cruel just because the gentleman isn't a giant like you."

Gillian stared at her cousin with a slight smile playing around her lips. "My apologies, Char. I had no idea you had a *tendresse* for him."

"Don't be ridiculous, I have nothing of the sort. Papa would never countenance a marriage between a poor baronet and me. I merely pointed out one of your husband's friends."

"Mmm, yes, thank you." Gillian made a mental note to ask Noble about his friend, and continued to scan the crowd.

"There's Wessex."

"Where?" Gillian spun around.

"Over there, just at the foot of the stairs. He's being given the cut by Lord Monteith. Oh, my, Gillian, that isn't good. I believe Lord Worcester just cut him as well. What are you going to do?"

Gillian looked across the mossy paths, meandering streams of water, manicured lawn, and Arcadian groups of shrubs lit from within by colored lamps to where a group of people had collected to watch her husband be ignored by the *crème* of the *ton*. Dressed entirely in black, with a brilliant snowy white shirt-front and cravat, Noble's austere beauty took Gillian's breath away. Instantly her anger refocused itself onto a new, and much more deserving, target.

"I'll show you what I'm going to do," she said grimly, her hands fisted as she walked quickly toward the group of people.

A hush settled over them as they watched her approach. Noble, standing alongside Lord Rosse, raised one glossy black brow as she walked swiftly toward him. Gillian suddenly grabbed the hem of her gown, speeded up her approach, and launched herself into her husband's arms, pressing her eager lips against his. She kissed him with all the fire and passion that had been smoldering in her ever since she had first seen him. She kissed him with every last ounce of love and devotion she possessed. She kissed him with an intensity that was readily apparent to those who stood by in astounded silence, watching them. She kissed him with abandon and joy and the warmth that only Noble could generate in her. It wasn't technically a perfect kiss as far as kisses went, but it was a monumental one in the eyes of the *ton*. It was a kiss that turned the tide of public opinion about the Black Earl.

And then she fell into the waterfall.

Two gentlemen strolled by as Noble tried to help her wring the worst of the water out of her gown. They both paused for a moment, watching the scene while drawing on their cigars, then proceeded on their promenade.

"Silly chits and their dampened muslins."

Chapter Seven

"Mmmm."

The Black Earl gritted his teeth and refused to lift his eyes from the latest threatening letter that had arrived in the morning's post. He had no need to gaze at his wife. He knew just how fetching she looked in a hunter green and cream dress, her fiery hair twisted into a simple chignon that he knew would immediately begin to disassemble itself into tendrils that would soften the planes of her face. He knew about the sweet swell of her bosom that led upward to the soft, rounded line of her shoulders, which in turn swept into the graceful curves of her arms, leading down to . . . blue hands.

He knew also what she would be doing. She was enjoying strawberries. In a manner guaranteed to make a saint fall. He grew hard just thinking about it.

He stared at the paper in his hand, not seeing the threats or the vile words, seeing instead the image of his wife as she had appeared the past night, curled up in his bed. He had been surprised to find her there after the scene at Countess Lieven's, and especially after he had lectured her the entire way home about his expectations for his countess's behavior. She had said not a word, sitting quietly as she listened to his reprimands until he began to feel he was an ogre, full of nothing but scolds and remonstrations. And yet she had sought his bed rather than her own. He had puzzled over this as he stood, candle in hand, gazing down on her for a moment that seemed to stretch into a thousand. Her hair had been loose, flowing over the white linen, flickering away from her as if she were a phoenix rising from the flames. His eyes traced a path down her satiny freckled cheek as it rested against her blue palm. She was asleep, and the sight of her so peaceful, so lovely, so very right did something deep inside him.

A tiny ray of light pierced the blackness of his soul and began to glow. He had wronged her, misjudged her. She was no Elizabeth, using his physical desire for her own gain; she was simply his Gillian, his wife, the woman who muddled her way through life with an impish smile and devilish twinkle in her eye. He sighed as he slipped into bed and curled up behind her, sharing her warmth, feeling suddenly as if a burden had shifted, lightening a little.

Why had she agreed to marry him? he wondered suddenly. Marriage to him offered security and a title, but he knew instinctively that neither mattered to her. He stroked the arm curled around her ribs and breathed in the seductive scent of sleepy woman. Why *had* she married him? The thought tortured him most of the night and into an indescribably lovely English summer morning.

"Mmmmmm."

Her voice caressed him in a manner that was almost physical, and yet his reaction to it was far more profound than any mere physical reaction could be. The light inside him strengthened, casting the far edges of his soul into dark, forbidding shadows. He stared with unseeing eyes at the letter as he looked deep into the heart of the light. The light was Gillian. She had somehow managed to work her way into the deepest recesses of his being, and there she burned like a beacon. Noble waited with a sick feeling for the black thing that slithered around in his soul to find the brightness, to extinguish it, but the black thing was miraculously banished to a far corner. Noble basked in the glow of the light, feeling for the first time as if life did hold some promise, as if there was some reason for his existence.

"Mmmmm. So good."

He sighed, unable to bear the torment any longer. He had to look. "Did you wish something, my dear?"

Gillian looked up from the pamphlet in which she was engrossed. "No, nothing, Noble. Thank you."

He watched her reach for another strawberry and hold it before her mouth, her mind engaged in reading the literature before her. He felt his breathing stop as he watched, waiting. Slowly Gillian parted her lips, the strawberry a hairsbreadth away from that luscious mouth, the very tip of her tongue emerging to lightly stroke the fruit's heavy round fullness.

Noble felt himself grow hard as steel at the sight. He swallowed back the tightness that threatened to choke him and tried to drag his attention from the erotic sight of his wife eating strawberries to the more important issue of who was threatening to do her bodily harm. The words swam before his eyes and he couldn't help but wonder what she was doing. Would she have finished licking the essence from the strawberry by this time? Would her small white teeth be pulling at the succulent fruit, tugging its globular, delicate flesh with little nips until it surrendered to the lure of her sweet, hot mouth? Would her tongue make a reappearance as she licked the juices from her soft, warm lips?

He couldn't help himself. He looked up. She was chewing, a green stem dangling between her long, delicate, albeit blue-tinted, fingers.

"More strawberries, my dear?" he asked, his voice strangely hoarse. She looked into the bowl he was offering. "Well, I shouldn't, but I do love strawberries so. Perhaps just one or two more."

He deftly turned the bowl so she would have to take the largest one, a veritable giant among strawberries, one that had two distinct hemispheres. He felt himself harden to a degree he would have thought impossible outside the realm of marble as Gillian's little pink tongue snaked out and caressed one side of the giant strawberry.

"Mmmm," she murmured happily, her eyes closed in bliss as she gave herself over to the pleasure of tasting the mammoth berry. Noble thought he would either shame himself or swoon when she took one half of the strawberry into the hot, moist, silky cave of her mouth and sucked the juices from its flesh. He shifted uncomfortably in his chair, aware only of his overwhelmingly intense desire to throw her down on the table and plunge himself deep into her womanly depths. Repeatedly. For a lengthy period of time, say a week or two. Maybe longer.

A small trickle of red juice escaped her lush, pink lips. Noble's tongue swelled up at the sight of it.

"Gark," he said, unable to tear his eyes from it as it traced a path down toward her chin.

"Pardon?" she asked, reaching for her linen napkin.

"Allow me," he croaked, and lunged awkwardly out of his chair toward her, his own cloth held clenched in his fingers. He glanced at it quickly, calculated the amount of energy it would take to unlock his rigid fingers, and leaned down.

"You have some juice. Just there." His voice was rustier than iron left in saltwater. "Allow me to attend to it."

She turned her head slightly, the tempting fruit still held before her lips. Noble inhaled the sweet smell of Gillian mingled with the earthy scent of strawberry just before his tongue touched her skin. He followed the path the juice had made up to its source and paused, looking into her fathomless eyes.

"Bite?" she asked, her voice strange and rough. It reached out and struck a resonance deep within him, like a harp string quivering after it had been plucked.

Gillian's lips parted. Her tongue pulled part of the strawberry

159

into the sweet darkness of her mouth. Noble was sure he would die if he didn't taste that piece of fruit. He gripped Gillian's chair on either side of her and forced her head back as he claimed both her mouth and the strawberry.

He hardened to granite. The juice from the strawberry mingled as their tongues twined around each other, dancing, teasing, sending Noble into a blissful state. Little warning bells began to chime in the back of his head as he slid his tongue along the inside of her silken cheek, tasting strawberry, tasting Gillian, tasting paradise. He started to reach for her, needing to feel himself buried in her warmth, drawing from it, merging himself into it, into the heat that was Gillian. He needed her warmth to feed the light burning so bravely inside him. He needed her at that exact instant.

" 'Ere be the kippers ye were wantin'—eh, take 'em back, lads. 'Is lordship isn't 'ungry for 'em anymore."

Noble snapped his head back from Gillian just in time to see the insolent grin on Crouch's face before the door closed. He felt as if someone had doused him with a bucket of ice water. He looked down at Gillian, down to where his fingers were white as they clutched the sides of her chair. Her breasts were rising and falling erratically, her eyes misty with passion. He tried to swallow but couldn't.

"Good, aren't they?" Gillian asked hoarsely, and plucked the remainder of the strawberry from between his teeth.

"What is that you are reading so attentively?" Noble inquired some minutes later, when he had managed to wrest control of his mind away from the demands of his body.

"It's an absolutely fascinating pamphlet I bought off a man in the square this morning when I was strolling with Piddle and Erp. It's called *Celestial Stimulation of the Organs,* and it explains how one might, by using special Oils of Araby and balmy, ethereal essences, restore elasticity and good health to those who are suffering from bad humors."

Noble, keeping his eyes carefully averted as she reached for another strawberry, asked if she were feeling ill.

"No, but you are."

He looked up at her statement.

"I couldn't help but notice that you were most restless last night, husband. And this morning, when I asked you why you were looking so peculiar and disgruntled, you said you had a pain in your head. All signs, according to Dr. Graham's helpful pamphlet, that your organs need attention."

Noble thought back to the night of torment he had endured, a self-imposed night of torment borne of his desire to show his wife that he was more than just a lustful beast who valued his own urges more than his wife's need to rest.

"I am quite well, I assure you, madam," he said, lying through his teeth. He *was* a lustful beast. He wanted her, needed her, had to have her. That very moment. "My organs have no need of stimulation, celestial or otherwise. I do, however, believe that we did not finish our discussion about the proper way of organizing and structuring your life."

Gillian looked surprised. "Would that be the lecture you delivered last evening?"

"It would. You looked tired, so I postponed the balance of the discussion until today."

Gillian sighed. Dabbing at her mouth, she sat back in her chair with her hands folded demurely on her lap. "Very well, Noble, if it will make you happy, you may lecture me now."

"Thank you. Now, as to—"

"It comes as news to me, of course, to find out my life is unorganized and unstructured."

"You may be assured it is, my dear. As for last evening's events—"

"Active, perhaps, or full of those marvelous little surprises that life always seems to offer, yes, I can see that, but unorganized and unstructured?"

161

Katie MacAlister

"It is. How else do you explain that?" He waved toward her blue hands.

She considered her hands. "Curiosity?"

"Curiosity, lady wife, when held unchecked by common sense and rational thought, is nothing more than chaos. And as we have discussed at length, a chaotic lifestyle is not one that is conducive to a happy home."

"But, Noble—"

He ignored her protests and spent fifteen minutes explaining again the importance of control and order in one's life. He paced back and forth before the sideboard, his stride lengthening as he gesticulated when making particular points. He waxed eloquent as he presented both arguments and examples for her edification. He was pleased to see he had her full attention. Her eyes never left him as he offered her rational and valid reasons why she would learn to suit her life to his, and how happy their lives together would be once that seemingly monumental task had been accomplished.

"Now, my dear," he finished, pulling out his pocket watch and consulting it, "I must keep an appointment, but before I go I will hear your plans for the day."

"Hmm?" she asked dreamily, her gaze still intent on him.

"Your plans, madam."

"Have you ever thought of wearing colors, Noble? Perhaps just a colored waistcoat? Not that you don't look elegantly delicious in black, but I thought perhaps you might like, once in a while, to don a bit of color."

He narrowed his eyes at her. "What has my method of dress to do with your plans for the day?"

She widened her eyes in response. "Why, nothing. I just asked a question. Oh, never mind, it doesn't matter. My plans for today—well, I believe Charlotte is coming to help me with ideas for the drawing room you said I might redecorate. And we plan on making a call to a . . . an acquaintance. And then I

162

thought I would take Nick to Regent's Park to see the zoological gardens. Would you like to accompany us?"

"No, thank you, I have my own schedule to attend to. Very well, my dear, I hope you keep the precepts we have been discussing in mind as you go about your day."

"Precepts?" She blinked at him.

"Yes, those that we've just spent the morning discussing. I will escort you to the Gayfields' rout tonight if I am able; if not, I will send Harry or Sir Hugh and meet you there later."

"But Noble, where—"

He was out the door before she could finish asking him about *his* plans for the day. And what precepts had they just discussed? Perhaps she should have been paying attention to what he was saying rather than woolgathering, but she couldn't help it. Whenever he started in on his pet lecture, which she seemed to have already heard as many days as she had been married, her mind wandered.

She really would have to watch that habit; it was not a wise one to indulge in around the Lord of Kisses. He had enough ways of distracting her from her goal without her helping him by not paying attention to what he was saying.

Noble settled back into an armchair in Boodle's and waved away the attendant. "Good morning, Harry. You look pleased with yourself. May I assume from that expression that you've had some luck?"

"Alas, not the luck you seek, my friend." Lord Rosse proffered a silver cigar case to the Black Earl. "But something interesting, nonetheless. Did you know that Mariah has disappeared?"

Noble paused for a moment in the act of lighting his cigar. "I had some suspicion she had, since she vacated the premises of the house in Kensington so quickly. Her sister has no idea where she's gone to ground?"

"None. She's quite worried about her, as a matter of fact. Ah,

Tolly, I thought we'd see you sooner or later. Come and join us."

Sir Hugh had another chair placed in a manner that would allow him to keep an eye on all who passed, and seated himself with a great show of care for his peach satin waistcoat and taffy-colored coat. "Rosse, Wessex. I wondered if you would take advantage of your good fortune, Wessex."

"What good fortune is that?" Noble puffed gently on his cigar and tried not to look bored.

"Why, the sudden reversal of opinion, of course! You and your Amazon are the talk of the *ton!* Surely even you must have heard the talk, Noble. Everyone is talking about *the kiss.*"

Noble arched one sable eyebrow. *"The kiss?* What kiss?"

Rosse smiled as Sir Hugh adjusted his intricately tied cravat an infinitesimal bit to the right. "Must think of letting old Hudson go. He's not as sharp with the Russian Waterfall as he should be. The kiss, man. The one she gave you in front of everyone at Countess Lieven's last night!"

Noble gave in to the urge and looked bored. "I find it difficult to believe that my wife demonstrating a spontaneous burst of affection for me can cause such a scandal, Tolly."

A spasm of distaste passed over the baronet's face. "That's where you have come up lucky. Her action, rash and indelicate though it might have been, has deemed her . . . has deemed you both . . . the toast of the Season. All the world loves a lover and all that."

Rosse laughed at the look of chagrin on the earl's face. "Now there's a role I never thought you to be in, Noble. The passionate lover, unable to keep from your wife's arms for the length of an evening."

A dull red flush washed over Wessex's cheeks.

"It's appalling!"

Both men looked surprised at the vehemence in Sir Hugh's voice. "That is . . . not that you have suddenly become the toast of the *ton,* but that her . . . but that your wife . . . you must admit, Wessex," he stammered, "her behavior is better suited to a Cyprian than a countess."

Noble's narrow-eyed gaze flashed silver as it pinned Sir Hugh back in his chair. "You are speaking of my wife, Tolly. I find myself warning you again to temper your speech when speaking of her."

Sir Hugh spread his hands in a sign of subjugation. "No offense was intended toward your good lady, I assure you, Wessex. As one of your oldest friends, I simply want to make sure that she does nothing—inadvertently, of course—that might damage your reputation more than it is. God knows I've bent over backward trying to smooth things over for you . . ."

Noble made a dismissive movement and glanced at the clock residing on a table a few feet away. "Apology accepted. I have an appointment to keep shortly, Tolly. If you don't mind, I'd like to hear what Harry has to say before I keep it."

The baronet flushed and shot an unreadable look at him, then settled back in his chair with an expression approaching petulance.

"You were saying, Harry?"

"Ah." Rosse raised an inquisitory eyebrow. Wessex had no difficulty in understanding the movement. "Tolly, I'm sure, can be counted on to keep private all that is said between us."

Sir Hugh's round face lost its petulant expression. "Of course, my word and all that. What is the big secret?"

"Harry has done a little investigating into an affair for me. It seems someone wishes me ill, and made an attempt to imprison me the other night."

Sir Hugh's jaw dropped. "No! Where? When? What happened? Good God, man, you weren't hurt, were you?"

Wessex explained the situation in a few succinct sentences.

Sir Hugh cleared his throat and put a hand on the older man's arm. "Anything I can do, Noble. I am completely at your service. And your lady's, too, of course."

Noble nodded and turned back to Rosse.

"Well, as I was telling Noble, there's not much to go on now. His mistress, who wrote the note that was responsible for him being lured to the house, has disappeared. No one knows of her whereabouts, although the servants report she left in a hurry."

"You've spoken with the servants?" Sir Hugh asked.

"Yes, I had some luck there and located the cook. All of the servants were paid two months' wages and told to leave immediately."

"That's very suspicious!" Sir Hugh said.

Noble ignored him. "You found no report of a stranger being seen at the house? No visitors who were beyond Mariah's normal circle of friends?"

"None. At least, none that I've heard from yet. I'm calling on a few men I know to help with the investigation, so perhaps they will be able to uncover something about her visitors."

"Excellent. I'm sure you'll have results, Harry. And now I must be off, gentleman. I have an appointment with a Mr. Stafford."

"Stafford?" Rosse asked, steepling his fingers together under his chin. "Bow Street Runners?"

"Yes. I need an additional pair of eyes."

"Focused on a certain Scotsman?"

"Among other individuals, yes," Noble responded and started for the door.

"Wessex—hold for a moment, man." Sir Hugh hurried after the Black Earl. "Allow me to be of assistance as well, Noble. I will do whatever I can to aid you in this. Is there some task I can accomplish for you?"

"Nothing, thank you, Tolly."

"Nonsense, there must be something." Sir Hugh put a restraining hand on the earl's sleeve. Noble, at the door, looked down at the hand on his arm, then up at the gently perspiring baronet. He bit back words of annoyance, reminding himself that Tolly was enthusiastic, if not overly bright. "I appreciate the offer, Tolly," he said, collecting his hat and stick from the attendant. "I will let you know when I have something for you to do."

Gillian was in the drawing room, holding up a piece of crimson Spitalfield silk against the wall and imagining a gilded ceiling with medallions formed from diamond and octagon shapes.

"What do you think, Nick? The crimson silk, or the bronze green silk? Or something else entirely?" Gillian asked, digging through a stack of wallpaper and fabric samples. "Here, look at this lovely blue. It's called smalt. Isn't it rich? Can't you just imagine this room in smalt, with the woodwork picked out in gilt?"

Nick looked at the fabrics and selected one he liked. "Peach Blossom. Yeees, it's lovely, but a little . . . well, pink, don't you think?"

"What's pink? Oooh, you have fabric samples? Did the earl give you permission to redecorate, then?" Charlotte bustled in through the door before Tremayne Two could announce her. "Let me see. No, definitely not pale colors, those are passé. You want a strong, vibrant color. I like this crimson."

Gillian looked at the butler. "Tremayne, will you order the carriage brought round as soon as possible? Lady Charlotte and I have a call to pay."

"Patent yellow, now there's an ugly color. Did you hear that the Duke of Wellington has yellow in his drawing room? Did you ever hear of such a thing?"

"As you wish, my lady."

"This sea green would be a good choice for a dining room. What color is your dining room now?"

Nick looked at the sea green and made a face.

"It's fawn. Oh, Tremayne? Would you have one of the boys bring Piddle and Erp around?"

Tremayne gave her a weak smile. Although the dogs' digestive extravagances had apparently ceased, they were still prone to occasional setbacks, and the staff considered themselves martyrs to her dogs. "Certainly, madam. Er . . . will the hounds be riding in the same carriage as you, or should I have their carriage brought around as well?"

"Walnut is nice, too. With the fussy bits picked out in cream or stone."

Nick nodded.

"Well, they can hardly protect me if they are in a separate carriage, Tremayne."

"Protect you, madam?"

"But I don't like this at all, this chocolate color. It's much harsher than walnut. This lilac number two is pretty. What do you think, Nick?"

Nick pointed to the lilac.

"Yes, protect me, Tremayne Two. His lordship made me promise I wouldn't go out without ample protection, lest his attacker try to kidnap Master Nicholas or myself."

"No, I've changed my mind about the lilac, Nick, despite your preference for it. Picture gallery red number three. That's a very popular color, I believe. Can't you see the walls done in picture gallery red number three?"

Nick eyed the walls with a speculative gaze, his lips pursed. He shook his head.

"I beg your pardon, my lady, but I hardly feel the hounds are suitable protection."

"No? I can see it. Well, perhaps picture gallery red number two."

Gillian's head began to spin as a result of the cross conversation. "I don't agree with you at all, Tremayne. They are ample protection. No one would dare accost either Nick or me when in their presence."

Nick tapped Charlotte on the arm and pointed out a swatch of sky blue.

"Mmmm. Yes, yes, I think you may have something there. Sky blue with the skirting boards painted in cream?"

"I hasten to remind your ladyship of the episode occurring just this morning in the park. If you recall, the hounds, when your ladyship was approached by the street hawker, dragged you a considerable distance to escape contact with the individual."

"Then again, you could go with a nice striped wallpaper."

"As I said, they were protecting me by removing me from what they thought was a threat to my safety."

"I like this one with the honeysuckle border. It's quite classical."

"I beg your pardon again, my lady, but I don't believe the hounds were attempting to remove you from a threatening person as much as they were attempting to remove *themselves* from a threatening person."

Nick pointed to a busy pattern of leaves and flowers.

"Hmmm. Hedgerow. Nice, Nick, but I don't think it would suit for the drawing room. A sitting room, perhaps, don't you think?"

"Are you calling my dogs cowards, Tremayne?"

"What do you think of this one—Kingston Market? I like the blues and reds in it."

Nick shook his head.

"Mayhap *coward* is too harsh a word, madam. Careful, perhaps? Cautious? Judicious in placing their trust in the kindness of strangers?"

"I don't like this Swakely one at all, though. Much too busy, and it has yellow as a background. It wouldn't do at all."

"Cowards, Tremayne?"

"This leaf foil is pretty though. It has some nice shades of green in it."

Tremayne sighed. "Cowards, madam. If I might be so bold as to offer your ladyship a suggestion, his lordship did mention in passing that he had instructed Crouch to attend your ladyship on all your outings. I would be happy to inform Crouch that you desire his presence."

Gillian had hoped to escape without Crouch, who had voiced considerable opinions the day before about the wisdom of her paying a call on Lord Carlisle. She had finally extracted a promise from him that he would not tattle on her to Noble by agreeing that she wouldn't visit Carlisle unaccompanied. That was what Charlotte was for.

"What am I for?" Her cousin looked up questioningly.

"Nothing, it matters not. Fine, Tremayne, tell Crouch we'll be going out."

"Well, that was fun," Charlotte said, pushing the samples off her lap. "I think you'll like our choices. Nick has a good eye for colors. Are we ready to leave? I made a list of things for you to ask Lord Carlisle, Gilly."

"What sorts of things?"

"Here's the list." She handed Gillian a folded-up sheet of paper, then peered over her shoulder at it. "You'll note the first item on the list is learning the names of Lord Wessex's mistresses."

"Ladybuds," Gillian said with a quick look at Nick.

"Ladybirds. Honestly, Gillian! The way you manacle the language is just disgraceful! Now, I'm not certain Lord Carlisle will know all their names, but you know how gentlemen are—they're worse gossips than we women."

"Exactly. Um . . . you have *Lady Wessex* written down here next."

"Yes, you said he made vague threats about Elizabeth, so he must have known her. Two birds with one bush."

Gillian blinked. "I beg your pardon?"

"You're killing two birds with one bush. It's an expression. Haven't you ever heard it? It means that you are taking care of two things at the same time. I would have thought that even in the Colonies such a common expression was used."

Gillian opened her mouth to correct her cousin, then decided against it. "Mmmm . . . *Income.*" She looked up. "Why am I asking him about Noble's income?"

"Not Lord Wessex's income, *his* income."

"Why am I asking Lord Carlisle about his income?"

"Because he's an earl, silly, and as everyone knows, an earl in the hand is worth . . . well, something. The point is that Mama would never forgive me if I was to let a perfectly good earl slip through my fingers because you were too obstinate to ask him what he's worth."

"Charlotte, the man may well be the one who is behind the attack on Noble! Would you want to marry someone with such a malformed and ill-natured character?"

"Oh, pooh, it's nothing that I couldn't take care of."

Gillian rolled her eyes and looked back at the list again.

"Does this mean what I think it means?"

Charlotte looked over her shoulder again. *"Padded?* Well, of course it does! You wouldn't want me marrying a man who pads his shoulders and calves, would you?"

"Well, of course not, whatever was I thinking?"

"Selfish, that's what you've become since you've been married—very, very selfish, thinking only of yourself. Now then, is there anything else you think we should ask this Lord Carlisle?"

Gillian chewed on her lower lip as she thought. "I would like to know the nature of his argument with Noble, but I'm not sure how forthcoming he would be about that."

Charlotte smiled a wicked smile, then suddenly the expression was gone, replaced by one of innocence so pure and sweet it would make an angel weep.

"Oh, you're good," Gillian said with a rueful smile. "You should really be on the stage, Char. Do you think it would work on him?"

Charlotte maintained the dewy-eyed, sweet expression for a few more seconds, then dimpled at her cousin. "Practice, my dear, it's all practice. I will be happy to show you how to do it on the way to Lord Carlisle's. It's just a matter of projecting innocence, if you will . . ."

"Some other time, perhaps." Gillian waved her cousin toward

the door and turned to hurry Nick along. She was rewarded by the sight of a nine-year-old boy frozen in a pose of humble meekness and submission. He gazed at her with an expression so pure of heart it positively radiated ingenuity and artlessness. He batted his long dark lashes slowly over his silver-gray eyes, then peeked out from beneath them to see her reaction. Gillian laughed and kissed his rosy, cherub's cheek. "Yes, yes, I can see you too should be on the stage. Come along, Mr. Kean. Your audience is impatiently awaiting your next performance."

"Is it absolutely necessary," Charlotte asked, squirming in the seat and managing to poke her elbow into Gillian's ribs, "that we bring those hounds? And your pirate? And three footmen? I feel as if I'm in the Lord Mayor's parade."

Gillian tried to expand her lungs enough to breathe a sigh, but was crammed in too tightly and had to make do with a tsk instead.

"Tsk, Charlotte! I tried to tell Crouch that it wasn't necessary to bring three footmen with us, but he muttered something about Noble leaving orders that Nick and I not go out without ample protection, and this is Crouch's idea of ample protection. I sincerely hope the carriage doesn't collapse under our combined weight. It seems a little frail."

Nick squirmed alongside her, flailed his arms and legs for a moment, then shot forward, gasping for air.

"Oh, dear, Nick, I'm so sorry. Could you not breathe? Are you all right now? It's this tiny old carriage—the landau would have to take this day to have a faulty wheel."

Charlotte pulled her head in from the window. "What?"

"Nothing. I was just explaining to Nick about the carriage, and why we have so much protection, although honestly, I would have thought that Piddle and Erp would be enough."

"They are outside of enough," her cousin replied, glaring at the seat opposite, where the two hounds were stuffed together, and with a sniff pushed the window open even wider. "This is ridiculous. I would have kept Papa's carriage if I had known you were going to squish me into this minuscule little box with those two beasts. What will Lord Carlisle think when he sees how wrinkled my gown is?"

"I believe he will have more important things to notice, Char."

Charlotte looked at her in horror. "More important than my gown? I think not!"

"Don't be so self-centered. Gentlemen like Lord Carlisle have other things on their mind than concerning themselves with the state—wrinkled or unwrinkled—of gowns."

"The gentlemen you know may have other things on their minds, but the gentlemen I know pay particular attention to a lady's gown."

"The gentlemen you know are fops."

"Gillian!"

Gillian didn't have the energy, or lung capacity, to argue the point any further, so she contented herself with running over the list of items she wished to discuss with the Scottish speeler earl.

The earl was just stepping into his carriage when they arrived. He paused, one hand on the carriage and a look of surprise on his face as it pulled up before him. He counted the liveried footmen clinging to the upper seats of the approaching carriage and almost bolted once he got a look at the behemoth who dangled from the rear.

"Crotch," he spat at his coachman, and stepped back down onto the pavement. The coachman promptly pawed at himself in an attempt to make sure nothing untoward was showing.

"No, you fool, not yours, that one. That giant one clinging to the rear of that blasted carriage. It's Crotch, Wessex's thug of a butler. What the devil is he doing here?"

There was a slight commotion as the carriage came to a halt. Several footmen leaped off the vehicle and surrounded it in a protective manner. The carriage swayed alarmingly from side to side, then a familiar red head popped out of the window.

"Lord Carlisle, how opportune our arrival was. Might I beg a few moments of your time?"

Carlisle blinked at the image before his eyes. She had escaped Wessex's clutches? A warm sense of satisfaction, coupled with a curiosity about her request, made him reconsider his morning's plans.

"My time is yours, madam," he replied with a courtly bow that was sadly lost on its recipient, her head having been retracted back into the carriage.

One of the footmen stood rattling the door to her carriage, and requested that the occupants unlock it. The carriage rocked violently back and forth, emitting periodic oaths and half-shouted exclamations that surprised Carlisle. What the devil was in that carriage? A bull? An elephant? Several elephants? The footman repeated his request, but it was lost in the cacophony from within. Curiosity drove him closer.

"If you would just move your leg, cousin . . ."

"Well, I'm trying, Char, but you're on my gown and I can't move. Argh!"

"Sorry, my elbow slipped . . ."

"Nick, darling, would you climb over . . . ow! Charlotte! . . . would you climb over Erp and slither through the window? I believe . . . Charlotte, if you poke me once again, I swear I'll . . ."

"Bloody hell!"

"Charlotte!"

"Well, you'd swear too if your lovely blond lace just ripped off your sleeve."

"Nick, you're standing on my hand . . . ah, thank you. If you would try the window . . . oh, dear. Dickon, will you stop shouting at us, we're trying. The door seems to be stuck! Blast!"

"Gillian!"

"Oh, don't *Gillian* me in that tone; you're the one who swore first. Will you kindly remove your elbow from my kidney, cousin?"

"Here, Nick, let me give you a little boost through the window, shall I?"

"Charlotte, if you hurt my child . . ."

"I shan't hurt . . . that was my hair!"

"Sorry. My hand slipped."

"I shan't hurt him, but I will push the little blighter through since you seem to be incapable of it."

"*Ow!* Was that absolutely necessary?"

"My hand slipped."

"Ha!"

Half of a small boy suddenly emerged from the carriage window. Lord Carlisle, watching with the same sort of fascination that sweeps over those who pass by hangings, accidents, and other gruesome sights, stood mesmerized. How many people were in there? And what was an Erp? Was the child alive, or had he been ejected for other purposes? It was difficult to tell whether he was flailing his arms of his own accord, or if the footman, attempting to assist, was bobbing the lad around.

"Nick, darling, if you could push all the way through, I would be most appreciative. It's not easy dodging your feet."

"Ow!"

"You see, dearest? You just clipped your cousin Charlotte on the chin."

"That little rotter! He did it on purpose! Scoot over, I'll push him through the bloody window."

"Charlotte, if you lay one finger on him . . . oh, dear God."

The carriage suddenly stopped rocking. Carlisle leaned forward, a chill running down his spine upon hearing the dread in Lady Wessex's voice. What had happened? A sudden illness? Had the boy, who, if the footman's unsuccessful attempts to tug him through the window were any indication, was stuck, collapsed? Had something happened to the lady named Charlotte, the one with the torn blond lace? Only a calamity of the most heinous kind could be responsible for the tones of horror echoed in Lady Wessex's voice.

"Dickon? Crouch? Will someone get the bloody door open right now? I think Piddle is going to be sick!"

The hairs on Lord Carlisle's neck stood on end at the blood-curdling scream that rent the air at Lady Wessex's pronouncement, but in the end, its owner was responsible for the resolution of the situation. After several loud wallops to the side of the carriage—Lord Carlisle assumed the lady Charlotte was kicking down the door—it popped open, and only the quick action of the footman named Dickon saved the small boy from crashing into the side of the carriage. Moments later the boy was pushed backward through the window, and two large, slobbering dogs shot out of the carriage, followed immediately by Lady Wessex and a woman with, he couldn't help noticing, an extremely wrinkled gown.

"Lord Carlisle." Gillian bobbed a curtsy and tried to ignore Piddle, who was being noisily sick on the pavement next to her. "How delightful to see you again. Have you made the acquaintance of my cousin, Lady Charlotte Collins?"

"Lord Carlisle," Charlotte curtsyed. "You must forgive my appearance. I seldom go out in public, my Mama being protective of my delicate sensibilities and naturally shy nature, but my dearest cousin begged me in such a manner that I was unable to refuse her request."

"You will notice how modest and retiring she is," Gillian said helpfully, unable to resist laughing at her cousin's expression of innocence and shy maidenhood. Charlotte had told her that particular combination of expressions had garnered her three proposals of marriage.

"Er . . . of course. Most modest and retiring. Perhaps we might continue this fascinating discussion inside? Is your . . . uh . . . dog finished there? Yes? Perhaps Crotch would take them around back to the stables."

"I beg your pardon?" Gillian didn't think she had heard the earl correctly.

"Crotch," he said, flapping his hands at the dogs, who had

ambled over to him to conduct a quick gender check on this new person.

Charlotte let out an innocent, maidenly sort of gasp and fanned herself in a manner most becoming to a modest, retiring person.

A blush burned up Gillian's face. God's spleen, would she never be able to go anywhere with her dogs? "Oh, yes, of course, crotch. Lord Carlisle, I'm so embarrassed. They always do that. Piddle! Erp! Naughty dogs! I hope they didn't . . . er . . . hurt you in their investigations. They like to smell people, you see, and try as I might I'm not able to break them of the habit of sniffing . . . er . . . of sniffing."

The earl narrowed his eyes at her.

"What the devil are you talking about?"

Charlotte clutched her arm and hissed a warning not to pursue the conversation. Gillian ignored it. "Your crotch, of course."

"My what?" The earl's voice rose as Erp decided to investigate again. "Down, sir! Down!"

"Erp! Bad dog! Nick, darling, grab Erp and keep him from doing that. I do apologize again, Lord Carlisle," Gillian said, holding on to Piddle's collar. "But as we've settled the question of your crotch, might we go inside?"

The earl stared for a moment, then closed his eyes and shook his head. When he opened them up again, she was still standing there, still smiling that charming, lovely, completely misleading smile. He began to feel sorry for the wife-killer Wessex. He had a suspicion that this time the Black Earl had met his match.

The Black Earl was beginning to believe the very same thing. He emerged from his consultation with John Stafford, the chief clerk for the Bow Street Runners, and was assured of help gathering proof that the bastard McGregor was behind the threats to himself and Gillian, and the attack of a few evenings past.

"Are you sure it's Lord Carlisle who is behind these letters?" Stafford asked.

"As sure as I can be without having his admission of the fact," Noble replied. "The man is a heartless devil who preys on women. He is responsible for the death of my late wife, and holds great animosity for me."

"I'm sure that is the case, my lord, but I must investigate the situation fully. Are you certain there are no other individuals who would wish to see you come to harm?"

"Any number, I'm certain," Noble replied with a wry twist to his mouth. "Half the *ton* believes I murdered my wife, the other half believes I'm a notorious rake. None of them, however, are privy to the information that is contained within the threatening letters."

"You will, of course, refuse to pay the blackmail sum demanded?"

"That goes without saying."

Stafford nodded his head and glanced down at the most recent letter Noble had received. "I can give you three men, my lord."

Noble stretched out his arm and retrieved his letter. "I had hoped for more."

"I'm afraid three is the best I can do at the moment. They will be round your house in the morning."

Noble wrote a few lines on the back of a calling card. "Have them present this to my butler, Crouch. Or Tremayne. Either of them; they're both my butlers."

Stafford raised his brows. "You have two butlers in one house, my lord?"

"Yes," he replied, pocketing the letter and standing. "It was my wife's idea."

His words echoed in his head a short time later as his carriage rolled toward a certain address near Russell Square. Was it really Gillian's idea to have the second Tremayne brother follow her up to his town house? She had said something about him helping Crouch learn to be less a pirate, which made no sense at all. Despite his hook, Crouch was not a pirate. Lord knew, the man got seasick just walking on a bridge over a river.

"Gillian," he said softly, gazing out the window, blind to all but the image of the tall, redheaded Amazon who had moved into his heart. How had she done it? He'd never expected to feel anything beyond mild affection for a woman again, and yet she was consuming his every thought.

Gillian. Just the sound of her name sent tendrils of heat through him; many of them, it was true, pooling in his groin, but he was also conscious of a gentle, soothing glow radiating out from the bright light she cast, warming him and making him believe he was human again.

Gillian. His wife, the woman who bore his name and would bear his children. He thought of her plump and round with his babe, and a spurt of base masculine pleasure added to the warmth already heating him.

Gillian. His lover, the woman whose passion matched his own so well that when they were making love, he found it hard to tell where he stopped and she began.

Gillian. His friend, the woman whose mishaps and accidents belied a mind too quick for her body, but also the woman whose heart was big enough to shelter both him and his son.

Gillian. The woman who was walking down the front steps of his most hated enemy's house, her arm linked through his, laughing up at that bastard murderer McGregor with a smile that should be reserved solely for him.

Gillian!

"What the bloody hell is this?" he roared, jumping out of the carriage before his coachman could bring the horses to a stop. "By God's ten toes, woman, what the hell do you think you are doing with that man?"

Gillian stopped on the last step, astonishment writ clearly on her face at the sight of her husband charging down the pavement toward her. "Noble?"

"Yes, Noble," he snarled, and lunged toward the Scot.

179

Katie MacAlister

"Noble! How wonderful you could join us! Nick, my dear,
your papa has come to join us, isn't that wonderful?"

Noble stopped, his hands a mere fraction of an inch from
Carlisle's throat. "Nick?" His voice was thick as he flexed his
fingers. She had brought Nick with her? She had brought Nick
with her while she kept an assignation with the man who was
responsible for the death of his wife? She had brought his son
with her while she tore out his heart and killed any last vestiges
of human kindness left within him?

"Good afternoon, Lord Wessex."

Noble blinked at the sight of a lovely blond woman, a familiar
blond woman, a woman who, if the maidenly blush and shy
eyes were anything to go by, had just been released from a
convent.

"You remember my cousin Charlotte, don't you, Noble?"

"Ah . . ."

" 'Ere ye are then, yer lordship. I was tellin' the mistress that
it weren't right 'er payin' this call without yer, but ye know 'ow
the ladies is."

"Er . . ."

"Charles, Dickon, 'elp Tremayne up there with those 'orses.
They don't like the looks of Piddle and Herp."

"Uh . . ." Piddle? Erp? Noble peered between his wife and his
enemy. Was there anyone from his home *not* present? As the
heat from the suspicions of a moment before faded, a new fire
roared to life when his eyes narrowed at the sight of that murdering bastard McGregor's hand resting possessively on Gillian's.

"Mine!" he roared, and scooped Gillian up and deposited her
on the pavement behind him.

"I beg your pardon?" Gillian asked, poking him in the back.
"Did you just shout *mine* in a voice loud enough to be heard in
Canterbury?"

"Be still, woman, while I deal with this bastard," Noble bellowed.

180

"Bastard, eh? That's a case of the pot calling the kettle black," Carlisle roared back.

"*Mine*? As in I belong to you, husband?"

"What the devil were you doing with my wife and son?" Noble yelled.

"As if I were your *possession?*"

"That's none of your business," Carlisle answered, his voice echoing off the houses across the street.

"I cannot believe you actually stood there and bellowed the word *mine* as if I were a toy and you a four-year-old child, Noble!"

"Like hell it's not! I demand to know what they were doing here!" Noble thundered.

"Then why don't you ask the lady?" Carlisle barked.

"I am not a possession!" Gillian raised her voice to match those of the two men.

"You keep my wife out of this! You'll answer my question, or by God I'll have my satisfaction over pistols!" Noble stormed.

"Name your seconds," Carlisle retorted, his black eyes dancing with enjoyment.

"They'll call on you this evening," Noble fired back, his hair standing on end. "Wife! Come with me!"

Gillian recognized that Noble was in a bit of a temper, and with a wisdom that had hitherto been unknown to her, bit back her angry protests at his arrogant display of possessiveness and took the hand he held out. He stalked back to his carriage and would have made a grand exit it if had not been for the others.

"Charles, Dickon, get those 'ounds loaded into the carriage."

Noble paused in the act of stuffing Gillian into his carriage and looked back. His gaze fell on that of his son, standing next to Charlotte, gray eyes shining brightly in the afternoon sun. "Nicholas, you will come with us."

Charlotte, who had been hard-pressed to maintain an expression radiating demure, maidenly horror at the thrilling manly display, fanned herself briskly and suddenly realized she would be left to ride home in an ancient carriage with Piddle and Erp as her sole companions.

"Lord Wessex!"

Noble handed Gillian into the carriage and turned to look at Charlotte.

She stood looking between Lord Carlisle and Noble.

"I . . . the dogs . . . you cannot possibly expect me . . . my lord, I . . ."

Gillian leaned out of the carriage. "I do believe this is a first, my lord. I've never seen my cousin at a loss for words."

Noble grunted and would have left Charlotte to the dog's carriage but for Gillian. There was a motive to her madness— she no more wanted to be alone with Noble where he would feel free to vent his anger on her regarding her visit to Lord Carlisle than she wanted to dance with a crocodile.

"I believe, my dear lady wife, your chances with the crocodile are substantially better," Noble said through gritted teeth, and proceeded to ignore her and everyone else in the carriage by staring out at the passing scenery.

"We were just off to the zoological gardens," Gillian started to say, but one look from Noble's icy gray eyes made it quite clear that the visit was canceled. Gillian sent her son an apologetic glance and was heartened to see the boy give her a warm smile and a little shrug.

She mouthed to him that they would go another time, and settled back next to Noble. Charlotte exchanged sympathetic glances with her cousin and was not in the least bit sorry when the carriage pulled up before her house. Gillian wished to have a word or two with her, but Noble grimly assisted Charlotte down, then leaped back into the carriage and gave the signal to be on the way.

In an attempt to forestall the inevitable tongue-lashing she was sure was due her, Gillian clasped Noble's hand in hers. His hand was unresponsive and stiff. Gillian mentally created, and discarded, any number of excuses and explanations for her visit to the earl. The carriage rocked as it bounced over bumps in the street, the familiar clop of the horses' hooves setting up a rhythm in her brain. Although within there was naught but injured silence, outside the carriage horses neighed, dogs barked, people shouted, coachmen and grooms talked to their charges, vendors shouted their wares, and a thousand other noises wove together into the intricate tapestry that was life in London. Gillian closed her eyes and leaned slightly toward Noble, her thumb tracing circles on the top of his hand, feeling suddenly safe and secure even if her husband was shortly to lecture her as she'd never been lectured before. She slid her thumb down to the underside of his hand and made little massaging circles on the pads of his fingers, sliding up and down the length, feeling the strength that lay in those long, elegant hands. Noble did not respond to her caress, but neither did he withdraw his hand.

She continued to stroke and pet his hand while she considered the results of her daring act in visiting the Scottish earl—she was now in possession of a list of four names, women who had been Noble's mistresses during the last fifteen years, as long as Carlisle had known him.

She hoped they could help her to figure out just what Noble's relationship with Elizabeth had been like before his dear wife died—or not his dear wife, if what Lord Carlisle had said was true.

Gillian chewed on her lower lip. The earl must be mistaken. She knew Noble, and no matter how strong the provocation, he could never have murdered his wife, not even if he found her with another man, as Lord Carlisle implied. And the hints he made about Noble's treatment of Elizabeth—well, those simply couldn't be true.

Gillian rubbed Noble's wrist and let her delicate, blue-tinted fingers massage the top of his hand. No, the earl had to be wrong about Noble. Clearly he had gotten hold of the same misinformation that had flooded the rest of the *ton*, and just as clearly it was up to her to uncover the truth and clear Noble's name.

A little sigh escaped her lips as she considered all she had to do, a sigh that went straight to Noble's heart. He stopped fighting the desire to respond to Gillian's gentle strokes and gave her hand a reassuring squeeze. She didn't look at him, but sighed again as she snuggled up against him, content in the knowledge that everything would be all right. Noble wasn't angry after all.

Noble was furious. He controlled himself in the carriage with an iron will that amazed even him, but once he arrived home, he demanded Gillian's presence in his library. By the time she left the room, her face pale and tear-streaked, he had made himself absolutely and undeniably clear as to his feelings about his wife visiting the man who was responsible for so much misery and unhappiness.

"But Noble, why can't I call on him if I'm suitably escorted?" Gillian cried after the bulk of his rage had been exorcised, tears trembling on the edge of her lashes.

Noble hardened his heart against the sight. "Because the man's a murdering bastard, madam, that's why you cannot call on him! From this moment forward you will have nothing further to do with him."

Gillian had blanched at the word *murderer*. Noble's accusations were so similar to Lord Carlisle's, it confused her. "He's a murderer? Whom did he murder?"

Noble's jaw set in a manner that Gillian was becoming all too familiar with. He placed his hands on the arms of her chair and leaned down until he was a breath away from her.

"It is of no matter to you. Hear me well, wife. On this you will obey me—you will have no further contact with McGregor. If you see him at a public place, you will ignore him. If he approaches you and attempts to converse with you, you will walk away. If he sends you any correspondence, you will immediately surrender it to me. Do I make myself clear?"

Gillian stared deep into his icy gray eyes and saw Noble's demons battling for control. There was anger and masculine dominance there, but there was also concern and something she didn't recognize—something that made her feel warm and feminine and at peace with him despite the fact that she was, at that moment, the target of his wrath.

"What am I to you?" she whispered, unable to keep the words back.

His eyes narrowed. "You are my wife."

The warm, peaceful feeling evaporated, leaving behind it the tears that had threatened earlier. "Is that all, Noble? It's true, then—I'm just a possession? Something you purchased with a specific goal in mind? I'm nothing more to you than an object to be kept in its place and brought out when it pleases you?"

Noble didn't know how to answer her, didn't know how to erase the pain he saw in her lovely green eyes. The words were written deep in his heart, but they were too new, too fresh to be spoken out loud. The light that glowed inside him, her light, was still too weak to banish all the darkness. He gazed into her eyes and said nothing, damning himself for his inability to speak, for his desire to have that which he'd sworn he would never again seek, and for allowing her into the secret recesses of his soul, where no one had been allowed before.

He watched with tormented eyes as she first pushed ineffectually at his hands until he released her, then raced, sobbing, out the door. God's eyebrows, what a mess he'd made of everything. Feeling his legs about to buckle under him, Noble sat in the chair Gillian had just abandoned and let his head slump into his hands. How the devil had things turned out this way? When had life slipped out of his control, turning it from a well-ordered and-structured, pleasant existence into this chaotic farce? How could a man be expected to function when all he planned, all he hoped for was dashed away and replaced . . . the thoughts suddenly stopped cold.

What was the use, why was he pretending to himself? His

life had been well-ordered and structured before Gillian came to it, that was true, but it had also been a bleak and hollow life, a life without joy or warmth or . . . love. Chaos might dodge her footsteps, but it was a small price to pay to be loved by her. And what had he done in the face of that love? He'd blown up at her, yelled at her until she sobbed at his cruelty, tears streaming down her face when she realized that he would not, *could not,* give her the words she needed to hear.

Another woman's tears came to mind, another woman's tears as a result of his cruelty. Noble clutched the arms of the chair until his nails gouged crescents in the wood, but he paid no heed to the pain in his fingers. He was too busy fighting the crippling pain that gripped his soul.

Dear God, please don't let me drive her away as I did Elizabeth, he prayed, his thoughts jumbled and confused, chasing each other in circles. Images of that night, that terrible night came unbidden to his mind, the image of finding his son curled up in a little ball in a pool of blood, almost out of his mind with terror. The night his wife died, the night he knew for a fact that hell existed, because he was in it. The feelings of guilt, once thought long gone, swept over him and merged with this new flood of guilt over his treatment of Gillian.

Noble Britton, the twelfth Earl of Wessex, sat alone in his library and at last faced the emotions he had refused to acknowledge for five years: sorrow for the horrors he had forced upon his son, remorse for failing his first wife, self-pity for the hell he had lived in for so long. And finally, and most recently, shame for hurting the one person who meant more to him than life itself.

Gillian stood in the doorway of the library and hesitated. She had knocked, but Noble had not answered. Was he ill? So angry still that he refused to acknowledge her? She took a step forward, afraid to draw his attention to her and yet unwilling to face his wrath if he thought she was concealing the letter she had just received.

"Noble?" The word was so soft, even she could hardly hear it. She stepped silently toward the head that rested against the back of the armchair. Was he reading? Asleep? She came around the side and stopped, stunned by the sight.

He was asleep, his head resting at an angle that looked most uncomfortable, his hands curled into fists. His face in repose looked so unguarded, so young, so peaceful, but it wasn't that unusual sight that made her heart constrict with pain. She bent forward and touched a finger to his cheek. Faint silvery tracks led down the angled planes of his face, down into the darkening shadows of his jaw.

He had been weeping. Her Lord of Rage had been weeping.

Chapter Eight

"Good evening, Lady Wessex."

"Oh, Lord Rosse, good evening." Gillian peered around the marquis, looking for Noble. "How nice to see you again. That's a lovely waistcoat. Are those dragons?"

"Yes. It is a gift from my betrothed."

Gillian looked at him, startled. "You are betrothed? I didn't know. Noble never mentioned it."

Rosse smiled. "I've been betrothed since I was sixteen. Our fathers arranged it."

Gillian's brow furrowed. "Is that legal?"

Rosse shrugged. "It matters not, I've pledged myself to the girl, and I'll marry her. Some day," he added with an irresistible grin. Gillian couldn't help but grin in response. She liked Rosse the best of all Noble's friends. He reminded her of a friendly puppy, all eagerness and enthusiasm.

"Noble had an important appointment, I'm afraid, but I managed to convince him to allow me to have the honor of escorting you to the Countess of Gayfield's rout, where your estimable husband will join us later."

Gillian was disappointed that Noble had not remained home

to escort her. She not only wanted to discuss the note she had received from Lord Carlisle, she wanted to find out why he had been weeping. Nick was in good health—that had been her first concern. Try as she might, she just could not understand why her Lord of Tempers ran hot one moment, then cold another. Perhaps it would be better if she stopped trying to understand him and just accepted his volatile emotions.

"Er . . . quite so, my lady," Lord Rosse said, and held the door open for her.

Gillian blushed, thought about explaining about her Unfortunate Habit, then decided it wasn't important.

"My lord," she said once she was seated in Lord Rosse's elegant carriage, "perhaps you would tell me—"

"Where your husband is this evening? I'm afraid I cannot, my lady."

Gillian looked annoyed. "I shouldn't dream of asking you such a thing," she said. "I have every faith in my Noble, and if he said he had an important matter of business to attend to, then I'm sure that is what he is doing."

Rosse thought back to the earlier conversation he had had with Noble.

"Just look at this, Harry," the Black Earl had demanded, waving a letter in front of the marquis's face. "How dare the blackguard impugn Gillian's virtue in such a manner? You'll act as my second, of course."

"Your second? You've called him out, then?"

"Yes, earlier, when I caught the murdering bastard with his hands all over my wife."

Rosse stared at him in surprise.

"Oh, not in that manner; it was all perfectly innocent on her part," Noble stormed, continuing to wear a path in the carpet before his friend. "She was suitably escorted by Crouch and three footmen, not to mention Nick, her cousin, and those blasted beasts. No, that was an innocent bit of folly on her part; her cousin wanted an introduction, and you know how Gillian thinks—in a manner so convoluted it's almost straightforward, she took Lady Charlotte to call on the man with some feeble excuse of seeking a referral from him. But the bastard's gone too far now. Just look at this!"

"I will if you stand still long enough for me to snatch it from your hand."

Noble tossed him the letter as he passed his friend.

"Hmmm. So she's to meet him tonight at the Gayfields' rout, eh?"

"So he says. Gillian won't meet him, of course. We had a discussion about that earlier."

Rosse could just imagine what form the discussion had taken. "It appears to be an anonymous letter. Are you sure it's from Carlisle?"

Noble snorted as he completed his circuit of the room and turned to begin it again. "Of course I'm sure; who else would send me a note gloating over the fact that Gillian had made an assignation to meet with him right under my nose? He's baiting me, Harry, and I refuse to be baited."

Rosse wasn't sure, but something didn't smell right about the entire situation. So far the added men he'd put on the investigation had found nothing to justify his intuition that there was more to the matter than just McGregor. He told Noble his suspicions, anyway.

"You've been out of the spy game too long. Your nose has lost its sharpness," Noble opined.

Rosse shrugged and took a sip of his friend's excellent brandy. "Possibly. But I don't believe so."

Noble thought about that for a moment; then his eye caught sight of the blasted note again and his attention was fixed wholly and completely on gaining satisfaction.

"Take Gillian to the Gayfields' tonight. I'll meet her there later."

Rosse looked into the hooded gray eyes of his friend, his mind quickly assimilating facts and trying to figure out Noble's scheme. "Where will you be until then?"

"In your shadow," Noble said grimly.

Rosse's pale eyes blinked behind the glass in his spectacles; then enlightenment darkened them. "Ah. I believe I see. You will pretend to be away this evening, leaving the avenue open for McGregor—"

"—to attempt to seduce my wife, whereupon I'll burst onto the scene and strangle the bastard on the spot."

A slow smile stole over Rosse's face. "And your wife?"

"Will believe I am still angry with her over this afternoon's debacle."

"A little hard on her, isn't it?"

Noble tugged at his lower lip, then sighed. "It can't be helped, and it will only be for a short duration. It is important that McGregor believe we are at odds, the better for him to succeed with Gillian."

The marquis warmed his brandy between his palms and inhaled the aroma. "Do you trust her?"

Noble paused in his circuit around the desk. "To not betray me with McGregor? Yes, I do. I've—" He picked up the paintbrush on his desk, his fingers running over the softness of the sable brush. As soft as that was, Gillian's hair was a thousand times silkier. "I've treated her poorly, Harry, and I intend to make up for that, but first I must deal with these incessant threats and attempts to drive us apart."

"I wondered if you had seen that," Rosse commented mildly.

"Seen what?"

"That the nature of the threats had changed from blackmailing you to promising harm to your wife and now to a blatant attempt to instill distrust and discord in your marriage."

Noble sat down suddenly. "McGregor's mad."

"Possibly. But I think it goes further than just McGregor's attempts at obtaining justice for Elizabeth. This strikes me as an attempt to destroy you personally as well as socially."

Katie MacAlister

"Personally?"

"I think, my friend," Rosse said as he stood and strolled to the window to look at the street beyond, "I think it is a good idea that you have sought additional protection. I fear you are going to need it."

What Rosse hadn't told his friend was that he himself had hired two more men with the sole purpose of following the earl and his countess. One of the men was even now in attendance at Lady Gayfield's, in the guise of a hired footman. The other had been given an invitation to the rout, procured at no small social cost to Rosse, and was in attendance at the party. Rosse went over his plans again, satisfied he had done all he could to protect his friend and his lovely lady.

"Lord Rosse?" That lady was now sitting across from him in his carriage and frowning in a most annoyed fashion.

"I beg your pardon, Lady Wessex, I was pondering a problem. What was your question?"

"About Noble and this silly duel . . ."

Rosse blinked at her in surprise. "You know about the duel?"

"Of course I know about the duel; I was there when Noble challenged poor Lord Carlisle."

"Ah. Well . . . ah . . . I don't believe it's customary to acquaint the wife of the duelist with the facts, my lady."

"Regardless, you will. You are Noble's second, are you not?"

"Yes, but—"

"Excellent. Then you must help me stop it."

"I understood that most ladies find it pleasing for their honor to be the subject of a duel."

"I am not most ladies, my lord."

No, she certainly was not. Rosse couldn't help but grin at her as she continued.

"I do not find the idea of my husband allowing another man to aim a pistol at him and fire a pleasant one, my lord, and I intend to move heaven and earth to make sure that he will not be in that position. Where and when is the duel to be held?"

Rosse shook his head. "I have not yet met with Lord Carlisle, my lady."

"But it will be you who suggests a meeting time and place, will it not?"

"As Noble's second, my first duty is to attempt to resolve the situation by means other than dueling."

Gillian snorted a most unladylike snort. "You know Noble, and I assume you know Lord Carlisle—two more pigheaded, obstinate, proud men I've never seen. Neither will back down."

"I am in agreement with you there, my lady. Assuming negotiations for a peaceable end to the challenge fails, then yes, I will suggest a meeting time and place."

Gillian chewed on her lower lip as she pondered the situation, her brow furrowed in thought, her fingers absently twisting the beads on her midnight blue overdress. Suddenly her brow cleared, her eyes sparkled, and her mouth formed a charming smile. Rosse was struck once again with a sense of rightness that she and Noble should have found each other. If only they could see how much love they had to offer each other, he thought, and voiced the question that rose to his tongue.

"You have thought of something to put an end to the duel, my lady?"

"Yes, my lord, I do believe I have."

"And that is . . . ?"

"Better left unsaid to you, Lord Rosse, lest at a later time my lord accuse you of having a hand in it."

Rosse spent the better part of the journey to Berkeley Square trying to convince her of the folly of whatever plan she had dreamed up, but it was to no avail.

Gillian needed desperately to see Charlotte. As the only person who knew she was investigating Noble's past, Charlotte's advice and help was invaluable, especially now when she had two immediate problems facing her—to find out what Lord Carlisle wanted, and to ensure that the duel did not take place. Since both items revolved around the same man, and threatened the health and happiness of her beloved husband, she felt herself perfectly within her rights to go against that husband's wishes and meet with the very man he had ordered her to avoid. She wasn't a fool, however, and knew that any meeting with Carlisle must take place in the presence of a witness to protect her reputation with both society and her husband. To be truthful, she didn't care a fig about the former, but the latter concerned her greatly.

Gillian greeted Lady Gayfield, who was delighted to have her present and asked whether the earl would be joining her soon. Lady Gayfield was newly married, and nervous about this, her second *ton* party. She was thrilled, however, that the two most talked-about members of society were going to be present.

"Lord Wessex will be here," Gillian told the viscountess. "He had an important engagement, but he promised he'd be along later."

Lady Gayfield, feeling one Wessex was good, but two would be better, especially if they could be counted on to do something scandalous like embrace publicly, was perfectly happy to wait until all hours for the arrival of the earl.

"May I be allowed to say how much I admired your actions the past evening?"

"My actions?" Gillian looked down at her faintly blue palms.

"Your . . . your affectionate embrace. It was so very romantic, so full of passion and *l'amour!* If the mood were to overtake you again this evening, and you wished to embrace your husband in such a manner, I want you to feel free to do so. You are among friends, Lady Wessex, friends who would not censure you for feeling what is right and natural for your husband."

Gillian tried not to let the corners of her mouth twitch. "Thank you, Lady Gayfield. Should I be overcome with emotion and find it necessary to kiss my husband, I will do so secure in the knowledge that I have your full approval."

"Indeed," Lady Gayfield smiled delightedly and pressed Gillian's hand, grand visions of the gossip that would fly from her party the following day should the Wessexes behave with suitably improper behavior, "indeed, I would not mind at all were you to give free rein to your emotions."

Gillian found the idea of the *ton* holding its collective breath waiting for her and Noble to display their affection very amusing.

"You are, after all, newly wed."

"Very true, and while I appreciate the offer to heed the call of our passions and desires, I believe Lord Wessex will draw the line at actually bedding me in front of your guests."

There were gasps behind her as others overheard her outrageous statement.

"Oh, yes, of course," Lady Gayfield gasped also, in mingled horror and delight. Who knew what Lady Wessex would say next? She almost hoped it would be something just as shocking. If only the Wessexes would see fit to conduct themselves in a scandalous fashion, her reputation as a hostess of the most interesting *ton* parties would be made.

Gillian made her excuses and escaped both Lady Gayfield and Lord Rosse and went in search of her cousin. She had passed from a reception room to the supper room but couldn't find her, and was just about to peer into the card room when she spied a familiar figure seated in a corner next to an enormous palm.

"Sir," she said, making a formal curtsy.

"Eh? Oh, it's you, gel. Thought I'd see you here this evening."

Gillian seated herself on the love seat next to the wizened figure and prepared to interrogate the old man about his connection with Noble.

His brilliant blue eyes sparkled at her from beneath his bushy white eyebrows, almost as if he could guess her thoughts.

"You look as if you'd just met with a highwayman."

"I believe I did. An honorable one at that."

"Eh? Oh, Carlisle."

Gillian stared openmouthed at the frail old man. "Yes, how did you know?"

"Bound to happen if you were looking in the proper place to uncover the secrets. Secrets and lies, I told you, and secrets and lies are what you've found."

Gillian reflected on that for a moment. "But which are the lies and which are the truths?"

" 'Tis for you to tell." The old man clasped his rheumy hands together and leaned back against the red cushions. "Your heart knows what's true and what's false. A smart woman would listen to what her heart tells her."

Gillian sighed. "That's just the problem. When I listen to my heart and try to act on its advice, I end up in trouble. Now Noble has challenged Lord Carlisle to a duel all because of my heart, and I have to save him. It's not easy being a woman, you know."

Palmerston snorted and closed his eyes. "No one said this journey would be easy, gel. If it's a life of ease you want, it's within your grasp. All you have to do is take it."

"But at what cost?" Gillian asked softly. "Noble's happiness? I'd rather struggle on with the journey if that's the price. He needs me, Palmerston, and I'm not about to give up on him when he needs me."

The old man didn't answer. Gillian wasn't sure if this was his way of dismissing her, or if he had actually fallen asleep. He was very old; it was probably the latter. She gave him a gentle pat on his knobby hand and slipped away quietly.

She found her cousin a few minutes later.

"Good evening, Aunt, Uncle."

Her aunt greeted her in a flustered, hesitant manner but didn't seem to have forbidden Charlotte to be in her niece's presence. Gillian curtsyed to her uncle, received a frosty look in return, and hurried over to claim Charlotte.

"Char, I must speak with you."

"Later, Gilly. Mama is fishing for an introduction to the most divine viscount, and I believe Lady Weatherby is going to finally admit defeat with her poor plain-faced Anne and introduce me to him."

"This is more important than your divine viscount."

Charlotte looked disbelieving. "I doubt if anything could be more important than a divine viscount." She snapped open her fan. "Unless, of course, it's a divine earl, marquis, or duke."

"This concerns an earl, and one whom you were, a few hours ago, making the most obvious sheep's eyes over."

"Lord Carlisle?" Charlotte asked.

"The very same."

Charlotte whispered a few words to her mother and then followed after her cousin to a secluded corner.

"I had assumed that Lord Wessex would have forbidden you to see Lord Carlisle again after that delicious scene this afternoon."

"It's hardly delicious when one's husband's life is in danger, Charlotte. And he did forbid me, but that's of no matter now, because I simply must save him. Look, this came a few hours ago."

She handed Charlotte the letter she had received.

"Oh, my," Charlotte said, a worried frown wrinkling her brow as she took in the few lines. "You're not going to do it, are you? Meet with him secretly? Tonight?"

"It says he has important information vital to our quest, Charlotte."

"Well, as to that, you weren't very forthcoming with him about your quest, you know."

"That's because Noble believes him to be behind the attack. I had to throw him off the scent by implying we believed it was someone else who planned such a heinous crime."

"But I thought you believed that."

"I do, but Noble doesn't, and if there's one thing I've learned, dear cousin, it's the importance of keeping an open mind. No, my duty is quite clear. I must meet with Lord Carlisle, and not only ascertain what vital information he has, but also—not that it will do any good—beg him to consider apologizing to Noble and thus halting the duel."

"And if he won't?"

Gillian sighed. "I shall take steps to ensure they won't meet tomorrow. I don't wish to—they're rather drastic steps—but I have Noble to think about."

"Why do I have a feeling your Noble won't be happy with you thinking about him in such a manner?"

Gillian waved off the question. "You must come with me once the meeting spot is named and be my witness."

"Have you been contacted yet?"

"No, but the note didn't say when I would be contacted, just that someone would let me know when and where I was to meet him."

"I will come with you, Gilly, but I think you should reconsider your actions. Lord Wessex—oh, Gilly, there he is!"

"Noble?"

"No, the divine viscount. Isn't he delicious?"

"Quite fashionable," Gillian said, viewing the dandified viscount with a giggle. "Those curls must have taken him forever to achieve."

"Mmm, but it's worth the effort." Charlotte started to move off toward her mother and the viscount.

"Don't forget, you promised you'd come with me!"

Charlotte waved a hand in acknowledgment and went to meet the sprig of fashion.

Gillian mingled, chatted, and even danced a few country dances before she received the instructions she awaited. A footman approached, bowed, and handed her a slip of paper. She read it quickly; then, with a glance through the rooms to make sure Noble had not yet shown up, she went to find Charlotte.

"Well, blast," she muttered when she found her. Charlotte was involved in a lengthy looking dance and was sure to be busy for some time. Gillian glanced at the note again.

Third room on the left, second floor. I'll wait ten minutes, then leave. Come alone. Well, she certainly wasn't enough of a ninny to go alone to a stranger's bedchamber with a man who was not her husband, but she did not wish to miss this chance to learn what Lord Carlisle knew, and to beg him to apologize to Noble. She waited until Charlotte was standing during a quiet moment in the set, and passed the note to her. Charlotte read it, nodded, and slipped the paper into her glove.

Gillian waited as long as she could, watching a gilt ormolu clock nervously, but there was nothing for it but to go upstairs by herself. Charlotte was still engaged in the dance with her divine viscount, and nothing was going to pull her from that sort of an opportunity.

Gillian toyed with the idea of asking a footman to accompany her but had a much better idea. She looked around for a servant, noticed a short, burly footman just behind her, and signaled to him.

"Madam?"

"I am feeling unwell, and Lady Gayfield has suggested I rest quietly for a few moments in a bedchamber upstairs. The third one on the left, second floor. I would like a maid sent to attend me."

The footman looked startled but murmured his compliance and left to carry out her instructions. She uncrossed her fingers and, feeling pleased with her cleverness, hurried toward the staircase.

She climbed the stairs to the second floor, popped her head around the corner to make sure there was no one in the hallway, and scurried down, counting doors. "One, two, ah, here it is."

She slipped into the room and was surprised to find it empty, although several tapers had been lit. There was a large bed with blue and gold bed curtains, several pieces of mahogany furniture, a love seat against a far wall, a screen with embroidered peacocks, and a large painting reminiscent of Botticelli's *Venus*.

Gillian looked at the painting closely. Was that cherub doing what she thought he was doing?

"I believe that's by Smollett," a voice from the other side of the room said. Gillian spun around and clutched her throat, then relaxed when she saw Lord Carlisle leaning negligently against the wall next to a wardrobe.

"You gave me quite a start, my lord, but I am pleased you are still here. I was detained and feared you would leave before I could meet with you."

"And deny myself the pleasure of a few stolen moments in your exquisite company, madam?" Lord Carlisle strolled into the room and grasped Gillian's hand in both of his, and brought it to his mouth. "I could not leave without gazing just once more into those deep, entrancing pools of emerald."

He kept his gaze locked on Gillian's as he turned her hand over and kissed her palm.

Gillian leaned closer. "You're very good, my lord, but not nearly as good as my husband."

The smile that had been playing around the earl's manly lips suddenly evaporated. He dropped her hand with a sigh.

"Well, it cannot be said that I did not try."

"No," Gillian laughed, "you did try. I'm sorry, my lord, but I do not wish to have an affair with you; I merely wish to know what it is you wanted to tell me about Noble, and to discuss this silly duel."

Carlisle said nothing for a moment, his black eyes somber. "Madam, will you accept advice from one who has known you but a short while?"

"Advice? What sort of advice?" Gillian glanced toward the door. Shouldn't the maid she asked for be arriving by now?

"As I said earlier, I have every reason to believe Lord Wessex murdered his wife."

"Oh, that," Gillian interrupted dismissively. "My lord, we've been through that. No matter what Lady Wessex told you, I refuse to believe that Noble acted as you have implied. He is simply not capable of such behavior."

Carlisle took her hand in his again but this time his eyes were serious and full of concern. "My lady, I know it is hard for you to admit, but your husband was responsible for his wife's death, and for her suffering before that untimely event. I cannot help but worry that should his substantial temper turn on you, you might suffer the same fate as my dear Elizabeth."

"I appreciate your concern," Gillian told him, giving his hand a slight squeeze. "But I am in no danger from Noble, nor will you ever convince me he had anything to do with his wife's death. Now, if you could tell me the information about the attack on Noble you wish to impart, I would be most grateful."

Carlisle closed his eyes for a moment and was just about to speak when someone knocked on the door.

"Oh, good, that will be the maid," Gillian said as she started for the door.

"Lady Wessex?"

It was a man's voice at the door.

"Oh, my," she said with a guilty glance toward the earl.

He held a finger to his lips and slipped into the wardrobe.

"Yes?" Gillian opened the door. It was the short footman. He looked nervously to either side, then pushed the door back slightly and squeezed through the opening.

"My lady, your husband has arrived and is seeking you. I would suggest you have your . . . rest . . . later."

"Oh, yes, of course. Um . . ." Gillian sent a concerned look toward the wardrobe. She hated to leave the earl without finding out what information he had about Noble's attacker. "Can you be discreet . . . uh . . ."

"Jones," the man replied, nodding. "Quite discreet, madam."

"Excellent," Gillian said with a relieved smile, and opened the door to the wardrobe. "Lord Carlisle, you may come out. Jones here will be discreet, so you may tell me what it is you know about the foul attack against Noble in front of him."

Carlisle rolled his eyes as he started to step out of the wardrobe, but a sudden knock at the door forced him to pause.

Gillian gave him an apologetic moue and, pushing him back inside the wardrobe, closed the door again. She waved the footman behind the screen and went to open the door.

"Am I too late?" Charlotte asked as she stepped in.

"Not too late, no, although I believe the problem has been taken care of," Gillian replied as she went to release Lord Carlisle. "Jones, you might as well come out too."

Charlotte looked with surprise as an earl popped out of the wardrobe, while a liveried footman emerged from behind the screen. "Gillian, I never would have thought you'd have it in you!" she teased.

Gillian ignored her and turned back to the earl. "Now, Lord Carlisle, if you wouldn't mind telling me what it is you wanted to tell me . . . oh, blast, now who's that?"

"I don't know, but I'll be damned if I go back into that wardrobe again."

"Yes, you will. I won't have Noble's reputation suffer because of you," Gillian said firmly and shoved him back into the tall enclosure, closing the door on his protests.

"Oooh, we get to hide?" Charlotte squealed, biting her lip for a moment as she glanced around the room. She gave a happy little cry and leaped onto the bed, pulling a bed curtain partially closed. Jones disappeared back behind the screen.

"Lord Rosse, good heavens, whatever are you doing here?"

"I . . . ah . . . heard you were here and wanted to arrive before Noble found you. Carlisle is here, isn't he?"

"Yes, in the wardrobe," Gillian said. Rosse nodded and opened the wardrobe. He was about to speak when Jones and Charlotte delurked.

"This is quite exciting," Charlotte said with a wicked giggle, then slapped an innocent and demure look on her face for the marquis's benefit. Rosse stared for a moment at the two additional occupants, then shook his head and turned back to the earl.

"Lady Wessex? Lady Wessex? You must let me in!"

"This is becoming ridiculous," Gillian muttered, marching over to the door. Rosse shoved Carlisle back into the wardrobe, while the footman and Charlotte reassumed their hiding places. Rosse looked around wildly for a moment and then threw himself under the tall bed.

"Yes? Who is it?" Gillian asked at the door.

"Sir Hugh. Please let me in, Lady Wessex. I have something of import to tell you."

Gillian opened the door to the baronet. "Something concerning Noble, no doubt?"

Tolliver pushed her back and closed the door loudly behind him. "The rumor is all over that you're up here with Carlisle. Where is he?" He looked around the room and settled on the tall mahogany wardrobe. "He's in there, isn't he?"

"Yes, he is," Gillian said, resigning herself to the fact that she was not going to be allowed to hear what it was Lord Carlisle wanted to tell her.

Sir Hugh gave her a sharp look. "In the future, madam, I would suggest you conduct your affairs with a bit more discretion. Noble is, after all, my dearest friend, and I hate to see him cuckolded in this manner. He knows what you're about and is on his way here now."

"It's a little difficult for her to cuckold him with all of us here, Tolly," Rosse said as he pulled himself out from under the bed. Sir Hugh exclaimed in surprise at the sight of him.

"A bit too crowded," Charlotte agreed, pushing aside the bed curtains and smiling fetchingly. "Oh footman, you can come out as well."

Sir Hugh stared with an open mouth as Jones emerged from behind the screen.

Rosse opened the wardrobe and faced the furious earl within.

"I'll be thanking you all to stop shutting me in that bloody thing! There's no air in there!"

"Quite," Rosse said succinctly, and turned to speak with Gillian.

"Gillian!" Her name echoed down the hallway.

"Oh lord, that's Noble," she said, wringing her hands. "He doesn't sound pleased, does he?"

"Gillian? Wife, where are you? Come out at once!"

Charlotte squeaked and ran back for the bed. The footman grinned and disappeared behind the screen but was immediately pushed out from behind it by Sir Hugh. He started toward the bed, but the earl beat it to him. "You can take the bloody Iron Maiden, I'll go beneath the bed."

Rosse and the footman looked at one another and around the room. Rosse was faster on his feet and made it to the area behind the love seat just ahead of the footman. Gillian stood by the wardrobe door as the footman, with a muttered oath, entered it.

She had just taken a step toward the door when Noble burst into the room.

"Hello, my love. Was that you I heard bellowing?"

Noble glanced quickly around the room and focused on the wardrobe. "Bloody hell, you're hiding him?" he exclaimed as he strode into the room, straight for the massive piece of furniture. "Did we not just have a discussion about McGregor, madam?"

"No," Gillian said as Noble threw open the wardrobe door and reaching in, pulled out the footman. He stared with a look of surprise at the short man who was dangling at the end of his fist. *"We* didn't have a discussion, *you* had a discussion. I just listened."

"Who the devil is this? And what is he doing hiding in Lady Gayfield's wardrobe?"

"It's her footman, Jones," Gillian answered.

"Er . . . actually, he works for me," Rosse said, pushing back the love seat and straightening up to his full height.

"Harry? What are you doing here? I thought we . . . ah . . . I thought you were to wait downstairs?"

"I felt it best to be on hand in case you decided to make good your threat to Carlisle," Rosse replied. "Do you mind setting Jones down? I don't think he can breathe with you holding his throat like that."

"Oh . . . er . . . my apologies." Noble set the man down and gave his rumpled livery a quick straightening. "So Carlisle isn't here?"

"No, he's here, somewhere," Rosse said, adjusting his spectacles. "Let's see, I believe that's Tolly behind the screen."

Sir Hugh stepped out with a red face. "Noble, I just came to warn your wife that you had heard the ghastly rumors about her and Carlisle—"

"That's enough, Tolly. I'm sure Noble knows you were here to protect him."

Sir Hugh nodded his head vehemently.

"And I believe Lady Wessex's cousin is in the bed . . . ah, yes, there she is."

"Good evening, Lord Wessex," Charlotte said, simultaneously dropping him a curtsy and fluttering her eyelashes at the marquis.

"And, of course, that's Carlisle poking out from under the bed."

Noble, who had been watching with an expression of sheer and utter confusion as people emerged from all sorts of furniture, narrowed his eyes and growled when the earl hauled himself out from under the bed.

"It's quite all right, old friend. Your wife has been amply chaperoned the entire time, as you can see."

"All's well that ends happily," Charlotte said as she dimpled at Rosse.

"I would like to have a word with Carlisle alone," Noble said in a gravelly voice.

Carlisle brushed himself off. "I don't believe I care for the odds of this situation. We have an appointment to meet at dawn two days hence, Wessex? Excellent. I shall arrange for seconds and see you then. Ladies, if you will excuse me." Carlisle bowed and left the room.

Gillian, who had taken hold of her husband's arm when Carlisle emerged from the bed, breathed a sigh of relief that quickly turned to one of worry when Noble, casting her a glance filled with portent, said, "If you would all excuse us, I believe my wife and I need to talk."

"Certainly," Charlotte said brightly, and instantly attached herself to the marquis. "Lord Rosse, would you escort me downstairs? I have no head for directions and am sure I would get lost without you to guide me."

Rosse waved the footman out before him and did his duty with a minimum of eye rolling and just the merest grin to Noble.

"Wessex, I feel compelled to plead Lady Wessex's case to you," Sir Hugh said, fidgeting with his quizzing glass. "She is young and quite impressionable, and I'm sure she had no intention that news of her assignation be spread among everyone—"

"That's enough, Tolly," Noble growled and, removing Gillian from his arm, he marched over and held the door open. "Gillian does not need you to plead her case."

"But Carlisle was here—"

"Good evening, Tolly," Noble said in a tone that even Sir Hugh did not dare challenge. Gillian wished she could escape the room with him. She knew Noble would have several things to say to her about meeting with Carlisle, and none of them would be pleasant or reasonable.

"Go ahead, Noble. I'm braced. You may proceed."

"I may, may I? And what do you expect me to proceed with, madam?" he asked, stalking toward her.

Gillian couldn't help herself—she backed up as he continued toward her. "Why, your lecture to me about meeting with Lord

Carlisle when you specifically forbade any such meeting," she said, then gasped when she ran up against the wall.

"Ah, so you *were* paying attention," Noble said, his gray eyes dark with emotion. Her Lord of Lectures stood toe-to-toe with her, then placed a hand on either side of the wall next to her head and leaned in until their noses were almost touching. "I was beginning to wonder if indeed you pay attention when I speak to you."

"Oh, my, yes," Gillian said breathlessly, affected by his nearness despite his irritation with her. She breathed in deeply, reveling in his scent. "Almost all of the time."

" 'Almost all of the time'?" Noble growled, brushing her lips carelessly with his. Gillian's heart raced. What was he doing? Was he not going to yell at her? Or was this some new punishment? A groan slipped past her lips as Noble leaned his hard body against hers, pushing her back against the wall. Oh, God, if it was a punishment, she'd be sure to encourage it every day!

"What?" she asked, unable to keep from licking the corners of his mouth.

"Hmm?"

"Nothing. Oh, Noble! Do you think you ought to? Here? Now? Oh, my, yes!"

"Yes," Noble agreed, and with one hand holding her head where he wanted it, he plundered her sweet, honeyed mouth.

"Are you sure, my dear?" Lord Gayfield, a pleasant, round-faced young man asked his wife as they came up the last of the stairs. "In your bedchamber?"

"Yes, yes, it's all anyone can speak of. Lord Carlisle and Lady Wessex were to meet in my bedchamber, and Lord Wessex has just left the card room to catch them in the act. Surely there will be a duel out of this, which is just what we need to put the right cachet to our parties." Lady Gayfield, almost beside herself with joy, paused for a moment and waved at fifteen or so of her closest friends, following her up the stairs. "We couldn't ask for anything better, Charles! It's almost as if Lady Wessex had heard my thoughts and was doing this just to please me."

Lord Gayfield looked doubtful, but obediently pushed open the door to his wife's bedchamber. They both peered in.

"Good lord!" Lady Gayfield said, one hand to her cheek.

Lord Gayfield spun his wife around and slammed the door behind them.

"There's nothing to see," he told the expectant crowd. "It's just Lord and Lady Wessex . . . uh . . . having a discussion."

It took a few minutes to dispersed the crowd, but at last the Gayfields were alone in the hallway.

Lady Gayfield put a restraining hand on her husband's arm as he started to follow his guests. "Charles," she whispered.

"Eh? What is it, Lydia?"

"Charles, did you see? How is that possible? Standing up? *Against the wall?*"

Lord Gayfield looked mildly embarrassed. "Er . . . yes. Against the wall. We'll discuss it later, Lydia."

"Well, I should hope so. And to think that Lady Wessex assured me her husband wouldn't bed her in front of the guests."

"Er . . . yes. Best let it go, Lydia."

"Well, I shall do so, but I will need to have the wallpaper redone in my room, Charles."

"Quite, my dear."

"Against the wall . . . Lord Wessex must be incredibly strong!"

Lord Gayfield put a supportive arm around his wife's shoulders and said nothing for a moment.

"Did you see Lady Wessex's stockings, Lydia? Quite charming embroidery. Eh . . . what say you get yourself a pair like them and we'll discuss the wall issue?"

Lady Gayfield giggled.

Chapter Nine

The Black Earl, that coldhearted, callous man who was rumored to have strangled, shot, and stabbed his wife to death (depending on with whom you spoke), the man who was well known to have a temper of astronomical proportions, the man who had, over the course of just a few years, challenged four men to duels (and subsequently put a lead ball into the arm of all but one), the man whose name was used by wise mamas to scare their silly daughters into looking at more appropriate suitors, sat back against the cushions of his well-sprung carriage and chuckled.

He felt light-headed, giddy almost. His arm tightened around his wife, snuggled up against his side, her head resting against his shoulder, her warmth wrapping him in a cocoon of happiness. She hadn't betrayed him, he gloated to himself as he breathed in the perfume that was Gillian. He had been right in judging her a suitable mate. She was everything he could possibly want in a woman—intelligent, loving, kindhearted, spirited—and she was his and his alone. She'd never give herself to any other man.

Noble felt a wellspring of happiness bubble up from the light that glowed strongly within him and rejoiced at its appearance.

Gone were the layers of ice that had held him in their frigid grip for so many years. Gone were the dark corners of his soul that harbored doubts and suspicion and distrust—her light had vanquished them. Gone was the crippling pain of loneliness that he had not known held him tight in its misanthropic embrace until she had destroyed that too.

Noble felt freer than he had since he was a young man. He was free to glory in all the emotions other men had: love, happiness, and joy. For the first time since he had achieved manhood, Noble purposely let the reins of control slip from his fingers and wallowed in the delightful feeling such an action brought with it. He kissed the top of Gillian's head while he mused that no more would he live by the mandates of order and rigid structure. He and Gillian and Nick would live in happy, glorious chaos, and he'd enjoy every damned minute of it.

He looked down at the cause of all his joy. She was sleeping, her face buried in his neck, her sweet, gentle breath feathering his skin with the softness of down. Good. She'd need her sleep. He had plans to honor this new happiness, and she'd need her strength to celebrate fully with him. He would have rubbed his hands together with glee but for his armful of wife. He contented himself with planning his celebration.

He would introduce her to all the ways of loving, all of the positions he knew, and probably a few he made up on the spot. He was feeling very inventive at the moment.

He would begin by loving her from the tip of her elegant toes to the top of that fiery crown, paying tribute to all the parts in between. He would kiss his way up those long legs, pause for a moment at the gates of heaven, then continue up over her gently rounded belly to those delicious twin peaks of pleasure. After paying his respects there, he would pause only long enough to make sure each graceful arm received its due attention, then move up to plunder that sweet mouth until she moaned and arched up against him.

Yes, yes, it was a good plan. First he'd start with mapping her terrain, then he'd be the stallion to her mare, and then, once she had caught her breath again, he'd let her ride him. He had planned on saving the activities they'd shared earlier in Lady Gayfield's bedchamber for another time, but that couldn't be helped. No, there was still much he could show her, but slowly, so as not to shock her. He reminded himself that she was new to the intimacies of the bedchamber, and with reluctance scratched off the list some of the more athletic variations. Simple was best. First the homage to her sweet, lush body, then stallion and mare, then he'd let her ride him, and then a long, long episode with them both on their sides, legs twined together, bodies moving in that delicious rhythm . . . perhaps that ought to move up on the list. First homage, then stallion and mare, *then* a sweet loving facing each other on their sides, followed by . . .

"My lord?"

Noble shook the images from his head with difficulty.

"What is it?"

A footman stood at the opened door of the carriage.

"My lord, do you wish to exit the carriage?"

Noble looked closer. It was Dickon, his footman. They were home.

"Ah, yes, indeed." Home. What a sweet word. Home and Gillian. Gillian at home. Gillian at home, in his bed.

"My lord?"

"One moment. Her ladyship is resting."

He waited until Dickon stepped away from the door, then kissed Gillian awake.

"Come, my dear, you are tired and need your rest."

"I'm not really that tired." Gillian yawned. Noble smiled to himself. She would be tired, oh yes, very, very tired indeed by the time he was through celebrating with her.

He helped her down the steps of the carriage and, giving into a carefree, wild impulse, swept her up into his arms.

"Noble! What on earth are you doing? I'm quite capable of walking, I assure you," Gillian protested, blushing at his actions in front of the servants and a passing carriage.

He smiled down at her and started for the three steps leading up to the front door when a loud noise shattered the calm of the evening. A sharp explosion echoed off the side of the house, followed immediately by the wild clatter of hooves as a small passing carriage suddenly raced away from them, the horses whipped to a gallop.

"What . . ."

Noble's mind snapped into sharp focus. He set Gillian down and hastily conducted a check of her person, then turned to instruct the coachman to follow the carriage from which the shots had been fired, but it was too late. Tremayne was on the ground, coming toward them, having recognized the sound for what it was.

"Noble, what was that? Surely not a rifle shot."

"Pistol, my dear," he said grimly, and waved Tremayne back to the carriage, ignoring the burning in his upper arm. "Follow him, you fool! Are you armed?"

"Aye, m'lord," Tremayne nodded and, leaping back into Noble's carriage, snatched the reins from the groom and set off after the culprits.

"Noble, you've been shot!"

His arms were suddenly full of wife, her hands checking over him as he had done moments before to her. "I think it's just your arm. Oh, my dear sweet Noble, let me help you in. Crouch! Crouch, send someone for a doctor. Dickon, help his lordship up the stairs. Charles, tell the kitchen I will need plenty of hot water. Good lord, Noble, put me down this instant, you've been shot and you shouldn't be straining your wound!"

Noble ignored her orders and carried her up the stairs to her bedchamber, then deposited her on the chaise. "It's not serious, madam. Tremayne will take care of it for me. Now have your bath and I shall see you as soon as this incident has been dealt with."

Gillian stared in surprise as her husband stalked out of the room as if nothing untoward had occurred, but soon rallied her wits enough to supervise Tremayne Three and Crouch in the care of Noble's wound. She was pleased to see that it was minor, just barely penetrating the outer edge of his arm.

"Perhaps you should have a nip, first, my lord," Tremayne suggested as he held the bottle of brandy preparatory to splashing the contents over the wound.

"Oh, that's an excellent suggestion, Three," Gillian agreed.

"No, I don't need it," Noble said, narrowing his eyes as his wife leaned over him to gaze at the wound. He had a clear view of her warm, enticing cleavage. He didn't need brandy. All he needed was her.

"Don't be foolish, Noble. It's bound to sting. Go ahead and sluice your gob."

Noble's head snapped back in disbelief. He looked closely at Gillian for a moment, then raised a sardonic brow at Crouch.

"Go ahead, m'lord, 'ave yerself a line of the old author," Crouch said with a weak smile, handing him a dram of brandy. Noble grimaced, muttered something about having a word with Crouch at a later date, and tossed back the fiery liquid.

By the time his wound had been tended to, Gillian felt the situation was well enough in hand for her to have the bath she'd ordered earlier. What had gotten into her Lord of Passion? His actions at the Gayfields' house, while appreciated and enjoyed despite the unusual circumstances, were bewildering. When Noble had pinned her up against the wall in Lady Gayfield's bedchamber the last thing she'd been expecting was for him to use that very same wall in a manner that still made her knees weak at the memory. No, she had not expected that; she'd expected Noble to rant and rave about her meeting with Lord Carlisle, and instead he had shared himself with her, giving her pleasure where she had been sure he would be cold and with-drawn.

She sighed over the confusing man she had married and scrubbed at her palms with a piece of pumice. Happily, the blue was almost gone, but it was a reminder of just how her heedless, foolish actions drove Noble to distraction. She sighed again, this time out of sympathy with him. Poor man; first his organs were out of humor and now an unknown villain had shot him. A frown marred her smooth brow for a moment as she contem-plated how she could ease his pain, then disappeared as she remembered the fascinating pamphlet she had forced the man to sell her earlier. It was the very thing!

Gillian padded around the room barefoot, gathering the items she would need; then, with her arms full of bottles and pots, she went through the connecting door into Noble's room.

She could hear his voice rumbling in his dressing room. Set-ting down her collection of oils and unguents, she stuck her head into the adjoining room.

"Did Tremayne Two catch up with the carriage?"

Noble turned toward her voice, his face black with anger. He stared at her for a moment, his gaze heating her even through her dressing gown. His expression cleared as the anger faded. "No, he did not. The other carriage had too much of an advan-tage."

"That's a shame. Will you be long?"

A curious spasm of emotion flashed across his face as he cleared his throat. "Not long, no."

Gillian beamed at him. "Excellent. I have a little procedure I'd like to try on you."

Noble seemed to be having some difficulty swallowing. His hands clenched and unclenched as he cleared his throat again. "I'm sure it will be most appreciated."

Gillian nodded and withdrew back into his bedchamber. She sat on the bed and reached for the pamphlet, then looked up as Noble shot through the door. He was across the room, his dressing gown removed en route, before her fingers could close around the pamphlet.

"Noble!" she shrieked as he pulled her into a passionate embrace. "My lord, your arm . . ."

"The merest of flesh wounds, I assure you, my darling," he said, his lips caressing her temples.

She looked down at that part of him that was pressing against her. "Husband, we couldn't possibly. You have been injured."

Noble murmured hot, passionate words in her ear, sending delightful little shivers of pleasure rippling down her spine and forming a hot pool at the very center of her womanhood.

"I have . . . your organs . . . celestial . . . Oils of Araby, Noble . . . stimulation . . ."

"Oh, yes, my love, it's very stimulating. Allow me to show you how very stimulating it can be."

Gillian, with an effort she didn't think possible, tore herself from her husband's arms and seductive, mesmerizing mouth.

"You are wounded, Noble. I cannot allow you to endanger your life by harming that wound."

Noble smiled at her, a smile that started fires all over her body. God's elbows, how was she to maintain any sort of control over the situation if her Lord of Smoldering Eyes was going to look at her with an obvious hunger that only she could feed?

She reached behind her and grabbing her pamphlet, holding it in front of his face.

"*The Celestial Stimulation of the Organs*, Noble. I thought we might, given the circumstances of your injury, use the special Oils of Araby and balmy, ethereal essences to restore your elasticity and good health."

Noble's smile increased in intensity, fanning the fire in Gillian's body into a raging inferno. She reminded herself sternly that he was hurt and knew not what he was doing, what with his being out of his head with pain, and it was up to her to ensure that he did no further damage to himself.

She stepped away from him and waved the pamphlet toward

the bed. "If you would lie down, husband, I will prepare the essences. They have to be warmed slightly, so as not to cause a shock to your system when they are administered. Once I have massaged the essences into your flesh, I am to apply the Oils of Araby to ensure that the humors are in balance. At which point—" Gillian consulted the pamphlet. She couldn't meet that look in his eyes without throwing herself on him. Shameful, that's what she was, wanton and shameful to think of engaging in such pleasurable activities while her husband was suffering so grievously. "At which point, I am to pay particular attention to those . . . er . . . parts of you so as to regain youth and vigor to your bodily endowments."

Noble suddenly looked interested and reached for the pamphlet. "Bodily endowments? You must pay particular attention to my bodily endowments? It says so?"

"Yes, that is part of the treatment. It's supposed to purify your blood if I conduct upon your . . . parts . . . those exercises shown in the back of the pamphlet."

" 'Imperial Exercises of Eros,' " Noble mumbled as he read the title, then turned the page. Gillian thought his eyes were going to pop right out of his head.

She fidgeted with the opening of her dressing gown. "It might be beyond your strength—"

Her words were cut off as Noble, with a move too swift for her eyes to follow, sent her dressing gown flying in one direction while she was tossed in the other, landing in the middle of his bed. He followed directly behind her, pinning her on the bed and holding the pamphlet in front of her.

"This one," he said hoarsely. Gillian hoped the trauma of his wounding hadn't caused an illness in his throat. "You'll do this one first, followed by the next one, and if I survive that, all the rest of the Imperial-bloody-Exercises of Eros."

She looked at the page he was waving in front of her. "Are you sure you are up to that? Your wound—"

"Purifying," he gasped, staring at her breasts, sending a fevered wave of desire washing over her. "My blood needs purifying. This minute."

Gillian pushed him gently onto his back and reached across his heaving broad chest for the Oils of Araby. "Well, if you are certain that you are up to it . . ."

"Noble?"

"Aaaaaaaaaaaaarg!"

"Noble, I'm not sure you are supposed to be having that reaction."

"Gaar."

"Yes, I understand you enjoy this exercise, but the pamphlet does not indicate that you should be panting at this point."

"Urrrrrr."

"Noble, my darling, we're only to the second Imperial Exercise of Eros. How do you expect me to go through all twelve if you are going to expend all of your blood-purifying energies on writhing about in that manner and moaning?"

"Eeeeeeeerm!"

"Oh, I beg your pardon; my hand slipped off your bodily endowment. My, those Oils of Araby certainly do heat up upon application, do they not?"

"Uuuuuuuung."

"One moment, my darling, I'm just reading the instructions for the third exercise. Let me see . . . apply the ethereal essences to the wellspring of vigor and manliness. I wonder where that is? Just here, do you think?"

"Nnnnnnnnaaaang!"

"Oh, my, yes, that certainly would appear to be a wellspring of vigor and manliness. Do you think you would have the same reaction if I touched you there again?"

"Nnnnnnnnaaaang!"

"Amazing! Once more?"

"Nnnnnnnnaaaang!"

"That's absolutely fascinating. Noble, I wish you could open

217

your eyes long enough to see this. I had no idea it was physically possible. You have tremendous muscle control."

"Gillian."

"Yes, my love?"

"Take me inside of you. Now."

Gillian looked down at her panting husband. His chest, lightly sheened with perspiration from the effort of purifying his blood, was heaving as he struggled to catch his breath, while his hands were compulsively clutching large quantities of the bedding. "I beg your pardon?"

"Ride me."

"Ride you?"

Noble opened his eyes just long enough to place both hands on Gillian's hips and hoist her over him. "Ride me."

Gillian looked down. "But you are covered in Oils of Araby and ethereal essences. I would hate for them to go to waste."

He moved her back and forth across his oiled, essenced bodily endowment. She felt so good, he almost spilled his seed right then and there. He gritted his teeth against the building rush of energy. Gillian's eyes darkened as she picked up the rhythm. "Perhaps it might benefit the purifying process if I were to . . . ah . . . ease you."

He lifted her up slightly and tensed his entire body as she slowly sank down upon him, her heat enveloping him with a pleasure that was so intense it was almost pain. As she slid downward on him, slowly, consuming him inch by painful inch, Noble shed the last remnants of control and thrust his hips upward, joining himself completely with her body and her soul. His spirit merged with hers and soared higher and higher until he thought he would shatter into a million bright, glittering pieces. At the highest point he shouted her name, pouring out the emotions of his newly opened heart, singing her praises and whispering words of love and joy.

He had left her behind on his journey to heaven, but still he felt her lips on his face, on his cheeks and eyes. Odd how comforting such a simple gesture was. He felt consumed by a strange lethargy that soon melted into something more elemental when Gillian shifted on top of him.

He opened his eyes and gazed into the bright, shining green eyes of the woman seated astride him. "My dear, let me tell you about a list I made earlier this evening. I believe it will go a long way in making up for my . . . er . . . appalling lack of manners of a moment ago."

Gillian smiled back at him and wriggled slightly. A streak of fire shot from his groin out to all points of his body.

"I will need your Oils of Araby."

A sudden line appeared between her eyes.

He smiled at her frown. "You look tired, my dear. I believe your blood could use purifying as well."

Chapter Ten

"M'lady?"

Gillian moaned slightly and buried her head deeper into the pillow.

"My lady?"

There was that pesky voice again, trying to draw her away from the sated, relaxed feeling that had held her in its embrace ever since her Lord of Araby bestowed his own ethereal essences upon her. Repeatedly. With much vigor and manliness.

"My lady, you have guests."

As mind-numbingly enjoyable as those Imperial Exercises turned out to be, what filled Gillian with happiness were the words Noble had spoken. Among the words of pleasure and passion, he had admitted that he loved her. She hugged those words to herself, cherishing them, holding them close in her heart. He loved her.

"The guests are in your sitting room, my lady."

Oh, it was true he probably didn't even realize he had spoken the words, but he *had* spoken them, and that meant that deep inside of him, probably in some small corner of his heart, she held sway over his beloved Elizabeth. If she could just nurture that love, it would grow, and he would come to love her as he did the former Lady Wessex.

"They've been waiting for half an hour now, my lady, and Mr. Crouch asked me to tell you that he'd prefer you not meet with the women."

Women? Guests? What on earth was Annie babbling about? "What time is it?" Gillian asked sleepily, burrowing her head deeper into Noble's pillow. She loved his scent.

"Almost noon, my lady."

"Mmmm." He smelled so . . . so . . . Noble-ish!

"Gillian!"

Gillian groaned. She knew that voice.

"Gillian, you lazy slugabed, get up! I've been waiting for you for almost an hour, and here you are lolling around in bed."

"Go 'way, Char. Sleepy."

"I don't care if you are sleepy, you've got to get up. Noble's mistresses are here!"

The mistresses! Gillian sat up in bed. God's shinbones, how had she come to sleep so late?

"The mistresses came? All of them? They all came? No one sent back a response; I didn't think they were coming!"

"Here, you, open a window. Gillian, you must instruct the servants to see to the airing of these rooms. This room is quite . . ." She sniffed and wrinkled her nose. ". . . stuffy."

Gillian blushed and pulled up the sheet.

"Yes, they all came, and they're all downstairs waiting for you."

"Water, Annie; I need water quickly. Have tea served to my guests, and tell them I will be along shortly. And tell Crouch not to worry, his lordship is out for the day."

"Good lord!"

Gillian paused in the act of reaching for the dressing gown her maid had laid across her feet as she left. "What?"

"Are you ill? Have you some sort of pox? You're covered in little red marks."

Gillian looked down at her arms. "Where?"

"There, on your bosom and neck."

Her blush deepened as she tried to pull the bedding up to her chin. "It's nothing, Char."

"It's not nothing, it's an epidemic!" Charlotte leaned closer, her eyes narrowed in concentration. "Lord, are those bite marks?"

Gillian thought her cheeks would burst into flames. "Charlotte, it's nothing. Please hand me my dressing gown so I may dress and welcome my husband's mistresses."

"They are! They are bite marks. Did Lord Wessex do that to you?"

"Charlotte!" Gillian hissed. "Please, you are embarrassing me."

"Do they hurt?"

"No, they're just little . . . love bites."

"Do you have them everywhere?"

"Charlotte—"

Her cousin tugged at the bed linens. "You do! Look, there's one there, on your stomach."

"Charlotte if you do not cease this unseemly examination of my person, I shall ban you from the mistresses conference."

"I can't believe you'd let him bite you. I should never let anyone bite me. Do you have them on your legs?"

"Charlotte, remove your hand from my leg this instant or I shall do something drastic!"

Charlotte dimpled at her. "What?"

Gillian thought for a moment. "I shan't introduce you to Noble's cousin."

"Faugh!" Charlotte said, and started to fumble with the bedding.

"He's a duke, and he's not married."

Charlotte stopped. "Age?"

"I believe he's in his forties."

"Children?"

"Two daughters. He needs an heir."

"Country seat?"

"Sussex."

"Very well, but I think you're being awfully mean about this. I shall go down and amuse Lord Wessex's ladybirds until you get dressed, but for heaven's sake, wear something with a high neck. We don't want you to shock them!"

Half an hour later Gillian stepped through the doorway to her sitting room.

". . . say, I can't imagine there can be any pleasure found in someone *biting* you. And my cousin was covered—oh, there you are."

Gillian looked at the women gathered. All four were crammed together on the pale blue sofa, each with a cup of tea held carefully in a gloved hand. Charlotte was seated in an armchair, one leg negligently crossed over the other, swinging her foot in an annoying and unladylike manner.

Gillian raised her chin as four pairs of eyes turned in her direction.

"Good morning. I can't begin to tell you how grateful I am that you could all take time out of your busy day to call on me. That is, I assume it's your days that are busy, not your evenings, although I cannot say for certain. When are your busy times, mistress-wise?"

The four women looked at one another, then back at Gillian. One, a dark-haired woman with porcelain skin, coughed gently. "You *are* Lady Wessex, are you not?"

Gillian smiled at her. The woman seemed a genteel sort for a lightskirt. Perhaps she had been misinformed about the character of such women. It made sense that Noble would consort only with a better class of women, not common doxies.

"Yes, I'm Lady Wessex. Oh dear, I suppose it would be best if we started with names first, so that I might know who you are."

Katie MacAlister

The dark-haired woman in the middle set down her teacup and rose. The other ladies rid themselves of their teacups as well. "I am Madelyn de la Clare, Lady Wessex, and I must admit that I'm a bit confused about why you've called us here. I can assure you that I have not seen your husband for several years. If you have something to say to me, I'd appreciate it if you could say it now, and I'll be on my way. My sister is watching my daughter, and I'd like to fetch her home again."

"You have a daughter?"

"I have three children, my lady."

"Are any of them Lord Wessex's?" Charlotte asked.

"Charlotte! Don't be impertinent. Noble would surely have acknowledged any of his children."

"Oh, yes, Nick. Beg pardon, I'm sure."

Madelyn looked from Gillian to Charlotte, her mien dignified. "No, my lady, none of my children belong to Lord Wessex. I am married now."

"How delightful for you." Gillian beamed. "I will be happy to tell you why I've called you all together, but perhaps I could meet the other ladies first?"

A pert, chestnut-haired beauty next to Madelyn bounced up and gave her a sketchy curtsy. "I am Beverly Grant, my lady, and I have not seen Lord Wessex in six years."

"How nice to meet you."

"I'm Laura Horn, m'lady," a shy blonde said, nervously twisting her gloves and keeping her soft brown eyes lowered demurely. "I met Lord Wessex eight years ago. He was very kind to me."

"I'm sure he was. And you are?"

The last of the four raised her chin and gave Gillian a long, level look. Her hair was the color of spun flax, and she had expressive hazel eyes that were thick with dark lashes. "Anne Miller, ma'am. Lord Wessex was my protector five years ago."

Gillian was pleased; the women seemed quite civil and accommodating. Then again, given their occupation, they probably had practice in accommodation.

The dark-haired Madelyn coughed again. "Yes, my lady, we have all had practice."

Gillian felt a blush creep up her throat. Charlotte rocked forward, clutching her sides with silent laughter. "Char, behave yourself, you're embarrassing me."

"I don't believe you need my help with that, cousin," Charlotte said, wiping back a tear.

Gillian ignored her and explained to the mistresses about the two attacks on Noble. The women all expressed surprise but seemed wary and uncomfortable, and Gillian sensed their hesitation.

"So you see, I have called you here to ask for your help."

"Our help?" Madelyn said. "You want *our* help? For what, exactly?"

Gillian explained her and Charlotte's plan. "In order to help Noble, I must first investigate his past. I intend to solve both mysteries, you see—how his beloved wife died, and who is attacking him now."

"Do you think they are related?" Laura asked quietly.

"That's a very perceptive question," Gillian answered thoughtfully. "Unfortunately, I don't know for certain, but I suspect they are. What other reason would someone have to suddenly plan a campaign against Noble? No, the source of the problem has to have its roots in his past, and that's where you ladies can help me."

"I'm sure we'd all like to help, madam, but it isn't possible at this time," Beverly said.

The other women voiced their regrets as well.

"Oh dear, I had so hoped you could help me," Gillian said with genuine regret. It seemed the closer she got to Noble, the farther back she was pushed in her attempt to find the answers. "I realize you are all busy with your . . . protectors . . . but I—"

"It's not that, my lady," Beverly interrupted her. "I have no protector at this time. It's a matter of finances, you see. We"—she looked to the other women, who all nodded at her—"we are at the mercy of the men we . . . accommodate, and once we lose that protection, we must rely on our own resources."

"Oh, well, that," Charlotte said with an airy wave of her hand. "Simply get another protector!"

"If it were only that easy, my lady," Anne said tartly, "we would all be more than happy to help Lady Wessex. But as it is, we must first find a gentleman who is willing to give us carte blanche, all the while hoping that he is not prone to abuse—"

"—or unnatural practices," said Beverly.

"—or has the pox," added Laura.

"—or gambles away his fortune," nodded Madelyn.

"Or a man who will find someone new and discard us as if we were nothing but rubbish," finished Anne.

Gillian was shocked at this side of the ladybird trade. "But surely there is something you can do to prepare for those eventualities? Save your funds earned . . . ah . . . in the course of your service?"

The women all laughed identical hard, bitter laughs. "We do save when possible, my lady, and sell any baubles given us, but that only goes so far, and then the time comes when we must again look for a protector or be forced into less desirable circumstances," Madelyn said.

"What could be less desirable than being a mistress?" Charlotte asked.

"Charlotte, if you cannot behave, you will have to leave. Ladies—" Gillian spread her hands wide in a helpless gesture. "I wish there was something I could do for you. I can, of course, pay you a modest sum for your time helping me."

"A modest sum?" Anne asked. "How modest a sum?"

Gillian calculated her next quarter's pin money and divided it into four. "Ten pounds?"

The women all looked at one another again; then Madelyn

spoke. "Since all the others are currently seeking protectors, and as my husband is . . . well, he's in gaol, we accept your offer. What is it in particular you want us to do?"

Gillian told them.

Charlotte offered her advice. "You should not forget this last mistress, the one who sent Lord Wessex the letter."

"Oh, yes, thank you, Charlotte. Noble's latest mistress was someone named Mariah. I don't know her surname, but I would imagine it would not be too difficult to find out."

The ladies agreed that it would not be difficult, and promised to find the whereabouts of the mysterious Mariah.

"As for the other thing," Gillian said slowly, nibbling on her lower lip. "Have you thought of organizing yourselves—mistresses, I mean—into a group? A guild, if you will, that would help members in times of need?"

The women, Charlotte included, stared at her as if she had suddenly sprouted wings. "A . . . mistresses guild?" Laura asked.

"Yes, a mistresses guild. For the . . ." Gillian gnawed on her lip for a moment. "For the welfare and betterment of the demimonde. You could arrange to have dues from those members who are currently . . . ah . . . employed, which go into a general fund to help those who find themselves unemployed and in need of assistance."

The women all blinked at her.

"Do you know," Madelyn said slowly, "that might be a thought. If we encourage enough women to join and subscribe for a set amount while they have carte blanche, we could set aside money for those women who are in between gentlemen."

"It's something to think about," Gillian said.

The ladies discussed it with increasing enthusiasm.

"We'd need someone to manage the fund," Beverly said loudly over the excited chatter. "Someone who could invest it for us, so that we could benefit from our subscriptions."

"That's our Beverly," Laura said proudly. "She was with Lord Cardwell, you know. The banker."

"Yes, she's right," Anne said, narrowing her eyes and giving Gillian a close look. "We'd need someone with connections to invest our money for us. No man would touch the money if he knew it was from us, but if it was from someone of the noble class, someone who might wish to invest her pin money, someone who had access to her husband's man of affairs . . ."

All five of the women's heads swiveled to look at Gillian.

"I'd be delighted," Gillian said graciously. "We can talk about the details at a later date, but first, I simply must ask you something that's been uppermost on my mind." Four brows rose in inquiry. "It's about you and Noble . . ."

The ladies smiled.

Noble was smiling as well. A silly, sated, smug sort of smile. He sat in a quiet corner of his club, his body blissfully at rest in the deep armchair. He had, he thought with amusement, all the strength of a newborn pup. His mind, the only thing that had the energy to function, wandered the merry paths of the memory of the past night's—and the morning's—activities. His smile turned into a cheeky grin.

"Will you look at that, Tolly?" Rosse said, prodding at Noble's outstretched legs with the toe of his boot. "It looks as if our friend here is suffering from a newly wed man's complaint."

Sir Hugh watched as Noble lifted a limp hand to wave the two men into nearby seats. " 'Pon my honor, Wessex, I don't know when I've seen you look so wasted. Are you ill? Ought to see a physician. Your color's not good at all."

"He's not suffering from anything other than paying tribute to the altar of Hymen." Rosse snickered, and waved for an attendant.

"Harry, if I had the strength I would thrash you soundly for that," Noble said, and instead demanded a whiskey.

"Ah, but you haven't, so I will take the opportunity to wish you a long and happy life with your lady, my friend." Rosse lifted his glass in a toast. Noble acknowledged the toast and sighed with deep appreciation as the water of life spread warmth throughout his limbs.

"About last night, Wessex—" Sir Hugh began. "It's a damned shame that had to happen."

Noble, thinking of his and Gillian's activities against Lady Gayfield's wall, murmured something unintelligible.

"But you'll take care of that blighter Carlisle tomorrow morning, eh? Noticed the wagers are laid evenly across you both in the books."

Rosse shot the baronet a questioning look. "Having a little flutter yourself, Tolly?"

Sir Hugh flushed and busied himself with arranging his fobs.

"What news do you have, Harry?" Noble asked, taking pity on the younger man's discomfort. Nothing could sour his present mood.

"Ah, well, a bit of information there, as it turns out. Mariah, your Mariah, or rather, formerly your Mariah, has been seen in the company of Sunderland."

One of Noble's sable brows arched. "Really? I hadn't imagined he would be interested in her."

Rosse nodded. "It surprised me too. Rumors are that he prefers his women a bit more . . . masculine."

"To say the least," murmured Noble.

"Sunderland?" Sir Hugh asked, a look of confusion crossing his face. "The Duke of Sunderland? What has he to do with your mistress?"

"That is the question, is it not?" Noble said, setting his glass down and stretching his arms high over his head. He still felt drained, but it was an extremely pleasing sensation.

"You forget, Tolly, Sunderland is a cousin of Noble's. Spent some time with him at Nethercote, or don't you remember that? Ah, but that was before your time."

"I'm not that much younger than you," Sir Hugh replied with

an angry glance at the marquis. "I remember Sunderland."

"No other word on the matter I wrote you about this morning, Harry?"

Rosse shook his head. "Impossible to trace."

"Other matter?" Sir Hugh asked, clearly peevish about being left out.

Noble gave him a quick accounting of the evening's shooting, and told Rosse that he had his Bow Street Runners in place.

"Excellent," Rosse responded, and rose with the others as they started off for the dining room. "With that much protection, I'm sure you need not worry about either Gillian's or Nick's welfare."

One of the footmen presented Noble with a note on a silver tray as they were about to enter the dining room. He paused for a moment to read it, and then swore loudly.

Rosse turned back, watching silently as Noble questioned the footman. The man repeatedly shook his head and tried to back away from the enraged earl, but Noble was clearly bent on gleaning what information he could. Finally the man made his escape.

Rosse raised his brows as Noble turned back to his friends. "Trouble?"

Noble said nothing but ground his teeth together as he handed the note to his friend. Sir Hugh leaned in to read the note.

Rosse whistled softly. "This fellow's really going for blood now, isn't he?"

Sir Hugh frowned. "I'm sure it's all nonsense. Why would anyone have wanted to shoot Lady Wessex? Unless . . ."

Noble snatched the note back from Rosse's hand. "There is no 'unless' about it. No one would have cause to hurt Gillian except as a means of hurting me."

"Hold on now, Noble," Sir Hugh cried as Noble spun on his heel and demanded his hat and stick. "You're not thinking clearly; your mind is muddled. There is someone who could want to see her destroyed."

Noble stopped so abruptly that the shorter man ran into his back. "Who?" he ground out, not bothering to turn around.

Sir Hugh danced to the side. "If you just apply your mind to the matter, I'm sure it will become clear, Noble. There's only one man—or at least there's only one at this point—with whom your wife has been disporting herse—"

The words stopped in his throat as Noble spun around and wrapped his hand around the baronet's neck, lifting him off the ground. "My wife did not disport herself with anyone, Tolly. Is that clear?"

"Noble, let him down, you're choking him," Rosse said, placing a hand on his friend's arm.

"Is that clear?" Noble said again, his eyes never leaving Sir Hugh's face. The baronet's eyes rolled back, but he managed enough of a nod to satisfy Noble.

"I will take care of McGregor tomorrow morning," Noble said, claiming his hat and walking stick and storming out the door.

"Where are you going now?" Rosse asked, following him to his carriage.

"Home," Noble told the coachman grimly, and then jumped into the carriage. "I'm going to make sure that bastard hasn't harmed my wife and son."

The mistresses looked at one another with chagrin.

"My lady," Beverly said finally, "that's . . . I don't believe . . . I've never been asked that question by one of my gentlemen's wives before."

The other mistresses nodded.

"In fact, while we are speaking on the subject, I can honestly say that I've never *met* any of my gentlemen's wives."

The other three mistresses nodded again.

"It's just not done." Charlotte nodded with them. "Bad *ton.*"

"Oh, Charlotte, what do you know about it?" Gillian said with a frown at her grinning cousin. "You shouldn't even be here."

"You asked me."

"I made a mistake."

"Ha!"

"Lady Wessex, perhaps if you were to tell us why you've asked that so very unusual question, we might better be able to answer it."

"Ah. Well, it's very simple, really. My husband loved his first wife very deeply—"

Laura gave a ladylike snort of disbelief.

"I beg your pardon, Laura? Did you say something?"

"I snorted in disbelief, my lady."

"Disbelief? Over something I said?"

"Yes, my lady. Gentlemen who love their wives very deeply do not keep mistresses."

Gillian thought about that.

"Good point, Mistress Laura," Charlotte said with approval. "If Lord Wessex loved his Elizabeth so very much, Gilly, why did he have a string of ladybirds?"

Gillian chewed on her lower lip.

"I saw her once, you know," Anne piped up. "At Drury Lane. She was in the box of another gentleman."

Charlotte leaned forward. "And?"

"She was . . . ah . . . fondling him."

Gillian blinked at her in surprise. "Elizabeth? Noble's Elizabeth? But if she . . . and if he . . . he engaged you all . . ."

It didn't make sense; even she, half-witted as she was from a night spent in Noble's arms, could see that.

"My understanding is that you wish to know your husband's favorite . . . ah . . ." Madelyn paused and sent a glance toward the enraptured Charlotte.

"Oh, you can say it in front of her," Gillian said with a sigh. "She's blackmailed me into giving her all of the pertinent details. I daresay by now she knows more than all of us combined."

"To be forewarned is to be small-armed," Charlotte said sagely. "Yes, do go on, Madelyn. We're yearning to know."

The drive to his house was a hellish nightmare. The streets seemed to close up before him, filled with reckless fools who did not know how to handle a coach and four, overturned carts, dogs leaping out and startling the horses, small children dashing hither and yon wherever Noble looked, and any number of other delays that stayed him from the side of his family, where he was most desperately needed.

He had deployed the three Runners in strategic spots around his house, each with a particular assignment, but upon reading the words now etched indelibly on his mind, he began to think three men were not enough.

Hell, a small army wouldn't be enough to protect his beloved Gillian. He thought of how she'd looked that morning when he managed to drag himself from his bed——on her back, her hair cascading a fiery path over the white linens, a rosy glow to her cheeks and a smile on her face as she slept the sleep of the well-loved.

He made a mental note to have his man purchase more of the Oils of Araby before considering again the problem of that murdering bastard McGregor. Could Harry be right in his suggestion that the real culprit might be someone other than the Scot? And if so, who? Who hated him enough to try to destroy first his marriage and now Gillian?

Gillian. Just as soon as he made sure she was in good health, he would take her upstairs and introduce her to more of the items on his list. For her security, of course, not for his own base pleasure—if he kept her so exhausted that she was unable to leave his bed, he'd have little worry that McGregor or any other murdering bastard could make good his threat and kill her. It was, after all, his duty to keep her safe, and if this was the only way he could do so . . . he grinned to himself as he acknowledged that the merits of such a plan were almost un-limited.

"Lord Wessex!"

Noble frowned at the footman blocking the door. *His* door, by God. "Yes, it's Lord Wessex, and he'd like to enter his house. Stand aside, Charles."

"But, my lord—we thought you were out for the day."

"Well, now I'm home. Is Lady Wessex in?"

Charles blanched and stepped back when Noble pushed past him. Tremayne wandered into the hall, saw the earl, gawked for a moment, and, with a stammered excuse, spun around and dashed for the green baize door.

Noble frowned. What the devil had bit his servants?

"Lady Wessex?" Noble reminded the pale Charles as he stripped off his hat and gloves.

"Ah. Lady Wessex?"

"Yes. Where is she?"

Charles swallowed twice and continued to stare at Noble with a chalky face.

"Are you ill, man?"

"No, my lord."

"Excellent. Then you can tell me whether my wife is at home."

"Ah . . ."

"Yer Lordship! Yer 'ome early!" Crouch shot through the door leading to the servant's domain so quickly he was forced to grab Noble as he skidded to a halt on the well-polished parquet floor.

"Eh, sorry about that, m'lord. I'll 'ave one of the maids sew that up."

Noble glared at the small hole in his sleeve where Crouch's hook had snagged itself. "Where is my wife?"

"Yer wife?" Crouch looked confused. "What wife would that be, m'lord?"

"The same wife who you have, for the past week, been dancing attendance upon. Where is she? Has she gone out?'

"Well, now, that's a right good question, m'lord."

Noble started toward the staircase. "Is she in the drawing room? Her bedchamber? Her sitting room?"

Charles made a choking sound and fell over backward in a dead faint.

"Fellow's ill; see to him, Crouch."

"Aye, m'lord, I'll do that. Eh—wouldn't yer lordship prefer sittin' in yer library while I find yer lady for ye?"

"I have a feeling it's better if I find her myself, Crouch," he replied as he marched up the stairs. He wondered what Gillian had done now to bring out the protective instincts in his staff, then chuckled over the thought. She had endeared herself to them just as quickly as she had to him. Although he couldn't let them think he supported such a notion, it warmed him to know they would protect her against what they perceived to be his unholy temper. He chuckled again as he turned down the hall toward her sitting room. Surely it would soon become apparent that no matter what outrageous act she committed, no matter what sort of a mess she embroiled herself in, he would bear it all with nary a word to the contrary. What could she possibly do, he asked himself as he opened the door, that could raise his ire now that he knew he loved her?

". . . once pretended that I was a wheelbarrow and he a gardener . . . oh!"

Blast it, she had friends paying her a visit. He smiled pleasantly and was about to make a bow when the woman who had been speaking, a chestnut-haired beauty with vivid blue eyes, caught his attention. She looked familiar. She looked very familiar, quite like . . . dear God, it couldn't be!

Noble stared at his former mistress, his mind doing cartwheels as it tried to manufacture a reasonable explanation for what Beverly would be doing in his wife's sitting room, talking about . . . *wheelbarrows?* A groan slipped past his lips as he recalled another time he had been feeling inventive, a most successful invention as far as he was concerned, but not one he wished discussed in front of his wife. Not with his co-inventor, anyway.

His eyes, feeling like a particularly sticky boiled sweet, swept the room to find her but stopped on the figure next to that of his ex-mistress. Surely that couldn't be . . . he closed his eyes and shook his head. No, he was seeing things. Perhaps the wound to his arm had given him a fever and he hadn't realized it. He must be delirious.

He opened his eyes again. No, there they were, standing together, Beverly and Laura. By dint of grinding his teeth together and squeezing his hands into fists he managed to keep from screaming, but it was a near thing. He took a deep breath and prepared to ask his wife just what the hell she thought she was doing, inviting his old mistresses to tea.

"Good afternoon, Lord Wessex," a smiling blond woman bobbed a curtsy. Anne, that had to be Anne; no one else had that saucy tilt to her head. Noble's mind started to go numb around the edges. Three mistresses? No, there was Madelyn; that made four. All together, here, in this room. How lovely. He peered suspiciously at a fifth occupant. No, it wasn't Mariah; it was Gillian's cousin. Which meant the other person, the sixth person, the person who was standing just behind his shoulder, no doubt chewing on that delectable little lip, was his wife.

"Gillian?" he asked softly.

"Yes, Noble?" She hurried around to his side. He was gratified to see he was right, she *was* chewing on her lip.

"Would you care to tell me why you have seen fit to entertain four women of whom, by rights, you should not acknowledge the existence, let alone know well enough to have to tea?" Noble was quite proud of how level and calm his voice was. The voice that spoke out loud, that is. The voice in his head was shrieking like a banshee.

Gillian thought about that for a moment. "Right now?"

"If you please."

"Perhaps it would be best if we were to leave," Charlotte said, making a quick dip toward the Black Earl and scurrying past him in a motion reminiscent of a startled crab. He looked, in her estimation, every bit as dangerous as his sobriquet, and she had no desire to be present to witness his reaction to Gillian's explanation. If she had the chance to make one; Charlotte sent a fervent prayer heavenward that Gillian would survive the explanation, and bolted.

"Perhaps we had better . . ." Madelyn rose and motioned to the other women. They all bobbed curtsies at the earl, who did not acknowledge them, his eyes at that moment being busy with the task of trying to bore holes into Gillian's head.

Gillian tried to avoid the Lord of Glares' eye but knew her goose was plucked, stuffed, and cooked. She opened her mouth to make an excuse.

"My lord?"

It was Dickon.

Noble snarled at him.

Dickon's eyes opened wide at the snarl. He picked at the trim on his jacket with bloodless fingers. "Eh . . . my lord, there is a matter that needs your attention belowstairs."

"What?" If Noble's lips had snapped shut any faster, Gillian thought, he would have bit the word in two.

Dickon looked as if he was going to be ill all over the carpet. "Mr. Crouch didn't say, my lord. He just said to tell you there is something that needs your attention belowstairs."

"Go."

The word shot out of his mouth with the velocity of a bullet. Dickon didn't hesitate. He went.

Gillian gave up avoiding his eye and raised her chin. "Before you commence lecturing me, I would like the opportunity to say one thing in my defense."

Noble almost didn't hear her, he was so busy trying to decide what to yell at her about first. "The choices are so tempting," he said softly to himself. "They are laid out before me in a vast panoply of Bad Ideas. No, I take that back; *Bad Ideas* isn't a good description of this particular venture. Taking hold of a wet, painted lantern was a Bad Idea. Bringing together four of my mistresses to discuss . . . my mind balks at the thought of exactly what you were discussing . . . bringing together my mistresses was not a Bad Idea. It was a Grievous Error of the highest degree."

Gillian licked her lips nervously.

"Lord Wessex? Lord Wessex . . . uh . . . there's an important note for you that's just come." It was Charles this time, a curiously pale and sweating Charles who repeatedly peered over his shoulder at something behind him. Gillian took a few steps to the side and looked beyond him. She could see a number of the staff out in the hall, huddled in a large group, evidently discussing something.

"Later."

"But my lord—"

"Later, I said!"

Charles almost stumbled over his feet, but he managed to make it out of the room without mishap. Gillian felt the odds were fairly good that she would not be so lucky.

"Lecture, madam? You believe I am about to lecture you?"

"Aren't you?"

Noble's eyes narrowed as he watched her lick her lips again.

"Oh, no you don't, my good lady wife! You will cease distracting me in such a manner."

"Yer lordship? I hate to interrupt ye there when yer about to rip a strip off Lady Wessex, but there's a matter of a small fire in the library, and we thought ye might—"

"You thought wrong, Crouch," Noble said, his eyes never leaving Gillian's face.

"But yer books and such—" Crouch waved his hook about in an expressive manner. Gillian gave him a tremulous smile of gratitude. It was a sweet thought, really it was, but surely Crouch must know that nothing could save her now.

"Let them burn. The whole bloody house can come down around our ears for all I care at this moment."

Crouch opened his mouth to say more but thought better of it. He closed the door softly behind him.

Gillian repressed the urge to flinch at the look in her husband's eyes and instead bit her lip nervously.

"None of that delectable lip biting, either," he said, shaking a finger at her. "It won't work this time. I am beyond such temptations. You, madam, have finally gone too far."

Gillian threw back her shoulders and raised her chin again. She wouldn't try to defend herself; she was, after all, technically in the wrong, despite the fact that she had done it to help him.

Noble stared at her out-thrust bosom, sending a wave of heat out from the deepest part of her. "You can bare those delicious strawberry-tipped breasts at me for all I care," he said, trying to snap his fingers but failing miserably. Gillian's color rose even more as his eyes wandered over her form as if he could see right through her gown. "It will have no effect on me whatsoever. I am impervious to your charms."

"Oh, my lord, my lady, you must come quick!" One of the parlormaids burst into the room, her eyes wild and filled with horror. She wrung her hands and tossed terrified looks back over her shoulder. "There's a terrible fight in the hall, my lord. The Tremaynes are at it again, and one of them has a hatchet!"

Noble didn't even flick a glance her way.

"Be gone!" he said, fluttering a hand at her.

"They're sure to kill each other, my lord! You must come now and stop them from murderin' each other!"

"One less person to interrupt me," he muttered, and narrowed his eyes at Gillian as she took a precautionary step backward. She wiped her damp hands down her sides. His eyes followed her movements greedily.

"Oh," she said breathlessly, little fires starting wherever Noble looked.

"You must come now!" the maid wailed.

"Out!" Noble said, turning to point at the open door. The maid glared at him for a minute, tossed her head, and spun around to face the hallway, her hands on her hips. "I hope you're happy! He didn't even *look* at me!"

An arm suddenly emerged through the opening, grabbed her by the elbow, and jerked her out of the room. The door closed quietly behind her.

Noble considered the closed portal for a moment. ". . . nine, ten," he said. The door flung open, and a rumpled Tremayne Two rushed in. "Highwaymen, my lord! Masked highwaymen at the door! Quick, you must come and . . ."

Tremayne Two quite accurately read in his employer's eyes his fate if he continued with that sentence. He turned on his heel and walked with stately dignity back through the door.

Noble tipped his head as he considered Gillian. "Do you have the feeling they are concerned for your well-being, my lady?"

"Should they not be, my lord?" she asked, hating the worry evident in her voice.

Noble pretended to think about her question. "Yes," he said at last with a decisive nod. "Yes, they should be very, very concerned."

He took two steps toward her and grasped her firmly by the shoulders. "Now, madam, now you will tell me exactly—" He froze as the door slowly opened behind him.

Over his shoulder Gillian could see a thin trickle of smoke gust into the room. The smoke seemed to possess a power all its own as it waved and eddied in an intricate smoke dance. It was almost as if someone were fanning it in through the door.

"My lord!"

Gillian was surprised to see Cook at the door. He cast a glance to his left, in the direction of the smoke's origin, and cleared his throat loudly. Someone beyond him began to cough. He raised his voice to speak over the noise. "My lord, the fire has reached the first floor. Mr. Crouch has been overcome by smoke and the rest of the staff is dropping like flies. You must come now!"

Gillian fought hard to keep the smile from her face. Noble's shoulders slumped briefly as he closed his eyes and leaned his forehead against Gillian's. She took the opportunity to wrap her arms around his waist. He sighed noisily at the fresh spate of coughing from beyond the door.

"Cook, tell Crouch if I ever catch him at my cigars again, I'll have his other hand."

Crouch suddenly appeared behind the cook. He opened his mouth to speak, was taken by a paroxysm of coughing, and ended up clinging to the door frame for support. Gillian couldn't help but notice there was a cigar stuck on the end of his hook. A long arm emerged from beyond Crouch, grabbed the cook, and slammed the door closed on both the cigar and Crouch's hook. Gillian watched with fascinated eyes as the hook wiggled back and forth to the accompaniment of muttered oaths and odd thumpings on the door.

"Are they gone?" Noble asked without opening his eyes.

"All but Crouch's hook and half of a cigar."

Noble's shoulders shook.

"There goes the hook now," Gillian said happily over a loud, wood-splintering noise. "Would you like me to lock the door?"

"No, they'd just break it down. I will put their minds at ease with respect to your safety, my dear, but if you are not in my library in five minutes with a suitable explanation, I will feel fully justified in reneging on my word to them."

"Five minutes? Would you consider, perhaps, an hour or two?" Gillian's mind spun madly around, formulating and instantly discarding a number of explanations. It would take her just five minutes to work off the expletives she wanted to say in private. Any half-believable explanation would surely take at least an hour to form.

"Five minutes."

"Half an hour?"

"Five . . . minutes."

He tipped up her chin and kissed her very gently on her lips. Gillian felt it was a warning—he could be gentle, or he could be a raging volcano of anger. The choice of how he would hear her explanation was hers.

"Five minutes." She sighed and began to think furiously.

In the end, she decided that the truth would have to suffice. She explained to Noble her plan to help him uncover the person behind the evil plots to harm him, and how the mistresses were to help. She pointed out that her sole motivation was to ensure his health and happiness. She mentioned that all the women were quite nice, really, and all had offered to help, although she did not mention the mistresses guild. Gillian was aware of her many faults but did not count stupidity among them. She expounded on Charlotte's idea of locating Mariah in an attempt to ascertain what she knew about the appalling incident. She brought his attention to the fact that women were often more successful in endeavors of a covert nature, since they kept their heads better in stressful situations, though one look at Noble's expression quickly ended that particular line of reasoning. She finished her arguments with a quick summation of the key points, made sure she stressed one last time that she was trying to help him because she loved him, and sat with her hands folded demurely and awaited judgment.

Noble had sat listening to her from behind his big mahogany desk, his fingers steepled and supporting his chin. Once or twice he had nodded as she made a point, but most of the time he watched her with an intensity that she found unnerving. His eyes glowed with a light from within their silvery depths, giving Gillian the almost overwhelming desire to shiver.

At first she listened carefully to what he was saying, as he was offering appreciation for her concern and her desire to help, but when it became clear that the rest of the lecture—and it *was* a lecture, despite the fact that he had assured he would refrain from lecturing—was headed for a detailed analysis of her conduct of the past few days, with particular emphasis on the outrageous nature of her plan with the mistresses, she let her mind wander. By the time he was through, however, she was unable to plan the dinners for the rest of the week, settle on what color wallpaper to use in the drawing room, or what shade of green to paint her bedchamber, as such useful lecture-passing musings were impossible to dwell upon when the Black Earl was storming around in front of her in one of his tempers.

At one point she thought he was finished and stood up to excuse herself. Noble, pacing by the window, spun around and pinned her with one silver-eyed glare. She felt her knees buckle beneath her and sank back down in her chair.

"Do not think I am through with you yet, madam," he said, breathing heavily and perspiring slightly about the forehead.

"Oh, aren't you? I thought perhaps you might be. It's getting late, Noble, and Cook is waiting to speak with me about the dinners."

"Damn the dinners!" Noble rubbed a hand over his eyes, and instantly Gillian's heart went out to him. The poor man; she was such a trial to him.

"Trial?" he snapped, his eyes wild. "Trial? Madam, you are a plague! You are a tribulation! You are an ordeal by fire!"

"Well, really, Noble," Gillian said crossly, her patience running thin, "I might be a trial, but I certainly am not an ordeal by fire."

"You've set two fires that I know of in less than a fortnight. That, my dear wife, qualifies you as an ordeal by fire."

Gillian compressed her lips into a thin line that said more than words ever could. Noble narrowed his eyes at her. "Do not don that obstinate look with me, my lady."

He stormed around to the front of his desk and leaned over her. "Hear me and hear me well, Gillian. I forbid you to meet with the four women you brought to my house today. I forbid you to investigate the unfortunate incidents. I forbid you to leave the house unless you are in my company. And I forbid you to have anything further to do with my son!"

Gillian gasped, horrified by his mandates. She could live with the first two and tolerate the third, but not to have contact with Nick? Her son? A fury unlike any other she'd known welled up deep inside her and threatened to spill over. She pushed Noble back until she could stand up, and faced him with her hands fisted on her hips and her eyes blazing.

"Why?"

Noble stared at her neck, his hands twitching as if with the effort to keep from throttling her. "Why? Have you not been listening to me for the last forty minutes?"

"Why may I not see Nick?"

"Because you are an unsuitable influence. He is a lad of tender years, and I will not have him exposed to the seedier side of life before he is ready to see it."

"The mistresses? He was not present, Noble!"

"It matters not. You took him with you when you had the harebrained idea to rescue me. You took him with you when you visited the man who was responsible for his stepmother's death. You ran the risk of exposing him this afternoon to women of a lower class. Clearly you cannot be trusted with the responsibility of seeing to his upbringing, so I shall remove him from your sphere of influence."

Gillian felt as if he'd struck her. He could rail at her all he liked, but to accuse her of being negligent where Nick was concerned—that was the outside of enough!

"I will not let you do this to me," she shouted, and punched him in the chest in an attempt to drive home the point. "You can lock me away, you can forbid me to see my friends, but you cannot take my son from me."

"He is not your son," Noble roared at her.

"He became my son the minute you married me," she yelled back, furious that despite all their intimacies, despite the fact that they loved one another, he still did not see them as a family.

"You cannot take him away from me. I won't let you."

"You have no choice in the matter," he snapped. "The decision is made. I will send Nick back to Nethercote in the morning. As you made a particular point about staying in town to be at my side, you will remain with me."

"You will not destroy this family!" She pounded on his chest again until he held her hands still; then, with a wordless cry of protest, she ripped them from his grasp and stalked toward the door.

"Gillian, I did not give you permission to leave. I have not yet finished with you."

"Oh, no, my lord," she said as she threw open the door, ignoring the startled faces of the staff gathered immediately outside. "You very nearly *are* finished, but you have not yet destroyed us completely. If you do not want to annihilate what was beginning to be a family, I strongly urge you to take back your words. I shall wait in my sitting room for your apology."

"Then you will wait for hell to freeze over," Noble thundered. "Gillian, come back here!"

Gillian turned and pushed her way blindly past the servants and ran up the stairs. At the top of the flight she paused when she saw Nick hiding in the shadows and clutched him to her with a sob.

"I won't let him take you away from me," she whispered, hugging him as tightly as she could. "You won't be alone again, I promise."

Nick looked up into his stepmother's eyes, and what he saw there warmed him down to the tips of his toes. He reached up to touch a tear streaking down her cheek and frowned at the wetness on his finger.

"My mother used to tell me a saying," Gillian said, bending down and kissing him on the forehead. "She said nothing worthwhile is easy. You, my darling son, are very worthwhile. I will do whatever it takes to make us a family, whatever it takes to make your father realize that he can't separate us. He's hurt and angry right now, Nick, and when people are hurt and angry they very often lash out at those people near to them. Do you understand?"

An urge bubbled up deep in Nick. He tried to ignore it, but it pressed up and up, higher and more insistent, until he almost gave in to the urge. Instead he nodded his head.

"Good." She pulled him into a hug again, and he let her warmth seep into him, comforting him. "I love you, my son," she whispered in his ear, and with a final kiss she was off, running up the next flight of stairs.

The urge inside Nick pushed higher until he thought it would burst right out of his mouth. He watched the hem of her gown flap briefly as she turned the corner on the stairs, and then he gave in to the urge. "I won't let Papa take you away," he whispered.

Chapter Eleven

Nick sat at the top of the stairs, a small huddled form hidden in the shadow cast by the wall. He picked at a scab on his knee from an injury he'd received when he tried to ride his pony up the steps to the veranda at Nethercote. The trouble with adults, he decided, was that they didn't come right out and say what was wrong, and how it could be fixed. He knew from the raised voices of his father and Gillian, audible even to him on the first floor, that they were arguing about something, and he had seen for himself that Gillian was crying again. But she didn't tell him what was the matter; she just talked about his father being hurt and angry.

Before he had much time to dwell on the subject, he saw his father storm out of the library, snatch up his hat and walking stick, and, with a growl, stomp out to his waiting carriage. The servants were standing in a group in the hall. He wondered if they knew what the problem was between Gillian and his father, and how it could be fixed. He was about to ask when Rogerson, his tutor, separated himself from the others and, spying Nick, came to herd him back upstairs to the room used for his studies.

Rogerson put an arm around his shoulders. "It'll be all right, lad." Nick thought of Gillian and how nice she made him feel, and he fervently hoped his tutor was right.

"Lord Wessex! I'm surprised to see you again so soon."

"I'm in the mood for a little exercise, Jackson. Can you accommodate me?"

Gentleman Jackson grinned. "There's an arrogant young blood in there just looking for someone to take him down a peg or two. Shall I tell him you'll oblige?"

Noble allowed the attendant to peel off his coat and reached for the buttons on his waistcoat. "By all means. I'd be very happy to beat the arrogance out of him," he said grimly.

"Well this is baffling!"

Crouch, Gillian noticed, had been hovering outside the not-quite-closed door of her sitting room. She smiled a little smile to herself. His interest and concern was really quite endearing, if a little stifling. She knew he was consumed with curiosity about the missive he'd just delivered to her.

"Did yer say somethin', m'lady?" he asked as he popped through the door.

"Why, Crouch, how opportune that you should be just there as I was speaking aloud to myself. As you have asked, yes, I did say something. This letter you brought me—it's quite baffling."

Crouch adopted a pose that indicated unadulterated interest. "Bafflin', m'lady? 'Twas sent to ye at Nethercote, but since yer 'ere, the steward 'ad it sent up by 'and."

"Yes, I understand how it came to be forwarded to me, but what I'm baffled about is the letter's contents. It tells me that if I should ride to London and call at a specific address in Kensington, I shall learn something of interest regarding my husband."

Crouch frowned. "Someone wanted ye to ride from Nethercote to town? Why would someone be wantin' that?"

Gillian tapped the edge of the note to her lips as she thought.

"This letter must have been sent to me in order to draw me into finding Noble shackled to his mistress's bed."

Crouch frowned. "Well if that ain't dicked in the nob."

"Um . . . yes, possibly, depending, of course, on whose nob it is that has been dicked. The question is, who sent this? The person who waylaid his lordship, or someone else?"

Crouch blew out his cheeks and scratched his belly with his hook as he considered the question. "Don't see 'ow anyone else could be knowin' what 'appened to 'is lordship unless they was the cull what smushed 'im."

Gillian blinked. "Ah, yes. I see your point. Only the smushing cull would have known where Noble could be found. But how would this cull know I was at Nethercote and not in town? Our removal to Nethercote wasn't in the papers."

Crouch sucked his lip. "That be a right good question, m'lady. A right good 'un."

Gilliam beamed at him for a moment. "Well, we shall put our minds to the problem. In the mean time, I have a task for you, but you mustn't tell Lord Wessex about it."

"Crikey, m'lady, 'is lordship'll be 'avin' my 'ead if I was to do somethin' against 'is wishes."

Gillian smiled. "It's not against his wishes. That is, it would be if he knew about it, but he doesn't, so that makes it all right. Do you see?"

Crouch groaned and rubbed his eyes with his good hand. "I'm afraid I do, m'lady. What is it yer wantin' me to do, then?"

Gillian removed a slip of paper from beneath a letter she had been writing and handed it to him. "I want you to go to Bow Street and hire some of those Runner persons. A half dozen should do, I'd think. They should be armed, and if they aren't, you should see that they are equipped with pistols. Or revolvers—whichever you think best. Then you are to take the men to be fitted for livery, and bring them home. We'll disguise them as footmen."

"What are you wantin' with a 'alf dozen armed Runner footmen?"

She gave the pirate butler a disgruntled look. "They're not for me, Crouch, they are for his lordship. For protection. Noble is in danger, and since I have been forbidden to leave the house, you must be my legs and see to all the arrangements."

Crouch thought briefly of telling her about the three Runners already in place in the house but decided against it. Lord Wessex was angry enough with her at the moment—if he were to find out she had subverted his Runners into protecting him, there was no telling what he would do.

"Aye, m'lady, I'll do my best, but I can make no promises that I'll be able to 'ire any Runners."

Gillian smiled a smile of pure sunshine that sent warmth clear down to Crouch's toes. "All I ask is that you do your best, Crouch," she said, turning back to her letter.

Charlotte sat in her bedchamber, staring into the mirror of her dressing table, her eyes unfocused and thoughtful.

"Very mysterious," she murmured to herself in a thrilled voice.

"Lady Charlotte?" Charlotte was jolted out of her reverie. "Lady Collins is asking for you. Shall I tell her you're indisposed?"

"No, tell her I'll be down in a few minutes."

She glanced at the letter in her hand. "Oh, Penny, one moment—tell Will or one of the other footman I will have a letter for him to take to my cousin."

She rose and went to a small writing desk, pulling out ink and quill, and while searching for a clean sheet of paper, she mused over the wording of her letter.

> *Dearest Cousin,*
> *The enclosed was sent to me because the writer feared it would not make it to your hand. I do hope you meet him at the*

*appointed time and place—I believe it would be to your benefit
to hear what he has to say, Gillian. Do let me know if you need
my assistance. Your loving cousin, Charlotte.*

Her smooth brow furrowed for a moment as she called the
maid back. "This is simply too good to miss. I wonder who I
could cozen into going for a stroll with me . . . ah, Caroline!
Just the person. Penny, I'll have another note for the footman
to deliver."

"Charles, I have a letter I'd like you to deliver for me."

"Certainly, Lady Wessex."

"The direction is on the front. You need not wait for a reply."

Charles looked at the front of the paper and blanched.

"Charles? You aren't going to faint again, are you? Are you
well?"

"Oh, my lady, please don't make me deliver this letter."

"Whyever should you not?"

"Lord Wessex'll string me up by my netherbits, my lady. He
surely will!"

"Nonsense. Your netherbits are perfectly safe in my hands.
Lord Wessex need not know anything about this unless you tell
him. And you aren't about to tell him, are you, Charles?"

Charles felt a cold, painful grip on his netherbits as he shook
his head that no, he would not be telling Lord Wessex anything.
He was powerless against her ladyship's smile and he knew it,
but he hoped for the sake of his unborn children that the Black
Earl would not discover what role he had played in the countess's plan.

"Nick, you are not attending me. What is it you are finding so
fascinating outside the window? Come, my boy, another hour
and we shall take a stroll in the park and look at the flora and
fauna."

251

Nick sighed and, patting Piddle's head, turned back to look at the book in front of him.

"Now as you can see, an equilateral triangle is one in which the length of all sides are equal. I shall draw one here for you, and assign a numerical value to one side. If we know the length of this side, what does it tell us about the lengths of the other two sides?"

Nick frowned at the triangle and muttered an expletive he'd heard his father use. Rogerson dropped the slate and stared.

"Where are you off to then, Crouch?"

" 'Er ladyship's off on one of 'er wild 'ares. She wants me to employ a couple of Runners for 'is nibs's protection."

"Does she really, now?" Deveraux rubbed his chin. "That's most interesting. Does she know about his lordship's newest footmen?" He nodded toward one of the Runners, currently engaged in chatting up one of the under parlor maids.

"No, I didn't tell 'er. I figure if 'is lordship wants 'er to know about them, 'e'll tell 'er."

"You're not actually going to go along with this wild scheme of hers, are you?"

"Aye," Crouch said, slapping a powered wig onto his head, adjusting it so it sat at a rakish, dashing angle. "I'm thinkin' it might not be a bad idea for 'is lordship to 'ave a bit of comp'ny when 'e's out and about."

"But, but—" the round little man sputtered. Crouch gave him a cheeky grin, saluted him with his hook, and sauntered down the back steps toward the mews.

"My lord, if you would allow me to call for my physician : . ."

"No need, Jackson. The swelling will go down in time. I believe your man set the bone correctly."

John "Gentleman" Jackson, that renowned pugilist and famed instructor of the science of boxing to half the men in the *ton*, the man who won the championship when he beat the infamous

Mendoza senseless, watched with worried eyes as the Black Earl tipped his head back to allow his neck cloth to be tied.

"I'd never have suggested you go against young MacDonald, my lord, if I'd thought he would give you a pasting."

Wessex flinched, but Jackson wasn't sure if it was due to the injury or the reference to having been bested in the ring by a much younger, and less skilled, man. "You'd best put something cold on that until the swelling goes down."

Lord Wessex nodded stiffly, muttered something, and left the establishment, Jackson sighed with relief as the earl departed.

"Did you ever think you'd see the day?" his man asked, peering out the window to watch Wessex get into his carriage. Jackson shook his head. He never wanted to see such a day again.

"The Black Earl taken down by a mere pup," the man said in an awestruck tone, loudly sucking his tooth. "What was it he said to you as he was leaving?"

Jackson's lips twitched. "He asked how the hell he was going to explain to his wife that he'd broken his nose."

"Do you think she'll come?"

Lord Carlisle looked at the smaller man standing so arrogantly before him and wondered for the hundredth time what his motive was for involving himself in the affair. He shrugged. "I have no idea. He might be keeping her prisoner in the house. I heard they had a terrible row, and Wessex threatened to send her away."

"If she comes, you know what to do."

"I shall do what I think best," the earl said with a frown. Upstart; who did he think he was to order his betters around?

"Yes, yes, certainly, I don't question that it will be for the best, but if you really wish to keep him from harming her, it might be better to move up our plans."

Carlisle's frown deepened. "That won't be necessary. I told you I was meeting with Wessex in the morning. I'll take care of the murdering whoreson then."

"Yes, there is that. Ah . . . is that the time? Should you not be on your way?"

Carlisle swore. "I don't need you acting the mother hen. I will be there on time."

"You're in a prickly mood today—I was simply trying to be helpful. I wouldn't want you being late. I doubt if the lady will wait for you."

"I'll be there," Carlisle ground out, and deliberately turned his head away from the garish figure. Why was the little man so interested in helping Lady Wessex?

"Good lord, man, what happened to you?"

"Nothing, Harry. What news do you have?"

"Hmmm?" Rosse stared at the swollen appendage that had all the earmarks of a break. "Oh, nothing other than the fact that Mariah is no longer with Sunderland. She's disappeared again, it seems."

Noble rubbed his head wearily, taking care not to touch his nose. "Why do I feel as if I'm running in circles, Harry?"

The marquis smiled. "Might be the result of the beating I suspect you took at Jackson's. Come." He stood up and clapped his old friend on the shoulder. "What you need is a bit of air to clear your head. Come along with me and we'll take a ride through the park while we discuss the problem."

Nick scooted over to the window seat and peered out the window at the mews. Normally the yard would be busy, but it was teatime, and most of the servants were in having their tea. He watched idly as a gray stable cat sat in the dirt lane and washed his tail.

"Nick . . . ah . . . Nick?"

Nick ignored his tutor.

"Come, my lad, just one word. Just a hello? My name? How about a greeting to that hound, there?"

Nick watched the cat finish his bath, stretch, and saunter off past the stable.

"Nick, I know you spoke. I heard you quite plainly. Now, if you could do it once, you can do it again. I'm thinking only of how happy your father will be, my boy."

Nick turned his head and gazed at his tutor with steely silver eyes. Rogerson blinked and rubbed his jaw. "I could have sworn you said . . . maybe I imagined it. Perhaps I just thought I heard you say it."

Nick looked back out into the yard and was surprised to see someone climbing down the water pipe that clung to the corner of the house. A strand of fiery red hair dangled down from the back of the dashing little hat with the long pheasant feather that complemented so charmingly Gillian's green riding habit. Nick jumped up and tugged on his tutor's sleeve, then pointed to the clock.

"Eh? Oh, yes, yes. I did promise you a visit to the park. Capital idea. Just what we both need—a bit of air to clear away the cobwebs. Come along then; let us be on our way."

"I don't understand your sudden desire to go for a stroll in the park, Charlotte, but I'm excessively pleased Mama said I might join you."

" 'Tis a bit of a mystery, is it not, Caroline?"

"A mystery?"

"Yes, a mystery. You know—something mysterious. Something dark, and secret, and fabulously thrilling!"

"And a mystery is a good thing?"

"It is wonderfully good, Caro. Haven't you read any novels with vengeful ghosts, mad men locked in towers, mysterious rooms with secret panels, poisoned wine, ghastly family curses, and frigid, sepulchral hands reaching through the bed curtains in the very dead of night?"

Lady Caroline looked horrified and glanced behind her to where their maids were following. "No, certainly not. Mama would never countenance my reading something so very provocative!"

Charlotte shrugged. "Your loss, Caro."

"But—but this mystery we are going to see in the park—it is nothing that has sepulchral hands?"

"You're a bit of a ninny, aren't you, Caro?"

"A ninny?"

"Never mind. Just come with me. I promise you'll enjoy yourself."

"With the mystery? Or with Hyde Park?"

"Saints preserve me from ninnies!"

Gillian sidled into the stables and looked around carefully. The stableboys and grooms were at tea. Excellent. It took her little time to get Ophelia saddled and slightly longer to convince her to stand still while she climbed up the mounting block, but all in all, she felt she was on schedule when she directed the mare toward Hyde Park. She sincerely hoped she could count on Charlotte's overwhelming curiosity to witness the scene with her and Lord Carlisle. Ladies, she knew, did not go riding without grooms in attendance, and she was more than a bit nervous about meeting the Scottish speeler by herself. Although if what the note Charlotte had included said was true, she would have a few choice things to say to him, things better said in private.

"Here, isn't that Lady Wessex?"

"Wot? Where?"

"There, riding off on that white mare."

"Bloody 'ell, it is! Get Johnson. 'Is bleedin' lordship'll skin us alive if'n we let 'er go out unprotected."

"Lord Carlisle!"

"Ah, Lady Wessex. I wasn't sure you would answer my summons. No footmen? No Crotch? No hounds or cousins or any of the army of attendants you seem never to be without?"

"No, my lord, it is just me today, but I will mention that I am here against my husband's wishes, and so desire you to be as quick as possible with what you have to say."

The earl made a slight bow and offered his arm. "Perhaps we might walk that way, away from the crowds?"

Gillian hesitated, and then took his arm. "Your letter was quite intriguing, my lord. You say you know the truth of what happened the night the late Lady Wessex died, yet your brief narration of the events does not make sense."

"In what way does it not make sense?"

"Quite simply, my lord, my husband was not responsible for the death of his first wife."

Carlisle snorted. "You are judging him by means of your tender woman's heart, my dear. I assure you that were you to take an unbiased view of the events, you would come to a much different conclusion."

"An unbiased view? Such as yours?"

"If you like, yes. My judgment is universally known to be trustworthy and free from any bias."

"Except where Lady Wessex is concerned."

Carlisle glanced at her from the corner of his eye but said nothing. Gillian felt the sparring had gone on long enough. She stopped and faced the earl.

"My lord, just what was your relationship with Lady Wessex?"

Carlisle squinted into the sky to watch two ravens fighting over a bit of food. "She was my friend."

"And lover?"

"And lover." He looked down into her green eyes and saw no censure, only curiosity and a bit of pity. A strand of hair blew over her cheek; he reached out and gently brushed it back. "So beautiful she was, like one of those Nordic ice maidens come to earth."

"You loved her?"

Carlisle put his hand on Gillian's back and gave her a little push. They resumed their walk. "He murdered her, my lady.

He shot her in cold blood. She had begged and pleaded with him for a divorce—it was apparent from the first that they were not suited, that his foul habits would destroy everything good and kind in her. She came to me during a house party and begged for my help, pleaded with me on her knees to save her from the nightly tortures he exacted upon her."

Gillian said nothing. The Noble Carlisle was describing wasn't her Noble; she felt that for certain.

"I was there that night, you know. I came in answer to a desperate summons from Elizabeth—she had overheard Wessex plotting to take her life that night, and she begged me to save her from him."

Gillian shook her head. "Not Noble."

"Noble, my lady. I saw him with my own eyes, swooned with blood lust, lying in a pool of his wife's blood, the pistol that killed her still clutched in his hand."

Gillian shook away the terrible picture Carlisle so vividly painted. "Not . . . Noble?" she whispered. "Perhaps . . . perhaps he just happened upon the scene and was struck down by . . . or perhaps he was defending her and accidentally . . . my lord, Noble would never hurt someone weaker than he, never!"

"I can assure you that I speak the truth, Lady Wessex. I saw the marks, you see. I saw the marks that fiend had left upon her body—bruises from beatings, stripes on her back where he had taken a lash to her, and . . . and worse. I won't be specific about the other things he did to my fair Elizabeth, other than to say that they were the most unnatural of sexual practices." The earl's face darkened as he was again swept up by the remorse and helplessness he had felt that night. "If I had been a peer then, I might have had a chance to bring him to justice, but as it was, I could do nothing. Your husband escaped unpunished for that heinous crime."

Gillian looked at two children running along the graveled footpath, a small terrier at their heels, barking excitedly as he chased the pair. They were so young, so innocent, so new and untouched and clean. Was she just as young and innocent as they were? Had she allowed her feelings for Noble to override her common sense? Was she being blind, not seeing him for what he really was?

Random images of him came to mind: Noble grinning at her the night he was shot, Noble ruffling Nick's hair as the two walked together toward the garden at Nethercote, the exasperated patience in the wry twist to his lips when he saw her blue hands, the love shining out of his beautiful silver eyes when they joined together as one.

"No." She turned back to Carlisle. "No, my lord, you are wrong."

"I *saw* him with the pistol! I had seen the marks—"

"Then they are from another, not Noble. If he had a pistol in his hand, there must be an explanation for it. An explanation other than the one you offer."

Carlisle shook his head. "You are allowing affection to blind you to the truth, my dear. Your husband is a consummate liar, a concealer of secrets of the most heinous sort, a vicious, cruel man who will think nothing of destroying you as he destroyed my Elizabeth. You are in danger, Lady Wessex, grave danger, and I wish to help you before it is too late." He took her hand and squeezed it. "I could not . . . I could not help Elizabeth, but I will not fail you."

"Secrets and lies," Gillian said softly.

"I beg your pardon?"

"Secrets and lies. That's what Palm . . . a gentleman told me." She looked up into the earl's face. "Secrets begetting lies. But what is the secret that started the lies?"

The earl held her gaze. "The only way to find the answer to that, my lady, is to ask your husband, and that is not an action I would recommend, for surely it will mean the end for you just as it meant the end for my dear Elizabeth."

Gillian stared wordlessly at him, unable to resolve the image of Noble lying in his wife's blood, the instrument of her death clutched in his hand, with what she knew of him. Which was the true Noble? Which were the lies? How was she to determine the truth?

"Gillian! Lord Carlisle! What a surprise! How delightful to meet you . . . in this wholly unexpected . . . and unforeseen manner," Charlotte panted as she galloped up to the pair. "Oh, my, it's quite warm out today, is it not? Lord Carlisle, may I make you known to Lady Caroline Ambermere? Caroline? Well, that's her back there. She's a slow walker."

Gillian rolled her eyes. There were times when Charlotte's manners fell far short of her own, rusticated and colonial though they were. She handed her cousin her handkerchief. Charlotte took it with a shy and demure smile at the earl, then turned to look back at Lady Caroline and deftly applied the cloth to her glowing face.

"We were just about to walk to the Serpentine, Lady Charlotte. I assume since you and Lady Caroline just came from that direction that you are headed elsewhere, so if you will excuse us . . ."

"Not at all," Charlotte said gaily, and grabbed her cousin's arm. "We love the Serpentine. Do let us walk there now."

Gillian gave the earl a rueful smile but was secretly relieved by Charlotte's appearance.

"Now, what were you discussing? The weather? The latest gossip? Whether Lord Wessex killed his wife?"

"Charlotte!"

Charlotte gave her cousin a sidelong look. "There's no use my pretending not to know anything about it, Gillian, Lord Carlisle did send me that note . . ."

"Which was addressed to me and only meant to be forwarded by you, not read."

"No! I must have neglected to notice that," Charlotte said, smiling shamelessly at the earl. He raised his eyes to heaven and, with a sigh, turned toward the Serpentine.

"Impudent as my cousin is, she does have a point, my lord,"

Gillian said as they walked toward the slip of water. "She is in my confidence, and you can speak freely before her."

"Absolutely," Charlotte said. "You may speak with perfect impunity and trust my discretion and naturally shy and unassuming nature."

"Too brown," Gillian whispered to her cousin.

"Do you think so?" Charlotte whispered back. "I thought it was just right. See, Lord Carlisle looks as if he's about to laugh."

The earl did laugh then, a bit ruefully, but still it was a laugh. "I have said my piece, Lady Charlotte. It is now up to your cousin to come to her senses and take the advice I so earnestly offer."

Gillian shook her head. "I'm afraid this discussion is at a standstill, my lord, so I will turn to another subject that I hold to be very important."

"The duel!" Charlotte said with satisfaction, and waved her hand toward the approaching figure of Lady Caroline and the two maids. "Caro, turn around, we're heading back that way."

"We are? But we just came from there."

"Never mind. Lord Carlisle here is going to tell us about the duel he's going to fight on the morrow with Lady Wessex's husband."

"Charlotte!"

"Oh, pooh, everyone knows about it by now." Charlotte made quick introductions. "Lord Carlisle was Lady Wessex's lover, and now he's to fight Lord Wessex because he had his hand on Gillian's arm."

"Charlotte, cease speaking this instant or we shall leave you!"

Charlotte looked hurt by the demand. "I'm simply trying to keep Caro abreast so she might appreciate the gravity of the moment when Lord Carlisle tells us his plans for murdering his rival."

Gillian spun around and grabbed her cousin by the wrist, her fingernails biting into her flesh. A bit of Charlotte's color drained out of her face when she saw Gillian's countenance. "If you ever again say anything so foul, I will never speak to you again."

"But—"

"Never."

"You are—"

"Not ever!"

Charlotte had never seen her cousin's eyes light up in such a manner before, and she decided it would be wise to humor her. After all, Gillian was in love with Lord Wessex despite the fact that he had probably murdered his first wife.

"I apologize, Gillian. That was unkind of me."

Gillian released her wrist and started walking again toward the water. A shout to the right brought her up short. "Oh, Nick, Mr. Rogerson. Are you out for a walk? How pleasant. That's a lovely flower, Nick, thank you. I just hope the groundskeepers did not see you pick it."

Gillian felt her heart constrict under the influence of her son's sunny smile. How on earth could Noble consider tearing such a wonderful boy from her? She put an arm around him, telling Rogerson they were going to the Serpentine to watch the ducks.

"I see you have your army with you after all," Lord Carlisle said softly. "As you are in such good hands, I will take my leave."

"Oh, Lord Carlisle—about the *event* . . . I know it will be unpleasant for you, but I would ask that you make your apologies to Noble and halt the plans for the morning. I'm sure you see no reason to ask his forgiveness—" she held up a hand before he could interrupt—"and in truth, the fault for the situation lies with me, so it is true you are not to blame, but you must excuse Noble for being a bit overprotective."

"Lady Wessex, I must beg you to discontinue your pleas. Alas, they are falling on deaf ears. This will not be the first time I've faced your husband over pistols, but I do fully intend that it will be the last."

Gillian's eyes turned frosty. She leveled an icy green gaze at him, and in tones that left him in no doubt as to her feelings, snapped out, "I see. You leave me no choice, then, Lord Carlisle. The consequences will be on your head."

He bowed and, with a polite farewell, took his leave.

"Er . . . Lady Wessex, perhaps I should take Master Nicholas home."

"No, it's quite all right, Rogerson. I believe the worst is over."

"I wouldn't be so sure of that," Charlotte said, looking over Gillian's shoulder.

"Why do you say that, Char?"

"Because Lord Wessex is headed this way, and he doesn't look pleased."

Gillian spun around. It was true, her Lord of Fire was walking toward them in a manner that made her knees quake. She looked beyond him to where Lord Rosse was handing over the reins of his horse to a groom and preparing to leap over the small metal fence that lined the edge of Rotten Row.

"Well, hell," she muttered.

Lady Caroline gasped. Charlotte looked worried and picked fretfully at Gillian's handkerchief. Rogerson blanched at the sight of the earl's face and prepared to spirit his charge away to safety. Gillian sighed and resigned herself to be yelled at yet again.

This time, she knew, she had no excuse to offer.

Chapter Twelve

Lord and Lady Wessex were given the sobriquet of the Battling Brittons that night by Lord Rosse. Gillian truly didn't know how he came to crown them with that title, since it was impossible to battle someone with whom you weren't speaking, and seeing as how Noble was positively icy to her, not saying a single, solitary word after he had escorted her home from the park, nor later while she was preparing for Lady Cowper's soiree, she felt Lord Rosse had taken liberties with the nickname.

Sitting next to the marquis, Gillian was particularly aware of her husband's eyes glittering dangerously whenever she caught his gaze as they rode to that evening's entertainment. After the chill that swept her the first few times she encountered his eyes, she did her best to avoid them altogether, turning her attention to the man next to her.

"Lord Rosse," she addressed him with a smile that was somewhat frayed around the edges, "as Noble is not speaking to me, perhaps you will tell me how he came by a broken nose."

Rosse shot his friend a pleading look. Noble ignored both it and his wife and glared out the window of the carriage as it rolled through the night.

"I believe, madam, that he acquired it at Jackson's rooms."

"Ah. Thank you, my lord."

"Not at all, my lady."

"Harry?"

"Yes?"

"Since my wife is behaving in a childish manner by making a point of not speaking to *me,* would you ask her just what the blazes she thought she was doing by ignoring my wishes and not only leaving the house but meeting with the very man I specifically forbade her to meet?"

"Ah . . ."

"Lord Rosse," Gillian said with an injured sniff and a frown across at Noble, "you might, since you are being so obliging as to act in a mature and intelligent manner, unlike some people I could mention, notably the irrational, emotional, and unjust man I married, would you be so kind as to tell him that I did not agree to abide by his dictates since they were silly, unreasonable, and unfair?"

"Silly? Unreasonable? Unfair?" Noble folded his arms across his chest and glared at her.

"Silly, unreasonable, and unfair. Noble you know full well that keeping me a prisoner in the house, forbidding me to see friends and family, and, worst of all, denying me my son, is simply intolerable. I will not stand for it!"

"Harry, please tell my wife that she will stand for whatever I tell her she will stand for."

"Um . . . no, I don't think I will tell her that, Noble."

Noble added Harry to his list of people to be glared at.

"See," Gillian said, tapping Rosse on his arm with her fan. "Irrational and emotional."

"I'm nothing of the sort," Noble snapped.

"You are, husband, just look at you! You're sitting there scowling and growling at us, and over what? A simple stroll in the park with my cousin, son, and others."

"You left the house by yourself, madam, without a footman

or groom in attendance, and," he said hurriedly, before Gillian could protest his statement, "you walked for some time alone with that murdering bastard."

"If you had three Bow Street Runners following me, then I was not alone," she said triumphantly, pleased with her logic. "So my going out to meet with Lord Carlisle was perfectly respectable."

"That's beside the point. You didn't know the Runners were in attendance . . ."

"Yes, and I'd like to discuss that with you . . ."

Noble waved her objection away. "The point is, you deliberately disobeyed my commands."

"Noble."

He glared at her gentle smile. "What?"

"You're speaking to me."

He swore under his breath. "Gillian, you will not distract me by smiling at me in that manner. The issue at hand is one of obedience. Without any concern for your health or safety, you left the sanctuary of our home to meet with that—"

"—murdering bastard, yes, Noble, we all know who he is." Gillian took a deep breath and reached out a hand toward him. He frowned at it.

"Oh, for heaven's sake . . ." Gillian moved across to sit next to her husband and, by wriggling her fingers, managed to work her hand under her husband's crossed arms. "Noble, I was perfectly safe. I knew Charlotte would be there, and I was in a public place."

She reached up with her free hand and ran her finger around the cleft in his chin. "Can you not see your way clear to forgiving my transgressions, and I shall forgive yours?"

He reached up to grab her fingers, his scowl growing blacker. "My transgressions? You will forgive me *my* transgressions?"

"Yes"—she pulled her hand out of his and placed it on his chest—"I am quite willing to forgive if you are."

Her hand slid up his chest and curled around the back of his neck, sliding into his hair. God's eyebrows but his hair was sinfully soft. It was like silk slipping through her fingers. She closed her fist around it and tugged his head toward hers, tilting her head back and offering up her mouth.

Noble tried to remember why he was so angry and why he had decided that a policy of indifference seemed like such a good idea, but the sight of her parted lips drove all other thoughts from his mind but the desire to sip her sweet nectar. He wrapped an arm around her and pulled her up against his chest as his mouth claimed hers, his tongue dipping in to revel in her taste. He stroked the roof of her mouth and saw stars when she suckled his tongue.

"I shouldn't be seeing this, no I shouldn't, so I'll just look out the window at the passing scenery. Or I would if I could see anything, but since it's nearly ten o'clock and black as sin out there, I can't see anything. However, since I'm sure if I were to look back at you, I would see . . . oh, yes, that's just what I thought I'd see, and I shouldn't be seeing that either, so I'll just keep my eyes looking elsewhere until you're both finished. I hope you finish soon," Rosse said wistfully. "It gets a bit tedious staring out into the dark when two people who are close enough to you to touch are engaged in an activity better suited to a private location."

"Harry."

"Yes, Noble?"

"Get shankered."

"Crouch?" Several hours later, Gillian peered out from her sitting room and waved the pirate in. "Crouch, where have you been?"

"Sorry, m'lady, the Tremaynes was at it again, and I 'ad to get my wager on Tremayne Three."

Gillian listened for a moment. No sounds of a battle reached her ears, so the fight must be going on in the servants' quarters. She knew she should intervene, but she hated to do so. The

Tremaynes all pouted so when she insisted they behave. "Three? Is he so much better than his brothers?"

Crouch grinned. "Nay, m'lady, worse, but I likes an under-strapper, I do."

"Well, I am glad you managed to tear yourself away from the excitement, but we have an important task ahead of us, and you know you are vital to my plans. Should you not be leaving to meet Lord Carlisle?"

"Aye, m'lady, I'm just about to do that." He yawned.

Gillian yawned back at him. "Don't do that," she snapped as soon as she could. "We both have work to do. Do you have the laudanum?"

He handed her a small brown bottle. "Ye know 'ow much to use?"

"Yes, just a few drops ought to do it. Do you have the Runners with you? All of them?"

"All five, m'lady. Yer two and 'is lordship's three, and we've all got barkin' irons with us."

"Barking . . . irons?"

"Aye, just as ye ordered."

Gillian tried to remember if she had asked specifically that the men be equipped with iron dogs that barked. She didn't think she had.

"Oh, pistols you mean."

"Aye." Crouch nodded, his gold earring swinging. "Snappers, just as ye've asked."

"Snappers, yes, excellent. You have the key to Noble's house in Kensington?"

He patted his waistcoat pocket with his hook. "Aye, m'lady, all's taken care of there, but I'm worryin' what I'll do if the murderin' bastard doesn't show up."

Gillian's smile brightened up the dark room. "He'll show up. He's been wanting to save me . . . well, now he'll have his chance."

"It's a right devilish mind ye've got yerself there, mistress."

Crouch saluted her with his hook. "I'm thinkin' 'is lordship, once 'e gets over being drugged, will thank ye."

"I wish you were right," Gillian said, her smile fading. "But I fear he's simply going to be too angry to see much reason for a while. Oh, well, there's just no helping it. If those two men intend on acting like stubborn little children and refuse to be reasonable, we'll just treat them as children and do what's best for them."

The rumble of masculine voices made its way up the stairs.

"Must be Lord Rosse leavin' 'is lordship," Crouch said as Gillian pushed him toward the back stairs.

"Then go, and Godspeed, Crouch."

"And to you, m'lady."

The two conspirators grinned at one another, then separated—Crouch down the backstairs, and Gillian skimming up the staircase to her bedchamber. She hugged the bottle tightly to her chest, planning just exactly how she would slip the liquid into a bit of brandy. Crouch had warned her about putting too much in brandy, since the liquor would accelerate the effects of the drug, so she had to make certain Noble didn't drink too much . . . just enough to guarantee he'd sleep through the dawn.

"That should take care of the Lord of Pigheadedness," she muttered a few minutes later as she entered her room and looked around for a spot in which to hide the bottle. As she walked toward the wardrobe, a sudden movement out of the corner of her eye had her gasping and stumbling backward in surprise. A small, thin figure unfolded itself from the corner and stood hesitant in the candlelight.

"Nick? Is that you? Is something wrong?" Gillian started toward the slight figure but rocked backward when he threw himself against her.

"Oh, Nick, my darling, did you have a nightmare?" Gillian wrapped her arms around the boy and swayed gently with him while he heaved huge sobs into her chest. She murmured soothing words and brushed the dark locks back from his forehead until the weaping lessened in intensity. "It's all right, my love. I'm right here, and nothing can hurt you now."

"But . . . if Papa sends you away . . ."

Gillian stared down into the tearstained face and blinked in surprise. Nick was talking? Now? Why? His thin little body shook against her as she held him. First things first, she told herself, and with an arm around the lad, sat down with him on her bed. "Your papa's not going to send me away, Nick. You're worrying about nothing. Now tell me." She handed him a handkerchief. "Did you have a nightmare?"

He nodded and blew his nose, then tried to hand the handkerchief back. "Er . . . no, you keep it," she said as she smoothed a hand over his hair. "Do you want to tell me about the dream? Sometimes it helps make it seem less frightening if you can talk about it."

He thought about that for a minute, then gave a minute shrug. "It was about that night."

"What night?"

"The night my mother died. My other mother."

Oh, lord. Had Nick been present when Elizabeth was killed? Gillian tried to remember what Noble had told her about the trauma that had sent Nick into self-imposed silence. He had said it had its roots in Elizabeth's death, and she had assumed he was traumatized because his beloved stepmother had been taken away from him.

"You can tell me if you'd like, Nick," she said, still stroking his head. He leaned into her and spoke in a soft, monotonous voice so devoid of emotion that it made her skin crawl. What he described made her sick. And furious.

"I was there again, in that room, her room, and she was there with him, and he was making me watch as he whipped her."

Gillian felt the blood drain from her face. Dear God, had she been wrong all along about Noble? Was the damning truth to come from the mouth of his own child?

"She screamed and screamed and wouldn't stop, and neither would the bleeding, and I thought I was going to be sick on the carpet when he started cutting her with a knife. I put my hands over my eyes, but I could still hear her screaming and begging him to stop, but he wouldn't."

Gillian clutched his head to her bosom and rocked him, squeezing her eyes closed over her tears. What sort of a monster was Noble? How could he commit such obscene acts, and in front of a child?

"She stopped screaming, so I thought it was all right to look, I thought he was done, but he wasn't, he had just tied something across her mouth, and tied her arms to the bed. Then he looked at me, and he laughed and laughed and told me to take off my clothes, that he wanted to leave Papa something to remember him by."

Gillian thought she was going to be sick for a moment, but then Nick's words struck her. "Papa? Nick, who was the man who was doing . . . who was doing those bad things?"

Nick shook his head. "I don't know his name, I just know him. He hurt her."

Gillian laid her head on his, relief swelling over the fact that Noble was innocent of such heinous crimes. She tightened her arms around the boy. "Was that the end of the dream?"

He shook his head again. "The man made me take off my clothes, and then he started laughing again, and I . . ." He tried to burrow his head into Gillian. She rubbed his back, overwhelmed by the waves of agonizing torment rolling off him. How could a child survive such a hellish scene?

"You don't have to tell me if you don't wish to, Nick."

"I wet myself," he said in a small voice. "Just like a baby, but I couldn't help it. The man stood over me with the whip and he laughed harder and said how just it was that Papa's son should be such a weakling."

"You're not weakling, Nick. The man was wrong, and you have nothing to be ashamed of."

"Papa saw," he whispered into her neck. "Papa came in and saw me. He saw me crying and he saw that I'd wet myself."

Gillian's mind chased around in circles. Noble was there? He saw what happened? How could this be? Why hadn't he killed this horrible monster who tormented Nick and Elizabeth?

"What did Papa do?"

"He fell down when the man hit him on the head with one of his pistols." Nick detached himself long enough to stare at Gillian with eyes filled with so much pain she wanted to weep. No child's eyes should look like that. "I tried to help Papa, but the man picked me up and threw me on top of her, and I was so scared I couldn't move. I couldn't move! I tried to help Papa, but I couldn't move!"

"Shhhh," she calmed him, holding him close again and stroking his back. "It's all right, my love, you aren't to blame for what that man did. No one blames you. Your father knows you tried to help him. He doesn't blame you."

Nick went suddenly stiff in her arms. "I couldn't move, and then the man shot her and there was blood everywhere and . . . I think I wet myself again."

"Oh, God," Gillian moaned, unable to keep the tears hidden now. She rocked the frail body of her son in her arms and wept for him, wept for the hell he had lived through, and wept for Elizabeth, who didn't deserve to die.

"The man was going to shoot Papa," Nick whispered so softly Gillian almost didn't hear it. "He was going to shoot him. Papa wasn't moving, he couldn't move, and she was dead and I didn't know what to do so I threw the candlestick at him, and he didn't shoot Papa because he shot the wall instead."

Gillian had a horribly vivid image of what happened that night. "Did the man leave then?"

Nick nodded, and his body sagged against hers. "He left, but she was dead, and I thought Papa might be dead until he started groaning. The man told me not to tell anyone or he'd come back and kill Papa. He told me it would be my fault if Papa died. I don't want Papa to die."

Gillian held him, rocking him and murmuring soft, comforting words in his ear until he fell asleep against her. She held him even after he slept, weeping silent tears for all that her brave little son had been through.

"I promise you, Nick," she whispered to him. "I promise you that your Papa will punish that man. He won't hurt you again."

Noble signed his name to the document, blotted it, and handed the thick sheet of paper to his secretary. "You'll be sure to destroy my prior will?"

"Of course, my lord. May I say, my lord, that I and all the staff hope that you will not need this document in the near future?"

"Thank you, Deveraux, I also trust it will not be needed for a long time." He and his man of affairs watched as Tremayne witnessed the document. Then Noble glanced at the clock and stretched as he stood. "I believe I will retire for a few hours before I am due to leave."

"Good night, my lord."

"Good night." Noble took the stairs two at a time. He was looking forward to spending the time before he had to leave covering as many items remaining on the list he had created for Gillian as was humanly possible. He was even looking forward to apologizing to her for trying to remove Nick from her care. Apologies did not come easy to him, but he had been wrong. The threat of taking Nick away had hurt his wife deeply.

He paused a moment as the thought snaked through him that he could die at dawn, leaving behind Gillian and Nick. Although he had every confidence in his ability with a pistol, only a fool did not feel fear when facing danger.

"If it's to be, then so be it," he muttered to himself as he stalked down the hallway toward his dressing room. That and other grim thoughts raced around in his mind while Tremayne removed his evening clothes. Gillian's words from earlier in the evening haunted him.

"This duel is simply ridiculous! It is not about a slight done to me or to you," she had said, her face flushed with anger. Noble thought her eyes were about to spit flames. "This is about your male arrogance; and Lord Carlisle's arrogance. Neither one of you wants to admit it was a simple misunderstanding, that no insult was done to either of you, except the ones you hurled at each other so publicly in the street. Is your stupid male pride worth dying for, Noble? Is it? Do Nick and I matter so little to you that you would throw away your life on something so trivial?"

He had defended his actions with the standard response about honor, but now, as he thought of what her life would be like without him, of how Nick would grow up without a father, he admitted there was some validity to her opinion.

It *was* ridiculous. It *was* about arrogance—his arrogance and pride and nothing more. Gillian had not betrayed him with Lord Carlisle, nor, from all accounts, had Carlisle behaved in an improper manner toward her. The fault for the entire situation lay squarely upon his shoulders.

He thought about this as he splashed water on his face and chest. What was to keep him from sending an apology to Carlisle and backing away from the challenge? It could be done; it was done all the time. He would have to take a little ribbing about the situation, but that would soon die down, and the promise of endless nights lying in his wife's arms would make even the worst ragging bearable.

Ah, those nights, he thought to himself. He wanted those nights, all of those nights with her, all of her forever. That simple realization made him breathe easier. Nodding to himself, he sat at a small writing table and wrote a note to Carlisle apologizing for his comments and accusations, then enclosed it in another to Harry, his second, with instructions to see that Carlisle received it immediately. He sent Tremayne out to rouse a footman to deliver the letter; then, satisfied that he had solved the problem in a manner that would greatly please his wife, he headed for his bedchamber to please her in other, more tangible, ways.

Gillian was waiting for him. After tucking Nick into her bed, she had disrobed, bathed her eyes, and hurried through the connecting door to have Noble's snifter of brandy ready when he arrived. Tremayne's voice filtered through from the attached dressing room, alerting her to Noble's presence. She tucked her feet under her as she sat before the fire, warming the brandy. First she would get him to drink the brandy, then she would tell him about Nick.

Noble threw open the door to his bedchamber and paused dramatically, one hand on the door, the other on his heart.

"Wife!" he said in a deep voice that rumbled around Gillian in a manner that made her knees turn to water. The look in his eyes made her own widen—God's drawers, how was she to get the brandy in him when he was wearing *that* look? How was she even to hand him the glass when his very glance made her tremble with anticipation?

"Noble!" she squeaked and, taking the glass in both hands, held it out to him.

"Gillian!" he answered and, raking those parts of her visible with a look that left no doubt in her mind as to his intent, he stalked toward her. Slowly. As he smiled. Gillian's hands twitched, sloshing the brandy around inside the rounded balloon of the glass.

"Brandy?" she gasped. He didn't even look at the glass as he plucked it from her hands and set it down on a nearby table, then turned and plucked her off the ground just as easily. Gillian blinked to find herself suddenly seated on her husband's lap, the soft satin of his dressing gown sliding sinuously beneath her fingers.

Noble cupped her head between his hands and gazed into her eyes. "I am about to make you very happy, wife."

Gillian squirmed against the protrusion poking her in the thigh. "Yes, I can feel that you are, you always do, Noble, but you know, I really think before you make me very happy, you ought to have a sip of brandy. It's been a long and strenuous day, and now that you're talking to me again, you probably need a little something to help you relax and calm your heated . . . uh . . . brain."

She held out the brandy to him again. He took the glass and leaned down to kiss her. Gillian heard the clink of the glass striking the table just before his tongue slipped in between her lips.

"Ah, yes, my darling, moan for me," he said against her lips. "I love it when you moan, Gillian. Your moans make my toes curl. Moan again."

Gillian opened her eyes and looked up at her Lord of Curled Toes. "Brandy."

He handed her the glass. "No, you must drink it," she said quickly and pushed it at him.

"I don't care for any; you have it," he said, taking the glass and putting it to her lips.

"No!" she squealed, and clamped her lips tight until he removed it. God's garters, he was making it difficult to get a simple little draught inside him.

"A simple little draught of what?" he asked, his eyelids low over his eyes as he bathed her in a look so seductive, she felt her skin tingle with excitement. His hands started those marvelous, familiar little fires all over her person, turning the skin tingles into a raging inferno. She looked down. How had he managed to take off her dressing gown without her knowing it?

"I'll tell you if you tell me what the draught is," he said, and began nibbling on her nape. "Is it something good for me? Something to improve my stamina? Something to bring the wellspring of vigor and manliness bubbling forth? Is it"—he traced the outside of her ear while she moaned softly—"something that will allow me to pleasure you all night long without a break?"

"Oh, yes," Gillian said, her mind refusing to consider anything but that one attractive thought. Noble's face hovered before her, his breath mingling with her breath, his lips so close she could feel the heat from his mouth.

"Then I shall take it, my lovely wife. And then I shall introduce you to yet another item on my list, and once you've shouted my name out to the heavens at least four times, then I shall tell you my secret."

Secrets. His name, making her shout it. *Four times!*

Noble tossed back the brandy with one quick movement, then scooped Gillian up and carried her to bed.

"And now, my little kumquat, I shall kiss you silly, then proceed to item number eight on the list."

"Item number eight?" she gasped as his lips nibbled a path beneath her breasts. "Number eight? Didn't that involve two lemon wedges and a pot of strawberry jam?"

"What a good memory you have," he said as his mouth made ever-narrowing circles around her breasts. Gillian felt her nipples harden to pebbles as his breath steamed over them.

"You would think," he said, his tongue snaking out to quickly lick a pert little nipple, "that if I were to breathe warm air on this little morsel, it would lose its wrinkles."

He breathed hot, steamy air over her wet nipple. Gillian's back arched as her hands kneaded the muscles in his shoulders.

"But I find that the opposite is true. How very curious."

"Yes, how very curious indeed, my lord." Gillian gave up trying to talk, or breathe for that matter. She just existed, one big, quivering mound of flesh whose sole purpose in life was to give pleasure to Noble. As he was exploring the strange phenomenon of nipple physics with her other breast, Gillian gathered her wits long enough to let her fingers roam over the muscled bulges of his shoulders and back, down over the silky skin on his behind, and lower, to that part of him he enjoyed having squeezed ever so lightly. She squeezed. He moaned against her breast. She squeezed again. He reared up, his eyes flashing silver, and with one hand spread her legs and entered her with a deep thrust.

She shouted his name.

"That's once," he groaned, and withdrew himself almost completely. Her hands were tangled in his hair, pulling his face toward hers, licking and nipping at his chin until he gave her what she wanted. Her tongue was wild in his mouth, twisting and twining around his, dancing an erotic tongue waltz, stroking and cajoling his tongue into joining with it in a celebration of tonguely love. He slid a hand down her sleek belly, spreading his fingers wide as they combed through her fiery curls, then seeking lower, parting, probing the hot, wet inner parts of her. Gillian writhed against his fingers and, tearing her mouth from his, shouted his name again.

"That's twice," he said hoarsely and, hooking her knees with his arms, pushed forward against her, reveling in the feeling of her silken sheath tightening and spasming against his hard length. He stared into her emerald eyes, made soft and misty with passion as he withdrew slowly, then surged back into her with short, powerful thrusts.

Her nails bit hard into his shoulders and raked long lines down his back. He felt the sting of sweat on the scratches, driving him on harder and faster. A fog started to settle over his eyes, a fog of lust. He shook the fog away and focused his eyes on Gillian's green, endlessly deep pools of emerald. She cried his name again.

"Three times," he grunted as the fog thickened. He was panting now, panting in time to the rhythm their bodies had set, groaning with each plunge deep into Gillian's body, gasping for air with each withdrawal. The world ceased to exist beyond the confines of their bodies. There was just Noble and Gillian and nothing else. He stretched and reached for the moment when even the two of them would no longer exist, replaced instead by the glorious being made up of their souls merged together.

The fog seeped into his mind, slowing and focusing his brain until there was just one thought that filled him.

He looked through blurred eyes at the woman writhing beneath him, twisting and turning, matching her thrusts to his, her green eyes blazing almost as bright as the fiery hair spread out above her.

"I . . ." He thrust his entire length into her, and then pulled back slightly.

". . . love . . ." Her hips lunged upward to meet his. He blinked, but the fog was too thick. He couldn't see her fire anymore.

". . . you . . ." His back arched as he lifted her up to him, plunging deeper than he'd ever been before. He heard her sob out his name just before he cried out hers, a light bursting from behind his eyes, blinding him to everything but the beauty and wonder and love that was his Gillian.

"Four," he sighed, collapsing on her as he slowly sank into a black pool of oblivion.

Chapter Thirteen

"M'lady? Pssst. M'lady, are ye awake?"

Gillian gently pushed Noble's arm aside and peered over his biceps. "Crouch? Is that you, Crouch?"

"Aye, m'lady, yer needed."

Gillian brushed her hair from her eyes, stole a quick glance at Noble to make sure he was still sleeping, sent another glance downward to verify that she was covered as decently as possible, discovered that the bed linens must have been kicked off sometime during the night, and blushed when she realized the only thing covering her womanly parts was her husband.

"Crouch, this really is the outside of enough! I don't believe it's proper for a butler, even a pirate butler, to come marching into one's bedchamber."

"I'ave m'eyes covered, m'lady."

"I can see that, Crouch, but I can also see that you are peeking, and if you think I won't tell Lord Wessex that, you are sadly mistaken."

Crouch's fingers slammed into tight formation. " 'Tis those bits o' 'is lordship's muslins. They're back and they won't leave."

"The mistresses? His mistresses, or rather ex-mistresses, since they are no longer in his employ, and even if they were, he wouldn't employ all of them at the same time, although if last night was anything to go by . . ." She gazed at her sleeping husband's face thoughtfully. ". . . but no, my mind is wandering. Crouch, please tell the ladies I will be down shortly."

"Aye, m'lady."

"Oh, Crouch?"

The butler tipped his head in question.

"You didn't really see anything you shouldn't have, did you?"

"No, m'lady, just 'is lordship's arse, and the sight o' that's nothin' that fills me with joy."

"Oh, I don't know," Gillian said, reaching a fond hand over and stroking Noble's lovely behind. "The sight of it fills me with joy. I think it's quite a nice behind, as behinds go."

"Mmmm?" Noble murmured, and tightened his arm around Gillian.

"Nothing, my love," Gillian cooed into his ear. "Crouch and I were just discussing your arse."

"Aye, m'lord. 'Er ladyship is of the opinion it's a sight to bring joy to the eye, but I've been debatin' the point with 'er." He eyed Noble with pursed lips, scratching at his chin with the sharp point of his hook. "Not that it ain't attractive on its own, I reckon. If you like that sort of thing."

"Crouch?" Noble breathed sleepily.

"Which I do, Crouch, and I'll thank you to keep your disparaging comments to yourself and be about your business. I will tend to his lordship's behind. And stop that peeking."

Crouch grinned and, feeling the way toward the door with his hook, made his exit.

Gillian slid out from under the arm and leg Noble had tossed over her and stood for a moment, admiring his derriere. It was a very nice one. She put out a hand and pressed gently.

"I don't know what Crouch is nattering on about. It's very fit. I bet I could bounce a shilling off it if I were so inclined."

With that happy thought she went to prepare to greet the mistresses.

Noble rolled onto his back and stretched carefully. His head felt like someone had been pounding on it with an anvil while his mouth tasted worse than something extremely nasty that he didn't want to go to the trouble to think of lest it make his headache worse and his tongue feel even thicker.

He rolled out of bed and, pulling the bell cord, staggered into his dressing room to attend to his morning ablutions.

It was while he was sitting in the armchair as Tremayne was shaving him that a faint thought wended its way through the fogged labyrinth of his mind and suddenly stood up and caught his attention.

"My arse?" he roared, startling Tremayne into dumping the basin of warm water down the earl's front.

"She had Crouch in admiring my arse?"

"I really couldn't say, m'lord. I wasn't present. Would you like me to consult Crouch about this grave question?"

"Don't be smart, Tremayne," Noble snapped, and allowed his shirt to be removed, the water mopped up, and a fresh garment reapplied.

"My arse," he said later as he strode down the hallway and leaped down the stairs. Midway to the breakfast room he passed his son.

"Good morning, Papa," Nick said.

"Morning, Nick. My arse!" Noble fumed, and stormed into the breakfast room. He would have a thing or two to say to his wife about conducting tours of his person when he was asleep. "Wife, I have a few—oh, hell. Where is she . . . uh . . . which one are you?"

"Forsythe, m'lord. I'm one of the Runners her ladyship hired."

"Oh, yes, well, have you seen Lady Wessex this morning?"

The slight little man in livery too large for him shook his head and endeavored to look like a footman. "I haven't seen her, no, my lord, although I did hear Mr. Crouch say something about a group of lightskirts calling for her."

The pounding in his head increased. She wouldn't dare. Not after he had made his feelings clear on the subject and given her a direct order. No, he shook his aching head; it must be some other group of lightskirts she was entertaining. Perhaps she had plans of reforming the entire demimonde. He wouldn't put it past her to try.

He took the stairs two at a time as he headed toward her sitting room.

Nick was still standing where he had passed him earlier. "Papa, could I talk to you?"

"Later, son. I have to go throttle your mother." Just see if he wouldn't. How dare she bring those women back to his house, exposing himself to ridicule and his son to . . . Noble paused a moment, then shook his head again. He must have imagined it.

He threw open the door of her sitting room, glared at the assembled women therein, and opened his mouth to deliver a scathing lecture that he would make sure Gillian never forgot. She turned to look at him, and the acrimonious words shriveled and died on his lips.

"What is it?" he asked instead, going down on one knee and taking her hand in his. It was cold.

Gillian squeezed his hand and tried to look a little less like the scared rabbit she knew she resembled. "Noble, Mariah is dead."

"Mariah?"

"Mistress Mariah. Your mistress, that is. Ex-mistress. The ladies here came to tell me that her body was found this morning, bobbing up against a pier. She had been . . ." Gillian looked as if she would be sick. Noble pulled her into a protective embrace.

"She'd been tortured, my lord, and then garroted," Anne said with a solemn face.

Gillian shivered in his arms.

*   *   *

Noble rallied his troops, explaining briefly to the staff that the danger to Gillian and possibly Nick had increased, and until further notice they were to maintain the utmost caution.

"No visitors, unless known to Lady Wessex or myself, are to be allowed in," he ordered as he paced before the line of servants. "No tradespeople will be allowed in the house for any reason. Likewise, servants from other houses, your personal friends and acquaintances, will be banned. Until we have the bastard responsible for the threats against Lady Wessex locked away in gaol, your sole responsibility will be to see to her safety, and that of my son. Are there any questions?"

The line of footmen, butlers, and other male staff members shook their heads. Crouch raised his hook.

"Yes?"

"Eh, m'lord, what should we do if 'er ladyship is desirin' to leave the 'ouse?"

"I have informed Lady Wessex that she will not leave the house except in my presence, or the presence of Lord Rosse."

Crouch rubbed his chin with the curved part of his hook. "Beggin' pardon, m'lord, but that didn't stop 'er last time."

Noble's face was grim. "It will not happen again. Are there any other questions? No? Excellent. Is everyone armed?"

The row of men nodded. One of the footmen coughed and stepped forward.

"Yes, Dickon?"

"My lord, shouldn't we have a watchword? Like in *The Mysteries of Limehouse*, where the watch captured an infamous band of pirates when they were spiriting away a group of young ladies for a sultan from a distant land, where they would be made slaves to his desire and forced to—"

"Yes, yes, I see your point, Dickon. Very well. We shall have a watchword. Any suggestions as to what it might be?"

"Testicle!" piped up Charles.

Noble frowned at him.

" 'E means tentacle, m'lord. 'Ad 'is 'alf day yesterday and saw

284

one of them octopantses at the zoological gardens."

"No, I mean testicle," argued Charles.

Noble considered his footman. "Is there any reason why you wish the watchword to be testicle, Charles?"

The young man sucked in his cheeks and bounced on the balls of his feet. "No, my lord."

"Just like the word, do you?"

"Yes, my lord."

Noble stopped pacing in front of the footman and narrowed his eyes at him. "There's nothing you should have told me that you haven't, is there, Charles?"

Charles's eyes widened. "Me, my lord?" he squeaked.

"Mmm," Noble said, giving him a close look, then continued his pacing. "Very well, our watchword is testicle. Should you encounter someone who does not answer your cry of 'Halt, who goes there?' with a snappy 'testicle,' you will restrain him and shout for assistance."

"A lady wouldn't say it," Charles said.

Noble spun around to face the interruption. "What's that?"

"You asked me if I had a reason for choosing the word testicle, my lord. I thought of one. A lady wouldn't say it. Therefore, any lady villains we encounter wouldn't say the watchword."

"Er . . . quite right. Are there any other questions?"

"They'd say something else," Charles said. Noble ignored him and gazed down the line of footmen.

"Like whirligigs," Dickon said with a nod. "That's what my mum used to call them."

"Dusters," said Crouch. "Jenny Hills. Flowers and frolics."

"Yes, quite. Are there any—"

"Gooseberries," said one of the Runners.

"No, they's jingleberries, they are," said another.

Noble rubbed his still-aching head. The pain seemed to be increasing again.

"Les accessories," said Tremayne Two in a perfect French accent.

"Orchestra stalls," offered Crouch.

"Twiddle-diddles. A lady would surely say twiddle-diddles," Charles suggested, looking up as the door opened. "Oh, my lady, could you answer a question? If you were asked to say the word—"

"Charles!" Noble bellowed. "That will be all! You are dismissed, all of you."

"If I was asked to say what word?" Gillian asked as the footmen filed out. Noble glared at the men and dared them to answer her.

"Whennymegs," Crouch muttered as he closed the door behind him.

Gillian turned to Noble. "Whennymegs? Oh, testicles. What about them? Are yours all right, my lord?" She turned her attention to the front of Noble's buckskins, concern writ across her face. "Did you damage them last night? You were quite enthusiastic, husband, but I thought everything looked hale and hearty this morning. Shall I check them for you?"

She started reaching for the buttons on his breeches. Noble caught her hand. "Everything is fine there, thank you. Did you do as I asked?"

"Yes, the ladies are gone, but really, Noble, you were quite rude, not even staying to chat. They do know you, and seem very fond of you. I think it would have been only polite if you had stayed to talk with them, find out how they're doing, who they're mistressing for, that sort of thing. Why, Laura had quite nice things to say about her time with you—"

Noble grabbed Gillian by the arms and pulled her up against him, ending the discussion the only way he thought would be effective. Gillian look bemused when he released her from the kiss, but he noted the sparkle in her eye was in no way diminished.

"And Anne said you were the best lov—"

He kissed her longer this time, deeper, dipping his tongue in and out of her mouth in a suggestive manner. She moaned into his mouth. He lifted his head and smiled smugly at her. She blinked several times, then touched a finger to his lips. "So soft, and yet so very demanding," she whispered, and gave herself a little shake. "Just how Beverly described—"

"Madam!" Noble roared in mock fury, shaking Gillian slightly. "You will cease this unseemly conversation!"

She giggled, then slowly the happy glow faded from her face. She placed a hand on his chest. "Noble, we must talk. About this morning—I know you are angry with me, and I appreciate you not lecturing me about interfering with your plans, but you were acting so very foolish, and I simply had to take steps. I couldn't allow you to face Lord Carlisle, not when there was the chance that he would harm you, or even kill you. You do understand that I did it for your own good, don't you?"

Noble stared at her with increasing bewilderment. "What are you talking about?"

Gillian blushed. "I can see you are being kindhearted by pretending it didn't happen, but I assure you, my darling husband, I am ready to hear your lecture."

Noble frowned. "What exactly did you do for my own good that had to do with Lord Carlisle? You haven't had time to see him." He looked around the library in mock suspicion. "I don't see him lurking in the corner, so you couldn't have invited him here as you are wont to do with people I'd rather not see. What is it you've done, wife?"

Gillian watched his expression closely. God's knuckles, he honestly didn't seem to be upset. Would she ever understand his moods? "I wasn't planning on telling you, but now I think perhaps it wouldn't upset you, as I had previously thought. I had him . . . that is to say, I ordered that Crouch and three of the Runner footmen . . . it was for your own good, you know, and solely to help you save face, so I don't think you should commence scowling in that manner, husband."

Noble counted to ten. "What did you do?"

"I had Lord Carlisle kidnapped."

287

Noble sank down into the nearest available chair, closed his eyes, and rubbed his hand across his forehead. "Why?" Even thinking the word made his head hurt worse.

"So that you wouldn't feel I was betraying you when I drugged you."

He stopped rubbing his forehead. "You did what?"

Gillian frowned. "You needn't act as if you didn't notice, husband."

"You drugged me? So I couldn't attend the duel?" Gillian nodded. "You drugged me? Ah, the draught. You drugged me with my own brandy? And then you let me make love to you?"

Gillian took a step or two away from him. Her Lord of Outrage looked as if he couldn't decide whether to laugh and kiss her silly, or to yell the hair right off her head, and if he settled on the latter, she wanted a little bit of distance. "It wasn't what I had planned, Noble, 'tis the truth I hadn't planned that you would . . . that you and I were going to . . . that we would . . . I just wanted you a little sleepy so that you would not wake in time for the duel, and . . . well . . . I must have given you a bit too much because you slept like the dead."

His indignation of earlier returned. "Do I remember correctly you engaging in a discussion of my personal attributes with Crouch?"

Gillian's face brightened and she stepped forward again. Here was safe ground. Surely he couldn't find fault with her wifely devotion in defending him. "Oh, yes, I did wonder if you were awake or not. Crouch said some rather rude things about your lovely behind, and I corrected him. It's not a good thing to let one's pirate have too much leniency where that sort of thing is concerned. With comments about one's behind, that is. Don't you agree?"

Noble opened his mouth to speak, realized he didn't know what the hell he was going to say to that, and closed it again. Tiny pinpricks of pain in his temples were dulling into a steady throb. If he concentrated, he could ignore them enough to continue the enlightening discussion of a moment ago.

"Let me see if I have this straight. You drugged me and kidnapped McGregor so that neither one of us could attend the duel, thereby making each think the other had absented himself from the duel?"

Gillian nodded. "I thought it only fair, you see. I didn't want one of you being accused of cowardice by not being present." She looked thoughtful. "It worked quite well, Crouch tells me. Lord Carlisle was most obliging and gave Crouch no trouble once he had a zoc. Crouch wouldn't tell me exactly what a zoc was, but I'm sure it must have been nice if it persuaded Lord Carlisle to go along quietly with him."

Noble considered telling her it was cant for a blow, then decided against it. She was picking up enough of the vulgar tongue from Crouch; she didn't need additional words. "I trust he has been released?"

"Oh, yes, quite early this morning. Crouch said he was furious, but settled down once he gave him another zoc. I do hope they are not habit-forming."

Noble closed his eyes and slumped back in his chair. He didn't know whether to throttle her for interfering or kiss her and then tell her his own actions. Perhaps he should do both. Just a quick little throttle, and then the kissing. Lots of kissing. He opened his eyes and looked at her standing in front of him, her face worried. Maybe the throttling could wait and he should start in with the kissing first.

"Oh, yes, I agree with that." Gillian nodded emphatically. Noble stared at her.

"You agree with what?"

"That the throttling can wait and you should start in with the kissing first. I like it when you kiss me. You make my knees turn to water."

Oh, lord, now he had picked up her Unfortunate Habit! He steeled himself against her hopeful look and frowned. "Wife, I will not have you interfering—"

"Noble?" she interrupted him, looking worried again. "Is this lecture going to take long? Because if it is, I'd like to talk about something else—"

"I am quite sure you would, madam—"

"I'd like to talk about Nick," she continued as if he had not spoken. "He told me about what happened that night when your Elizabeth died, and I do think he needs to be reassured that you do not blame him for anything. He was most distressed by the thought that he had failed you, or shamed you in some manner."

Noble stared at her, unable to believe what she was saying. "He told you? In the same manner he told you he liked being in London?"

She frowned. "No, of course not, he told me. That is, he spoke—"

Noble was up and out of his chair before he knew what he was doing. "He told you? He spoke?" He had both hands on Gillian's shoulders and glowered into her face. "He actually spoke to you and you didn't bother to mention the fact to me?"

"I had to drug you," she started to explain, then threw up her hands, muttered something about him not understanding, and, turning, bolted out of the library. Noble stared at the spot where she had been standing, trying to grasp this miracle she had worked; then her words sank in. Nick had spoken about that night?

He passed her on the first flight of stairs, racing up to the second floor, where Nick's rooms were. If Nick was remembering the facts of that night, he needed more than just simple reassurance—he needed every ounce of love his father could give him. As Noble leaped up the last few stairs he sent a prayer of heartfelt gratitude that God had sent him Gillian. Without her, he wouldn't have learned how to love again.

He paused in the doorway to Nick's room, sick with the thought of what he would find. His son, his innocent little boy, exposed to horrors Noble fervently hoped he'd never understand, events so traumatic that it had stripped him of speech. He stood with his hand on the doorknob, willing himself to enter the room and face the boy who fought his devils just as fiercely as Noble fought his own.

"He needs you, Noble," Gillian said softly behind him.

Noble nodded, still unable to open the door. Gillian leaned into him for a moment, then put her hand on his and waited. Noble took a deep breath and pushed the door open.

Nick leaped up from the window seat and stared at his father. Noble's silver-eyed gaze held that of his son for a brief minute, then the boy was flying across the room crying, "Papa!"

Gillian smiled even as she wiped discreetly at the tears that overflowed at the sight of Noble sitting with his son on his lap, the boy sobbing into his chest, reliving once again that horrible night. She met her husband's eyes briefly, then slipped out of the room with Rogerson.

"He'll be better now, ma'am," the tutor reassured her.

"They both will," Gillian responded, dabbing at the last few tears. "They've learned how to climb walls, I think."

"Walls, my lady? I don't understand."

Gillian beamed at him as she started down the hall. "It doesn't matter, Rogerson. They understand."

"Good lord, man, you look like death warmed over. No man looks like that who's spent the night worshipping at the feet of his lovely bride; therefore you must have drank yourself silly instead. Noble, my boy, we really must have a talk one of these days."

"My lovely bride," Noble said as he settled himself across from Lord Rosse, "drugged me last night so I couldn't attend my dawn appointment."

Rosse stared at him. "You didn't tell her you'd apologized and called it off?"

Noble explained about Gillian's plan to save both his and Carlisle's honor. Rosse laughed over the tale until he realized that his friend was looking even more grim than before, if that was possible, which he would have doubted had he not been looking at proof.

"Well, that explains where Carlisle had disappeared to last night when I delivered your note. But don't tell me you are angry with the charming Gillian for her attempts to save your worthless hide?"

Noble didn't react to his gentle teasing. "Nick's talking."

Rosse looked at the Black Earl's tight jaw and the eyes that glittered a hard, cold silver. "He remembers that night?"

Noble nodded. "There was a second man there, Harry. It . . ." Noble seemed to be having difficulty making his jaw work. "It wasn't McGregor. Nick saw it all; he saw Elizabeth and this other man, and he saw their little games. So help me God, if I ever find the bastard, I'll gut him alive. He was going to abuse Nick simply to strike at me."

Rosse looked ill, but not as ill as Noble felt. That black thing that had once roiled around inside him was back, but this time it had a target, a reason for being, and its name was vengeance. "God damn her soul to eternal hell! How could she do that to him? He was just a little boy."

"I'm sure she's rotting there now," Rosse said, thinking that if anyone deserved eternal damnation, the late Countess of Wessex did. "Did he . . . did Nick understand everything?"

"No, thank God," Noble said, suddenly exhausted. He felt drained, squeezed dry, as if he were an old limp washrag. "He doesn't, and Gillian is doing her best to make him forget, but I doubt if he ever will. My God, Harry, the man was going to . . ." The thought was too foul, he couldn't even put it into words.

Rosse noticed the tears in his friend's eyes and felt a lump forming in his throat. "What can I do, Noble?"

"We've got to find out who this other man was. The one who played those foul games with Elizabeth." Noble stared out the window for a moment. "She had so many lovers, Harry, where do I begin looking?"

"Did Nick give you a description of the man?"

"Just a brief one—an average-sized man with no outstanding features, brown hair, dark eyes—a description that could match more than half the men in the *ton*."

"Perhaps if I were to question him—"

Noble shook his head adamantly. "No. I'll not have him relive that night again. We'll have to find the bastard without upsetting Nick. Gillian's taken him out to the zoological garden to see the octupantses."

Rosse looked startled. "To see the what?"

"Octopus."

"I thought you said . . . never mind, it doesn't matter. Is it safe for them to be out?"

"Gillian said it would be better for him to be out of the house for a bit. I didn't send her out alone; she's got all five Runners with her." A smile flickered across Noble's face as he remembered her outraged objection to taking all five with her. "Do you know that she hired two Runners to protect me? With your two, that makes seven all together. It's a wonder the thieves and murderers aren't running rampant in the city."

Rosse grunted, and continued tugging on his lip as he considered and rejected paths of inquiry. "You'll be safe enough at White's. You may not like this, Noble—I know you want justice for your boy—but I think we should finish up with this first problem before starting on one five years old."

Noble looked obstinate, and it took Harry until the pair had reached White's to convince him that to divide their attention and forces would be foolish. "After all," he pointed out as they handed over their hats and sticks, "you lose Carlisle as your main suspect if Nick is correct and there's a second man involved. I'd be willing to wager it's this man who is behind the attacks on you and the threats to your lady, rather than Carlisle."

"He's tried to convince Gillian I am an ogre," Noble protested. He hated to give up the idea of McGregor as villain but had to admit it was looking less likely with each passing day.

Katie MacAlister

"All he's tried to do is warn her against what he believes is your vicious temper. Gillian told me last night that he believes you murdered Elizabeth most foully and are going to do the same to her."

Noble looked startled. "By God, I'll thrash the . . . she didn't believe him, did she?"

Rosse nodded to an acquaintance, was pleased to see that no one cut his friend, and headed for his favorite quiet corner. "No, of course she didn't, but she did point out that all he's ever tried to do is to protect her from you."

"So she thinks," Noble said darkly, and glowered at his boots.

"About that night, Noble—I know you don't want to talk about it, but have you told Gillian what happened? What really happened, not what Carlisle is sure to have told her what he saw?"

"There wasn't time," Noble answered. "After I spoke with Nick, Gillian thought it was best to fill his mind with happier thoughts and took him off to the Gardens."

Rosse adjusted his spectacles. "I can imagine what Carlisle told her he saw—I had the devil of a time pulling him off you. I thought I was too late after I heard the pistol shots and found you in a pool of blood, with Carlisle's hands digging into your throat."

Noble grimaced and rubbed at his neck. "I couldn't speak for weeks. Thank God you were staying with me then."

"It wasn't a pleasant time for you," Rosse said easily. "You needed a friendly face around that dour ancestral pile. I never did find out why Carlisle was there that night—did you?"

"Yes. He showed me a note from Elizabeth, saying she'd overheard me plotting to kill her. He had come to play knight-in-shining-armor to her maiden-in-distress."

Rosse blinked carefully, noting the anger in his friend's voice. "Do you mean . . . she arranged to have him there?" His mind raced on, quickly leaping over false impressions and jumping to the logical conclusion. "Was she arranging for you to take the blame for something? Something to do with Carlisle?"

Noble shook his head and rubbed his hands together. Even thinking about that night made him feel cold. "No. I think now—now that I know about the second man—I think he and Elizabeth were planning to use Carlisle."

"For what purpose?"

"As a scapegoat for my murder."

Rosse's jaw dropped.

"There you are! Lud, Wessex, the news is all over the clubs— you called the duel off? You apologized? 'Pon my honor, I never thought the day would come when you backed down from a challenge!"

"I apologized," Noble said evenly, sending the marquis a look that let him know their conversation was at an end.

"But . . . but why?" Sir Hugh stammered. "That is . . . it's not like you, man, not like you a'tall. You feeling quite the thing? Not ill, perhaps? Sickening over something?"

"I'm quite all right, Tolly, there's no need to hover over me like a giant mother hen."

Sir Hugh flushed at the look of distaste Noble gave his plum waistcoat with its scarlet embroidery. "I couldn't credit it, but if you say it's true . . ." Sir Hugh shrugged and made himself comfortable in a nearby chair. "Why the long faces if you've settled this affair?"

Noble was about to explain when a shadow fell across them.

"I accept your apology," Lord Carlisle said, standing before Noble and clutching a pair of soft leather gloves. "Consider that score settled. However, I inquired. It was your house. If you think you can disguise that Crotch of yours by tying a bit of black silk over his ugly face, you're mistaken."

Noble didn't flinch as Carlisle laid the gloves across his cheek with a snap of his wrist. "Consider yourself challenged."

Noble pursed his lips for a moment, then bent and retrieved the gloves from where Carlisle had thrown them at his feet. He handed them back. "No."

Sir Hugh gasped. Carlisle stared. "No what?"

"No, I don't accept your challenge. You are quite right to be outraged over my wife's actions. I apologize on her behalf."

Carlisle gawked at him. "You . . . apologize?"

Noble nodded. "I do. Her plan, motivated by her desire to see no blood shed between us, was carried out solely upon her orders. However, as she is my wife and I am responsible for her actions, I apologize."

"You won't face me over pistols?"

"No."

Carlisle looked as if he wanted to pout. "Well, dammit, man, you have to give me satisfaction for this slight!"

"There's always Jackson's," Rosse pointed out. "You could beat your frustrations out on each other."

Noble looked at Carlisle, noting that although the Scot was shorter than he was, he had more bulk to his chest. Even dressed in a kilt, as he was now, Carlisle was the picture of masculine power. Carlisle, likewise engaged in an assessment of his would-be opponent, wasn't fooled in the least by the elegant picture Noble displayed—after all didn't his nose looked to have been recently broken? Carlisle knew that beneath that tastefully cut, skin-tight coat, Noble had the strength to match him.

"Done," both men said at the same time, then agreed to meet in the early afternoon to settle the matter once and for all.

"I liked the elephant the best, didn't you, Gillian? Didn't you think the elephant was the best? I thought he looked very sad, though. Perhaps he misses his home. Do you think he misses his home? If I were an elephant, I'd miss my home."

"Yes, I'm sure that's it. He did look homesick."

Nick thought for a moment. "But I also liked the lions, didn't you like the lions? And the camels. And the zebras. But I didn't like the jackals. Did you like the jackals, Crouch?"

"Eh, well now, Master Nick, that's a right good question—"

"I liked the giraffe, too. Did you see how long his neck was, Gillian? How does he drink with such a long neck? I wonder if Rogerson knows how a giraffe drinks. I bet if my neck was that long that I could figure out a way to drink."

"You weren't fast enough," Gillian told Crouch as she handed him her bonnet and parasol.

"Aye, m'lady, that I weren't," he answered her with a cheeky grin. "But it's nice to see the lad talkin' again."

"That it is, Crouch. Nick, why don't you go upstairs and ask Rogerson about the drinking habits of the giraffe? Is that for me?" she asked as Charles the footman brought a note on a silver tray.

"It's from Lady Charlotte," Charles said helpfully.

"Yes, I can see that," Gillian said, examining the note. She slid her finger under the wax as she started toward the library.

"Her ladyship's maid brought it just a bit ago. Her ladyship's maid said it was quite urgent, and that you were to send for her ladyship if you wanted her."

"Thank you, Charles." Gillian smiled at him as he held open the library door for her.

"If there's anything you want, my lady, just let me know," he added helpfully. "Anything at all. Say, for example, you wanted a message sent to Lady Charlotte. Well, then"—he puffed up his chest and thumped it importantly—"Bob's your uncle!"

"No, my uncle's name is Theodore," she said absently as she read the note. Charles hovered hopefully around the door. His curiosity was rewarded when Gillian suddenly crumpled the note and said, "Bloody hell! Will someone *please* explain to me how that man's mind works?"

Charles quickly stepped back into the room. "I would be happy to be of assistance, my lady, if you were to just tell me which man it is you seek information about."

Gillian stifled the desire to roll her eyes and instead commanded that the carriage be brought around immediately. "I have a few letters to write, Crouch," she said to the butler as she hurried out into the hall and toward the stairs. "I'll want a footman . . . no, four footmen, ready to take them immediately. I'll want the notes delivered as quickly as possible, so have them ride."

"Four footmen, m'lady?"

"Yes, four," Gillian replied as she leaped up the stairs. "I shall go to Lady Charlotte myself, and the four footmen can deliver the notes to his lordship's ladybats."

"Ladybirds," Crouch corrected her softly as he watched her fly up the stairs; then he turned his attention to the louts standing about watching with nothing better to do but scratch their arses. " 'Ere, you, Dickon, you 'eard the mistress. Go tell Tremayne to 'ave the carriage and four 'orses brought 'round. Coo lummey, what 'is lordship'll 'ave to say about this, I don't want to think."

"I thought that bit of news would bring you at a gallop," Charlotte said as she entered the small sitting room. "Good afternoon, Nick. You look well."

Nick bowed. "Thank you, Lady Charlotte."

Charlotte stared openmouthed at him for a moment, then raised a brow as she looked at Gillian.

"Nick has decided he likes talking," she answered the unasked question. "Now, tell me where you heard this news."

"Papa told Mama when he came home from his morning at the club. He said the books are filled with wagers on whether Lord Wessex will trump Lord Carlisle, or vice versa. Papa didn't know who to bet on—he felt as if he should back Lord Wessex, since he's his nephew-in-law, but he thinks Lord Carlisle has the advantage and so . . . well . . . he's wagered on both."

Gillian couldn't keep the smile back. "That sounds like Uncle Theo. He doesn't like to be on the losing side of any venture, least of all those concerning a few groats."

Charlotte snorted. "A few groats—after what Lord Wessex

settled on you, I should think he would cast his lot with your husband."

"Char, you make it sound as if Noble purchased me!"

Charlotte shrugged and daintily picked at a cuticle. "He did, more or less. Oh, don't get your feathers in a hackle, cousin; I assume you are not here to debate the hows and whys of your marriage. What are you going to do about this terrible fisticuffs duel the men have planned?"

"I shall stop it, of course! I have no intention of allowing Lord Carlisle to beat the tar out of my husband."

"What makes you think Lord Carlisle's tar won't take a pounding?"

Gillian made a moue. "Normally, I'd back Noble's tar against Lord Carlisle's, but in the last few days Noble has been kidnapped, shot, received a black eye, broken his nose, and been drugged. The last, I'm annoyed to say, was completely without need, since Noble informed me this morning that he had actually apologized to Lord Carlisle and canceled the duel the night before."

Charlotte nodded. "Papa told Mama about that, as well. But how do you intend to stop them?"

Gillian smiled. "I have a wonderful plan."

Charlotte dimpled at her in return. Nick looked worried.

Lord Carlisle sauntered over to where the smaller man was sitting. He glared at his companion's arrogant posture for a moment, then allowed himself to be waved into an adjoining chair. "You wanted to see me?"

The smaller man nodded his head. "It's about this silly challenge you've issued Wessex . . . you don't intend to go through with it, do you? The man is known for his abilities in the boxing ring."

"As am I," Carlisle said with a scowl. Impudent upstart. Who did he think he was, cautioning him against Wessex?

"I have no doubt, but you seem to be forgetting the goal of

the exercise—to protect Lady Wessex from his inhuman rages. How do you think she'll fare once he takes out his anger on her?"

"Anger at my beating him in the ring? She won't be responsible for that."

"No, but she is responsible for having you detained, and forcing Wessex into a public apology. No man in his right mind would let his wife get away with such brazen actions, especially a man of Wessex's pride. She'll pay for her little plan and pay dearly, unless I miss my guess."

Carlisle digested this unpalatable news. "She was trying to protect him; surely you don't think he'd—"

"He has every right to beat her for interfering, and when his humiliation at your hands is added to his rage, well . . ." The smaller man spread his hands and shrugged. "It will be all over for her. Perhaps you can save the next bride."

"No, dammit, I'll save this one!" Carlisle snarled, his face twisted with pain. "I couldn't save Elizabeth from that monster's wrath, but I'll save this Lady Wessex."

The small man sat back with a satisfied grin, his fingers steepled together. "I have an idea about how you might just do that. I've taken a house in the country. If we move up the plan to tonight, I will place my house at your disposal. There's no safer location for her—Wessex'd never think of seeking her there."

Carlisle waved away a man offering libations and watched the smaller man fidget with his watch fobs, wondering if he should chance speaking bluntly.

"I thought you were on your uppers? The word around town is that you can't meet your vowels, yet you've taken a house?"

The man flushed angrily. "My finances are no concern of yours. Now, do you want to save Lady Wessex or not? Be quick, man, her life is at stake! You should know that more than anyone!"

Carlisle narrowed his eyes at the impudent manner in which he was addressed. He was tempted to walk away from the plan, but the memory of his failure to save Elizabeth haunted him still. He couldn't allow that history to repeat itself.

He nodded his agreement.

"Ladies, we have an emergency!" Gillian declared as she strode into her sitting room, Nick on her heels. "Lord Wessex and Lord Carlisle are going to—"

"—have a duel by fisticuffs, yes, we know," Beverly interrupted her.

Gillian frowned. "How do you know? I just learned of it from my cousin!"

Beverly shrugged.

"We tend to hear things of import in the *ton*, my lady," Madelyn said. "We have to be current with the latest *on-dits* if we are to be successful."

"Sort of an occupational necessity, you mean?"

The ladies nodded.

"I see. Well, be that as it may, the fact remains that we shall need to take immediate action to bring this unendurable situation to a close."

"What can we do?" Laura asked hesitantly. "Do you wish us to disguise ourselves in men's clothing and descend upon Mr. Jackson's rooms?"

Gillian eyed the women's lush figures. Disguising them as men was clearly not an option.

"I'm sorry I'm late," gasped Anne as she burst into the room ahead of an unhappy-looking Tremayne. "The White Dove was telling me the most amazing bit of news about Lord Wessex—"

"We've heard it," Madelyn said, scooting over to make room on the love seat.

"Oh," Anne said, pouting a little at this turn of events.

"White Dove?" Gillian asked.

"The Duke of Marlborough's mistress," Laura explained.

"She's the undisputed leader of the demimonde. Anne, Lady Wessex needs our help to stop this silly duel."

Anne's pout disappeared as her eyes began to sparkle. "Shall we nobble them? I've always wanted to try my hand at a bit of honest nobbling."

"Anne!" Beverly said with a frown. "I'm sure Lady Wessex has a plan that does not involve something so very crude."

"Yes, indeed, I do," Gillian said with a smile for her mistress friends. "It's much nicer than nobbling, and really very simple."

Five faces turned to her expectantly.

"I want you to seduce the men at Gentlemen Jackson's."

Three hours later Gillian alighted from the carriage. She looked at number 13, Bond Street, and gave a little sigh. "It doesn't look like much, does it?"

"Mmmm, no," Charlotte said, watching a handsome young blood enter the next-door establishment. "Let's go there instead. Fencing. Gilly, you know how you love swords!"

"Oooh, Henry Angelo's school," Anne trilled as she stepped out of the second carriage. "I've been there. You'd like it, Lady Charlotte. There are ever so many young gentleman who learn to fence there."

"No," Gillian said firmly, tugging her cousin toward the proper door. "Later. Perhaps. If you behave."

"Pooh, who wants to behave? You don't have any fun that way." Charlotte shot longing glances toward the second door.

"You do, or you shan't come with us and watch the mistresses seduce the gentlemen. Honestly, Charlotte, it's a full day's work trying to keep you proper!"

Crouch, standing next to them, blanched at her words. "*You* want to go inside the boxing saloon, m'lady? Am I 'earin' you correctly? *You* want to go in?"

"Yes, Crouch, that's correct. I plan to—"

Crouch shook his head and raised his hook. "No, m'lady. I can't allow it. 'Is lordship would be stringin' my gut out thinner'n a blue-eyed cat's smellers. Ye'll not be wantin' to see me with my guts like that, now would you, m'lady?"

"That pitiful tone in your voice is very effective, Crouch," Charlotte said in a stage whisper. "If you like, I can show you an expression that would highly complement it. You might have better luck that way."

"Charlotte, I forbid you to subvert my pirate!"

"My lady." Madelyn put her hand on Gillian's arm and inserted herself between the two cousins. "Do you not think we should be about your plan? Even now, Lord Wessex could be—"

"Dear God, yes, of course! Off you go, the four of you. We shall follow once you've had suitable time to seduce the men." Gillian pulled a watch from her reticule. "About how long do you anticipate that will take? Three minutes? Four?"

Beverly shot her a look of patent disbelief. "To seduce someone? My lady, that could take upwards of an hour—"

"Oh, no," Gillian argued. "We don't have that sort of time. I want the quick version." She looked at the blank faces gawking at her. "You know, the *quick* seduction. Heavens, I can't believe I need to tell you four how to do your job. The quick one, the one that makes a man's eyes bulge out and his breathing stop and his hands clench and unclench spasmodically. It only takes a few minutes for Noble to reach that state, and surely you are ever so much more effective at seduction than I am."

Madelyn opened and closed her mouth a few times before she got the words out. "We'll do our best, my lady."

Gillian beamed at her. "Excellent. We'll follow you in a few minutes." She smiled a reassuring smile at Crouch as he shook his head at the sight of the mistresses disappearing through Gentleman Jackson's door.

Gillian took a firm grip on her cousin's arm to keep her from wandering. "Crouch, when we go upstairs, you and the footmen may stay out here."

"Nay, m'lady, yer won't be doing that. Remember my gut! 'Ere Charles, Dickon, 'Enry—ye three guard 'er ladyship. Frank,

'Arrison, ye take the 'ounds. Thomas, Jim, the two of ye stay with the 'orses, and make sure no one does anythin' funny like to either carriage. I'll stay by Master Nick's side. And we'll all be stayin' out 'ere where it's safe!"

This last was said directly to Gillian. Charlotte looked over the line of footmen as they leaped down from the two carriages necessary to carry them all, then turned back to Gillian. "If you could get them all on top of horses, you could join Astley's!"

Gillian rolled her eyes. "Really, Crouch, I appreciate your concern, but my plan is quite sound, I assure you. We'll be perfectly safe; his lordship will be there, after all.

Crouch crossed his arms over his chest. "Aye, m'lady, but who'll keep ye safe from 'im once 'e discovers ye there?"

"Testicle!" Charles shouted suddenly, tugging at the pirate's sleeve. "Testicle, Mr. Crouch. Look, over there, testicle!"

"Why the devil are ye yammerin' on about yer cods?"

Charles danced up and down before Crouch's unbelieving eyes. Was the man actually wringing his hands?

"Testicle! Look, coming down the street—testicle!"

Crouch suddenly remembered the watchword and spun around, his eyes narrowed, looking for any threat to his mistress's safety. A carriage was speedily bearing down on them, the horses lathered and wild-eyed. Immediately footmen began running to and fro, stumbling over each other, over the dogs, and over their own feet. Crouch shouted orders to form a circle around Gillian, but the orders were lost in all the noise and confusion.

"Oh for heaven's sake," Gillian said, shaking her head as she stepped over a prone footmen. She grabbed Nick and pushed him up the stairs. "Quickly, Charlotte, before they regroup. Oh, I do hope the mistresses have seduced all the men by now."

Charlotte panted behind her as they dashed up the steps. "I'm sure it takes more than two minutes to seduce a man, let alone a whole room full of them. Even Lord Wessex must take longer than two minutes to be seduced."

Gilian recalled several occasions when Noble had proved that statement false but kept that bit of news to herself, concentrating instead on how they would stop the ridiculous boxing match. They paused at the top of the second flight of stairs to catch their breath.

"I still don't understand why you want the mistresses to seduce every man present, cousin. Other than for the sheer pleasure of watching their expertise in action, of course."

"Charlotte!" Gillian scolded, and tucked several strands of hair back into her chignon. "They are there for distraction. You don't think we're just going to be allowed to stroll into Mr. Jackson's rooms without being questioned, do you?"

Charlotte tugged at her gown and pinched her cheeks. "Certainly I thought so. Why shouldn't we?"

"Because ladies are not allowed in. Hence the mistresses. Nick, darling, you have a bit of dirt smudged on your chin . . . yes, thank you, that's got it. Are you ready?"

Nick squeezed her hand. "I'm ready."

"Excellent. Char, ready? Oh, blast, that would be Crouch and his reinforcements. Shoulders back, everyone. This is a glorious cause we fight for!"

"Lord Wessex?" Charlotte asked as Gillian pushed open the door. "Glorious? Good-looking, I'll admit, but glorious? I—oh, my! Will you look at that gentleman! He is bare-chested! What a magnificent figure of a man! Beverly, you cannot possibly want that gentleman, he's much too young for you. I'll take care of him for you, shall I?"

Gentleman Jackson's rooms were in an uproar. Several gentlemen of the *ton* had arrived to watch the battle royal, and they had made themselves quite comfortable as they strolled around the outer room, carrying out loud conversations with each other over the deafening noise of the other gentlemen gossiping, arguing, and wagering over the outcome of the duel. Into that sea of masculinity the mistresses had sallied, flags flying and sails unfurled. The result was utter pandemonium.

"Excellent!" Gillian cried upon viewing the chaos, her hand tight on the back of Nick's jacket. It wouldn't do at all to lose him in this crowd of hot bloods. "Look, Char, the mistresses are a smashing success!"

"I'm looking, I'm looking," Charlotte muttered, quickly donning an expression that pronounced her a shy, frightened, innocent young maiden who suddenly found herself in an unsuitably masculine environment. "Why, Lord Beckman, what a surprise to find you here!"

Lord Beckman looked equally surprised to see two ladies push their way through the crowd. He stuttered an excuse and slunk away.

"Hrmph. What a weakling Beckman is. Never did have any backbone. Oooh, look, Gilly, Anne is sitting on the Duke of Firth's lap! How very clever of her. I wonder how she did it?"

"Excuse me," Gillian said politely as she slipped past two men. "Char, come along. Stay with me lest you be confused with one of the ladybuns."

Charlotte's eyes glittered as she followed reluctantly behind. "Do you think there's a chance of that?"

"Here's a door. Nick, stay behind me. Charlotte, you're responsible for keeping him safe."

Charlotte saluted and put a protective arm about the lad.

Gillian threw the door open without preamble and stood staring at the sight within. There were several men inside, one of whom was a tall, burly fellow who could only be the famous Gentleman Jackson himself. He was talking with Noble, while Lord Rosse and Sir Hugh stood nearby.

Noble was in the act of removing his upper layers of clothing, his back to the door. Directly in front of Gillian was Lord Carlisle, handsomely garbed in a colorful kilt. She spent no time in admiring the attractive ensemble, for he was in the act of removing his hand from his hose and looking toward Noble. In his hand he held a small dagger, which he hefted in a manner that clearly indicated he was going to throw it.

At Noble.

In his back.

The result of such a heinous act being that her beloved husband would surely die.

Not if she had anything to say about it! Gillian thought as she leaped toward the Scot. Just as she did so, he stepped forward, her hand just missing his arm but ending up with a handful of woolen kilt. She didn't hesitate even a fraction of a second—Noble's very life was at stake, and only her actions could keep him from coming to harm. She took a firm grip on the material with both hands and yanked as hard as she could.

"I would say that answers the question of what a Scotsman wears beneath his kilt," Charlotte said over her shoulder, her eyes wide and sparkling.

Nick pushed his way into the room. "He's not wearing anything," he said, puzzled, looking up at Gillian.

"Exactly," she answered, distracted by the scene before her. It wasn't the horrified look on Lord Carlisle's face that worried her. It was the steel-blistering scowl on her husband's handsome countenance that suddenly made her wish she were miles away.

"Good afternoon, Noble," she said with a weak smile. "Fancy meeting you here."

"It won't happen again, Jackson, I can assure you of that. If I have to lock my wife away, I will make sure she never comes here again."

Gentleman Jackson was adamant. No matter how important Lord Wessex's patronage was, he couldn't be having a repeat of the day's chaos. "I'm sorry, my lord. It would be best if you found another of the boxing schools to patronize."

Noble glanced around at the debacle. While most of the bloods had left after it had been made clear the duel was off, they had not left peaceably. Chairs had been smashed against the floor, cups of wine and other libations had been dashed against the walls, occasional tables were thrown through the windows, and the famed gold curtains had been ripped down and thrown out to the crowd gathering below the windows. In the midst of this destruction, what looked to be a full phalanx of his footmen were milling around the remains of the crowd. Gillian's two dogs were running from man to man conducting their own investigation, while his ex-mistresses—he didn't want to even begin to ponder what they were doing here, although he knew Gillian had a hand in it—were busily chatting up the remaining gentlemen present. He wished them well. Perhaps if they all found the protectors they sought, they would be out of his life once and for all.

"Papa?" His son tugged at his hand. Noble put the hand on the boy's head, surprised at his lack of surprise at seeing him. Why should he be surprised? Hadn't Gillian included Nick in every other of her harebrained schemes?

"Not all of them, Papa," Nick answered solemnly. "She didn't let me meet your ladybuds."

"Ladybirds," Noble said without thinking. "Er . . . that is . . . oh, hell, never mind. It doesn't matter. Where is your mother? I don't see her anywhere."

"She went out the door with that man who didn't have anything on underneath his skirt."

"Kilt," he replied absently, then suddenly grabbed Nick by both shoulders. "She what?" he bellowed at the boy. "When did she leave?"

Nick's face turned pale. "Just a few minutes ago, but Papa, I want to tell you about—"

Noble was off before Nick could finish his sentence.

"—the man who hurt you," he said softly.

"McGregor!" Noble roared as he pushed his way through the remaining gawkers, his heart feeling as if it was going to burst out of his chest. "McGregor!"

He'd done it; the bastard had done it. He'd taken Noble's soul and crushed it to a lifeless pulp. If he'd done anything to harm her . . . Noble choked on the thought. He rounded up his men and, after giving them a brief tongue-lashing for letting Gillian out of their sight, raced down the stairs and out onto the street, the entire population of Jackson's following swiftly on his heels.

Noble paced back and forth in front of a house in Cheapside, muttering to himself just what he'd do to that murdering bastard McGregor when he caught up with him. He wanted nothing more than to be on the back of the nearest horse, hunting for his Gillian, hunting for the man who had spirited her away directly under his nose, doing something—anything—to find her.

"If he's harmed a single hair on her head," he threatened, shaking his fist at the sky, "by God, I'll—"

"Tear his head off and spit down his neck, yes, Noble, we've heard that already," Lord Rosse said as he strode down the front steps and toward his friend.

Noble spun around and took the marquis by the neck cloth. "What have you found out? Where did the devil take her? What did the murdering bastard's man have to say?"

"Noble, calm yourself, you're upsetting your son."

Rosse waited until Noble released him before continuing. "Carlisle's man doesn't know where he's gone, but he did verify that he had ordered a small case packed earlier, so evidently he'd planned this all along."

"No, not this," Noble said, resuming his pacing as his mind wheeled and turned frantically, trying to make sense of it. "He couldn't have known Gillian would appear at Jackson's. No, what he planned was something else, a plan he decided to abandon once he realized he could take advantage of Jackson's madhouse to kidnap her."

He combed an agitated hand through his hair as he stopped in front of his friend. "Where, Harry, where has he gone to earth?"

"I don't know, Noble. I wish to God I did. I never thought—I was sure Carlisle was innocent—but I suppose you were right. My nose has gotten cold."

Noble clapped a hand on his friend's shoulder, then resumed his pacing. "It's not your fault, old friend. She was my responsibility—what is it, Crouch?"

"M'lord, one of the Runners 'as returned."

Noble raced over to where the Runner, still dressed in his livery, was jumping off a horse. "They've gone toward Colfax," he said breathlessly. "We followed them to the east road. Davey's on their heels, but I'd wager a year's worth of blue ruin that they've gone to the Nag's Head Inn at Colfax."

Noble was in the carriage before the man had finished, ordering the coachman to spring the horses.

"Papa! Don't leave without me!"

Noble swore and threw the door open, grabbing the small figure of his son and hauling him into the carriage just as the horses leapt off.

"We'll be right behind you," he heard Rosse shout as the carriage barreled down the road, the coachman bellowing oaths at the people who were foolish enough to block his path. Noble closed his eyes briefly against the pain that threatened to overwhelm him, pain at the thought of losing Gillian. She was his very soul, hers entwined so tightly with his that he didn't think he could survive the separation. His mind repeated a litany in time to the horses' hoofbeats, "Please God, let her be all right."

A small, cold hand slipped into his. Noble opened his eyes and looked down at his son.

"She'll be fine," he said, wiping off a lone tear streaking down the boy's cheek. "Don't worry, son, we'll rescue her."

"Just like she rescued you?" Nick asked, squeezing his father's hand tight.

A small smile flashed over Noble's face. "Yes, just like that. We'll save her and take her home and keep her safe for the rest of her life."

Nick burrowed his head into his father's side. "That man will hurt her like he did Mama," he said into Noble's coat.

"What man?" Noble asked, the idea of locking his wife away in a tall tower beginning to look very attractive.

"The man who hurt Mama. The man who hit you on your head when you came in to help me."

Noble felt his blood turn to ice. Gently he pushed the boy back until he could see his face. Nick's eyes—those eyes that made him feel he was looking into a mirror—gazed back at him filled with pain and worry.

"The man you saw who . . ." God, he hated to do this to him, but it was Gillian's life at stake. "The man you saw shoot your mama?"

Nick nodded, a tear spilling over his brimming eyes.

"Where did you see this man?"

"At Gentleman Jackson's. He was watching Gillian."

The ice turned to fire deep inside him. "Was the man still there after Gillian left?"

Nick nodded again, looking even more worried. He twisted the material in his short pants between nervous fingers. "Did I do something wrong, Papa? I tried to tell you, but you wouldn't listen."

Noble hugged his son fiercely. "No, son, you didn't do anything wrong. Now, I want you to tell me from the very beginning when you first noticed that man at Gentleman Jackson's."

Lord Rosse, riding one of the Black Earl's horses, was surprised to see Noble's carriage suddenly stop. He rode up and leaned down to ask if everything was all right.

Noble stepped out and handed Nick up to John Coachman. "You can ride up there with John for a bit, son. If you're good, he'll let you handle the whip."

Noble turned back to his friend. "Tie him off." He nodded at the horse as he climbed back into the carriage. "We have to talk."

"What's all this about?" Rosse asked a minute later as the coach once again started off at a fast clip. "You'll have to change horses at Rowley at the rate you're pushing them."

Noble ignored the comment, his face hard and bitter. "It's Tolly."

Rosse stared at him, not understanding his cryptic comment.

A spasm of pain swept across Noble's face. "God help me, I thought the man was my friend, but it's been Tolly all along. He's been behind McGregor's attacks on me, I'm sure of it. *Tolly* was the man who killed Elizabeth."

"Tolly?" Rosse asked, disbelieving. "Our Tolly? Are you sure? He's the one who told us to look at Carlisle's house . . . oh."

"Exactly. Nick identified him, right down to those blasted seals and fobs he always decks himself out with. He told me . . ." Noble's voice choked to a stop. It took him a few moments before he could continue. "He told me how Tolly would visit Elizabeth and they'd play their little games in front of Nick. My God, Harry, how could she do that to him? How could she hate him so much that she'd want to see him suffer like that?"

Rosse swallowed back his own lump. "She never liked him, Noble, you knew that."

"I knew it, and I thought I'd protected him from her wrath at not being able to have children . . . but I didn't. I failed him, Harry, and that thought will haunt me till the day I die. And now—" Noble stared blindly out the window. "What if I fail Gillian, too?" he whispered.

"You won't," Rosse said in a hearty voice. "We'll stop at Rowley and change horses, and see if the Runner left any message about their direction. We'll find them."

"You know what he did to Elizabeth," Noble said hoarsely. "He beat her. He cut her. He abused her in ways no man should abuse a woman. He must be mad—mad with jealousy or hate or—God knows what. What's to stop him from taking out his rage at me on Gillian? What's to stop him from doing the same inhuman things to her that he did to Elizabeth?"

His last words were almost a sob. Rosse put out a hand and grasped his friend by the arm. "Noble, stop torturing yourself. It won't do you any good, or Nick, or Gillian. Now get hold of yourself, man, and let's consider all the places Tolly might have gone."

Gillian was not amused. When she had spied a familiar wizened figure beckoning her, she'd followed without hesitation, leaving her apology to Lord Carlisle half-finished. Noble was busy raging at an ill-looking Crouch, and Charlotte still had Nick in her grasp, so she left Lord Carlisle and Sir Hugh and slipped out through the door to a small anteroom.

"Palmerston, I'm surprised to see you here. I wouldn't have believed that you would be interested in such goings-on."

The old man slowly lowered himself onto a bench with the aid of his stick. He wheezed a chuckle at her. "Now, gel, you don't expect me to let my godson do battle for his honor without being present, do you?"

"Your *godson*?" Gillian exclaimed, seating herself next to him. "I didn't know he was your godson."

"Aye, godson and great-grandson-by-law."

Gillian raised her eyebrows. "You're Elizabeth's great-grandfather?"

"Aye." A look of distaste crossed his face. Gillian was reminded of an ancient wrinkled and brittle parchment that she had once seen. Like it, Palmerston's face seemed to have survived more than its fair share of years.

"Elizabeth, now there was an evil gel. Truly evil."

Gillian stared in surprise. "Your own great-granddaughter? Evil?"

"Aye, that she was. She'd liked to hurt things, ever since she was a little gel. Cruelty was a sport to her. Caught her more'n once tormenting my dogs. Took a switch to her for it once, but she just moaned and squirmed and begged me to thrash her again."

Katie MacAlister

Palmerston's brilliant blue eyes peered out from twin bushy white eyebrows. "You know what I'm talking about, gel?"

"I—no, I guess I don't," admitted Gillian.

"Some people—sick people, people sick in their minds—find pleasure in inflicting pain on others. Other people gain pleasure from their own pain."

Gillian wrinkled her nose in disbelief.

Palmerston nodded. "Elizabeth was like that. She took enjoyment from pain, and she took great delight in hurting others." He leaned back and closed his eyes. "She particularly liked to hurt your husband. And his son."

"But why?"

Palmerston shook his head. "No reasoning with their kind. They're not sane. Mind yourself, gel. There's others like Elizabeth who would hurt you if they could."

"Me? Who?" Gillian asked. Palmerston didn't reply; he just closed his eyes and leaned back against the wall. "Is it the same person who has tried to harm Noble?"

She gave the old man a gentle shake, but he refused to say any more. She sat back next to him, ignoring the sudden crashes and harsh voices from the room beyond. Elizabeth had hated Noble? If that was the case, perhaps he hadn't been mourning her death; perhaps she had misinterpreted his dislike of his first wife for grief. Perhaps there was hope for her after all.

The noise swelled into the room as the door opened and a figure slipped through.

"There you are, Lady Wessex. I thought you might have come here."

Gillian glanced at Palmerston, but he was still sleeping despite the noise. "Yes, but I should return," she said, standing. "Noble will be wanting to leave . . ."

"He asked me to escort you downstairs," Lord Carlisle said, grasping her arm and pushing her toward a back door.

"*Noble* asked you?"

"Yes. He's taking his son to his carriage and asked if I would see you safely down. You don't want to go out into the main rooms—they aren't safe for a gentle lady."

"But my cousin—"

"Has been taken outside already," Lord Carlisle said with a worried smile. He pushed her gently toward the servants' stairs. "We'll go down the back way, then meet up with Wessex outside."

Ha, Gillian thought to herself some time later. What a fool she had been to trust Lord Carlisle. She hoped Palmerston would be sure to tell Noble who had urged her away. She struggled briefly against her bonds and wished she had the common sense God gave to slugs.

He had kidnapped her! Face down on the floor of his carriage, her arms bound at her sides, a foul taste in her mouth from the horribly musty black cloth that encased her, Gillian came to terms with the fact that the man she had thought was a friend was, in fact, a villain. Noble had been right all along.

"Just because I tried to stop the duel," she muttered, spitting out a mouthful of the cloth and trying to work a foot out of the bottom of the canvas bag, "he decided to pay me back in kind. Well, he'll soon see what a mistake he made in underestimating me!"

The carriage lurched over a hole in the paving stones, sending her flying into the side wall. She saw stars for a few minutes, then managed to curl herself up so her head didn't pound against the wall interior of the carriage with each bump and jolt. Once she was satisfied she had enough air, she concentrated on trying to work her arms free of the ropes, but it would be hopeless until she could remove herself from the bag. She struggled for what seemed to be days until she had one foot free.

"Excellent," she said to herself, and spent the next two years working her second foot free. Just as she emerged from her chrysalis, exhausted and sweaty but triumphant, the carriage swayed and jounced to a halt. She cautiously peeked out the window. They were in the yard of a posting inn, and it looked as if the horses were being changed. "More than excellent," she said as she tried the handle of the carriage door. It was unlocked. She sent up a little prayer and threw the door open, leaping out of her prison.

And straight into Lord Carlisle's arms. Or what would have been his arms if he had known she was going to come bursting out of the carriage just as he was opening the door to check on her. Instead she hit him head-on, knocking him backwards. Together they hit the ground with a resounding smack.

Gillian scrambled off the earl and stared at him for a moment. There was a pool of blood growing from beneath his head. She prodded him. He didn't move. She put a hand to his mouth but felt no breath stirring.

"Bloody hell! I've killed him!"

"Aye, that you've done," a raspy voice said from behind her. Gillian turned around to see a coachman backing away from her warily.

"But I didn't mean to . . . he kidnapped me, you see . . . and then this . . . he was opening the door as I was coming out . . . it was an accident. You can see that, can't you?"

The coachman looked at her with wide, nervous eyes, which widened even more when he looked around her again. "Here, I'm fetching the landlord. If you've gone and murdered my lord, it'll be the three-legged mare for you, lady or no!"

"But, wait—" Gillian started toward the coachman, but he turned and fled before she could get near him.

"Well, now what do I do?" she wailed to the still figure of the earl. "I can't just leave you here—good lord, Sir Hugh! Whatever are you doing here?"

A small yellow curricle raced into the yard and pulled up directly before her. The baronet leaped from the seat, took one look at the scene before him, and ordered his tiger to tend his horse. "I shall assist Lady Wessex home in this carriage."

Gillian felt like kissing him for saying such a nice word. *Home.* "That would be excessively kind of you, Sir Hugh, but I'm afraid

I'm going to have to stay. You see, the magistrate will be sure to want to know how I came to kill an earl . . ."

Sir Hugh peered down at the recumbent figure. "Dead, is he? Shame, but still, I'm sure it was an accident. He did kidnap you, after all."

"Kidnapping or not, I don't believe I should leave until I've spoken with the authorities," she said with a reluctant look toward the inn. She had no desire to see the gallows, let alone make use of them.

Sir Hugh pulled his lip in thought. "I have an idea. I have a house not far from here—an hour's drive at most—I'll leave word inside as to your whereabouts, and you can come along and have a rest until Wessex arrives."

"Noble is coming?" Suddenly the situation didn't seem to be quite so terrible. Surely he would be able to help her out of this horrible mess. "Is he right behind you?"

"No, he had to tend to some business first. I'll just go inside and leave Noble a message where we're going, and then we can be on our way."

Looking back on the day, Gillian realized she should have been suspicious about Sir Hugh's antics when he insisted on leaving the body of Lord Carlisle lying in the courtyard, but she had wanted to be away just as badly as Sir Hugh seemed to, so she accepted his explanation that the innkeeper was sending for a doctor before Carlisle was moved.

She also felt she should have seen signs of Sir Hugh's madness before it became disastrously evident, but she hadn't. She rode along with him, pleased with her savior up until he escorted her into a darkened bedchamber.

"Thank you, Sir Hugh," she said politely, wishing he would leave her so she could tidy herself up. "I'm sure this will be most . . . oh, my. What . . . er . . . what exactly is that?"

"What?" Sir Hugh asked politely as he slid the bolt home in the door and began to light candles.

Gillian pointed at the raised circular platform. "That. That large thing, just there, taking up most of the room."

She began to feel something was very, very wrong.

"Ah, that." Sir Hugh came up behind her and put a hand to her back. "That is a little something I devised myself. A modified Catherine wheel. Notice that it spins."

Gillian noticed that, just as she also noticed the four leather straps and what looked suspiciously like dried bloodstains. She tried not to sound scared to death when she spoke. "Ah. It's . . . most ingenious, Sir Hugh."

He smiled. Gillian's stomach dropped into her boots. She was looking at a madman; she knew that just as well as she knew her own self.

Sir Hugh laughed. "Mad? I don't believe so, my dear, although I should by rights be after suffering what your husband has done to me."

Gillian took a step backwards. "Noble is your friend, Sir Hugh. He's been your friend for many years."

"Friend," he snarled, stepping toward her. "Enemy, my dear, my bitterest enemy. Did you know he stole the fair Elizabeth from me? She had been promised to me, you see, by my papa. But then Noble came along, and suddenly he had to have her and no one else."

Gillian stepped back again, but the madman followed. "If she was in love with him . . ."

He snorted. "She didn't know how to love anyone but herself, the coldhearted bitch. No, first he took my Elizabeth, then he took my land."

"Your land?"

A tic started beneath the baronet's left eye. He rubbed at it absently as he spoke. "The solicitor blamed the gaming debts, but I know the truth. Wessex bought him out, forced him to sell my land, my inheritance, forced me from my birthright!"

Gillian gasped as Sir Hugh screamed the last word. He was staring past her, his fists working, his face livid and twisted with hate. "He had everything. He had it all, handed to him by his dear papa, but still he had to take what was mine. Everything, he took everything."

Suddenly his hand lashed out and he grabbed her by her arm, tugging her forward until she could feel his heated breath on her face. She tried to turn away from the horrible sight of his face tortured and knotted with madness, but he pulled her even closer.

"I showed him, though, didn't I? Poor Hugh, nothing but a wastrel's son, they all said, but I proved them wrong, didn't I? Didn't I?"

He shook her with the last words.

"I—"

"I did, I did and you know it! I even did away with that grasping, greedy bitch Mariah when he came close to tracking her down."

Gillian stared at him with blank horror. He killed Mariah? Simply to keep her from speaking to Noble? She swayed for a moment, feeling as if she was going to be sick with the realization of just how mad Sir Hugh was.

"You cold bitch, you never did want me to succeed at anything either!" he snarled in her face. "I knew what you had planned, you know. I knew how you plotted with McGregor to have me shot in place of Wessex." Sir Hugh barked a short laugh. "I thought you'd learned your lesson the last time, but I see I shall have to punish you yet again, my dear Elizabeth."

Gillian tried yanking her arm away from the baronet but wasn't prepared when his fist shot into her face. Her knees buckled and she fought to catch her breath as mind-numbing pain radiated out from her jaw. She shook her head and tried to keep her heaving stomach contained but ended up retching onto the carpet. When she was finished, Sir Hugh yanked her to her feet and threw her onto the wooden platform. She was too dazed and stunned by the pain to do more than struggle feebly.

* * *

Katie MacAlister

"What do you think?" Lord Rosse asked, watching through the window as their carriage raced down the drive toward the house. "Are you sure Carlisle was telling the truth? That Tolly's brought her here? He wasn't in any shape to know what he was about, what with that big dent in the back of his head."

"He knew what he was saying," Noble said grimly. He flexed his fingers. If what Carlisle said was accurate, Gillian was utterly without resources, believing the baronet to be her friend, not a deadly enemy. He just hoped he got to her in time. If not—he couldn't face that thought. "Tolly fooled him just as he fooled me."

Rosse shook his head. "Carlisle believed everything Elizabeth told him?"

"Yes," Noble said, leaning forward in an effort to urge the carriage faster. "He believed every last damned lie that fell from her treacherous lips. She had to have something to explain the marks made by her sick games with Tolly to her lovers—who better to blame than her own dear husband?"

Before Rosse could speak, the carriage rolled to a stop, and both men were out and leaping up the stone steps to the door. Noble pounded on it, demanding entrance. Rosse reached around him, tried the doorknob, and threw the door open.

"You're such a gentleman," he told the Black Earl as Noble shot him a surprised look. They pushed their way into the small hall. A scared-looking footman was just scurrying off into another room, but Noble was on him in two steps.

"Where is she?" he roared, almost deafening the poor witless man. "Where has he taken her?"

The man's mouth opened and closed, but no words came out. Noble shook the smaller man and demanded to be told where his wife was.

"Here, let me have him, you're doing more damage than good," Rosse said, pulling the man out of his enraged friend's hands.

"Where has your master gone? Is he upstairs? Is he in the house? Where is he?"

The man blanched and shook his head. "I don't know. I don't know where the master is."

"Liar!" Noble snarled. Picking the man up, he threw him out one of the windows next to the door. "You!" He pointed at the slight figure of an obviously terrified footman. "If you don't want to join your friend there, tell me where to find your master."

The footman stared with an open mouth at the broken window, swallowed hard, and pointed upward. "Second floor, my lord. Last room on the left."

Noble and Rosse were up the stairs before John Coachman and Nick even entered the house.

Noble's mind was empty of all thoughts but of saving his Gillian. As his foot hit the top stair, a scream ripped through the air, rending Noble's heart in two. He snarled vicious threats as he charged down the corridor, Rosse hard on his heels.

"Here," he bellowed and, trying the doorknob, began to throw himself against the door.

"Noble, stop a moment," Rosse pleaded. "Stop a moment before you knock yourself silly."

"Gillian . . . scream . . . in there . . ." Noble panted as he threw himself again and again at the door.

"Look at the door, man, it must be at least five inches thick. You can't break it down." He grabbed Noble and shook him until his eyes lost the panicked look. "You can't break it down, but there has to be another way into the room."

Noble stared at his friend, his chest heaving, his eyes clouded with tears. "He's hurting her, Harry."

"I know. We'll get her out, but you have to use your head."

Noble froze for a moment, anguish written into every line of his face; then suddenly he spun around and raced down the darkened hallway.

Rosse watched him for a moment before turning his attention to the lock. He fiddled with it to no avail. Perhaps they would have to break down the door after all. If so, they would certainly need something stronger than brute strength.

Gillian had discovered quite early on that her screams gave great pleasure to Sir Hugh, and a pleased Sir Hugh was a Sir Hugh who did not hover over her with that wicked-looking knife, threatening to do all sorts of unspeakable things to her. He had already carefully sliced off her gown and was now taking enormous pleasure out of cutting great chunks of her shift off as well. She knew Noble would save her, but she hoped he'd hurry. She was quickly running out of shift, and her attempt to delay the baronet with talk was not meeting with great success.

"Sir Hugh, won't you tell me, please, why you are doing this? I understand you think Noble has done you a wrong . . ."

"Noble," Sir Hugh growled, and waved the knife uncomfortably close to her face. "Your *dear* husband. Ah, Elizabeth, if only you'd chosen me, but I was a mere baronet and not worthy of you, was I?"

Elizabeth? This was the second time he'd referred to her as Elizabeth. Perhaps if she humored him . . . "Certainly you were worthy of me, Sir Hugh, but I fell in love with Noble—"

"Love! Love? Don't make me ill, my dear. You no more know what love is than you know what makes up the moon. No, my dear, I shall first punish you for your naughty ways, then we shall continue with our original plan. You will use that lush body of yours to bring McGregor to bay, and then we'll arrange for your dear husband's demise."

Gillian felt sick, but not as sick as when the baronet began to describe what sorts of "games" he wanted to play with her. Did people really do those sorts of things to one another? And he made it sound as if Elizabeth enjoyed it—how could she have been so wrong about Elizabeth? Did Noble know about his first wife's plot against him? Did he know what Elizabeth had really been like? Did he know that Sir Hugh had killed Elizabeth that night so many years ago? Did Noble know that his first wife had taken Sir Hugh as her lover? And Lord Carlisle; there was no forgetting him. He had admitted to being Elizabeth's lover, and it was evident from Sir Hugh that he and Elizabeth had planned to use Carlisle as a scapegoat for Noble's murder. Gillian's head began to spin with pain and confusion. Secrets and lies, lies and secrets, Palmerston had said. The lies—those were Elizabeth's words to Lord Carlisle. The secrets—Sir Hugh and Elizabeth and their secret plan to do away with Noble.

"It's time, my dear. I haven't heard your fair voice raised in terror in far, far too long." Sir Hugh ran a thumb down the knife and stepped toward Gillian's outspread legs. He had cut the shift off, leaving her exposed almost to her torso. She closed her eyes and sent up a prayer, jumping at the sudden cold feeling of the blade as Sir Hugh ran its flat side up the length of her thighs.

"Now, Noble, now is a good time," she whispered, trying to brace herself against any pain. "Please, Noble, I need you now."

"Praying, my dear? You know how futile that is—I shall have to flog the blasphemy out of your soul once we are through with this little game."

"Noooooooooooble!" Gillian's voice raised to a shriek as Sir Hugh grabbed the edge of her torn shift and ripped it open wide. A sudden explosion of light and sound burst into the hellish darkness of the room as a figure crashed through the window, and then Noble was there, his hands around Sir Hugh's throat, squeezing tighter and tighter, lifting the madman off the ground, his hands never loosening their grip. Gillian closed her eyes again, but she still heard the sickening crack as Noble twisted the baronet's head, snapping his neck.

"Noble," she whispered, and he was there, looking her over for signs of injury, then slicing the leather restraints and carrying her to a chair.

"It's all right, sweetheart, I have you now," he crooned, rocking her as he held her tight. "I have you my darling, you're safe now."

"Don't let me go," she whispered into his neck, trying to stop the shaking that wracked her body. "I knew you'd come, Noble. I knew you would find me, my darling, adorable, beloved husband. But don't you think you could have found me a little bit sooner?"

Noble let out a shaky laugh and squeezed the breath out of her. "Wife, you are the only woman I know who could suffer what you just suffered and still have enough breath to lecture me."

Gillian pulled out of his embrace just far enough to see those dear, lovely silver-gray eyes with the marvelous black flecks. "I do not lecture, my lord. *You* lecture. I just listen. Oh, Noble! You are bleeding! Your poor legs are cut! You must let me attend them before you become ill."

Noble laughed again, stronger this time, and released her only long enough to drape a bedsheet around her before opening the door. "Nothing can harm me now, love, especially not a few scratches."

Rosse stood outside the door with a hatchet, panting with the effort of trying to break it down. "She's all right?" he asked as Noble pushed past him, Gillian settled comfortably in his arms.

"Unhurt, just frightened."

"And . . . ?" He nodded toward the room.

"He's in there. You're welcome to him. What's left."

Rosse smiled. "I will take great pleasure in cleaning up after you."

Gillian took one look at that smile and burrowed her head under Noble's chin. She didn't want to think how Lord Rosse intended to "clean up."

"Papa?" Nick squirmed out of John Coachman's grasp and ran up the stairs as Noble carried Gillian down. "Is Mama all right?"

Gillian untucked her head and beamed at her son. "I'm fine, Nick, just a little embarrassed in the clothing department." She tipped her head back to look at Noble. "Did you hear, husband? He called me 'Mama,' " she said against his lips. He stopped in the middle of the staircase and kissed her as he had wanted to kiss her ever since he laid eyes on her walking across the ballroom with Charlotte.

"Papa? Papa, you did rescue Mama just like we did you."

Noble tore himself from Gillian's mouth and gathered his wits enough to smile down at his son as he started down the rest of the stairs. "Did we, indeed?"

"Yes." Nick jumped down the stairs and pranced around Noble as he headed toward his carriage. "You see? Mama is wearing a bedsheet just like you wore when we rescued you. We did it right, Papa, just like you said."

Noble looked down at his wife, so warm and soft in his arms, her curves melting into him, her breath gently splaying across his neck. Her scent surrounded him, filling him with warmth from his crown to his very toes. "Yes, we did it right, Nick. This time we did it right."

Epilogue

"That concludes this, the fifth monthly meeting of the Greater London Mistresses Guild," Gillian said with a satisfied sigh, and closed the brown calf account book before her. She smiled at the eighteen women present. "The emergency fund is growing at an astronomical rate, thanks to Deveraux's investments, and you all should see some rewards for your involvement in the next few months. Are there any questions as to the holdings of the Guild? No? I believe then, ladies, we have accomplished our agenda for this month. I will be traveling to Nethercote for the Christmas holiday, so I won't be in attendance at the next few meetings." She glanced down at her rounded belly. "And probably not for a few months after that, but I will be in contact with Madelyn, who has accepted the role of acting director during my absence."

The room of demi-reps all nodded understandingly, and smiled benevolently at Madelyn.

"No further business? Very well, then. I wish you a happy Christmas and a very prosperous New Year."

Gillian levered herself out of the chair, hugged Noble's ex-mistresses, and wished them a particularly nice holiday, then made her way out of the small house in Kensington to the coach waiting outside.

"Home, Crouch."

"Aye, m'lady. As fast as the 'orses will take us."

She smiled at him as he handed her into the carriage. Hands from within reached out and pulled her inside into an embrace. Lips, warm, soft, passionate lips, nipped and kissed hers, until she parted them with a little laugh.

"Noble, what on earth are you doing here? I thought you didn't like knowing what went on with the Guild."

The lips kissed their way over to her ear. "I don't, but I've learned to live with it. You do remember your promise?"

Gillian slid her hand up the hard length of his chest and around his neck into his hair. "I remember. It's only until the Guild gets off the ground." She tugged until his lips were almost touching hers.

"According to Deveraux," Noble said with a groan as her other hand went exploring, "the Guild is growing richer each day. It's time for you to step down, Madam Director."

Gillian didn't answer, at least not with words. Her Lord of Love wouldn't let her. He had other plans for her lips, and she wasn't about to dispute them.

"Noble," she said later that evening, when they had separated at last, their bodies coated with sweat, their minds and bodies sated and happy and warm. Noble grunted and hauled her over until he could wrap an arm about her swollen belly. He had felt the baby kick a few days before and hoped it would happen again. His mind drifted with pleasant thoughts of home and family, and he wondered that he could ever have felt cold and alone.

"Noble, might we invite your godfather for Christmas? I would dearly love to see him again, and I think he would enjoy Nethercote. Nick would like him, too, I think."

Noble opened one eye and looked at the flushed figure of his delicious, delectable, wonderfully warm wife. "My godfather? You mean Lord Palmerston?"

She frowned and snuggled closer to him. "I knew he was a lord. He wouldn't tell me that, though."

"Tell you? Gillian, what are you talking about? My godfather's been dead for several years now."

Gillian sat up and stared at him with a horrified face. What had gotten into her now, talking about Palmerston? And how had she found out about him?

"Dead? He's . . . *dead?* But he can't be dead. I've spoken with him!"

Sometimes she got the strangest notions. Noble smiled to himself. Fancies. He'd heard about them from other men with children. Wives who were expecting often had strange fancies. Ah, well, he had learned to live with her heedless method of attacking life, he had learned to enjoy the chaos that dogged her every footstep, and he had reveled in the blinding passion that characterized her concern for others. He'd learn to live with this particularly charming quirk of her imagination, too. He sighed happily and pulled her back into his arms, close to his heart where she belonged.

"You're not an ordeal by fire after all," he murmured sleepily. "You're my saving grace."

Gillian smiled into his chest despite her confusion, then gave a little shrug and snuggled down for sleep. So they had a family ghost. Didn't all the best families boast a ghost or two? She made a mental note to mention it to Palmerston the next time she saw him, and let herself drift off into sleep as she felt her heartbeat slow and match that of Noble's.

Downstairs in Noble's library, the small, wizened figure of a very old man sat back in Noble's favorite chair and rubbed his gnarled hands together as he chuckled wheezily to himself. Saving grace, yes; the boy had it right this time. Gillian was Noble's saving grace. He wondered if he should visit Noble and warn him that his children would bring even more chaos and joyous confusion into his life, then decided against it. Noble was going to earn every single gray hair those young'uns would be giving him—why have him worry about it in advance?

Palmerston chuckled again. He was looking forward to the next forty or so years. They promised to be very entertaining.

JENNIFER ASHLEY
EMILY BRYAN
ALISSA JOHNSON

Invite you to

A Christmas Ball

It is the most anticipated event of the ton: the annual holiday ball at Hartwell House. The music is elegant, the food exquisite, and the guest list absolutely exclusive. Some come looking for love. Some will do almost anything to avoid it. But everyone wants to be there. No matter what their desires, amid the swirling gowns and soft glow of candlelight, magic tends to happen. And one dance, one kiss, one night can shape a new destiny....

ISBN 13: 978-0-8439-6250-5

Alissa Johnson

"A bright star." —*RT BOOKreviews*

McAlistair's Fortune

To Miss Evie Cole, ignorance was never bliss. That principle had driven her to become quite adept at a most unladylike pursuit—eavesdropping. And it was while honing this skill that she heard her guardians' elaborate scheme to find her a husband. Too bad she'd vowed never to marry. At least she knew the peril they were planning to help entrap her was only pretend.

What she didn't hear would change everything. James McAlistair wasn't supposed to be part of the bargain. Not only was the retired assassin dark, silent and intimidating, but Evie also happened to know from an accidental encounter on a warm, moon-drenched night that the man was an exceptional kisser. Now the danger was real. Because now Evie might fall in love.

"Filled with rapier-sharp repartee, passion and espionage."
—RITA Award-winning author Sophia Nash on
As Luck Would Have It

ISBN 13: 978-0-8439-6251-2

Dawn MacTavish

"...An enthralling, non-stop read. 4 ½ Stars!"
—*RT Book Reviews* on *Prisoner of the Flames*

Counterfeit Lady

"NO, MY LADY, I COULDN'T—"

But Alice could—and did. Against her better judgment, she allowed herself one night at a masquerade ball, playing the role of her mistress. When else might she, daughter of an austere Methodist minister and a servant, sample the pleasures of the ton? She had but one obligation: deter the coxcomb and would-be suitor, Nigel Farnham.

"WHEN HAS 'NO' EVER STOPPED ME?"

She vanished in a swish of buttery silk and left behind the scent of sweet clover and violets. Mischievous and bold, Lady Clara Langly was a chit who desperately needed to be taken in hand—but she had left Nigel abruptly, fled into the night, and he'd had no chance to see her pretty face unmasked. If he was right, and dancing was nothing but making love to music, their quadrille was just the beginning. . . .

ISBN 13: 978-0-8439-6321-2

GERRI RUSSELL

To Tempt a Knight

Brotherhood of the Scottish Templars

"Gerri Russell writes with a passionate intensity that will sweep readers straight into her richly imagined world."
—Jayne Ann Krentz

Sir William Keith owed allegiance to no one save the mysterious brotherhood of the Scottish Templars. But his task to protect the legendary Templar treasure brought him straight into the path of a bold lass who demanded he help find her kidnapped father, the treasure's previous guardian.

William dared not abandon Lady Siobhan Fraser to her enemies. She was his best hope for finding the holy artifacts—and a dire temptation to his vow of chastity. How long could he deny the ecstasy that awaited him in her arms? For he knew all too well it's the forbidden fruit that tastes the sweetest....

Coming this Fall!   ISBN 13: 978-0-8439-6259-8

✂ □ **YES!**

Sign me up for the Historical Romance Book Club and send my FREE BOOKS! If I choose to stay in the club, I will pay only $8.50* each month, a savings of $6.48!

NAME: _____

ADDRESS: _____

TELEPHONE: _____

EMAIL: _____

□ I want to pay by credit card.

□ **VISA**   □ **MasterCard**   □ **DISCOVER**

ACCOUNT #: _____

EXPIRATION DATE: _____

SIGNATURE: _____

Mail this page along with $2.00 shipping and handling to:
Historical Romance Book Club
PO Box 6640
Wayne, PA 19087
Or fax (must include credit card information) to:
610-995-9274
You can also sign up online at **www.dorchesterpub.com**.
*Plus $2.00 for shipping. Offer open to residents of the U.S. and Canada only.
Canadian residents please call 1-800-481-9191 for pricing information.
If under 18, a parent or guardian must sign. Terms, prices and conditions subject to
change. Subscription subject to acceptance. Dorchester Publishing reserves the right
to reject any order or cancel any subscription.